# *The* King *of* Lavender Square

## Susan Ryan

POOLBEG

Published 2018
by Poolbeg Press Ltd
123 Grange Hill, Baldoyle
Dublin 13, Ireland
E-mail: poolbeg@poolbeg.com
www.poolbeg.com

1

A catalogue record for this book is available from the British Library.

ISBN 978-1-78199-8373

Typeset by Poolbeg in Sabon
Printed and bound by CPI Group (UK) Ltd, Croydon, CR0 4YY

www.poolbeg.com

# About the Author

Susan Ryan grew up in Gorey, County Wexford. After graduating with a degree in Social Science from University College Dublin, she worked in Greece, Germany, London and Australia in jobs as varied as "menu translation" in Greece to "cook" in the Western Australian wheat belt. She now works as an advertising copywriter, on campaigns ranging from banking to beer, and has won a number of industry awards. In 2012, she was commissioned by Ireland's only two-star Michelin restaurant to write *Restaurant Patrick Guilbaud: The First Thirty Years*. She lives in Dublin with her partner, Stéphane, and their daughter Sophie.

*The King of Lavender Square* is her first novel.

# Acknowledgements

When you decide you want to be a novelist (in my case it was age 12) for some reason writing this part, the thank you's, seems like the pinnacle of the achievement. It means something: that you're an author at last. I, myself, always read an author's acknowledgements when I've finished reading a book. It gives an insight into the writer as a person, their influences, who is important in their lives, who they feel they need to thank.

For me, I need to thank my family first and foremost – my dad Fergus, my sister Lisa, and my brother Colin. My mother, Elizabeth, is no longer around and I miss her. She was magnificent. She always was and continues to be my Muse. Thank you to her family, the Mahers, and to the Ryans for being there for us.

Thank you to all my wonderful friends (U.C.D., Carrick, Australia, Guinness, D.C. and beyond) and family and indeed anyone out there who's ever had to listen to me drone on about wanting to be a writer, particularly those who've read manuscripts before they were anywhere near polished or picked up by a publisher: Mary Delaney, Anna Delaney, Kate Murray, Ann Moloney, Bernie Hackett, Shay Hackett, Emma Hackett, Claire Hackett, Deirdre Hickson, Laura Reynolds, Karen McGuinness, Deirdre McDermott, Deirdre Picard, Lisa McMahon, Fergus Ryan, Gail Keane, Trina Keane, Liz Hutchinson, Jean Hogan, Ciara Considine, John Reynolds, Julie Reynolds, Louise LeClaire, Monica Haechler, Joan Haechler and the über-talented Djinn Von Noorden. Thank you to Marcus who was there from the very start and to John and to Tony. Thank you to fellow author, Patrick Chapman, for encouraging me all the way over pizza on Parliament Street and to my fabulous fellow Toastmasters at Hellfire.

A special thank you to Ricco Reynolds and Dave Elliott for their football expertise and to Transport FC for the inspiration and for enduring my terrible attempts at the game.

Thank you to all the advertising agencies I've worked for, for encouraging creativity and tolerating talk of the dream between screaming deadlines – Chemistry Advertising, Dialogue Marketing, Forza, Irish International-Proximity & Target Marketing.

Thank you to Patrick Guilbaud, Stéphane Robin and Guillaume Lebrun for trusting me to write their book, and to Niamh O'Dea for recommending me, to Tim O'Dea for listening and to Eileen Pearson for believing.

A special thanks to Paula Campbell at Poolbeg for taking a chance on me, and to Caroline Maloney, and very importantly my hardworking editor, Gaye Shortland.

An extra special shout-out to Annette Foley, Daniel Robin, Sophie Robin and all the Robins, Lemorvans and Freys in France.

Above all, thank you to Stéphane for all your love and kindness and for believing in me all the way.

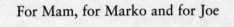
For Mam, for Marko and for Joe

# PART 1

# Chapter 1

On the day she first spoke to the boy, there was an accident in Lavender Square involving a cat and a dog and it was her fault. It wasn't intentional but the guilt hit her immediately just the same. Guilt came naturally to Saskia Heffernan.

If she had been "fully aware" at the time, or "living in the now", as her shelf of self-help books suggested she ought to have been, she might have seen it coming, drawn a line through the sequence of events that led to the inevitable moment. But she was neither, so she didn't. Years later, when she was a different person altogether, she would look back and trace the first stirrings of change to a certain Friday in September, to the day of the runner. It was just before the dog arrived and the incident with the note. Before that, no one knew anyone. In a heartbeat, it all changed.

She had seen the boy plenty of times. They shared the same building but his mother didn't encourage chatter. If they passed each other in the hallway, the woman, who looked exotic in her colourful African dresses, lowered her head and dipped it slightly in a kind of an attempt at a nod. Sometimes the boy looked up and smiled a white toothy grin with gaps where he was missing his milk teeth, which always made Saskia smile back. But that was it. Any information she had about them was gleaned from watching, listening and weighing up the odds.

She knew they didn't like the dark. Because when the communal lights didn't work, which was often enough, she heard them pause at the top of the stairs which led to their flat below and count to three, keys jangling at the ready – *un, deux, trois* – before hurtling down to the gloom of the lower unlit hallway where any potential natural light was kept at bay by the doors of the flats and utility room that were housed there. She wasn't sure where the woman worked except that she took the boy with her. She knew he was eight. She'd overheard the landlord muttering to another tenant that a boy of eight was surely old enough to be at school. At the time, Saskia thought that a man who made his living from collecting rents would be better off minding his own business.

She liked to watch people and listen. But not in a way that could get a girl arrested, although she did own a pair of binoculars. Her "ground floor" flat, which was actually considerably above ground because of the steep flight of steps that led up to the front door, awarded her with a view of Lavender Square and amphitheatre acoustics that made it impossible not to spy on her neighbours. Even hushed conversations had a way of resonating from footpath to window in perfect clarity like sound over water. The sizeable sash window of her flat allowed her to earwig on stoop-style conversations where people could be surprisingly open. This feature helped compensate for the cheap carpet, lumpy wallpaper, mock-pine furniture and bandaged-together kitchenette. What had once made a fine drawing room made a small flat. As a result, a permanent assortment of knickers, bed sheets and jeans hung in semi-aired state.

On that particular Friday in late August, the view was quite spectacular. The sun rose into a cloudless sky and tinged the world a blue-pink. A mist hung above the walled private garden and, far away in the distance, a haze blanketed the Dublin Mountains.

When she had first moved in, years before, Saskia had made a point of reading about Lavender Square in the local library. Built as "Victoria Square", the intention was a modest development of terraced townhouses, two storeys over garden level, and a salute to the then queen who would have approved of the *Upstairs, Downstairs* architecture with its granite steps that delivered callers to the main front door. These steps had bypassed the messy business of kitchens and sculleries below. Another door, a lesser front door, which was set into the side of these steep steps at garden level, had dealt with all that, maintaining the household's equilibrium – either receiving guests above or catering for them below.

The said queen would have been less pleased that the name never took – "Lavender" seemed more appropriate. The shrub's abundance and presence in several of the front gardens and in the walled garden was often observed but rarely questioned, although there was a story about a broken-hearted young woman who, on losing her lover in the Crimea, had paced the square nightly clutching a handkerchief laden with sprigs of lavender to calm her frayed nerves. Saskia sometimes thought about her, the girl who had experienced a love so intense she was insane with grief, and wondered what such a love would be like. She wanted to reach out and comfort her, ease her pain, tell her that each stray seed had been destined for greatness, to colour the air over a century later with a musky sense of love. Saskia often had thoughts like these. They weren't ones she mentioned aloud. Not that there was anyone to mention them to.

At first glance, the houses in the square were pleasant: red-bricks, their two storeys rising proudly above the granite-skirted garden level. The walled garden at its centre was maintained by a solitary gardener but rarely used even though each of the private residences owned a key.

North, south, east and west: front doors, front gardens and gates faced outwards to form the symmetrical square – best side out like true Victorians. While out back, behind the terraces of houses, a shady and forgotten lane lined with rusty, dusty lock-ups, weeds and debris hemmed the ends of the gardens and yards, snaked past the walls with back-garden doors now shut, padlocked or bricked up.

Each house had railings and a wrought-iron gate that squeaked satisfactorily. And visitors could either brace themselves for the climb to the big front door or, if not, avoid the steps altogether, and tap on the smaller door that nestled into the side of those very steps.

Up close, alongside the Victorian gems and daintily manicured gardens, there was also shabbiness. The houses on the north face of the square had been converted into flats and looked less well loved.

Most of the doors underneath the front steps had been bricked up for security purposes, removing some of the charm and certainly convenience from the residences which were optimistically advertised as "garden flats". Rusting bicycles were chained to crumbling railings and overflowing bins set on low-maintenance concrete. There were two to three flats or bedsits per level. If you could afford it, your flat was at the front of the house, on the ground or first floor. The cheaper flats were at the back and darker and less airy.

It was in one of these houses, at the end of the north terrace, that Saskia lived. On sunny evenings she sat and marvelled over the irony that she, a lowly flat-dweller, lived in a coveted south-facing building that caught the afternoon sun, unlike the private residents who were forced out onto their front steps to grab the best of the light. Every morning she sat and watched the square come to life over toast and marmalade and a large pot of tea.

That Friday in August was no different.

Her best view was of the east face of the square and she felt like she knew the inhabitants through their daily routines.

At half past seven, like clockwork, the green door of Number 5 swung open and the woman stepped out. She leaned back against the door and paused to tilt her face towards the sun but her foot tapped impatiently. She was always well turned out: a revolving door of well-cut suits and dresses and jackets that looked as if they would be pleasing to touch. Saskia imagined a walk-in wardrobe, one that warranted the term "closet". Today the woman wore sunglasses and something cream.

She was not a natural beauty. Her hair was professionally blonde and clipped short, and she was well-groomed, hard and polished like teak, sharp and haughty, the kind with a list of requirements and high demands that necessitated ambition and expense. She was a high-flyer, a finger-clicker, not the breed to acknowledge Saskia's lowly existence for even a second. The type who wore sunglasses indoors and donated her clothes to charity shops, thinking she was doing the planet a huge favour. Saskia knew this because she'd seen her in the local second-hand shop, side-stepping the rails of unwanted skirts, slacks and shirts, taking care not to touch anything in case she caught something like an incurable strain of leprosy or bird flu. The woman was also a café regular.

A little girl arrived at the woman's side. She was a miniature edition of her mother and, if the twosome had started singing, stepping out in time to some carefully choreographed routine like in a Doris Day movie, it wouldn't have seemed out of place. Not in Lavender Square where the birds sang from the telegraph wires, butterflies made a pattern against a perfect blue sky, the postman whistled by on his Raleigh Chopper, and fourteen steps from front door to pavement provided a suitable stage setting for such light-hearted footwork.

Instead, the woman turned and spoke to someone behind her, someone not visible, and the door swung shut, no smile or kiss goodbye. Then mother and daughter, laden with satchel, sweater, handbag and briefcase, hurried down the steps and piled into a jeep capable of pulling up to an Andean base camp. It revved up and shot off, and this morning it narrowly avoided the runner. A wrenching gear-change followed a screech of brakes and long-drawn-out wail of horn.

Saskia raised her binoculars for a closer look.

"You again," she murmured. "You wagon. You'll kill someone yet."

The runner gave the jeep-driver a look and dusted himself off before running on and out of the square in the wake of the obnoxious vehicle. His legs were long and tanned and athletic, and there was something about them that made her feel light-headed. His face was handsome too, though intense and Heathcliff-like under a careful mess of dark hair. He lived a couple of doors down from the jeep woman but they barely acknowledged each other. From what Saskia could make out, he lived in a plush flat on the garden level of his parents' home. The flat had once been a General Practice, his father's she guessed. The brass plate with his name and letters was still screwed into the wall. And sometimes the doctor's wife still wandered outside to polish it absently with a rag as though a quick rub might genie back their youth.

The runner seemed to live a dashing life of sharp tapered suits, quick phone calls and coffee on the go, which all seemed very impressive to Saskia who had nothing that required dashing to even though she and he were certainly around the same age. She imagined he might be a future "captain of industry", a phrase she puzzled over whenever she read the business section of the paper, which wasn't often, while knowing vaguely that she would never be the captain of anything.

He was going places, that much was clear. The runner wore his ambition with the same confidence he drove his shiny two-seater classic convertible which he parked tidily at the curb each evening. Saskia was not a fan of such silly little cars but, judging by the constant supply of equally shiny brunette girls that arrived into Lavender Square sitting in the passenger seat of the very car she loathed, she was in the minority. Each new girl looked like a slightly improved clone of the last and they all wore the same expression – hope. Hope that she might be the one to stop the runner in his tracks. None of them did. They were expelled early the morning after, something Saskia had initially thought was out of respect for his aging parents who lived above him, but she was mistaken. It was so he could get his daily run in. Nothing got in the way of his run wherever it took him – towards the mountains, along the canal or deeper into southside suburbia – Saskia was always gone by the time he got back so there wasn't a chance to catch a glimpse of those great legs again. Not until Saturday at least. That's when he washed his car wearing a worn "Massive Attack" T-shirt and ripped surfer shorts, clothes that suited him far better than the ugly rugby shirts, jeans and deck shoes he wore otherwise when off duty. Saskia liked the T-shirt. It was like a window into another part of his life that was less south-side, less private-school boy, less predictable.

Predictable or otherwise, the runner was well gone by the time another neighbour of his opened her front door. Hers was white and in need of a coat of paint. Saskia knew she was a teacher because the older children of the square sometimes waved and called out "Hi, Teacher!" to her as they passed. Other times, at night, they crept up the steps to her front door and rang the doorbell only to tear away laughing. At first, the teacher would pull open her door and stare out into the nothingness, the porch light creating a halo over her head. Then for a time she stopped answering the front door altogether, even when one day a couple of Jehovah's Witnesses stood patiently for twenty minutes because they spotted a smoke plume and thought "What's a little wait when you just might rescue someone from the fires of hell?"

Saskia knew the teacher's name was Nuala. She seemed to be known and acknowledged by everyone yet had no friends. This was unsurprising. The teacher's thin-lipped mouth was set in a permanent line, her elbows dug rigidly into her sides as if in an effort to keep her insides intact, and she owned a collection of cardigans that had been in fashion once – some time around the outbreak of the Great War.

The woman lived alone, with only a well-groomed ginger cat for company, and Saskia imagined she lived a frugal life. Tea well stewed, bread and margarine, an existence foraged out in a small corner of the big, old house: swept, wiped down and maintained, punctuated only by copybook-marking and soap-watching.

This morning she wore a faded sunhat and a dress that reached her ankles. She wasn't taking any chances with the last of the summer sun, even if a bit of sun wouldn't have done her any harm. She was grey and washed-out like the pink roses on her dress, and she seemed sourer than usual. For a moment she contemplated a set of pruning shears but then put them down in order to remove an envelope from the pocket of her dress. It contained a letter, the words of which seemed to pull her downwards until she was sitting on her steps. She read it over and over and it was clear that, whatever was in the letter, it wasn't informing her of a Prize Bonds windfall.

Saskia refilled her cup.

In the flat to the rear of hers, the musician strummed on his guitar, taking pauses presumably to scribble down notes or words to the melancholy melody. He dressed "hipster" and acknowledged her in grunts which seemed to say: "You're not on my level."

Above her, the floorboards creaked and she pictured the tenant and shivered unconsciously. He was a recluse, rarely seen, but his malignant presence permeated the house through a tiptoed trail of unsigned notes written in green biro which he stuck to doors, walls and light switches if someone did something to displease him. When he was agitated he paced, over and back, over and back, and sometimes late at night he whimpered low and mournfully like a ghost dog, but Saskia could never be sure whether she was imagining this or not. She had calculated that his name was Joe. It was a detective game she'd played at the start, matching names to the other tenants with the help of the post on the hall table. Joe Delaney received nothing but bills and welfare-related letters.

She heard the front door open and saw the boy and his mother step outside into the sunlight. He carried a shiny blue football and she sat on the steps to watch while he had a kick-around in the small front garden, which was really a patch of hardened earth, and his legs and bare feet were like flashes of black magic in the sun.

Like the other tenants, the Kimbas kept to themselves, and the local priest seemed to be their only visitor. The woman had moved in when she was pregnant and now the boy was eight. She seemed to teach him at home because sometimes, when Saskia went downstairs to use the washing machine, she heard him recite spellings and tables and rhymes in sing-song through the door of their flat. Mrs Kimba was tall, slender and beautiful and carried herself elegantly. She maintained a perfectly coiffed pageboy hairstyle which was always shiny and never seemed in need of washing or taming unlike Saskia's which had a mind of its own. In the beginning her letters had carried brightly coloured stamps from the Congo but those letters were fewer now, and she looked permanently hunted and often unwell. Sometimes, when she was supposed to be watching her boy play ball, she drifted off to a semi-conscious state from which the boy had to shake her awake. There was no evidence of a Mr Kimba.

The sun rose higher, cutting a path across the perfect blue sky and Saskia watched the day unfold before her. The echo of footsteps and conversations rang up to her as the world went about its business, and by eight the square was a hive of activity. Curb-side spaces were filled by local workers in search of free parking. The later starters drained out of the buildings, magnetised to the exit of the square. Office workers in heels and skirts and shirts and ties, checkout assistants, the pharmacy assistant in white, the beautician in pink, the beefy security guard in black, the bicycle courier, the pizza delivery guy and the librarian. The window cleaner wheeled his bike, balancing his ladder precariously across the handlebars. A woman walked her dog.

Saskia knew them by habit. She'd watched people come and go – the professionals, the students, the backpackers, and now the immigrants. And just as she matched tenants to envelopes, she matched people to professions and trades.

Saskia liked to watch other people as she herself was a disappointment. Over the phone, people were delighted when they heard her voice and then her name. "Oh – Saskia – how Hollywood!" they said, but delight turned to crudely hidden displeasure when they met her in person. They expected something exotic. Instead they got a plump, pale and shy bespectacled girl with slumped shoulders and eyes that refused to meet theirs. Most concluded she was "harmless" in response to her mild manner and lack of words. She was for the most part quiet and even-tempered, but what they overlooked was a subdued intelligence and a simmering rage that at times erupted, but rarely in public.

Her name made her a magnet: it created equal poles of attraction and rejection. Saskia hated it. The surname, Heffernan, didn't help. It was like a punchline to a farmhand joke. It was her voice that was good, although this too let her down. While her name conjured up notions of a Russian princess hooded in silver fox furs, her husky voice sealed the deal. Until, of course, you met her face to face and found yourself looking over her shoulder for the dream you'd spoken to on the phone regarding a reorder of disposable cups. Still, its huskiness meant she was hot-to-trot as a voiceover artist and she hoped that soon she would be in a position to leave the mock-Tuscan café where she worked as a "barista", a job title she couldn't utter without spluttering into her own coffee.

Later that day, she was due at a radio recording. The advertising agency liked her demo, the studio had explained. Her huskiness would suit the script and all going well she would be the new voice of an organic cider brand, meaning regular work. She shrugged.

"We'll see," she said with the resignation of someone used to being let down.

Behind her, her mobile phone rang. She glanced at the number, ignored it and finished her toast. It was delicious but she really would have to give it up. Anyone with a brain knew that if you wanted to be lean, you had to omit wheat from your diet. She sighed, dragged her hair into a ponytail and climbed into the shower.

# Chapter 2

The studio was light-filled. It was polished, white and minimalist. It was also oppressively hot. On her way there Saskia had recited mantras, made a Sign of the Cross passing the church, and reasoned with herself. It was her voice they wanted and its huskiness, not her face or her lumpy body or the lack of a sparkling personality – just her voice, and she had faith in that. She wore a pair of linen pants, which had a miniscule slimming effect and she had painted her toenails. For some reason, toenails in coral pink gave her a confidence boost and made her feel calm, almost.

Naturally, all that carefully constructed composure went out the window the moment she stepped through the door. They were all waiting for her in a line like a guard of honour, smiling a little too widely, and they spoke "south side". Saskia had been around long enough to know that too-wide smiles spelt trouble.

There was the cider client, a blonde who had an air of corporate brutality about her, the copywriter who wore cycling shorts and a faux-shabby T-shirt, and the engineer, a resigned longhaired youth who you could tell from ten paces wished he was producing Beyoncé albums instead of radio ads.

The account executive from the advertising agency was the last to shake her hand. He was tall, tanned, toned and dark-haired and immaculately tailored into a navy suit. He introduced himself as

Tom Winters and she recognised him immediately. It was the runner from the square. Up close he looked different. He looked magnificent and smelt magnificent, and it was overpowering. She opened and closed her mouth a couple of times like a carp, her legs buckled slightly and her nerves split into a million little shreds. He shook her hand. His was dry; hers was wet. He unconsciously wiped his on his pants. Then, script in hand, he ushered her into the airless recording booth, where without dropping his smile or drawing a second breath, he explained that the client was a demanding horse's ass who expected award-winning radio ads at the flick of a switch and, after all sorts of string-pulling, this ad (no pressure) was to be aired next day in a last-minute bid to cash in on the unexpected warm weather.

Saskia didn't understand a thing he said but he abandoned her before she could get a word in, to join the others and observe her through a window. She felt like the solitary attraction in an aquarium. She pulled on her headset and instantly felt a thousand degrees warmer; a slick of sweat made a river down her back and her linen trousers transformed into a limp rag. It was a bad start and things went rapidly downhill after that.

Meeting the runner face to face had floored her. There was a good chance he'd noticed her staring down at him from her window in the mornings. He could easily have said, "Hey, aren't you that crazy fat chick who spies on me from your breakfast table?" But she needn't have worried. If he'd seen her in passing, he didn't let on. She could tell cool Tom Winters made a habit of forgetting fat girls whose faces were unmemorable, their perhaps otherwise distinctive features lost in plumpness.

After the first few takes his coolness quickly began to dissipate. He grew increasingly impatient with the copywriter's laidback method of instructing Saskia even if he tried hard to disguise the fact by making a grand show of carefully removing his tie and suit jacket. On the fifth take, the client pulled Tom Winters into a huddle and spoke in silent, urgent mutterings. It was clear, by the way she flicked her hair and kept touching his arm, she fancied her chances with the handsome account executive. Saskia could have told her to save her efforts. His body language did not reciprocate hers. His hand made a white-knuckled fist for one, and this was never a good sign.

11

Post-huddle, he took over. The copywriter shrugged and reversed his chair away from the desk to check his phone. Tom Winters wore the same intense expression he did when running and he demanded take after take after take, breathing deeply between each. When he addressed her he was cold now, and she knew that every time the engineer silenced the speaker between them, they were talking about her, questioning her ability. You didn't need to be able to hear them to know that.

He looked up then and straight at her. The engineer flicked a switch.

"Saskia?" said Tom Winters, the runner, and she blushed.

He studied her for a moment and frowned and then his expression changed to one she was familiar with. It was disappointment. And when he spoke again, she did not like the patronising edge to his voice.

"I need you to be more suggestive."

"Seriously," Saskia said. "You need me to be more suggestive with a script like this. You don't think it's suggestive enough already to cause an outrage?"

"No, I don't," he said snappily. "Could you dial up the 'husky mysteriousness' too, please – channel your inner Scarlett Johansson?"

"Sure," she said unsurely. "'Husky, mysterious' and 'Scarlett Johansson' – so does that mean you want 'American' now too?"

"No," he said, vexed. "I'm just using her as an example."

"Yes, I get it," she said. "As an example of 'husky mysteriousness'."

"And try to get into character a little more," Tom Winters urged. "You're Eve, the first woman on earth, you are the *main* woman, the only woman. You are recounting your story – the first time you spotted Adam and led him astray."

Like Eve was a real person, Saskia wanted to scream back, but she didn't. Instead she breathed deeply. She felt easier. The runner no longer seemed attractive. Not as handsome as he had from a height, from her window perch. Nor did his legs seem so good and she imagined feeding his expensive suit into a shredder.

"And we're rolling," said the engineer, bored.

Saskia leaned into the microphone, upped the "husky mysteriousness" and read from the script suggestively.

**STARTS**

FVO: It was a long time ago, oh centuries – it was late summer, and a Saturday, I think. It must have been because there was a rumour that the seventh day would be a day of rest. The first time I saw him he was naked, standing under a tree. To me, he was the only man. Perfection, as though he had been made for me.

"Hello, stranger," I said. "You look thirsty."

"Yes," he said, "I am."

I picked him an apple.

"I've made you something out of this fruit," I said.

I threw it to him. He caught it.

"That's a sin," he said. "It's not even fully ripe."

I smiled at him and poured him a drink.

**SFX: Drink being poured.**

He took a sip.

FVO: "Mmmm, refreshing," he said. "I think that might keep me up all night," and he gave me that look.

"Well, here's hoping," I said and I laughed.

"Up and adam!" he said and we kissed for the first time.

**ENDS**

Saskia made a note to never again fantasise over a guy who was associated with such egregious scripts.

On her way back into the flat she passed the boy and his mother on the steps. They were eating and did not look up. A bottle of wine bored a guilty hole in her bag. It was a little early but she didn't care.

The front door was already open. This was a rare occurrence. A chair, jammed between the frame and the door, prevented the strong spring from slamming it shut, and the sunlight fought hard to penetrate the dimly lit dust motes in the dank hallway. The recluse would not approve. Changes in the house made him uneasy.

Her flat was stuffy. She put the wine in the fridge, opened the window wide and looked out over the square which was shiny with leaves and trees about to turn. A copper beech shimmered in the dead heat, inviting all who passed into the walled garden which was closed off to the world by a dark-green door. Birds chattered and poked their heads out of the nooks and crannies in the masonry of the more dilapidated houses; a single white feather billowed and sank to earth.

She sat at her table perfectly still and for a long time, and her heart hurt. She unconsciously picked off the coral-pink nail varnish as the sun travelled west, pulling the harshness out of the light. In the offices, the afternoon slump would have set in and workers would be restless, itching to get out into the sun and down to the pub.

She poured a glass of wine and then another and watched the afternoon slip by into evening. The sun hit the east and north faces and the red bricks glowed warm. People sat on their steps, fanned themselves and drank wine. A bunch of noisy Italians attempted a barbecue next door and billows of blue smoke and the aroma of sausage wafted up to her window. Cars returned to roost and the square got busier.

The blonde lady appeared happier this evening, relaxed by the sense of Friday. No horns blowing now or brakes screeching. Now, she listened patiently to the little girl who was no doubt recounting her day. They took their time climbing their steps and then sat to bask in the evening and finish their ice creams. The woman looked tired and thoughtful, her sharpness softened with each slow breath, and when she combed her fingers through her daughter's locks they caught the sun like corn.

A few doors down, the teacher sat on her steps on a cushion and drank from a cup. She wore monstrous sunglasses and her cat curled into her. She acknowledged her blonde neighbour with a bare tilt of her chin.

The Kimba boy played with his blue ball again after tea and before bed. Up and down, over and back he tottered on the postage-stamp of space, giggling when he tripped. His mother watched him, chin in hands – dozing and waking, dozing and waking.

Stars appeared in a mauve sky and Saskia carried on watching and noticing. She noticed how people gently ignored each other, went about their business as though surrounded by ghosts brushing through. From where she sat it seemed strange somehow. That in a perfectly proportioned square, with its trees and birds and proud houses all living in harmony, its souls moved in detached lonely universes. Then, from a height, life seemed more manageable. It had perspective. It was at ground level that things became more complicated.

When the sky turned navy, moths fluttered above the teacher, but still she did not go inside.

Saskia watched the group of Italians sitting on their steps, all beauty and gestures, glasses of wine and open camaraderie. On another, two Polish men played cards in silence and drank cheap beer from cans. Their overalls were clouded with dust and their boots, heavy with clay, lay in an untidy heap. Women smoked companionably in their slippers, leaned on the railings and doorjambs and spoke in the low-curled tones of the east, swapping recipes and stories and childhoods in Vilnius, Kiev and Krakow.

The teacher hugged her knees. An old cardigan draped her shoulders like a shawl and her cat stalked, his eyes like two fireflies dancing amongst the rosebushes.

Saskia lit a cigarette and blew smoke-rings out her window. Between inhalations, she let tears roll down her face. She poured more wine. It eased her guilt, coloured the world in a softer shade so it seemed almost containable. Her guilt stemmed from a sympathetic temperament. She felt sorry for people. For the homeless man on the corner for whom she once bought coffee and he asked her if she had a can of lager instead, for the starving millions, for the old men who shuffled and had blank stares; for the old women with stoops who were riddled with loneliness, for the little black boy who played football from morning to night and seemed to have no friends or football boots; for his beautiful mother who was most certainly unwell and seemed terrorised by memories, and for the window cleaner who looked too old to work. Sometimes, but not often, she felt sorry for herself.

Her phone rang and she cleared her throat.

"Mam?"

"Hi, love. How are you?"

"Fine. How are you, Mam?"

"Oh, okay," she said a little shakily. "Today wasn't a good day."

"In what way, Mam?" she asked and she inhaled carefully to hide her impatience.

15

"I didn't sleep last night and everything seemed to go wrong today, you know the way?"

"Of course," Saskia replied and nodded at the receiver to show she did. "You need to get some sleep, Mam. It will help."

"There'll be no sleep for me," her mother reassured her bitterly. "And how was your day?"

"Grand. I recorded a radio ad."

"Good girl. What's it for? Will I hear it?"

Saskia paused to light another cigarette.

"You will, Mam – it's for 'Adam's Apple'."

"What's that, an aftershave?"

"Close, a cider."

"Oh," her mother said quietly.

"Yes."

There was a brief silence.

"I suppose it's a start," her mother added. "Sure it might get you out of that café?"

"I really hope so, Mam."

"I always thought you were capable of more, Saskia," her mother said with a hint of hurt.

"I'm only twenty, Mam – starting out really."

"I was married at twenty," her mother reminded her as though this were some tremendous achievement.

Saskia sighed softly.

Her mother rang off.

Night seeped in and the streetlights grew brighter and she wondered and worried at how small the world seemed when you were Irish. Was it only Irish people who could connect two perfect strangers within minutes? Was it because they had dozens of relatives or because the island was just so small or was it plain bad luck? Whatever it was, she thought it disturbing that one moment you could be admiring a runner from your window and the next sitting face to face with him and dialling up the "husky mysteriousness". She had concocted him into an intelligent and compassionate man. In reality, he was a stereotype: a spoiled private schoolboy who still technically lived with his parents, a beautiful but empty vessel who only saw beauty on the surface. It was disappointing, but then again life was disappointing.

She drank her wine and glanced over at the teacher and wondered if she ever changed her expression. She seemed to own just one: sour. She felt bad then for thinking that, because the teacher reached into her pocket for the letter and read it once again. Then she put her head in her hands and left it there for a long time. When she looked up, she seemed to look straight at Saskia, and that's when Saskia drew the curtains. She'd seen enough for one day.

# Chapter 3

Next morning she woke early to the floorboards creaking overhead. The recluse was up and pacing. Something was bothering him. She compared him to a caged animal, with senses not quite yet dulled, and he scared her. Saskia hated him without knowing him and sometimes, not often, she felt guilty about this. She sighed and got out of bed. The air was heavy with static and heat. She pulled open the window and heard a car engine. It moved slowly, in first gear, and it circled over and over: north, south, east, west. It was unusual for someone to be looking for free parking so early on a Saturday.

She put on the kettle and tied open the curtains. A gold mist rose from the walled garden. The trees stood motionless, the copper beeches, the oaks, the sycamores and the majestic horse-chestnut. It was as if they were waiting for winter: middle-aged men, aware of their frailties and the prospect of thinning foliage.

The recluse paced, the car continued to circle over and over, and she watched, curious now. Eventually, when it had passed for the fifth time, it slowed and came to a stop and the passenger door opened so that a black object could be dumped right out onto the middle of the street. Saskia bet it was someone dumping their rubbish but, when she pulled up the window further for a better look, the car door slammed, the driver stepped on the accelerator and the black shadow moved and trotted forward. Saskia reached for her glasses and saw that it wasn't rubbish at all but a black Jack Russell type mongrel with a white belly and it looked after the car until it disappeared. Then it sat down and scratched itself, sure that its owners would be back to collect it.

Upstairs, the floorboards creaked again. Saskia guessed the recluse had seen the dog being dumped too but she knew it would be up to her to ring the animal rescue people. She sighed sadly. The little dog would have to wait. It was far too early to ring anyone and there was no way she was bringing him inside. She went back to bed. It wasn't a happy start to the day and she took the abandoned dog as a bad sign.

Later, she woke to the mutterings of a conversation on the steps. It was still quiet. On Saturdays, the square awakened slowly, yawned and stretched. This morning a scorching sun soaked the slates, doors and brickwork, turning them orange then pink then yellow. Blackbirds lined themselves in rows on the rooftops and sang sweetly. Seagulls circled inland and swooped and cried out mournfully. Crows perched and cawed like old women. Magpies chattered and made a racket and finches dashed in and out of the hedgerows. They fluttered and chased and tittered to each other as though harbouring a secret joy.

Mrs Kimba was sitting with the priest just outside on the front steps and her boy was playing with his football. The front door was open again and a hint of fresh air circled the house.

The priest was middle-aged and dressed priest-casually. He wore a woolly diamond-patterned cardigan and Saskia imagined he smelt like a parish house, of polish and carrots and gravy, and that divine intervention was what was preventing him from melting in his cardiganed heat. His voice was kind. He called Mrs Kimba by her first name, Tessa.

Saskia leaned closer to her window and listened in.

"I understand the pain of separation for you, Tessa," the priest said, "but it is for the best. I know you've taught Patrick well. I only have to look at how bright he is and how well he's done with you. But school is about more than books. It's his First Communion year and your son needs to meet people his own age."

The woman clutched her elbows, lowered her head and looked at her feet. She nodded slowly.

"The parish will help you out with the uniform and other expenses," the priest added.

"I will not hear of it," the woman replied proudly. "We're going shopping today."

"Well, the offer is there," he said and he got up to kick the ball around with her son.

They kicked it over and back. The deserted dog joined in and barked and chased. Tessa Kimba dozed.

Upstairs, the floorboards squeaked once more. The man was pacing again, right above Saskia's head. Today he was more agitated than usual. A door opened and closed and there was tiptoeing on the stairs. He was on the prowl. Someone was about to receive a note. This was the way he worked.

The priest did not last long running around. He sat down and mopped his face with a large, spotted handkerchief. Mrs Kimba woke up. The priest took off his shoe and shook out a pebble.

"You seem tired of late," he observed.

"I'm perfectly fine," she replied stiffly.

"Maybe a check-up wouldn't do you any harm."

The African lady laughed. "It is not top of my list, not when there are school trousers to be bought."

"I told you we can help out. We've a good parish."

"We can make our own way, thank you."

The priest coughed and stood up.

"Maybe some adult company would give you some extra support, Tessa," he suggested. "There are groups of women just like you all over the city. I can put you in touch with them."

"You mean other Africans, don't you, Father, other Congolese?" she said tetchily. "That's what you mean when you say 'women just like you', isn't it?"

The priest hesitated. He chose his words carefully.

"Not necessarily," he said. "I don't mean to seem patronising, assuming you'll automatically get on just because you're from the same continent. But it can be pleasant to meet people from home when you're away from home. Lord knows, as Irish people we're well aware of the fact."

"Thank you, Father, but I have no intention of making us more separate than we already are. Why do you think I chose to live in this white middle-class suburb in the first place?"

The woman was firm. The priest inhaled and exhaled.

"If that is your intention, then it is a good thing you've decided to send Patrick to school."

Mrs Kimba looked up and she smiled, just a crack.

"Yes," she nodded. "I suppose you are right, Father. You win."

"I don't see it as winning."

She lowered her voice then and Saskia had to strain her ears to hear.

"I also want Patrick out of the house," she whispered. "There is a man ..."

"A man?" asked the priest and he sounded alarmed. "What do you mean?"

She raised her hand to silence him.

"It's nothing, Father, thank you. I'm sorry I mentioned it."

"If you're sure," the priest said doubtfully.

Saskia drew back from the window and was thoughtful as she sorted her washing. Tessa Kimba was wary of the recluse too. This made her feel like less of a paranoid lunatic.

She picked up her laundry basket, opened her door and readied herself for the stairs down to the washing machine. She waited momentarily at the top of the stairs. Like the Kimbas, Saskia did not like the floor beneath with its lack of natural light and timed light switches and dodgy wiring. The murkiness lay below like a black well and a boiled mixture of worn carpet, air freshener and years of old cooking rose to the surface. The Polish couple that lived to the rear of the Kimbas had a taste for overcooked cabbage.

She hit the light switch which gave her time to race down the stairs and past the two flats to the utility room. She speedily loaded the washing machine, turned it on and made for the stairs.

It was then she saw a familiar yellow note stuck to the door of Number 1, the Kimbas' flat.

MUD HUTS MIGHT NOT HAVE FRONT DOORS
BUT JUST KEEP OURS CLOSED

Somewhere above her a door closed and Saskia's heart beat faster. She stood motionless, poised in indecisiveness and then the light timed out, leaving her in the dark. So instead of grabbing and destroying the note as she should have, she felt her way to the light switch – *pat, pat, pat* – flicked it on and then she bolted, stumbling back up to the yellowy daylight of her own flat where she breathed more easily.

But the moment she sat down, she got straight back up again. The boy could not see the note. She opened her door only to discover it was already too late because mother and son were quickly disappearing back down the stairs to their flat. She tiptoed to the banister, leaned over and waited and listened, hoping the note might have magically become unstuck and disappeared. It hadn't. She heard the boy's voice and Saskia knew it was yet another moment in her life she would relive and be haunted by. Tessa Kimba never forgot the note and Saskia never forgot the hurt in her voice when she answered her son.

"What does the note say, Maman?" he asked.

"Nothing, nothing important at all," his mother said.

Later, when Saskia was getting ready for work, she saw the Kimbas leave the house. They hurried down the steps and out of the square. The woman kept her head down and the boy trotted to keep up. Under his arm he carried his blue ball.

She lit a cigarette. Outside, the dog lay on the footpath and waited, the runner ran by and, above her, the floorboards creaked once more but less frequently now, and Saskia thought it was a cruel world indeed that allowed an innocent dog to be abandoned and a mother and son receive horrible notes while the likes of cool Tom Winters with his expensive running shoes and horrible Joe Delaney were still allowed to draw breath.

She picked up her phone and thought about calling the landlord but instead she called Animal Rescue. There was no answer. Joe Delaney she would have to think about. She wasn't sure what sort of a creature she was dealing with. There was always a chance she would be murdered in her bed if she reported him. The landlord would want proof he was the note-writer and she had none.

# Chapter 4

Patrick Kimba and his mother walked into town. There were things to do, places to see and a uniform to be bought. Patrick would have preferred to play football but he knew better and kept quiet. Saturdays made his mother happy, put a smile on her face. She said Saturdays were good for the soul. Besides, his mother wasn't a lady you argued with.

They walked briskly along the canal where the trees dipped into water that flowed so slowly you could hardly tell it was moving at all. A tram rumbled past and made a whispering sound along silver tracks that sparkled in the sun. Patrick dawdled and watched the mysterious streetcar until it curled around the corner like a crocodile's tail. He preferred to stroll, but his mother was always in a rush and today she was in an even bigger rush.

In the National Gallery, they went straight to the painting 'A Convent Garden, Brittany'. It was his mother's favourite. She liked the way there was lots of sunshine in it because Ireland had hardly any. A man in a uniform came over to them.

"You like this painting," he said. "I've seen you look at it before."

"Yes, we do," his mother said. "It looks like a beautiful garden, peaceful."

"It was a secret garden," the man said, "hidden to the world behind high stone walls."

"The best ones always are," his mother said strangely and they walked on.

In Stephen's Green, they laid out their rug under a tree and unpacked lunch: a sweet potato each with a little salt, washed down with lime cordial that was now warm. They chatted in French, then English, and afterwards they played cards. There was no breeze.

"Maman?" Patrick asked.

"*Oui, ma puce.*"

"Did my father ever play football?"

"He had no time for football. There was a war on."

"Do war heroes not get to play football?"

His mother smiled.

"He must have been brave," Patrick said.

"He was."

"Is he dead?"

"Probably, *petit*."

"But you don't know for sure?" Patrick said, hoping for a new answer.

"No."

"But couldn't you find him on Facebook?"

His mother shook her head.

"He's never met me, Maman."

"No, that's right," she smiled although her smile was fading now, "but he saw you as a bump."

"And he doesn't know we're here."

"No."

"When I play in the World Cup he will know where to find us then, won't he?"

"*Bien sur*," his mother said and she closed her eyes, meaning she didn't want any more questions.

Patrick thought adults made an awful mess of everything. There would be no wars at all if he were in charge. And if his father were around, he would have someone to play football with. There might even be money for tram rides and Coco Pops. He lay down on the rug beside his mother and looked up at the sky. Clouds moved slowly like giant caravans on their way somewhere else and he thought about his visit to Mister Singh the week before.

It had been his first ever visit to the dentist. It was a check-up and nothing to be scared of, his mother told him, which had left him feeling more scared than he already was. Mister Singh had skin like his, but his hair was different. He was from a place called Mumbai and his voice went up and down like a song. He had a very white smile and his mother said it was good for a dentist to have such a smile.

"Are you scared, little man?" Mister Singh had asked when the nurse brought him into the room.

"No," Patrick lied. The surgery smelt of medicine and the drill had sounded loud and painful from the waiting room.

"Well, then you are the first – a brave young man, very good. Please sit." He indicated the chair and Patrick wondered if he should say something about being scared after all in case Mister Singh started to torture him but, before he could, the dentist turned up the volume on the television set which sat in a corner up high. The nurse didn't look too happy about it.

There was a football match on and Mister Singh was immediately engrossed. "*Pass the ball, man!*" he loudly said to the telly. "*Ach, what is the point of giving it to him? He is no good at all! Are you blind as well as stupid? Frey was waving at you wildly!*"

The dentist sounded angry. He looked down at Patrick and shook his head.

"The beautiful game," he said sadly. "It sucks you in. My wife does not approve, my daughters have no interest – that is why I watch it here. Is your papa a fan?"

"I don't know. My maman does not know where he is. She does not know where to find him. He does not know where to find us," Patrick recited.

"I see," said the dentist wisely and he looked back at the screen. "Your papa does not know where to find you. This is a problem. Slide back in here now and let me take a look."

The light shone above Patrick so brightly he couldn't see anything. He hoped the dentist could and that he wouldn't stick the drill thing somewhere it wasn't meant to go.

The dentist spoke as he poked around.

"I know a good way to find your papa."

"*Arg,*" Patrick replied because the dentist's hands were stuffed into his mouth.

"You see these football stars on the telly?"

"*Arg*," Patrick said, although he couldn't see anything at all.

"They can't go anywhere without a snapper taking their photo. The whole world knows them, their names, their wives, their children, their shoe size and the way they take their tea. Even in India, the children have posters of Laurent Deschamps on the walls of their shacks. You know Laurent Deschamps?"

Patrick shook his head carefully.

"He was a god, yes. Once played for Innskeep United. You know, you look like him a bit." The dentist chuckled. "You become a professional footballer, my boy, and mark my words your father will know where to find you. A beautiful wife who knows how to spend your money will also know where to find you, just like a cobra in the Ganges."

Mister Singh laughed out loud then and Patrick couldn't see what was so funny.

When he was leaving, the dentist handed him a blue football. "Here, I keep this in here for when I need to kick something. It's yours now, the first of many, I trust. I will be looking out for you, Master Kimba. Play fair."

And just like that, a dream was born.


Patrick opened his eyes. His mother was packing up to leave. They were going shopping now for his school uniform. Someday his father would be there with them to carry the picnic rug and pay bills. He was absolutely sure of it.

The department store was hot and stuffy and packed with people and elbows and handbags. His mother looked through the rails of pants and Patrick sat and kicked his heels, watching other kids picking anything they liked off the shelves: cool shiny rucksacks, bundles of socks and pairs of shoes. And then their mothers just strolled up to the counter and took care of it all with a plastic card like magic and they went home quick-smart. Not like his mother who was taking hours and hours.

A little bit away from him, a girl sat with her nose stuck in a book. Her mother wore massive sunglasses and spoke loudly, waving a list about, until a lady with an orange face and big smile grabbed the list. She returned armed with stacks of skirts and shirts and ties and jumpers and shoes and a heavy winter coat and a blazer with a crest of two lions. It was all done very quickly and the girl and her mother disappeared behind the curtains of the changing room and now the lady was helping someone else, this time a boy with his father. The boy sat in his socks and played on his phone. The woman disappeared again, and when she came back she was carrying the most beautiful pair of football boots Patrick had ever seen. His eyes widened and he drank in the black leather, the gold strip, the long laces, the clean studs and the smell of brand-new newness.

Then his heart thumped as he caught the woman with the orange face looking at him. She was not smiling now and then she looked away to where a crowd had a gathered. Something was wrong. Before the crowd would let him through, Patrick already knew it was something to do with his mother.

The shop people wanted to fetch a doctor but she kept saying no. There was a lot of fussing and cooing and tea-making but she just wanted to pay for their things and go. The manager put the uniform into a bag and handed it to Patrick. As long as Mrs Kimba was *absolutely* sure she was okay? He didn't want any money. People gave them funny looks and his mother was embarrassed. She stood up, grabbed Patrick's hand and they fled. In their hurry they hopped onto a bus going in the wrong direction and ended up in the Phoenix Park. They got out and spread their rug in the meadow and his mother lay down and closed her eyes.

Patrick played with his ball and watched the deer in the distance and mothers and fathers with their kids. He waited for his mother to wake up. Her chest moved slowly up and down as the clouds in the sky got bigger and darker.

There was no need to worry, she had told him. The heat was just too much for her. That was all. He thought this over as he kicked the ball. He wasn't stupid. If he was, he might have believed her. His mother, Tessa Kimba, was from Africa and everyone with a brain knew that Irish heat did not get to African ladies.

The deer moved on and people packed up and went home, fathers and their sons, mothers and babies. He could see the tip of light on The Spire on O'Connell Street until it disappeared behind the clouds.

## SUSAN RYAN

On their way home they heard thunder and he knew he wouldn't forget the strange day as long as he lived even though his mother told him to erase it from his mind completely.

# Chapter 5

Saskia's day was busy. There was a run on iced coffees and a queue out the café door. The air was thundery and people's hair frizzed wildly in the humidity. Customers were mentallers at the best of times, moronic about their coffee, mega-fussy, as though a lifesaving blood transfusion was at stake. They studied her over the counter, craned their necks to make sure she was getting their order right, not using full-fat milk instead of skinny, before ordering a full-fat cream-cheese bagel with extra bacon. Today they looked uncomfortable and were more crotchety than usual, and they took it out on her. Her manager was no better: a woman who smiled ruthlessly and spoke to Saskia slowly in the way you might to someone in a remedial class.

The hours rolled by and the day wore on and she served, wiped and smiled until her face and feet ached. It was afternoon when the thunder started to roll and she first heard her voice over the airwaves. It made her jump and then she smiled. It was the radio ad and she thought it sounded good despite the dumb script and fraught recording experience. She raised the volume and someone snickered. She looked up.

It was a woman wearing sunglasses so large she looked like a giant fly. It took a moment for her to realise she was the jeep driver from the square. Her husband, a man who looked henpecked, and her daughter chose seats at the counter right under Saskia's nose.

The woman ordered two iced coffees and a milkshake and said please. She had manners but they weren't genuine, used out of habit rather than class. If a burglar was helping himself to the family silver, she would have said: "Get out of my house, please, or I'm calling the police."

The woman was fond of her own voice. "Did you hear that radio commercial?" she asked her husband loudly. "Religion, alcohol and sex all in one go – how did a little time bomb like that slip under the radar, I wonder? There is no way broadcasting cleared that."

The husband scooped the froth off his coffee and for a moment he said nothing. Then he took a sip and spoke quietly. "I heard it," he said and he smiled. "One of your clients too. Aren't they lucky to have such a high-flying troubleshooter, who loves a good challenge, at their disposal? You'll have your work cut out for you though, won't you, darling? Every craw-thumping anti-alcohol pro-life creationist nutjob will be burning up the phonelines with bones to pick. What angle will you take on this? That cider is made from apples and hence is good for you?" He was smiling at her, but his tone was cynical. "How lucky for you that you don't let pesky morals get in the way of good spin."

"Get a grip!" his wife snapped.

Saskia's heart twisted sharply and the air in the café compressed. Another rumble of thunder grumbled overhead.

The husband and wife glared at each other and the little girl interrupted. She expertly changed the subject by telling her father about the African lady who'd fainted in the department store.

"She fell into a rail of trousers and it fell on top of her," she explained. "The crowd around her wouldn't stand back to let her son through. He thought his mother was dead."

"The poor fella. Did they call for an ambulance?" asked her father.

"Daddy, she only fainted because of the heat," the girl said indignantly. "Anyway, she just wanted to pay for her things and go home."

The mother stirred her coffee and laughed to herself.

"Indeed," she remarked, "a clever woman, that one. From the

flats – I recognised her. The shop gave her the items for free, you know – the full school uniform, would you credit that? Terrified out of their wits she'd sue while the rest of us idiots, who actually have to work and pay for every single thing, stood by watching the whole affair." She laughed and shook her head and stirred her coffee.

"Charming," her husband remarked.

The little girl looked at her feet. Her face burned and she sucked her thumb.

"Emma!" the woman scolded and the girl removed her thumb from her mouth.

They finished their drinks and, as they were leaving, the ad came on the radio again. The woman listened carefully, and Saskia didn't like the look of the smile that curled onto her face. The door shut behind them and it started to rain.

She was glad to get home that evening. On her way, she picked up another bottle of wine. She believed she deserved it. It had been a bad day from start to finish.

She sat at her table, kicked off her shoes and watched the thunderstorm. People scurried home.

The teacher raced into the square, pulling a shopping cart of groceries behind her. Tom Winters parked and got out of his car, carrying shopping bags from an expensive Italian deli. No supermarkets for the runner; only the finest ingredients would do, preferably ones harvested and prepared by genuine Italian peasants. The Kimbas arrived home at dusk, wet through, with a bag from a city department store. Tessa Kimba was limping slightly and looked weary. The boy reached down to pet the lonely dog which had scampered out from under a sad little shrub in the garden. Someone had left a bowl of something out for it. It was empty now. His mother shooed it away.

The sky grew darker and more ominous. Lightning flashed frequently and the thunder grew louder and nearer. The storm was terrific and it seemed to mark the end of the summer. The wind picked up, the rain beat down, doors closed and curtains were drawn.

Saskia poured a hefty glass of wine and knelt on the floor by her chest of drawers. Then, drawer by drawer, she looked through her precious things. It was part of her Saturday-night ritual. The first drawer contained three tablecloths with corresponding sets of napkins neatly folded and never used. Each layer was sprinkled with sprigs of lavender to keep them fresh. She patted down the pristine collection, pushed the drawer closed and pulled open the next.

This one held pottery, hand-made roughly hewn plates and mugs carefully painted, and still in their tissue paper. Sets of sheets and pillowcases sat a drawer down from that: white with woven-in ribbon, waiting to be shaken out, tucked in and used. The last drawer contained gifts, all from foreign countries, none of which she'd been to. It was her sister who wandered, eternally running. Sketches from Prague, reed-woven placemats from Thailand, wooden carvings from Cape Town, a Boab nut from Western Australia, tiny Malaysian vases, Vietnamese chopsticks and a Balinese jewellery box. This last she removed from the drawer and began to slowly trace the flower pattern on the lid. She opened the box and spilled the contents into her palm: forty-five perfect white pills, enough now. She put them back, closed the box and slid the drawer shut.

Upstairs the man paced again, over and back across the floorboards, in an agitated fashion. Perhaps he was concocting fresh notes and she was next on his list. "STOP BREATHING – IT'S ANNOYING." If Saskia had had a gun in her chest of drawers, she would have grabbed it, raced upstairs and shot him, or lamed him or at least waved it about to put the frighteners on him.

She sat back at her table. Outside, the little dog still waited under the shrub. As night drew in and doors closed, it grew confused and scared. It curled into a ball and didn't move unless it heard a car. Then it lifted its head hopefully and let it sink down again once it passed. There had been no answer from Animal Rescue. It was distressing. Saskia knew nothing about dogs and was a little scared of them, but she knew enough to know it had to be hungry. She chopped up some cooked ham and fetched a bowl of water.

She was about to pull on her coat when she heard the front door open. The outdoor light flickered on. She switched off her own light and peered out the window. A man stepped out of the building into the rain. She knew by his stance that it was the recluse. She pulled open the window a crack. The air felt electric and smelt of rain. The man wore a baseball cap that advertised calf feed and an anorak, and he was greasy and stooped. The dog ran up the steps to him and wagged its tail hopefully. It was less energetic now, less optimistic.

"Come here, girl," Joe Delaney said softly.

He crouched down and the little black dog with the white neck and belly cocked its ears and came to him. He picked up the wet bundle, pulled it close and sat down on the steps in the rain. Then he rocked back and forth, whimpering quietly as the rain beat down and the gutters bubbled.

"I don't know what I can do for you, girl," he said into her wet hair, "but we'll start with a bit of grub."

# Chapter 6

Sunday passed lazily. It was sunny again, though cooler. People washed their cars, picked weeds and sat on their doorsteps lapping up the last days of summer. Saskia watched and listened.

Throughout the day the recluse made sporadic appearances, darting out of the building and out of the square with the dog bundled under his coat. His expressions were varying shades of terror. He had a dog now and dogs had to do their business out in the open. He hadn't bargained for that. It almost made her smile.

She heard her radio ad several times but the jeep woman's comments had taken the shine off it. She was right: her voice sounded ridiculous and the script cringier than ever. Now it irritated her. Each replay deepened an impending sense of doom and on Monday morning she woke up feeling anxious, already knowing it was going to be a bad day. She was on an early shift and got ready over toast and tea.

In the flat beneath her, Patrick Kimba pretended to be asleep. Curled up in a ball, he faced the wall and imagined all sorts of shapes and patterns working their way out of the darkness. He could hear a dog barking. It sounded like it was somewhere in the house but he couldn't be sure. He could also hear his mother's breathing and could tell she was already awake. The breaths weren't deep enough. They were careful and gentle. He didn't dare to move. The fold-up bed was noisy and the springs sounded like a circus trampoline even if you turned very slowly. One sound and his mother would call out to him and that meant curtains drawn and the day beginning and, although he was excited about starting school, he was a little nervous too. He wondered what the other kids would be like. He wasn't sure about wearing a school uniform either. It hung from the wardrobe like a navy monster and looked as though it might be itchy. The trousers, shirt, tie and jumper were new but his shoes weren't. The lady in the charity shop said they were as good as new and smiled like that was a normal thing to say but he knew it wasn't normal to put your feet into shoes where another boy's feet had been. It didn't feel right and they were a bit smelly even after his mother pressed in a new pair of insoles. He would have preferred old trousers and new shoes.

The day was bright, fresh and light and the square was a carnival of activity. Added to the office staff and shop girls and civil servants and labourers and bricklayers, were the schoolchildren. Trussed up in their shiny uniforms with ribbons and coloured fluffy bits in their hair, they were sparkling clean. The small ones took careful steps in their new shoes and held their mothers' hands for guidance. The older ones were more confident and made jokes and laughed and pulled on the sleeves of their new jumpers to stretch them out of shape into something that resembled cool.

At the school gate Saskia waited to cross with a group of parents and children. The lollipop lady was a plump and jolly sort who took pride in her work. The responsibility of ferrying her charges across the road to safety was one that weighed heavily on her broad shoulders and she wielded her lollipop stick as though about to chair a meeting at the UN.

The gate was a loading bay to a zoo where an assortment of transport – bicycles, people carriers, saloons and four-wheel drives – offloaded their occupants. Kids climbed out and climbed down and there were shouts and greetings and all manner of exchanges. Some mothers were glamorous and cheerful, others looked pale and exhausted and others wore pristine gym gear. All were jittery with a mixture of delight and guilt at the prospect of getting their kids out of their hair. In the middle of them all, Mrs Kimba and her son picked their way through the crowd. They were like two black pebbles on a beach of white stones. The boy held his mother's hand and was brave. Saskia hoped the other children would be nice to him.

In the café, she arranged the papers. The jeep woman was already there, sitting over a double espresso, reading a tabloid through her sunglasses. She spoke on her phone with a clipped urgency.

"Fiona Fox here," she stated, and she seemed very pleased with the alliteration her name created. "Yes, I've seen it," she said and she flicked through a couple of pages. "It's bad, needs to be managed. Heard the radio ad too, unfortunate timing all of it."

Saskia pretended to wipe down a table and glanced over the woman's shoulder. The paper was opened on a double-page spread about the perils of alcohol advertising. The headline read, "WOULD YOU ADAM AND EVE IT?" and there was a picture. It was a group of blind-drunk teenagers surrounded by cans of Adam's Apple cider. The woman spoke again.

"You know, the agency should have known better. Rookie mistakes here. Religious and sexual connotations in the script along with an article like this will do untold damage to the brand. Someone's going to have to take the flack."

There was a silence. The woman nodded.

"I'll get working on it," she said and she hung up.

When she left a mist of heavy perfume lingered and Saskia smiled. The thought of Tom Winters getting a bollocking made the situation ever so slightly less unbearable.

She cleared the table and wondered how the little Kimba boy was getting on during his first day of school.

As it turned out, Patrick's day started out well enough. He was put sitting beside a cross girl with a ponytail who picked her nose, and across from a girl called Emma who kept staring at him. There was a boy called Brad beside her. He had red hair and freckles. The classroom smelt of chalk dust and was stuffy.

"This is Patrick," Miss Hennessy told everyone.

"*Dia dhuit, a Phádraig!*" they all chorused in Irish.

36

They did sums and religion and spelling and wrote a story: "What I did during my summer holidays."

Brad was funny and kept trying to make everyone laugh. When the teacher turned her back to write on the blackboard, he pulled faces at the cross girl. She folded her arms and ignored him but he didn't stop.

Without turning, the teacher knew who was making everyone giggle. She kept writing on the blackboard.

"Brad Flanagan, if I get down as far as you, you'll be one sorry boy," she said.

That was saying something. Miss Hennessy was nice but she was very tall and very huge and could easily flatten any of them.

At break time they ate under the watchful eye of the teacher before being released into the yard to play: peanut-butter sandwiches, mini-pizzas, cheese straws, crisps, smoothies, bars of chocolate, biscuits and soft drinks. Patrick's sweet potato was eyed with suspicion and outside he was left on his own. He sat in the shade under a huge horse-chestnut tree and drew shapes in the dirt with the toe of his second-hand shoe. He was hot, but he did not take off his jumper. His mother had warned him not to. Other kids chased each other in the sun and the older ones sent texts on their mobiles.

When the bell went they all trooped back inside and that's when the trouble started. Brad Flanagan started making fun of Patrick's accent and had somehow found out that he had got his uniform for free. He wanted to know how come. Patrick said nothing.

But, even worse, his shoes had really started to smell. Brad Flanagan sniffed the air like a dog trying to trace the culprit.

The teacher got cross.

"What's the matter with you, Brad Flanagan?" she asked. "Can't you sit still for a second?"

"There's a smell! It's from him, Teacher," he said and he pointed straight at Patrick. "His feet stink."

Heads turned and all eyes landed on Patrick. He felt hot and dizzy and looked down at the desk.

"That's enough, Brad," the teacher scolded. "It's stuffy today so we're all a bit smelly. After a good wash tonight we'll all be right as rain again."

She opened all the windows and Patrick hated his stupid shoes more than ever.

Later that day, as she steamed milk, Saskia had to admit that although the Fox woman was on the radio lambasting her *husky mysteriousness*, she was impressed by her polished ability. Aul' ones and mothers and fathers and teachers and doctors and teachers and priests bayed for blood and called for a ban on alcohol advertising. The woman defended the cider company without appearing to defend it and then cleverly shifted the blame. She explained that there had been a mistake, an oversight and some bad decisions made by someone too junior for the job – the script, the husky voice, unnecessary and ridiculously overplayed, clearly an amateur. The advertising agency would no longer be working on the account. The commercial was being pulled. Everyone was terribly sorry.

The queue lengthened and Saskia sprinkled chocolate through a star stencil on the froth of a cappuccino. She shrugged in resignation.

"Feck that for a game of soldiers anyway," she said.

Later, she opened a bottle of wine and wondered what the parameters for alcoholism were, which was interesting, because plenty of people seemed to be drinking on that warm Monday evening.

Nuala Murphy, the teacher, sat on her steps and drank whiskey from a tumbler. She stared into the middle distance and absently stroked her cat. Perhaps her first day of term had been a bad one. Two doors up, Tom Winters swigged beer from a bottle and had a vacant look about him. And two doors up from him, at the house with the green door, star troubleshooter Fiona Fox sat on her steps with a huge glass of wine, one she felt she'd earned no doubt, after a day of destroying careers. Saskia watched her through her binoculars and a tiny ball of anger curled inside her. She poured more wine.

Before bed, Patrick Kimba and his mother sat outside and drank glasses of milk. The front door was shut firmly behind them now. And although the little boy tried not to sound downhearted, Saskia knew he was. His mother did too.

"What is the matter, *ma puce*?" she asked and pulled him close.

He shrugged and drank from his glass. It left a white moustache. He wiped it away with his pyjama sleeve. His mother tickled him and he squirmed.

"It's nothing, Maman," he said. "They just make fun of my accent."

But his mother knew there was more to it than this and she probed.

He shrugged again as if to dismiss the weight of what he was about to say.

"Everyone in my class knows I got my uniform for free."

His mother sat up straight and suddenly, as though she'd been shot.

"But how?"

The boy shrugged again.

"There was a girl from my class called Emma Fox in the shop that day and her mother said you pretended to faint."

"But I didn't."

"I know, Maman," he said.

"Jesus help us," she whispered.

The two of them sat there for a long time and said nothing and Saskia felt a dart of pain in her heart. Her schooldays had been cruel. Spectacularly unfashionable spectacles and pudginess had left her wide open, easy pickings for the sharp-tongued bullies. It still did. People still mistook fatness for stupidity.

She raised the binoculars again to observe the Fox woman and made the connection. "Like mother, like daughter," she muttered and the ball of anger turned and expanded. The more she drank, the bigger it grew. Fiona Fox needed a comeuppance. She would sleep on it.

She opened her jewellery box and played with the white pills before selecting two which she swallowed before going to bed. Her mobile rang several times, but she slept through.

# Chapter 7

There was a turn in the weather after that. Metallic grey skies marked the end of the summer. The rain beat down. Petals and leaves fell to earth, doorsteps emptied and fires were lit.

Up until then Saskia had always watched over the square with a detached perspective but since the "cider fiasco" her radar worked on overdrive and she couldn't shake Tom Winters, the Fox woman, the teacher, the recluse or the African mother and her son. They appeared to circle one another like animals. Where one had walked five minutes previously, the other brushed through five minutes later, placing new footprints where the others had just been. Each unaware and unconscious of anyone's existence except their own.

Tom Winters had a look about him that suggested his star had burnt out. There were fewer female callers. He often sat in his car when he returned home as though he was reluctant to get out. When he did, he sometimes paused at Fiona Fox's gate with a murderous look on his face.

One day she caught him circling her jeep and kicking the tyres and there was a bust-up.

"*What on earth are you doing skulking around my car?*" Fiona shouted from her steps.

"*I'm not skulking!*" he shouted back.

"*That's exactly what you're doing!*"

"*And so what if I am? You're the woman who ruined my life!*"
he thundered.

"What?" Fiona said impatiently as she walked right up to him.

"You're the weapon who got me fired over a radio ad."

"What for?"

"Cider. Adam's Apple."

She shrugged. "I was employed by the client to clean up a mess.
I did. There were casualties."

"Aren't you noble?" he said.

"Aren't I noble?" She laughed. "You work in advertising – get
real."

"Now, because of you, I work in sales promotion," he said and
he walked away.

Saskia saw the teacher cuddling her cat, growing paler and sourer
by the day, and she watched as Tessa Kimba grew weaker.

Every afternoon, the African woman collected her son from
school and Saskia waited for the boy with his bobbing satchel to
emerge from the lane into the square, running ahead of his mother,
all the way to the front door, eager to get on with the real business
of the day: playing with his football. Saskia watched him and
smiled and felt a fondness for the boy who grinned toothily even
when there wasn't much to smile about. She had overheard him tell
his mother that his nickname in school was now "Smelly". It was
because of his shoes. It broke Saskia's heart. It also made her very
angry. She directed this anger towards Mrs Fox, who she
scrutinised daily, noting her movements and her careless driving.
She also focused her anger on Joe Delaney who had started to walk
his dog late at night when the square was dark with shadows. She
began following him. She wasn't sure why. Perhaps she wanted to
frighten him, pay him back for the note, all of the notes.

She discovered that the square was a strange place at night. The
streetlights cast spooky shadows, cats stalked, and urban foxes
prowled. There were late-night revellers, drunken stumblers, mad
men, mad yokes, taxi drivers, shift-workers and canoodling couples
that sneaked around and spoke in urgent whispers. Words floated
out from windows and there were strange goings-on in the walled
garden: dots of torchlight, voices and giggles which was interesting

considering the door to it was locked to all but permanent residents.

Every night she tracked man and dog from a safe distance and imagined shaking Joe Delaney until his bones rattled. Then she felt bad because he seemed to really love the dog. Certainly the dog loved him.

And every night she passed the Fox woman's jeep and considered puncturing her tyres but thought better of it. The woman was an ignorant driver and the type who ruined careers at the drop of a hat, but it was hardly tyre-slashing territory. She changed her mind about this when the jeep narrowly avoided knocking down Patrick Kimba. This happened shortly after he began playing football in the dark.

# Chapter 8

Halloween approached in a crossfire of premature fireworks and bangers which filled the air with the pungent smell of burnt powder. Youngsters scavenged for flammable items for their bonfires: tyres, branches, sacks, bags and rags. The enthusiastic carved out pumpkins and made lanterns. They hung skeletons, witches and ghosts from their doors or mastered intricate artistic displays of cobwebs, leaves, twigs and crab apples.

Patrick took to chewing on his lip. His mother was sleeping more and, with her in bed most of the time, there was less and less time for getting outside with his football. She kept the keys with her too, pinned to the inside of her dress pocket, even when she was sleeping. It was a habit, security, she told him, and he understood that but it made sneaking out difficult. The big front door had a spring and it clicked shut, locking you out unless you had the keys. If the other door, which the posh houses still had, wasn't bricked up it would have been perfect. It was right outside their flat, but there was no use thinking about that. He mulled over the problem, watching passers-by from their window which was barred so it wasn't an option either. He sat on the couch while his mother slept and tapped his ball from foot to foot, over and back, over and back, softly so it wouldn't wake her. He chewed on his bottom lip and listened to car alarms, raindrops and early fireworks and the solution came to him.

He was pleased with himself. Now every evening, once his maman dropped off, he carefully pulled open the drawer of odds and ends and removed the roll of Christmas sticky tape. Then he pushed open the flat door silently, listened and crept upstairs. Two strips of cheerful dancing Santas tape pinned back the front-door latch long enough for him to kick his ball around in the brighter corners cast by the street lights. It gave him fifteen minutes – maybe longer but he didn't risk it. If his mother caught him outside there would be hell to pay. She had warned him, made it clear, that if he left the flat without her permission, nothing but bad would come to him. That was all very well but Patrick saw the situation differently: if he didn't practise, then nothing good would come to him either. No matter what, by the time she came to and started asking questions about homework, he needed to be back at the kitchen counter scratching his head over sums.

Each time he kicked the ball he imagined it was Brad Flanagan's fat head. Because of him he had the nickname. Now, every time Patrick said anything, everyone in the class started sniffing. He liked lunchtimes, because that's when he was left completely alone under the giant horse-chestnut tree. He had no one to talk to but he didn't mind so long as he had his blue ball.

School was terrible and some days were worse than others like the day Miss Hennessy brought them up to the top of the classroom one by one to tell the class what they wanted to be when they grew up.

"I want to play football for Ireland," he stated quietly and everyone laughed.

Even Miss Hennessy smiled. "Anything else, Patrick?" she asked gently. "Something less glamorous?"

"I want to play for Innskeep too," he said.

"Innskeep?" said Miss Hennessy, and this time she smiled even more widely while the class sniggered. "Well, it's good to dream!"

Patrick sat down and Brad kicked him under the table.

Then there was another day when Brad Flanagan cornered him and demanded information about his father. He had a friend with him, a skinny older boy called Chad, who was from the same estate and had very close-together eyes.

"What's the story with your father?" Brad barked, his hands on his hips.

Chad said nothing at all, just looked at him, waiting for an answer.

"He's a soldier," Patrick said and that shut Brad up. Patrick didn't want to go into detail. He knew his mother wouldn't like it.

Saskia thought Halloween was a pointless celebration made even worse by her dumb boss who thought it would be a good idea to put orange food colouring into the milk so people could enjoy frothy festive orange cappuccinos and lattes. Unfortunately, no one else thought it was a good idea and their regulars practically ran out of the café screaming. Saskia was given the job of cleaning out the milk tank and discarding the orange mess. Afterwards, the sink looked as if someone had murdered a pumpkin. Worse still, they were all "encouraged" to wear face paint, to get into the spirit of the day that was in it. She was administered with Aunt Sally cheeks which really looked preposterous when you were trying to talk your way out of an orange-milk situation with an angry customer.

At home, she watched the fireworks from her window and they made her feel lonely. She put her head in her hands and cried but just for a moment. Crying was an indulgence she could not afford to slip into. She wiped her eyes roughly and raised her binoculars to scan the square. No jeep yet. Its driver was no doubt off somewhere making someone's life a misery. The boy was out playing football. He was dressed up as a little devil and looked cute. Tonight, he was alone again.

Patrick had been excited about Halloween. The priest pulled him aside after Mass and handed him a bag which contained a devil costume and a devil mask with horns and cuts and scars and yellowed teeth. His mother thought it was a strange thing for a priest to give a young boy but she promised to bring him to each of the doors around the square once it was dark. It was all arranged. She would hang back in the shadows and let him knock on the doors. If he was asked to perform, he would say a little poem in French that warded off evil spirits and then collect his loot in a bag. A load of sweets and crisps – he could hardly wait.

But when it came to trick or treating time, his mother wouldn't wake up. He stood over her in his devil outfit and mask and watched her sleep. Her breathing was heavy and a tiny trail of spittle made a river from her mouth and, even when he shook her gently, she didn't budge.

He watched the other children with their parents, going from door to door: witches, ghosts, wizards and princesses, giggling and calling out to each other and comparing their bags. Fireworks lit the sky like waterfalls: pink and blue and silver. He tapped his ball from foot to foot, over and back, over and back, and wished his father were there to take him round the houses. He decided he was going outside, if not to trick or treat, then at least to kick his ball around. He took the tape from the drawer, crept downstairs in the dark and taped the door latch into place. The sky was festooned with fireworks and smoke and he could hear sirens. He kicked his ball down the steps and it rolled out onto the street. Without thinking, he ran out after it. There was a screech of brakes and the jeep driver let down her window and screamed abuse when she saw the miniature devil. He quickly retrieved his ball but when he ran back in through the gate his mother was waiting for him and her face was like thunder.

"Inside," she said, "*now*." He started to sob. "And you can stop that immediately! I told you there would be trouble if you disobeyed me."

Saskia saw it all and, after drinking far too much wine, she walked the square purposefully. Trailing Joe Delaney for a bit she tingled with rage as she bent down to pick up a stone. She closed her fist tightly around it. It was sharp and it pierced her skin. The pain brought her to her senses and she stopped stalking. Instead, she walked straight over to where Fiona Fox's jeep was parked and stood over it for a while, contemplating. Being a snob or a mindless troubleshooter hardly merited a destroyed car. But as far as Saskia was concerned, dangerous driving did. She could have killed the boy and that was unforgivable. She took the stone and casually walked by the driver's door digging in and dragging the sharp edge of the stone along it without once looking back. Then she went home.

# Chapter 9

The next morning, Saskia woke abruptly and with a pounding head. Upstairs, the dog barked. A horrible sound sawed its way through her skull. The noise was coming from outside and it seemed to go on forever. It stirred everyone. Blinds snapped up, doors opened and slammed, heads popped out windows, eyes watched. Saskia pulled open her curtains and at first the sunlight dazzled her. When the black spots cleared, she saw Joe Delaney and his dog slip out of the house. She could also see the cause of the commotion.

It was the Fox woman, sitting in her jeep, leaning on the horn and screaming her head off in a most unflattering way. From a distance, it looked comical, but Saskia knew she had made a mistake when she saw the woman's daughter. The young girl stood white-faced on the steps of their house and looked on while her mother had what appeared to be a nervous breakdown. When the horn-blowing persisted, she fetched her father. He ran out of the house, through the gate and banged on the bonnet of the jeep with the heel of his hand. The noise stopped but only to allow an uncivil exchange of words. Fiona Fox got out and pointed at the door.

"*Someone has destroyed my car and you don't care!*" she shrieked at her husband.

"They're well gone at this stage, whoever they are," he replied with a steely calmness.

"How the hell do you know? They could be looking on, laughing."

"And do you think that by sitting on your car horn like a maniac you'll lure them out of their hiding place as opposed to just annoying the neighbours?"

"Fuck the neighbours!"

Her husband laughed.

"*If you had any balls,*" Fiona Fox shouted venomously, "*you would hunt down the person who did this!*"

Mr Fox put his hands on his hips and studied the sky, counting to ten.

"That's right, say nothing," she continued. "Useless – no, actually," she reconsidered, "you're worse than useless."

She slammed the car door and kicked a tyre.

"*Emma, hop in, I'm already running late!*" she yelled at the little girl before turning back to her husband.

The square was starting to get busy. It was time to go to work and to school. Passers-by watched with bemused interest, glad it was someone else and not them involved in so public a scene of domestic disharmony.

The front door opened and the Kimbas stepped outside: the boy in his uniform, ball under his arm. His mother looked weaker today, sickly, frail and miserable. The boy took his mother's hand.

A few doors down, Nuala the teacher watched Fiona Fox and shook her head. A stack of compositions weighed heavily in her arms. Her cat curled around her ankles.

Tom Winters returned to the square from his run and slowed to get a closer look at the car damage and Fiona turned on him.

"*Was this your handiwork?*" she screamed, pointing at the keyed door of the jeep.

"Nope," he said loudly, "I'm not a criminal," but he smiled just so Fiona Fox was absolutely clear that he didn't feel the remotest bit sorry for her.

And Saskia looked on at all of this with a kind of fascinated guilt. There was something pleasing about seeing the Fox woman suffer – but not her daughter. She wondered what had possessed her. She pulled on her dressing gown and went outside to sit on the step.

Afterwards, she would say she sensed something terrible was about to happen. Every action had a sharp clarity and each followed the next in a slow-motion domino-effect.

As the Kimbas passed through the gate, the engine of the four-wheel drive roared to life and Joe Delaney and his dog rounded the corner. The teacher opened her gate, her cat stopped to lick its fur. The jeep accelerated, Tom Winters hopped onto the footpath off the street, and just as his feet made contact with the ground, the dog spotted the cat. It shot out of Joe Delaney's grasp, hurtled gleefully down the footpath and made a beeline for it. The teacher screamed, Tom Winters turned and the dog chased the cat, out onto the street, right into the path of the four-wheel drive.

There was a yelp and the nervy sensation of the life being knocked out of something hung in the air. The teacher's papers fell and scattered. The recluse with the cap and the dirty coat ran howling towards the scene of the accident. His face was distorted in grief. Tears rolled down his haggard cheeks and his glasses slipped off onto the ground. He picked up his dog, which was twitching but then went still, and scuttled away, disappearing down a lane and out of the square, and all the while the little girl in the passenger seat of the jeep wailed. Tessa Kimba pulled her son closer, shielding his eyes from the bloody scene. Tom Winters slipped inside, the teacher sank to the ground and knelt over her cat. It was like a very low-budget horror film.

Saskia went into her flat, grabbed her rubber gloves and a refuse sack and crossed the street. The cat was placed carefully into the bag. The teacher took it from her gingerly, bending down to pick up the dog-owner's glasses. She was a pitiful figure as she made her way back to her house in her old cardigan and blotched face, but before going in through her gate she turned and addressed the driver.

"I always hated you, Fiona Fox," she said quietly and she climbed the steps with the plastic bag that contained her only friend.

Saskia went back inside. It was time to stop drinking.

All day long, the accident replayed in her head and she couldn't shake the images of the squashed, lifeless cat and the dead dog. After her shift, she sat at her window and thought about the teacher who was now completely alone. She also thought about Joe Delaney and how she, Saskia Heffernan, was worse than the crazy recluse was any day. He might have been a racist weirdo and a low-rung human being to boot but at least he'd been kind enough to take in an abandoned dog. She wondered where he would bury the body. There was no sign of him – no creaking floorboards or agitated pacing. This evening, she would not drink.

Tom Winters had other ideas. He sat on his steps and sipped from a bottle of craft beer. He appeared dishevelled and hopeless. His father watched him from a window before coming outside. He paced in front of his son with his hands cupped behind his back. At times he stopped and looked at him in a disappointed fashion.

"What's got into you?" he asked.

Tom Winters shrugged.

"Don't shrug at me, young man," his father hissed and Tom laughed. This enraged the older man. "You've had a setback. Get over it," he said and he plucked an imaginary weed.

"What would you know?" his son replied through gritted teeth. "It's not a setback, it's a demotion – out of advertising and into the sales promotion department, the gulag of marketing. I've been made a scapegoat, taken the hit for everyone because of that hoor Fiona Fox!"

"She was doing her job. And don't you know she's always had it in for you ever since your football smashed through her kitchen window? Take it on the chin."

He climbed the steps then halted before going back inside.

"I always said you would have been better off going into medicine like your sisters and me before them. Lord knows you had the brains for it."

Tom Winters ignored him and opened another beer.

Saskia made a pot of tea and sat back in her chair. The boy and his mother were late. Guilt clawed at her. That morning, Tessa Kimba had looked terrified as she pulled her son away from the scene of the accident. Saskia watched the lane, willing them home, and was relieved when she spied the small figure bobbing along the lane towards the square. It was Patrick Kimba and he was in a terrible hurry. He burst into the square and kept running until he arrived at the front door. He was alone, no Mrs Kimba. They were having another race. Today, the boy had won by a long shot. His mother was nowhere to be seen.

Saskia heard him knock on the window of their flat below, calling for his mother, but there was no answer. He sat on the doorstep until he caught his breath, then he shrugged off his rucksack and kicked his football in the confined patch of front garden. The street would have been better, Saskia thought, but no doubt his mother would kill him if she caught him after the Halloween night near-accident. Dribble, kick, shoot.

Saskia watched him with a smile. He was as cute as a button, his face a perfect smooth form of innocence, his skin a velvety brown. For some reason, he was wearing odd pants. They were beige, not the uniform navy.

Time passed and there was still no sign of the mother. It was not like her to leave the boy alone. Saskia considered going out to him but decided to wait another while. She guessed Mrs Kimba would be prickly about intrusion.

An hour went by. He took a break, sipped from a water bottle and then lay back and watched the clouds pass overhead. Saskia was mesmerised by him. There was something different about the boy. He was wise somehow and self-contained. Time ticked and he waited patiently. He played with his ball again, lay down again. A cloud passed over the sun and cast a shadow and he sat up. He stood up and surveyed the square: north, south, east and west, no sign.

Saskia decided it was time to check on him. She slipped her feet into her shoes and pushed back her chair. Then, as she stood up she saw Joe Delaney push the gate open. He was carrying a shovel and he hissed something as he passed the boy. Whatever it was, it made Patrick pick up his ball and bag and run.

Saskia flew out of her flat past Joe Delaney in the hall – a blur of greasiness, a whiff of sorrow– but by the time she got outside the boy was running down the road. And he might have kept on running only his football stopped him. He dropped it and it bounced, skipped and rolled through a gate and came a to stop at the feet of Tom Winters who looked up and came face to face with

Patrick Kimba who was out of breath and panting.

Saskia held back.

Tom Winters and the boy studied each other silently.

"Hello, what's up with you?" Tom Winters asked eventually.

"There's a man," the boy replied, still out of breath.

"Oh. What sort of a man?"

The boy lowered his voice to a whisper.

"He's old and wrinkled and his eyes roll like a wild horse's. He has a bag and a shovel and a dead dog and he knows where I live because he lives there too! He called me a dirty brat."

"What?" Tom Winters said and he sat up. "Did you rob his orchard or kick his dog or something?"

"No!"

"Well, then, why are you running?" he half teased. "You must have done something to annoy him."

"I didn't," said the boy and that was when he started to cry. He dug his fists into his eyes and sobbed quietly.

"Jaysus, what's wrong?" Tom Winters asked and he patted Patrick on the shoulder. "I was only teasing. Where do you live? I'll take you home."

The boy cried harder then and Tom couldn't get any sense out of him. A breeze rustled the leaves in the trees. It would start getting dark soon. He scratched his head, at a loss.

"My maman's not at home," said the boy whose nose had begun to run. "I walked home on my own and I don't know where she is and I looked into the flat and she's not there and I'm hungry and I was playing football and that man came and I ran off!"

He delivered this in one long wail of distress and that's when Saskia walked over to them.

"You?" said Tom Winters. "I thought you looked familiar that day at the studio."

"That's right, Tom Winters, me," Saskia replied. "I live in Lavender Square too, imagine."

"I appear to have found an orphan," Tom Winters said.

Saskia crouched down to Patrick Kimba's level.

"Patrick, isn't it?" she said kindly and he nodded. She turned to Tom. "He and his mother live in the same building as me."

"Well, have you seen his mother today?" Tom Winters asked

and Saskia could tell he was impatient, keen to wash his hands of the inconvenience and get back to his evening.

"No. Not since this morning. Do you know where your mam could be, Patrick?"

He shook his head. His wiped his nose on his sleeve and looked glum. "She wasn't there after school and she always is."

"Did you tell your teacher?"

"No, I just ran. I wanted to get home. I hate school."

"She works, doesn't she?"

He nodded.

"Where does she work?"

"Different places. She cleans houses."

"Do you know where she worked today?"

He shook his head and began to sniffle again.

"Do you have a mobile number for her?"

"She doesn't have one."

Saskia sighed. "Okay, well, we're going to look after you until she comes back or we find her. I'm sure there's a simple explanation."

He nodded.

Saskia took Tom aside and tried to figure out what to do. She told him her flat was too small and she didn't want to risk running into Joe Delaney in case it set Patrick off again. Tom said his place didn't suit either which Saskia knew wasn't true. But when he suggested his neighbour, the teacher, Miss Murphy, Saskia thought it was a good idea. Teachers seemed to always know what to do – even griefstricken ones who'd just lost their cats. She removed a tissue from her pocket and wiped the boy's nose.

Tom Winters stalled.

"Look, you seem to know what you're doing here," he evened with her. "Could you take him in there do you think and fill the teacher in? I'm no good at this."

"No, I couldn't," Saskia said. "You know the teacher, I don't." And she would have laughed at his attempt to wriggle free only the little boy looked so distressed and he started to cry again. He had wet his pants. "We'll go together. Come on. But first I'll slip a note under Mrs Kimba's door in case she shows up. And I'll ring the school."

But the school knew nothing about Mrs Kimba.

When Saskia got back the boy was co-operative and went with them to the teacher's. He seemed relieved to have two grown-ups taking care of things, and he took them both by surprise by taking a hand each. His felt tiny and they were cold, like small stones.

The teacher answered the door. She wore a plastic apron and gardening gloves and had a trowel in her hand. She regarded the three of them suspiciously and brushed away a stray tear.

"Can I help you, Mr Winters?" she asked.

"I hope so, Miss Murphy," Tom said. "We have a young man here who seems to have lost his mother."

# Chapter 10

Nuala Murphy filled the bath with water and bubbles. The little boy still held Saskia's hand. He seemed to trust her and it felt nice. The teacher had a disapproving sniff and she sniffed at intervals as the bubbles worked their way into a foamy mountain. She tested the water temperature with her elbow.

"You seem to know what you're doing, Miss Murphy," Saskia observed.

The teacher sniffed again and dried her hands.

"Nuala," she said. "Please call me Nuala." She stood up and winced.

Nuala Murphy had the gestures of an old woman even though she was in her early fifties at most.

"I nursed both my parents through long and lingering illnesses, God rest them," she explained and sniffed.

The boy had never been in a bath, only a shower. The bubbles helped and after a while he seemed happier with the situation.

It was difficult not to smile.

"Have a little splash about," the teacher said, more kindly now. "I'll try to find you something to wear and we'll find your mammy for you."

They left him alone. Saskia followed the woman across the landing into a box bedroom. It had peeling aeroplane wallpaper, a poster of a footballer and an ancient wardrobe stuffed with sheets and shirts, jackets and men's pyjamas. Saskia wondered who the previous occupant of the room had been, but somehow shied away from asking Nuala.

Nuala pulled out a pair of flannel pyjamas and shook them out. There was a distinct smell of mothballs.

"We'll have to put his uniform in the wash," she said and she sniffed again. "Also, we should check his schoolbag for a pair of school trousers. I'm willing to bet he had an accident already today. That's why he was wearing those odd-coloured pants. The school would have some spares."

Saskia fetched his schoolbag. It was neat: a pencil, two copybooks, a water bottle and a raggedy football sticker. His uniform trousers were rolled up inside a plastic bag. They were still wet and Saskia wondered what had caused the little boy to wet his pants the first time round.

They went down a flight of stairs, past an ornate arched window into the hallway where the front door and drawing room were. It was strange being in another house with the same layout but without all the flats, bedsits and grubbiness. The air in the house was cool and smelt of old and musty ghosts. Dark patterned carpet hugged the staircases and hallways, damask wallpaper lined the walls, and furniture, old and impossibly heavy, sagged.

Down another flight to the kitchen which was quiet, save for the steady tick of the clock. It smelt of years of stewed tea, seasonal spices, memories and nostalgia. A bottle of whiskey, half full, sat on the counter, a fruitcake cooled on a wire tray and a votive light glowed red beneath a picture of the Sacred Heart. An oilcloth covered the long kitchen table and a window-seat, stacked with Mills and Boon paperbacks, overlooked a maintained back garden where healthy rose plants swayed in the breeze. Piles of student comprehension, an impressive collection of red biros and a number of remote controls sat on an old range cooker. It was dusty and unused. An electric bar heater, plugged in but not switched on, stretched from the wall socket to an armchair that faced the TV which Tom Winters was watching.

Nuala flicked off the television and the three of them were looking at each other, wondering what to do next, when the phone started to ring in the hallway above them. Nuala jumped, tutted and sighed. She let it ring and it rang persistently. Whoever the caller was, they weren't giving up without a fight.

"You don't want to get that, Miss Murphy?" Tom asked.

"No," Nuala snapped.

Saskia noticed she didn't ask Tom to call her by her first name.

"It would only be poor relatives that would be looking for me," the teacher added, and she laughed nervously.

Saskia looked at Tom who raised his right eyebrow.

Eventually the phone stopped ringing and then the doorbell rang. A few moments later, Tom scowlingly led the jeep-driving Fiona Fox and her daughter into the kitchen. They were bearing flowers and chocolates.

Nuala sniffed and folded her arms.

"Emma just wanted to see how you were after your poor cat," Fiona Fox said. "It was a terrible accident."

"You drive like a maniac," Nuala snapped. "Everyone with sight in their eyes knows it. You're a road hog."

Fiona puffed out her chest like a belligerent pigeon.

"Nuala," she said impatiently, "might I remind you that a bloody dog chased your cat right under my wheels."

"Yes, Fiona," Nuala replied sarcastically, "but you also mangled the bloody dog, didn't you?"

The women glared at each other, Emma Fox looked at her feet and, in the kitchen, with its ticking clock and aroma of stewed tea, there was an awkwardness between people who were used to their own routines and space and didn't want any messy interruptions. Nuala dug her hands into her apron pocket.

"Dogs and cats aside, we have other fish to fry," she said wearily. "You had better sit down."

Fiona did so reluctantly and, while Nuala put on the kettle and cut cake, Saskia filled them in about the little boy whose mother hadn't shown up at the school gate. The school had no information, she'd slipped a note under the door of the flat to let Mrs Kimba know where her son was, she wasn't sure what to do next.

Fiona Fox folded her arms, sat back in her chair and pursed her lips.

Saskia looked at her steadily.

Fiona frowned.

The little girl watched them over her mug of tea.

"Don't I know you from somewhere?" Fiona asked Saskia indignantly.

"I serve you coffee," she said. "You're 'Large Americano with an extra shot'."

"But why are you here, in Lavender Square? Do you offer a takeout service?"

"I live here," Saskia said.

"Right, in one of the flats," Fiona said as if that explained everything.

Saskia noticed how they were all slow to suggest anything that might lead to taking responsibility for the boy.

They chewed and sipped and watched the clock ticking.

Tom Winters made the first move to leave.

"Well, it's time I got home," he said, scraping his chair back over the tiles.

"Where do you think you're off to, Sonny Jim?" Nuala snapped.

"Well, sure, there's no point in us all hanging around looking at each other."

"Sit back down on your backside. No one is going anywhere. He's as much your responsibility as he is any of ours," Nuala said, nodding at each of them.

"Well, I hardly think that's altogether true," Fiona began, but then she stopped mid-sentence because the boy was standing at the kitchen door, wrapped in a bath towel. They had forgotten him.

"The water went cold," he said.

"It's you," said Emma Fox.

They got busy then. Guilt spurred them into action. Tom was steered in the direction of the freezer.

"Find what you can in there and defrost it in the microwave," Nuala ordered.

She told Fiona to ring the Guards and she and Saskia listened to her make the call in the hallway as they ferried Patrick back upstairs to get dressed. She was impatient as she explained the situation and gave her details, unused to having to adhere to anyone's system except her own.

"Yes, Garda," she said after a moment with a heavy sigh, "I'll ring the hospitals."

Nuala closed the door of the box room.

Patrick observed Saskia solemnly as she towel-dried his hair. Nuala snipped the ends off the legs of a pair of huge pyjamas that had been her father's and took a good chunk off each arm. She dressed him, pulling the cord until the bottoms tightened around his belly. The pyjamas were still enormous but it worked. The mothballs made them both sneeze and they smiled at each other.

"I look like I'm wearing a dress," he said, examining himself in the mirror.

"It looks more like a nightshirt really," Nuala observed. "Lots of men wear them."

"Like who?"

"Men, like him," she said, pointing at the poster on the wall.

"Pelé?" he exclaimed. "No way."

"Sure. You know about him?"

He nodded. "We saw a programme about him on telly, Maman and me. He was the best."

"Yes. You play football too – I saw your ball. Are you as good as Pelé?"

"Not yet, but I will be. I'll be better," he said and he sounded very sure of this.

In the kitchen, Tom had assembled an assortment of pre-cooked and labelled meals for one: lasagne, shepherd's pie, chilli, beef stroganoff, stew, beef paprika and chicken curry. He'd also helped himself to a whiskey and somehow managed to pull out all the good silverware, china and napkins. It made the table look oddly festive.

Nuala glared at him. "I didn't mean for you to feed the whole street, just Patrick," she said.

"Well, seeing as you're not letting us go home, I thought you might feed us," he said.

"Well, you've no problem making yourself at home anyway, do you, Mr Winters?" Nuala said, eyeing his whiskey glass, and he reddened a bit.

Saskia smiled slightly. Tom noticed her smirk.

"What's so funny?" he snapped.

"Nothing," she said innocently and they all sat down to eat.

It was a pick-and-mix affair. Tom swapped his shepherd's pie for Saskia's lasagne. Fiona swapped her chilli for Emma's beef stroganoff and Patrick picked at his curry. They were pensive, quiet, save for the scraping of cutlery against plates.

"Did you find my maman yet?" Patrick asked.

There was a momentary pause.

"Not yet, mate," Tom said, "but we're working on it."

Fiona had rung all of the hospitals to no avail. There was no Tessa Kimba registered anywhere.

They resumed eating.

Emma watched Patrick from across the table.

"Maybe your mum fainted again?" she suggested out of the blue.

Patrick looked up from his curry.

"What do you mean?" Nuala asked.

"His mother fainted in a shop one day in town."

"Is that right, Patrick?" Nuala said, turning her attention to the little boy.

"Yeah," Emma said, "she did, and Patrick got his uniform free, didn't he, Mum? You said she was clever."

The table looked at Fiona with interest. Fiona coloured and then, luckily for her, the doorbell rang.

It was the Guards. Nuala brought them into the drawing room. The boy's mother was in Vincent's, the guards explained. She was brought in, having collapsed in a local park and no one knew who she was. She wasn't carrying any ID, only came to a few hours ago, distraught, had no English. Only spoke French and it took a while to organise a translator. Turned out she thought the boy might have returned to the square.

"Which he did," said Nuala.

"Which he did," the Guards said, snapping their notebooks shut, case closed.

After Nuala called the hospital, she beckoned to Fiona.

"You have the car, I have the French," she said emphatically.

Fiona had hoped to slip off home now that Tessa Kimba had been located. But that was not on the cards apparently. Nuala had got it into her head that, as neighbours, they were in this together.

"Your mum had a little fall," Nuala told Patrick. "She's staying in hospital overnight just to get checked out. She wants you not to worry and to go to bed. It's late."

Patrick was doubtful.

"We're going in to see her now and these two," she pointed at Saskia and Tom, "are going to tuck you in. Your uniform is in the washing machine and it will be squeaky clean in the morning."

Fiona couldn't get through to her husband. He wasn't at home and his mobile was switched off. It meant leaving her daughter behind and she wasn't happy about it. She eyed Tom and Saskia warily.

Nuala was practical. "Sure, Emma will be company for little fellow. Aren't they in the same class? There are two beds in that room. Let her sleep for a bit, we don't know how long we'll be."

Fiona rolled her eyes. Everything was simple as far as Nuala Murphy was concerned.

Tom and Saskia were instructed to dress the other bed in the box room and to put Patrick's clothes in the dryer. Everything was organised. The teacher didn't leave much room for argument.

"This is a perfect room for a boy," Saskia said, as they shook out sheets and pillowcases. "It's got that attic-adventure feel to it."

"This house is like a morgue," Tom said, slipping an ancient pillowcase over an equally ancient pillow.

"Isn't that a little uncharitable after the woman's just fed you?"

"I didn't ask to be here," Tom replied childishly.

"I'm sure Tessa Kimba didn't ask to collapse," Saskia responded.

"Well, it must be great to be perfect," Tom Winters said and he left the room.


"Will you play football with me sometimes?" Patrick asked him when they were putting him to bed.

"Of course, mate," Tom said. "Who do you support?"

"Ireland."

"Well, we all support Ireland, but do you have a Premier League team?"

"Innskeep."

"Could be worse," he said and he tousled his hair.

"I'm going to play for Ireland though," Patrick said, making himself clear.

"Sure, but it's probably best to play for a Premier League team too. That's where you'll earn your crust and it's how you'll be discovered. You need a profile to be found in the first place."

"I know. But when I told Teacher that I wanted to play for Innskeep she kinda laughed at me."

"Well, you'll have the last laugh, mate."

"Okay."

Tom switched off the light and he and Saskia left, closing the door behind them.

Even though it was dark Patrick could still see the outline of the wallpaper aeroplanes and across the room he could hear Emma breathing.

"Are you awake?" Emma asked.

"No."

"Do you miss your mum?"

"Leave me alone," Patrick said and he turned over.

Downstairs, Tom washed up and Saskia dried. The silences made her feel self-conscious and, being in such close proximity to all that dark stubble and moodiness, she found herself making inane conversation.

"Isn't it mad? One minute we're recording a radio ad, hardly knowing each other from Adam, the next we're doing the washing-up."

"It's mad altogether," he shrugged. "Nice pun, by the way."

"What?"

"Know each other from Adam – Adam's Apple," he said, spelling it out like she was the thickest person alive.

"Oh yeah," she said flatly. "Clever me." She ploughed on. "So what's happened since the famous cider incident? It seems to have caused all sorts of fuss."

Tom sighed and scrubbed vigorously at a stubborn stain.

"I was demoted. I've been relocated to the agency dungeon to work on sales promotions."

"Sounds grim."

"It is. It's where failed account executives go to die."

"I'm sure it's better than making coffee for a living," she laughed.

"That Fiona Fox shafted me rightly," he said, ignoring her. "I despise her."

"Right," Saskia said, not pointing out that she, Saskia, had also been sold down the river by Fiona Fox that day.

"Look it, do you mind if I leave you to it?" Tom said, drying his hands. "I think I've done my share here and I've stuff to do."

"Course," said Saskia, and he was gone.

It hadn't occurred to him to ask whether she had things to do herself. Chubby country girls who served coffee for a living didn't count.

She switched on the electric heater and sat back in the armchair. It had been a strange day and she was contemplating the collection of remote controls when there was a gentle knock on the kitchen door. It was Patrick. He looked worried. She pulled over a chair and put some milk on to boil. She made him a cup of hot chocolate and sat down again.

"You've had quite an adventure today," she said and he nodded. "You're a brave boy. Braver than I've ever been."

"I wet my pants," he said.

"That's okay."

"Not really, but I was scared."

"Everyone gets scared. I'm scared all the time."

"Why?"

"I live on my own. Sometimes I leave the light on all night."

Patrick nodded. The answer seemed to satisfy him.

"Do you want to tell me what scared you?" she asked.

He took a sip of his chocolate and contemplated.

"A mean boy in school said I can't play Joseph in the Nativity play this Christmas because I'm the wrong colour."

"Did you kick him?"

"No. I said, 'You can't either, Brad, because you're the wrong colour too. Jesus lived in the desert so he definitely had a tan'."

Saskia smiled. "Good for you, Patrick. What happened then?"

"He pinched me and I dropped the Busy Lizzie and Teacher shouted so loud I wet my pants. Some of the boys and girls started whispering, '*Oui, oui, oui, oui*'."

"If Brad Flanagan pinched me and my teacher was shouting at me on top of it, I'd wet my pants too."

Patrick looked solemn. "Emma told the whole class I got my uniform for free."

Saskia topped up his chocolate and sat down.

She pulled her chair in closer and whispered conspiratorially, "Can I tell you something?"

"Yes," Patrick whispered back.

"When I was in school, the people who were the horriblest were the unhappiest. Does that make sense?"

Patrick shrugged.

"People who are sad sometimes pick on people who are happy. Often they have problems at home. It doesn't mean it's not wrong or that you have to put up with it but it's good to know."

He took this in and the two of them sat there for a while, quietly. The clock ticked and it was peaceful. Patrick seemed more at ease. Saskia wondered how she should broach the subject of Joe Delaney and decided to ask him straight out.

"Patrick, the man with the shovel earlier – did he do something to you? You ran away from him like the clappers."

He looked across at her and gauged her level of trustworthiness.

"You cannot tell Maman," he said.

"Why?"

"She has bad dreams. I hear her at night. She talks in her sleep. You have to promise not to tell, Saskia."

When he said her name, it sounded French. The emphasis was on the second syllable: Sas-*kee*-a. She wasn't sure it was appropriate to bargain with an eight-year-old but she crossed her heart and made a promise anyway.

He told her he'd run into the man on the way home from school, down the lane, the shortcut.

"He had a shovel and was crying. I tried to creep past but he saw me and he jumped and he shouted, 'Go on, yeh dirty brat, or I'll bury you too along with the dog!' and that's when I ran all the way home without stopping. So when I saw him at the house I ran again."

"That's a terrible thing to say to anyone," Saskia said and she swallowed down the nausea.

Patrick drained his cup.

She regretted making the promise. Joe Delaney deserved to be strung up – dead dog or no dead dog.

Patrick yawned. It was time for bed. Again.

She tucked him in and sat on the bed.

Emma was asleep so they spoke in whispers.

"I really am going to play football for Ireland when I grow up," he told her and she could see his eyes shining in the dark.

"Well, you are a very good footballer," she said and she kissed him on the forehead. "I've seen you play. Plus, I've also seen you run, and you've some sprint on you."

On her way down to the kitchen, she took a peek at the drawing room. Neglected armchairs waited for companionship. Gold-foil glassware gathered dust in cabinets that also gathered dust. Victorian portraits regarded with disapproval fireplaces that had long forgotten the warmth of cinders and everything wore a layer of loneliness.

On the hall table, there was a pile of unopened, official-looking letters.

# Chapter 11

Nuala arrived home at three in the morning. Saskia was dozing in the armchair and woke up to the sound of the kettle. She rubbed her eyes. It was cold and Nuala flicked the switch on the electric heater. She looked tired and bewildered as she made a pot of tea.

"How did you get on?" Saskia asked.

Nuala sniffed.

"Casualty for six hours with Fiona Fox, sure the craic was only mighty."

She poured two cups of tea and put one beside Saskia together with milk and sugar. Then she sat down, crossed her ankles and sipped her own tea.

"How is Mrs Kimba?"

"Well, she got a bed – which is nothing short of a miracle. They say she's got blood clots – it's why she collapsed. What they don't know is why she has those clots."

"Was she relieved when she heard Patrick was safe?"

Nuala shrugged. "I couldn't tell you. The woman is cold or something, guarded. I spoke to her in French and she haughtily informed me she spoke English perfectly well, that she'd only had momentary memory loss when she hit her head."

Saskia thought the teacher seemed wounded. Perhaps she didn't get much of an opportunity to flex her French in front of real

French speakers.

"How does she feel?"

"She feels tired and weak. They think it could be a pulmonary embolism, a clot in the lung."

"What does that mean?"

"It could mean a lot of things, cancer for one."

"Christ."

"That's what she's worried about. That and hospital bills."

"The poor thing," Saskia sympathised.

Nuala looked at her. "Saskia, the woman seems to have nothing set in place, no plans or safeguards, friends or relatives. It's irresponsible. Who did she think was going to look after her son if something happened to her?"

"I suppose it's lucky we were around then," Saskia said and the teacher gave her another look.

"Lucky? That's one way of putting it, I suppose," she said.

When the teapot was drained, Nuala announced she was going to bed. Saskia started to rinse the teacups. The teacher watched her.

"Tessa Kimba has asked that her son go to school as usual in the morning," she sighed.

Saskia folded the tea towel.

"I'm on an early shift but I can collect him from school," she offered. "It's no bother."

"Good," Nuala said. "I'll manage the morning. Tomorrow evening we'll see what the state of play is. And if you see that Tom Winters, you can tell him to clear his diary for the next few days. It's up to all of us to help out."

Saskia pulled on her coat.

"You don't like him," she said.

"No," the teacher said without hesitating. "He was a pupil of mine. Impossible to teach, a spoiled little pup. His mother ruined him. He's the youngest in that house, of course. Tom Winters is the type of man who thinks that life is one big party."

One big party seemed preferable to thinking that life was no party at all, Saskia thought as she crossed the street back to her own flat.

The teacher certainly had a long memory.


Patrick woke up with light streaming in through the bedroom

window. It felt strange being in a different room with Pelé on the wall. Emma Fox was gone. Patrick had heard her mother come to collect her in the middle of the night. His uniform was laid out carefully on the chair: shirt, tie, jumper, trousers, like a flat person with no body. It looked like he was going to school like any other day. He didn't want to go. He wanted to see his maman. What if he wet his pants again? Brad Flanagan would never leave him alone. He turned over in the bed and hid under the covers. Maybe Nuala would forget about him and he could stay there all day.

No such luck. He heard a toilet flush, followed by footsteps on the stairs and she knocked on the door.

"Time to get up," she announced as she came in.

"Do I have to go?" he asked in a muffled voice. "It's not fair."

"It's what your mam wants, Patrick, so get your skates on. Life's not fair. I have to go to school too and teach a herd of wild animals. So get dressed like a good boy and then come down for breakfast."

They sat across from each other at the table with the oilcloth. Patrick drank milk and ate toast carefully. Nuala buttered bread for their sandwiches.

"What do you normally have for breakfast?" she asked.

"Coco Pops," he said chancing his arm, his big brown eyes observing her between the teapot and the milk jug.

She eyed him carefully. "Chocolate for breakfast – are you sure about that?"

"Yep."

"Okay, I'll get you some today. Just in case you're here for another night. And if not, you can take them home with you."

"Cool," he said but without enthusiasm.

Nuala had guessed correctly that his mother would never buy Coco Pops in a million years.

"My clothes smell nice," he said, sniffing his sleeve and changing the subject.

"That's something," she said.

He drank some tea and bit off some toast, looking thoughtful.

"Do you miss your cat?" he asked.

She looked up from the sandwiches and straight at him. She blinked quickly several times.

"Yes, I do," she said and went back to the buttering.

Patrick sat in the corridor while Nuala had a word with his teacher in the staff room. It was early so the coat hooks were empty, the halls deserted and the floors shiny. It was nice, peaceful. Pictures covered the walls, bright with shiny stuck-on bits, butterflies, stars, sunshine, houses and flowers. There was a smell of disinfectant.

Nuala came out and sat on the chair beside him. She looked funny because the chair was small, kid-size.

"I have to go to school now myself, Patrick, to the big school, so Miss Hennessy is going to look after you, okay?"

He nodded and looked at his feet.

"After school, Saskia will collect you and we'll organise going out to see your mam. Be good now."

He leaned in and hugged her and she patted his back. She was stiff like a board and not used to hugs.

Miss Hennessy was kind. He helped her set the tables in the staff room for morning tea, laying out cups and saucers and plates of biscuits, and she told him he could eat one or two of the nice chocolate ones if he liked. When the bell rang for class, she sent him on an errand.

"The housekeeper in the convent will give you a big jug of milk," she explained. "It's down the gravel path and through the gate and you just knock on the red door. Leave the jug on this table here when you come back and then come into class. Be sure to take your time now or you'll spill it."

The housekeeper was a fat jolly sort with rosy cheeks. Her apron was floury.

"Well, who do we have here?" she asked with her hands on her hips.

"I'm here for the milk," he said.

"Well, you'd better come in then, I suppose."

She sat him up on a high stool and buttered him a hot scone. "Munch away on that now and I'll fetch the milk for you."

Patrick swung his legs under the stool. It felt nice to be out of the class. Things were looking up. He would tell his mother all about it later.

At lunchtime, he dribbled his ball around the horse-chestnut tree.

He was hungry. The tomato sandwiches Nuala had made were soggy and he couldn't eat all of them. But at least he'd been left alone. Mysteriously, Brad Flanagan was keeping his distance, Chad with the too-close eyes too.

He sat down to take a rest and saw Emma Fox approach. She stopped short of him and spoke.

"I've to give you a message," she said. "My mum and Tom Winters are going to drive all of us out to the hospital this evening."

Patrick squinted up at her and wondered why Emma had to go out to the hospital too. She shuffled and balanced on the sides of her feet.

"Do you want me to play ball with you? I'm not any good, but you could teach me."

He stared at her.

"Why are you mean to me?" he asked.

"I'm not."

"Yes, you are. You told everyone I got my uniform for free. And you laughed at me when I wet my pants."

Emma looked at her feet and bit her bottom lip.

"I'm sorry," she said. "I'll stop."

"I dunno," Patrick said.

"I promise I will never say a mean thing to you again. Cross my heart."

He shrugged.

"I heard you tell Saskia you're going to play football for Ireland – is it true?"

"Yes."

"Cool."

Patrick threw her the ball. She caught it.

"Good catch," he said, "but the first rule of football is no hands."

Saskia collected him after school. She was waiting at the gate with a smile and a fistful of chocolates swiped from the café. She took his hand and they walked through the little park by the duck pond, around the beds of flowers, under the archway of trees and out onto the road where they waited for the green man. At the canal they sat on a park bench and fed the swans stale bread rolls. They chatted.

He liked Saskia. She was kind and funny and he didn't mind telling her things. So when she asked if his mother was from the Congo, he told her his father was from there too.

"He is a soldier," Patrick explained. "A war hero."

"Oh," Saskia said because it was all she could think of saying.

"I never met him but he saw me as a bump, that's what Maman says, before we came to Ireland."

"Is he alive?" Saskia asked and then wondered if you could be locked up for asking a young boy such a question.

He seemed unfazed.

"*Oui*, but Maman doesn't know where he is."

"I see."

"When I grow up, I'm going to find him," he said solemnly. "Mr Singh said I could when I'm playing for Innskeep."

"And who is Mr Singh?"

"The dentist."

"Right. So he knows a lot about football?"

"Everything."

Saskia picked a bread roll into a million tiny bits, Patrick tapped his blue ball from foot to foot, and they stayed there like that in companionable silence until it was time to go back to the square.

After homework, they played Snap and drank lemonade. He was a polite boy and gentle, not like normal eight-year-olds who thumped and slammed and bellowed. His movements were tidy and adult-like. He didn't whack his hand down violently, yelling *"Snap!"* when a match appeared. He seemed to understand the notion that good things come to those who wait.

They bundled up and went out front with the ball and she realised she liked being with him. There was a wisdom about him for someone so young, so she was embarrassed by her own childish jealousy when she saw how excited he got when Tom Winters drove past in his silly car. He ran out through the gate to greet him. She trailed behind.

Patrick caught up with him.

"Oh hello, mate," Tom said. "How was your day?"

"Fine."

"Good."

"And how is your mum?"

"We're going out to see her soon."

"Good for you."

"Will we play football now?"

"Now?"

"Yes."

"It doesn't really suit, mate."

"Why, what are you doing? Last night you said you'd play football with me."

"Oh, I didn't literally mean any goddamn time."

"Well, goddamn you," said Patrick and he turned to walk away with his ball under his arm.

Tom called after him. "Okay, okay! Fifteen minutes, but don't swear like that again or you'll get me into trouble."

Nuala found them out on the street, using coats for goalposts, with Saskia looking on.

"It's yourself," Nuala said, acknowledging Tom with a disapproving sniff.

"Hello, Miss Murphy."

"Hello, yourself. We need to head off soon, so gather your things together."

"Oh, I'm not going to the hospital," said Tom. "It doesn't suit."

"Yes, you are," Nuala said in the tone of someone who was well used to dealing with pups like Tom Winters, and she turned on her heel. "We're all going. You were the one who found Patrick first so his mother will be eager to hear the whole story. I'll take a lift with you in that sports car of yours. I'd enough of Fiona Fox last night to last me a lifetime."

Saskia sat in the passenger seat of the jeep. She wanted the visit over with. She didn't fancy her chances with Fiona Fox's poor driving record. Fiona drummed on the steering wheel in traffic and fumed. Twice she asked if she was the only resident in Lavender Square with a suitable mode of transport. Twice, Saskia ignored her. She was flustered and flushed and her hair was in a frizz. She didn't like hospitals. The smell always made her heave. She turned in her seat to look back at Tom and Nuala travelling behind them. Nuala looked comical sitting stiffly in the two-seater. Tom's bad mood was palpable. Charity runs to hospitals were beneath him.

She waved back at him knowing it would annoy him and he gave her a look. Tom Winters had a way of looking at you like you were a piece of dirt on the side of the street.

Tessa was overjoyed to see her son. He climbed up beside her and put his arms around her neck. They spoke in French and it sounded like a song. Her eyes shone. The others stood back momentarily, reluctant to disturb them.

They were all carrying bags except for Tom who was empty-handed. He stuffed his hands into his pockets awkwardly. The bags were emptied and wares brought forth.

Nuala handed over grapes, Lucozade and a dressing gown; Saskia, slippers and a book. There was a card from Patrick and Emma's class, a huge, cluttered and colourful mess.

Fiona's bag was the biggest and from an expensive department store. She gave Tessa a washbag filled with creams and potions and gels and smells and handed Patrick a paper carry bag.

He pulled out a shoebox. He lifted the lid cautiously and folded back a double layer of tissue paper to reveal a pair of blue-and-gold football boots. His eyes opened wide in disbelief and he swallowed.

"Emma told me you didn't have a pair," Fiona said.

"Thank you, thank you very much," he said quietly. "Can-can I wear them now?"

"Why not?"

He looked to his mother and she nodded and it seemed as though he might explode with excitement. Everyone was smiling at him.

Tessa had spent the day being prodded and poked. She still managed to sit up straight and look elegant and dignified and well groomed in a hospital gown, her pageboy hairstyle still perfectly intact. Her French accent added a layer of intrigue and, if you didn't know better, you might have thought she was a French diplomat who'd fallen ill on a business trip.

Saskia noticed Tom admiring Tessa from a distance, beauty admiring beauty, like one impressionist painter admiring another's brushstrokes. After a while she suggested taking Emma and Patrick for a walk to get fizzy drinks. She urged Tom to come with her.

"Don't worry," she said as they walked down the corridor. "It's not because I want to play house with you, it's because I'm pretty

73

sure Nuala would like to try and get some more details on Tessa's results."

"Fine," he said. "Man, do I hate hospitals!"

Saskia laughed. "All men say that."

"Do they now?"

"Yes. Without fail every time a man steps inside the door of a hospital, he absolutely *always* says that."

"*Always*?" he asked and his eyes flashed.

"*Always!*"

"And what about women? Where do you stand on the whole hospital thing?"

"Personally, every time I step inside a hospital I feel nauseous. I can't answer for other women but I gather they accept that hospitals are a part of life. Men think that life is one big parade."

"Oh, for fuck's sake, woman, give over! Let's get these two some drinks," he huffed, rooting in his pockets for change.

When they got back to the ward, the space between the Nuala and Fiona was bristling. It appeared Fiona had held out and Nuala had drawn the short straw.

"You're going to stay with me until your mam gets home," she told Patrick and her smile was hesitant. She turned to glare at Fiona. "Maybe Emma could come around now and then for company?"

"Sure," Fiona said and she exhaled in relief.

They left Patrick alone with his mother for a bit and shuffled around the corridors, waiting.

When Emma went to use the bathroom, Nuala pulled the four adults into a huddle.

"Now listen here," she whispered furiously, "I know you're all keen to wash your hands of this little situation but let me tell you now: I'm not taking sole responsibility for this child." She turned and pointed at Fiona. "If you think you can swan in here with your big bag of tricks and presents like Daddy Warbucks, thinking that somehow it lets you off the hook, you're wrong. And you, pretty boy," she said, turning to Tom, "if you think that by playing the 'sure the ball only happened to land at my feet' card, you have another think coming too. We're all busy so let's share the load: minding, collecting, dropping off, homework and entertainment, even bloody football, the whole shebang. And hopefully it won't be for too long."

In the carpark Nuala halted beside the jeep.

"That's some gash you have on your door," she remarked to Fiona. "Is that what all the racket was about yesterday morning?"

"The gash you're referring to," Fiona replied huffily, glaring at Tom, "is going to cost me thousands to get fixed."

"I told you I didn't do it," Tom said loudly, "so quit glaring at me!"

Saskia squirmed and she caught Tom looking at her strangely.

"What are you looking at?" she snapped.

"Nothin'," he said.

They drove home in silence, each resenting the other, except for the children who slept soundly in the back seat of Fiona's jeep. The dual carriageway was a runway of sodium and over the city there was an orange glow.

# Chapter 12

A week went by without any news and rolled into the following week. There were delays sorting out paperwork and medical coverage. As a group they tried to be polite around each other but this soon dissipated and they rowed. They rowed over everything, particularly the hospital visits, each eager to protect their own time, territory and space. Nuala was savagely resolute that they all take turns. She knew, given half a chance, they would offload the boy on her.

"Why should I have to go at all?" Tom asked. "What the hell do I have to say to the woman?"

"Don't be such a big baby," Nuala hissed. "I wash and cook and read and bring the boy to school every day, so get over it."

"Well, I didn't ask for this."

"None of us asked for this."

"This is not on at all," Fiona Fox barged in. "How is it that I'm the only one here with a car that can carry more than one passenger? It's just not fair," she said childishly. "I mean my work schedule does not allow for these little evening soirées."

"Could you stop mentioning your work schedule?" Tom snarled. "We totally get it that your work is far more important than everyone else's. But here's the thing, you're hardly a neurosurgeon."

And so it went around in circles.

Only Saskia kept quiet. The hospital visits were difficult, she slept badly afterwards, but it was the right thing to do. How else did they expect Patrick to get to see his mother – shove him onto a bus with a note and hope for the best? It was only an hour or two out of their day. Tessa would be home soon and then they could all go back to the way they were: neighbours that ignored each other.

Eventually, they worked out a schedule as diplomatically as possible, and after all the bartering and bargaining, Tessa often ended up having four visitors each evening. Patrick needed to go every night and the rest took turns, but because Tom could only carry one passenger, when it was Saskia's turn to visit Fiona had to carry her, the same with Nuala. Emma went along on those nights too. It was in Fiona's words, "a shit show".

Each visit had the same format: salutations, Patrick's news and then an update on Tessa's medical situation.

Procedures moved in slow motion. There were X-rays and CAT scans booked but no one seemed to be in any hurry. The nurses were vague, doctors vaguer still and nothing was clear. Her blood was being monitored and she was on blood-thinner which was the main thing apparently. It would make sure she had no more clots. Each visit ended with Tessa reassuring them that she'd be home soon.

The novelty of having a cute black boy to look after wore thin and Patrick sensed the strain. He longed for his mother to come home, yet at the same time loved his room at Nuala's with its picture of Pelé and aeroplane wallpaper. Every morning he woke up and counted the aeroplanes until he reached one hundred. He liked the way the sun curled through the curtains and lit each of them up. The wallpaper was old of course and torn in places but somehow it still felt like his. He liked having his own room that looked out over the walled garden, the square and the mountains, and his bed was cosy, not like the noisy fold-out one at home. Thinking about this made him feel guilty.

Nuala and he had a little routine. She told him that a system was important if things were to be done right, that they needed to work together or everything would fall asunder.

Each morning, after counting aeroplanes, he stood up on his

bed, pulled back the curtains and watched the day start. Before the sun came up and the streetlights went off, tiny lights sparkled on the mountains. Often the sky was grey and it rained but when the sun broke through, it made the clouds pink or orange or red. On these days, the walled garden looked enchanted. And he had a perfect view. Locked to the world, it was empty except for the robins, blackbirds, magpies and worms. To Patrick, it was mysterious and magical. He imagined it was cursed, protected by a spell that kept people out. Nuala said it was a waste of space. That no one ever used it except for the gardener, a cranky old ferret who everyone paid but avoided like the plague.

The mornings had started to get colder and he always climbed back into his warm bed and waited for Nuala to call him.

She'd tap on the door and call out, "Patrick, are you awake?" and he always was. She wore a huge soft white dressing gown and he liked her when she was sleepy and her hair was messy. Once she was dressed, in her skirt and thick cardigan, she was all business and chop-chop, and there was no time for hanging around looking at aeroplanes.

Over breakfast they listened to the radio. Nuala made cheese or ham sandwiches now instead of tomato and poured tea, tutting over the news, and he ate Coco Pops. He liked the kitchen with the glowing red lamp under the picture of Jesus and the big table and window seat. He liked Nuala too, even though she was cross and never smiled. Tom sometimes called her a hatchet behind her back and Emma told him that her mother and Nuala had gone to school together but were not friends because Nuala was uptight. Patrick didn't say that if he were Nuala he wouldn't want to be friends with Mrs Fox either. Her perfume made him feel sick and she was always smiling but it wasn't a real smile. It was the kind of smile that bad guys on the telly had before they shot a good guy in the head.

After breakfast Nuala washed the dishes, Patrick dried and they recited tables. Nuala never chose the easy ones like the two times tables. She liked to keep him on his toes and his brain ticking over. It made him nervous. It was difficult to stick your fist into a cup and dry it without dropping it and think of the answer at the same time.

"Seven sevens?"

"49."

"Seven eights?"

"56."

"Seven nines?"

"63."

"Good," she'd say, rinsing a cup under the tap.

They walked to school together, under the umbrella if it rained, down the lanes through the park, no time for the ducks. Nuala walked briskly. Patrick trotted to keep up. She looked straight ahead like an army major. The lollipop lady always nodded at her and winked at Patrick. She was round like a snowman in her white coat and she had something to say to most of the children.

"How are you today? New coat, new bag, hair in plaits? I might plait mine tomorrow, wha'?" which was funny because her carroty hair was as short as a man's.

Nuala would deliver Patrick safely to the school door and with a squeeze on the shoulder she'd carry on to her own school to teach French and Irish to the wild animals. It was probably because of the wild animals that she never smiled.

Saskia smiled more than Nuala. Most afternoons she collected him from school and waited for him at the gate with her hands stuffed into the pockets of her huge coat. She was always early, there before any of the parents, and sometimes she looked worried. Maybe she thought he might fall down a hole on his way from the classroom to the gate. But she always smiled when her eyes found his and then she looked pretty. She took his hand and held it tightly and wanted to know absolutely every detail about his day.

Did Miss Hennessy throw a stick of chalk at Brad Flanagan again and tell him that he had her heart broken? Did Patrick get another gold star for getting his spellings right? How was Emma? Did they manage to get out at lunchtime between showers to kick the ball around? Was he warm enough? Was he hungry? Did he want to feed the ducks?

Most days they walked to the canal where she reached into one of her big pockets for the chocolates from the café. In the other she kept a bag with stale scones, croissants or rolls for the birds. She'd sit on a bench and smoke while he tore the old bread to pieces and fed the ducks and swans. The birds got used to him and once they heard the rustle of the bag they'd paddle over.

Saskia often thought it was like a scene from *The Lion King* only she never said that in case it was considered ludicrously inappropriate and racist to boot. The ducks would quack in appreciation and he'd giggle, delighted with himself, and he'd look back at her. She'd smile through a cloud of smoke.

Afterwards they'd go back to Nuala's for a glass of milk and a snack before clearing the table for homework. Nuala had given Saskia a key but warned her not to answer the phone. It would only be someone Nuala didn't want to talk to.

Saskia told Patrick he was a clever boy. What she didn't tell him was that he left her feeling like a semi-literate thick. Her Irish was out of practice, and her times tables were rusty from an over-reliance on a cash register. English reading was his favourite and she loved listening to him read in his boyish voice with its French pronunciation. He ran his finger under each word as he read, hesitating only over the new words. He usually worked them out, shaping his mouth around the vowels and consonants until the word emerged, brand shiny new.

Homework over, they'd pack up and watch cartoons until Nuala came home. Patrick loved cartoons and when he laughed out loud it made Saskia laugh out loud too. But once five thirty passed, he became distracted and glanced continuously at the clock. At first, Saskia thought he was counting off the minutes until she went, until she discovered the clock-watching was in anticipation of the highlight of his day: Tom. It disappointed her. Patrick adored Tom despite the fact that Tom always looked put out when he arrived in the door. There were no pleasantries or thank-you's between her and him. They were like shift-workers that brushed past each other: Tom clocked in and Saskia clocked out, home to her flat with its solitude.

She had never minded the flat particularly, but now she began to hate it: the cramped space, the grubbiness and floorboard creaks even though there hadn't been a sign of Joe Delaney since the day of the accident. Not a note, whimper, pace or creak. Perhaps he was grieving in his own way, silently, or maybe it was because he couldn't see. His battered glasses still sat on Nuala's windowsill, unclaimed. Saskia had considered handing them in to him or leaving him a note, but then thought better of it. Taking the glasses would lead to questions from Nuala and questions would lead back to her flat and being in some way associated with a cretin like him. Besides, she had promised Patrick not to say anything about the man with the shovel and she wasn't sure she could trust herself not to if his name came up.

She began to linger longer at Nuala's. The teacher wasn't exactly open arms and jam sandwiches but she didn't run Saskia either. They drank tea, watched a soap or secretly spied on Tom and Patrick playing football in the back garden and giggled over Tom's mithered man expression. He had tried to cry off, beg work commitments, hide or sneak out but Patrick always found him and hunted him down. If there was no answer from Tom's flat he would ring Tom's parents' doorbell, ball in hand, football boots laced up, and wait patiently until one of them answered.

Mr Winters wouldn't cover for his selfish son.

"If you think I'm going to lie to an eight-year old, just so you can sit on your backside, you've another think coming," he spluttered.

Tom stopped trying to avoid the young footballer after that and stopped off at Nuala's every evening after work.

Patrick was always ready for him, waiting like a puppy, wagging with energy. He was good with the ball, determined and eager to please. They kicked the ball over and back to each other, soft first, then harder, two-touch then one, from five yards then ten. They practised headers. Patrick appeared to have a knack; Tom did not. Their attempts at a one-a-side game was a chance for Patrick to run rings around Tom, dodging and dribbling and circling to reach the back wall and score. More than once Tom was sure he heard Nuala and Saskia laughing at him though he never saw the teacher's expression change from one degree above misery to verify this. She didn't give him a moment's let-up either. She fixed him with a diamond-cutting gaze and shook her head as if she expected nothing better. She warned them to avoid the roses. The rose bed was where her cat was buried. He was always relieved when she called them inside and the chore was over and done with for another day. That was until she started the post-match cup-of-tea routine. And when Tom tried refusing it in an attempt to head straight home, she ignored him.

"There you are now," she'd insist, shoving a mug into his fist and folding her arms so there was no escaping and no confusion.

Saskia thought it was worth hanging around to see this alone. Spuds boiled on the cooker, chops sizzled under the grill, the Sacred Heart watching closely in case Tom had any ideas. He was expected to stay and drink the tea, even if it meant Nuala had to funnel it down his gullet and scald him. Saskia guessed the forced tea-drinking exercise was punishment for Tom being disruptive in her French classes all those years ago. She found it interesting that he obeyed her now.

Unsurprisingly, it was Tom who complained about the hospital visits more than anyone else. He told Saskia, after a single evening of having to take a lift with Fiona Fox when his own car was being serviced, that it was like being in the Seventh Circle of Hell. The woman was an unashamed snob and the journey to the hospital consisted of numerous speakerphone calls where she routinely terrorised those on the receiving end. She seemed to destroy people's lives for a living and bandied around words like "immediately", "obviously"', "terminated", "executed", and "dead man walking", with ease. She was also on first-name terms with ministers, journalists, musicians, actors, models and socialites. She forced a smile when she spoke to them so they would hear the smile in her voice and drop their guard. What they didn't realise was that Fiona Fox was evil and smelt of a perfume so vile he was certain it was the type normally used by embalmers.

"She smiled at me," he told Saskia, "tried to encourage conversation, to get me back on side like I was some sort of potential ally. 'Nuala!' she said and rolled her eyes. I'm not Nuala's greatest fan, but I despise Fiona Fox. She's the type of power woman you come across in marketing departments, a ruthless self-seeker with a hair-flicking habit like she's some sort of impossible beauty. And that accent of hers, it's so gnarled up, it sounds like she's chewing on a wasp."

With all the open obnoxiousness of Fiona Fox, Tessa Kimba was the complete opposite: Fiona Fox's yang, a natural beauty, tall and willowy with a fine bone structure, and she had discretion. The woman did not feel the need to fill gaps of silence. Nuala complained about this. She thought it was rich that a woman whose son was being taken care of by strangers would make them work so hard to make conversation during their visits. Saskia saw it differently. What the others saw as arrogance, she saw as fear. She knew Tessa Kimba was afraid, not just of one thing, but of a million things she had no control over. Privately each of them was curious about Tessa. They itched to know more, but she was not the type to confide or sit around having cosy chats. She disclosed information purely on a need-to-know basis. They managed to find out she was a refugee from Kinshasa in the Democratic Republic of Congo. They knew Patrick was Irish-born and that both mother and son spoke French, English and Swahili – other than that, nothing. Tessa neatly diverted questions about her past, skirted enquiries about her family and avoided any talk to do with Patrick's father. She was, in essence, a mystery woman.

Patrick was more open. He told them he was born in the Coombe hospital after his mother carried him over from Africa in her belly. He told them cleaning houses made her very tired because in the Congo she had been a schoolteacher. This was why she taught him at home and also why he'd no friends because he'd only just started in real school. He told them his grandparents and aunts and uncles had died from a disease called cholera and that one of his mother's neighbours had been eaten by a crocodile. He also told them his father was a soldier. They did not know where he was nor did he know where they were. This raised a few eyebrows among his neighbours. He did not tell them what he'd told Saskia, that he planned to find his father, track him down and bring him to Ireland. He knew Saskia wouldn't mention it. She kept her promises.

The little boy was devoid of self-pity and this made all of them feel guilty. For someone who'd been brought up with little contact with other people, he showed an admirable trust and faith in others. He trusted the neighbours who were looking after him and chose to see only kindness. He believed his mother would get better and trusted the hospital to make her well again. When he asked questions, he listened to the answers and accepted them and he was polite, thankful for everything done for him. It made it more difficult for his minders to moan so they got on with it, consoling themselves that their act of charity would soon draw to a close.

# Chapter 13

It got colder. The big house was draughty, the windows rattled and Patrick was always cold. He slept on later in the mornings and Nuala often found him curled up in the duvet like a hibernating squirrel, fast asleep. It made her cross. There was no time for tardiness on school mornings.

The others commented on the cold house. Tom said it was about as warm as an autopsy lab and Nuala told him to feck off home with himself. Fiona shivered visibly each time she stepped inside the door and Emma wore a fleece whenever she called over. It wasn't until Nuala arrived home and found Saskia and Patrick watching telly in their coats that she paid any attention.

"What's wrong with the two of you?"

"We're cold," Saskia told her.

"Turn up the heater, then," Nuala snapped but the heater was already at its highest setting.

"It mightn't do any harm to light the range?" Saskia suggested when Patrick was out of earshot.

That was a mistake. Nuala turned on her.

"Might it not? And tell me this, who will pay to fix it up? The chimney probably has a hundred birds' nests in it not to mention leaves and grit." The teacher was incensed. A fine mist of spittle sprayed from her mouth as she aired her grievances. "Do you know what it costs to maintain one of these houses? Victorian restoration and preservation, my arse! You'd be better off digging a big hole and fecking all your money into it. If I'd had any sense I would have sold this pile years ago to some builder with a load of cash and no taste so he could convert it into a dozen bedsits."

Saskia was sorry she'd mentioned it. The range was a subject to be avoided. She muttered an apology and picked up her things. She was tired of bearing the brunt of other people's gripes.

That night Nuala made Patrick a hot-water bottle. He was so grateful she felt really bad for failing to notice he'd been feeling the cold.

"You should have told me you were perishing, you know," she said gently. "You're my guest. A guest should not feel cold when paying a visit. It shows me up as a bad hostess."

Tessa remained in hospital. Patrick remained in Nuala's. Everyone was kind to him but it was not like the soft kindness of his mother. Theirs was impatient and, somewhere deep inside, he knew he was now in the way and an inconvenience – particularly to Tom who was often impatient when they drove to the hospital together in his little car. It wasn't a nice feeling. Sometimes at night he stood up on the end of his bed and peered out the window to see if by any chance his mother had come home from hospital and was about to walk through the gate. She never did. And often he lay awake, terrorised that she would never come back. Saskia was different. He told her things. Like how late at night, when Nuala thought he was asleep, she walked through the house, up and down the stairs over and over until she got tired. Then she sat at the arched window, which looked out over the back of the house, over the garden, roofs, chimneys and spires all the way to a line of twinkling lights in the distance which she'd told him was the sea – reading the same letter, over and over. It was strange.

Saskia told him everyone had their own secrets and that he didn't need to worry about Nuala. She would tell him what was on her mind if she felt she needed to. Patrick wasn't so sure about that. Saskia was right about the secrets though. He soon concluded most people were riddled with them, Emma more than anyone. She was nicer now. At lunchtimes in school they kicked the ball over and back to each other under the tree. One day she told him she sometimes wished her parents were dead. She knew it was wrong to wish such a thing.

"Which one do you want to die more," Patrick asked, "your mother or your father?"

Emma considered the question carefully, steadying the ball with her foot.

"It's different all the time," she said and she drew back her leg and gave the ball an almighty kick. It hit the tree and came back and landed at her feet.

Patrick was impressed.

"They fight a lot," she said and her mouth twisted in a funny way.

"About what?"

"Everything. I sleep with my fingers in my ears."

They sat down under the tree. Emma started to cry. Patrick put his arm around her. He felt sorry for her living in that big house all alone except for a couple of parents who fought all the time. She wiped her nose on her sleeve and took a folded and battered postcard from a pocket in her mobile-phone cover.

"When they shout, I dream about running away, to here, this place. It's an island."

She handed him the postcard. The photograph was of a dark-blue sky and a small island with a perfect town on a hill.

Patrick read the caption. "Mont-Saint-Michel."

"Is that the way you say it?" Emma asked.

"*Oui.*"

"Wee?"

"*Oui.* Why would you run away there? It's in France."

"It looks like a peaceful place."

"It does. Maybe I could run away there myself if I ever needed to."

"We can share it as our runaway place," Emma said seriously.

His mother had secrets too, Patrick discovered. Tessa had been slow to hand over the key of their flat to Nuala. It was only when she realised she wasn't being discharged that she reluctantly handed it over.

She pulled Patrick aside and told him to make sure Nuala didn't root through their things. "Don't show her our *cachette*," she warned.

The *cachette* was a secret space under a loose floorboard. It held their passports and a credit card for emergencies.

"Everything we own is in that flat, *ma puce*," she reminded him.

Nuala was annoyed by Tessa's reticence. Patrick needed clothes. What could the Kimbas possibly have to hide? Saskia didn't comment but she did accompany Patrick and Nuala to the flat. She was interested to hear what the teacher would have to say about the garden level of their building.

Nuala peered over the banister suspiciously like a monk down a well. The hall lights were on the blink again and, before she knew what was happening, Patrick grabbed her hand and pulled her down the stairs so quickly she thought she was going to fall to her death.

"*Are you trying to break my neck?*" she shouted into the darkness, and her voice made an echo.

"We normally run," Patrick said timidly. "Maman is scared of the dark."

"Jesus wept," Nuala said and she sniffed. "Well, I'm scared of that smell. It's dog."

Saskia fumbled until she found the keyhole of the Kimbas' flat and they stepped inside. It was the coldness that hit them first, then its size. The flat was as cold and as small as a tomb but Tessa had gone to great trouble to make it a home. It was filled with pretty odds and ends and it was neat. The shelves were lined with books, and there were plants and cushions and vases, a china tea set in the kitchenette, a cheerful red kettle on the hob and sprigs of dried lavender hung from the ceiling. A myriad of prints adorned the walls. One took centre stage. It was "A Convent Garden, Brittany" by William Leech. Its white light and speckled sunshine exuded calm.

"It's Maman's favourite," Patrick said, disappearing up a short ladder to a loft-style platform which held a bed. "She likes the walled garden."

Nuala lowered herself gently onto the couch. She looked semi-stunned. Saskia stood at the barred window.

"My clothes are up here!" Patrick called down.

"Give us a second, pet," Saskia called back and she and Nuala exchanged glances.

"Is this the alternative if you don't own a home?" Nuala whispered. "This flat is the size of a corner of my kitchen."

They climbed up to the loft sleeping area with its single bed and foldaway camp bed. In silence, they packed a bag with some things for Tessa and clothes for Patrick. There was very little to choose from, just a few rags of things, and that left a sharp lump in Saskia's throat. Nuala picked up a basket of dirty laundry and took it with her.

They pulled the door closed behind them. When they got home, Nuala called the chimney sweep. It was time to light the range. The next day she went out and bought an electric blanket.

# Chapter 14

When Patrick caught a throat infection Nuala sat by his bedside watching him sleep and felt his forehead at intervals, wishing his raging temperature would stabilise. In the middle of the night, she went in her dressing gown to get Saskia out of bed and then she dragged Doc Winters out of retirement to make a house call.

He was a solemn man who looked over his glasses as he examined his patient.

"Deep breath – another one – now say *ahhh!*"

"*Ahhh!*"

He prescribed antibiotics, a few days in bed and some cough syrup.

"It tastes terrible but a mighty footballer like you will keep it down no problem," he said.

Afterwards, the doctor sat by the range with Nuala and Saskia. They sipped tea companionably and the clock ticked in the cosy kitchen.

"God, isn't it lovely to meet a little chap like that," he said. "Old-fashioned really, not in the slightest bit spoilt. That little fella barely has an arse in his pants and he's all the better for it in some ways. You were good to take him in."

"No real choice in the matter," Nuala said.

"Any news on the mother?"

She shook her head.

"If it was anything serious they'd have probably found it at this stage. Having said that, hospitals have changed since my day. Any mention of the father?"

"Not around – a soldier apparently, in the Congo. The mother is as secretive as the day is long."

"Really? What type of soldier, I wonder?" The doctor frowned and was thoughtful. "Did she mention which part of the Congo she was from?"

"Kinshasa," Saskia said.

"So she speaks Lingala then as well as French?"

"Not sure – I know she speaks Swahili though," Saskia said.

"And she's from Kinshasa? That's odd."

"Are you some sort of a specialist on the Congo?" Nuala asked half-jokingly. She wanted to get back to bed and was keen to wrap up the conversation.

"Not an expert but I worked with a chap who spent time with *Médecins Sans Frontières* there – told me some hairy stories." He shivered at the memory of them.

Saskia would have liked to have heard more but Nuala changed the subject.

"What do working mothers do when their child is sick, Dr Winters?" she asked.

"They stay at home."

"Even if they're teachers?"

"Especially if they're teachers. You have a state job, don't you? I'll bet you've never taken a day off in your life."

He was right.

Nuala stayed at home and Saskia noticed she nursed the little boy lovingly. She brought hot drinks up the stairs, took his temperature on the hour and read to him from *Great Expectations*, the only suitable book in the house for an infirm boy.

"Am I like Pip, do you think, a young boy on an adventure?" he asked.

"Why not? As long as I'm not like Mrs Joe Gargery with her grated red face," Nuala responded, and they laughed at this.

At some stage in her life, Nuala had been a softer woman.

Tom and Fiona took Patrick's throat infection as an opportunity to lay off the hospital visits. It was Patrick who Tessa wanted to see anyway, so there was no point. Nuala was too preoccupied to argue with them. Patrick's being laid up also meant no football and Tom was thrilled with the unexpected holiday. There was a chance the break in routine might change things. That he might be released from his contract. Just to be sure, he kept a low profile. It didn't occur to him to visit the boy in sick bay. Instead he went shopping at a safely-out-of-the-way shopping centre and bought a single item: an expensive shirt with a tiny logo. He revelled in the attention from the shop assistants, like a cat being stroked, and went for pizza and a glass of wine. He people-watched and women watched him. He was like a marble sculpture they were drawn to, exquisite and unattainable. He clocked the glances, smiled secretly and locked eyes with a girl in the crowd. It was Saskia Heffernan. She was looking straight at him from a distance. His smile fell away.

Laden down with shopping, she moved slowly through the crowds like a clipper. She stopped and bent down to rearrange her bags and to shove down an eager teddy bear. They regarded each other across the concourse for a moment and then, without an acknowledgement of any sort, she picked up her bags and walked on. He shrugged and ordered a second glass of wine.


Saskia took a taxi to the hospital and found Tessa alone and looking out the window into the darkness. She looked confused when she saw her.

"I didn't think any of you were coming."

"I was in the neighbourhood."

"Really?"

"No. I just wanted to give you this," she said and she handed Tessa the teddy bear. He wore a jumper and the ribbon around his neck read "*Get well soon*".

Tessa took it and looked at it strangely as though Saskia had handed her a jar of dead flies.

"Thank you," she said and she put the teddy aside.

Saskia sat down. Tessa was not the most comfortable person to be around. It was easier when Patrick was there.

"Patrick is much better," she reported cheerfully. "He'll be back in to see you soon."

"I hope to be out of here soon," Tessa replied coldly. "I have to get back to work. The rent is due and I need to pay you all back."

"You're probably entitled to sickness benefit, you know?"

"Charity?"

"No, social welfare."

"I prefer to make my own way, thank you."

The woman appeared insulted. Saskia shifted uncomfortably in her seat.

"How are you feeling?"

"Not any better, not any worse. I just want to get back to the way things were. I have things to be getting on with."

"We all do, Tessa," Saskia said and stood up to leave. She was sick of the whole lot of them.

Tessa called her back.

"Sorry," she said. "I know you hate hospitals."

"How?"

"I just do."

Saskia stalled at the end of the bed and chewed on her lip.

"I'm having terrible dreams," Tessa confided. "Dreams about dead relatives and I'm afraid I might be dying."

Saskia took the chair and sat, pulling it closer.

"Are these the relatives that died of cholera?" she asked.

Tessa's expression darkened.

"Patrick told us," Saskia explained. "He also told us you'd a neighbour who was eaten by a crocodile."

Tessa frowned.

"He can be such a *pipelette*, a blabbermouth, but yes, it's true. My family were wiped out by the disease. The neighbour was a different matter. He was a fool, went wading with his net in the wrong part of the river. Everyone knows that the river, the Congo, has crocodiles. Fewer now but they're still there." Tessa was unsympathetic. Her face was hard.

"You have a tragic past," Saskia said gently.

"Don't we all, all of us refugees?" Tessa replied impatiently. "Isn't that why we're here? Does anyone ever leave their home country out of choice unless things are terrible?"

"I never thought about it like that."

"People don't. They think we are here to sponge. Most people think about themselves."

"I know they do but I'm not one of those people."

Tessa sighed.

"Don't dwell on the dreams," Saskia said. "Hospitals are terrible places and the dreams are only mirroring your worries. If you were dying, don't you think the doctors would know?"

"They don't know anything. I haven't spoken properly to a doctor in what feels like days. I'm just waiting, waiting, waiting."

Saskia changed the subject and told her they'd been to the flat.

Tessa tensed ever so slightly.

"You have it so pretty," Saskia added quickly.

"Thank you," Tessa said.

She relaxed and told Saskia how she'd discovered charity shops when she arrived in Ireland. How she had spent days rummaging through what to some was attic junk but to her was a treasure chest of undiscovered delights: vases, crystal glassware, rugs, blankets, irons, china crockery, pretty prints, books, plant pots, clocks and figurines. Everything.

"You have to have a good eye to be able to do that," Saskia said in admiration. "I could visit a hundred charity shops and bypass whole shelf-loads of Ming vases."

Tessa smiled. "You're hard on yourself," she said.

They chatted more easily, about Patrick and school and Lavender Square.

"I've been doing Patrick's homework with him," Saskia said. "He's a very bright boy. You've taught him very well."

"I was a teacher once."

"He told me."

"I want him to do well."

"He will. Of course, football seems to be his priority."

"School comes first," Tessa said insistently and she sounded exactly like a teacher.

As Saskia was leaving, she glanced back and saw Tessa pick up the teddy. She squeezed his belly and fondled his ears and then clutched him to her chest. The worry had returned to her face.

On her way home, she knocked on Tom's door.

"You look like a woman on a mission," he said dryly.

"I am," she said and she smiled. "You see, up until now, I've been covering for you, told Patrick you had a life-threatening bout of diarrhoea after some dodgy foie gras, explained it's why you haven't been around to say hi."

"You don't need to cover for me," he replied angrily. "He's not my responsibility. I'm not his father."

"I'm aware of that but funny you should bring up the *dad* subject. It's just unfortunate, and jaysus knows I can't credit the boy with taste here, but he likes you. In fact, I think he kind of idolises you. But, really, I put it down to the lack of males in his life. It wouldn't matter if you were Tony Soprano: you're male and you're all the male he's got."

"Spare me the pop psychology, could you?" Tom said and he went to close the door.

"He'll be well enough to play football again on Saturday," she shouted in through the keyhole and she walked away laughing.

On Saturday morning, Tom awoke to the sound a ball being kicked – *thump, thump, thump*. The sound persisted. He pulled the curtains a crack and caught his father gambolling about in their back garden with Patrick. His few strands of grey hair flapped about in the wind and he looked happy, like a big kid. Tom got back into bed and flicked on the telly.

Later, when the house was quiet, he went downstairs. His mother was in the kitchen arranging tea and biscuits and aspirin on a tray. He went to the fridge.

"A tray? We must have visitors." He took a biscuit and his mother slapped it out of his hand. "Where's the old man?" he asked.

"In bed," his mother replied coldly and picked up the tray. "Heart palpitations. He's too old to be chasing after an eight-year-old." She left the room and closed the door.

Tom sighed and drank milk straight from the carton.

"Fuck it," he said.

# Chapter 15

The routine resumed. In Nuala's peaceful kitchen, time, measured by the slow steady measure of the clock, *tick, tick, tick*, slipped past, and outside the wind howled around the house and hollered down the chimney. Logs fell and sparked and collapsed in the newly resurrected range and the smell of turf turned up old memories and comforts.

Nuala grew attached to the little boy, protective even, and when Patrick started calling Nuala *"Tata"*, short for *tante* or aunt, she did not correct him. Nuala's fondness for the little boy had crept up on her, and she wasn't fully aware of her feelings for him until she found the note. Its venomous words written in green winded her.

She came across it crumpled up in one of Tessa's dress pockets when she was putting on a wash. She tossed it aside, switched on the washing machine and leaned on the worktop to watch Patrick and Tom play ball in the back garden.

"He is such a handsome, useless lump," she remarked to Saskia and absently unfolded the note and read it. Her face darkened. She looked up.

"What's wrong?" Saskia asked. "You look cross."

She handed the note to Saskia. Saskia read it and put it down. They looked out into the garden. Patrick ran around giggling.

"It was in her dress pocket," Nuala said. "Who would write such a thing?"

Saskia looked straight ahead. "I know who wrote the note," she said, "but I've no proof."

Nuala's head turned like a whip. "How?"

"It's a man in our building – he's a recluse."

"I'll bet he is," Nuala barked. "I'm calling the landlord – give me his number."

"Nuala, you'll have to talk to Tessa first. It's her business, not ours."

"I have every intention of talking to her first." Nuala cursed loudly and fetched her coat.

Saskia looked out into the garden just in time to see Patrick fall. She knew Tom sometimes tripped him up on purpose. He got some sort of kick out of seeing the look of surprise on the boy's face and Patrick always took it well. He picked himself up, dusted himself off and grinned. Not that night though. He fell hard. He went flying through the air and landed on his chin. When he pulled himself up he looked at Tom, puzzled, but he didn't cry.

Saskia opened the door and switched on the light.

Nuala arrived at her side with a scissors. She looked furious.

Tom looked up and for the first time Saskia saw something different in his expression. It was the tiniest hint of guilt.

"Aren't you the real big man?" Nuala hissed ferociously.

She made a dash for him and waved the scissors under his nose.

"For that little trick, you can play for an extra half hour. I know it's your turn to go to the hospital but tonight I need to speak to Tessa alone so I'm taking a taxi. One word of protest," she warned "and I'll kick the backside off you."

Tom didn't argue.

Nuala pulled on a pair of gardening gloves, quickly snipped a half dozen of her precious roses, bundled them up in newspaper and left.

Patrick asked if Tom could stay for tea.

Saskia shrugged. "He can stay if he wants to. There's plenty for everyone. It's just fish fingers, beans and mash. Nothing fancy," she said as if Tom might be expecting something elaborate, something that involved flambéing or a pasta-maker.

At the hospital, Nuala arranged the flowers in a vase. Tessa admired them and thanked her. She seemed happier this evening, practically chipper.

"You know, before this hospital stay, I'd never been given flowers before," she said, amused.

"You live in Ireland, what do you expect?" Nuala said with a grim smile. "The men are worse than useless. How are you this evening?"

"Good," she said brightly. "I was given some good news. They think I'll be home on Saturday."

"Oh," Nuala said.

"You don't seem pleased?" Tessa said. "I thought you'd be keen to get your life back? An eight-year-old has a lot of energy."

"He's no trouble," Nuala said and she picked a leaf off a stem. "Have they a diagnosis now?"

"Sometimes, clots just happen. Sticky blood."

Nuala sat down and took the note out of her bag.

"I found this in one of your dresses when I was doing the laundry," she said. She handed the note to Tessa.

Tessa flinched and handed it back.

"Please burn it."

"Burn it? You should report it to the landlord – it's bullying."

"The landlord? I have more than enough on my plate," Tessa said firmly.

"A man in your building wrote this, Tessa. It's wrong."

"They're words, Nuala, only words. Words can't hurt us. He knows nothing about us."

Nuala was unsure.

"I don't want any more talk about it," Tessa said and Nuala knew the matter would not be mentioned again.

"Okay," she said, and she put the note back into her bag.

After dinner, Tom and Saskia sat by the range with a glass of wine. They watched the news with the volume low. Patrick was finishing his homework at the kitchen table and Saskia wondered why Tom was still hanging around. He was unusually chatty. He told her the fish fingers and beans had struck a reminiscent chord and stirred a childhood memory, a trip to the zoo with his sisters. He looked comfortable and she gathered he was waiting until the last drop of wine was drained from the bottle.

She was on tenterhooks. The day had gone badly. A customer had scalded himself and was threatening to sue and the finger was being pointed in her direction. Her phone was on silent but was ringing incessantly and she was hormonal.

"How did you end up with a name like Saskia?" Tom asked quietly so as not to disturb the homework. "Did you get grief in school?"

"What do you mean?"

"I mean, you're from Galway – 'Saskia' is hardly native." He chuckled.

"No, what you mean is, I'm not exotic enough to have a name like Saskia," she snapped.

"Steady on, dude. Don't be so sensitive."

"Don't be so sensitive? It's *my name*."

"Okay, okay, forget it."

Saskia folded her arms over her stomach. She was conscious of her spare tyre and conscious of the way Tom sized her up with a critical eye.

"My father liked Saskia Reeves," she said apologetically.

"The actress?"

"Yes. He liked the name," she said, lowering her voice. "Thing is, he didn't hang around long enough to see if I liked it."

"Is that why you hate men?" he muttered. "Because your father left."

"I don't hate men," she whispered. "I dislike men who think they're God's gift."

"And what's that supposed to mean?" he whispered back.

"Nothing," she said innocently, making a mental note to once again cut down on her wine-drinking. It brought out the honesty in her. "It's just I know how you see me: an overweight rhinoceros with a name that doesn't match. But at least I don't swan around in labelled clothes thinking the world owes me something."

"Feck you," Tom said.

"Feck you too," Saskia replied. "You criticise Fiona Fox but you're as bad as her. In fact, the two of you were made for one other. Maybe you should run off together and start a colony."

Tom got up from his seat.

"If you're sensitive about being overweight then maybe you

should stop eating," he whispered, more ferociously now. "And who are you to cast judgement on me? You know nothing about me."

"I know enough," she said.

Tom left, slamming the door behind him.

Patrick looked up from the table.

"What's wrong?" he asked.

"A silliness," Saskia replied and she smiled in such a way that Patrick knew this wasn't true.

A few moments later there was a knock at the door.

Saskia went out and hesitated.

"I'm not interested in talking to you any more tonight!" she shouted through the letterbox.

There was a momentary pause. The letterbox pushed in.

"You'll have to talk to me at some stage, Nuala," a voice replied.

Saskia jumped. She opened the door but kept the chain on.

Through the crack, she saw a middle-aged man.

"Nuala's not here at the moment. Can I help you?" she asked.

"You can," the man said. "You can tell her that her brother called."

When Nuala arrived home and saw her brother at the kitchen table helping himself to fruitcake, she stood still in the doorway like a startled rabbit.

Saskia thought she'd done the right thing inviting him in but evidently not. It was not a warm family-reunion moment.

Nuala crossed the room and filled the kettle.

"I always liked the range," Frank Murphy remarked. "It never ceased to draw a crowd." His accent had a mid-Western American twang.

Nuala folded her arms and observed him from the sink.

"I've nothing to say to you, Frank."

"I'm sure you don't, Nuala, but I've plenty to say to you."

"Who do you think you are coming around here in the middle of the night?" she snarled.

"Had no choice. You weren't responding to any of the attorney's letters or answering my calls."

Saskia noticed the manipulative smile in his eyes and Nuala caught her eye.

She frowned. "Please leave us be, Saskia, thank you, goodnight," she said in one breath.

Saskia said her goodbyes and pulled on her coat. She closed the kitchen door but lingered to eavesdrop.

"I've enough on my plate, Frank," Nuala said.

"So I see," Frank Murphy replied. "Took a look in my old room and saw that little African kid asleep – cute."

"*How dare you!*" Nuala shouted.

"It's my home too, Nuala, and you know it. Why else would you have left my room unchanged? Same wallpaper and everything for years. I'm touched."

"Don't be. That room is used for storage so there's never been a need for new wallpaper. It is in its arse your home too! Get that out of your head. I gave my best years nursing our parents, administering bed-baths and medication, only to be left on the shelf in repayment, and you ride in here on your high horse with your Americanisms and expect open arms and an inheritance just because your life has gone belly-up? Get out and go to hell!"

"I'm going," he said smugly, "but you have no hold on this house, Nuala. It's as much mine as it is yours no matter how often you play the Florence Nightingale card. I suggest you take your head out of the sand and get some legal advice."

A chair scraped against the tiles, footsteps approached and Saskia fled.

That night, Nuala couldn't sleep. She floated down the stairs like a ghost in her voluminous nightie and sat at the arched window, hugging her knees. Patrick's door opened with a creak, there were tiptoes and then he was beside her. They cuddled together and looked out over the moonlit rooftops, past the shadowy cathedral to the bay where the lighthouse blinked.

"*Tu es triste, Tata?*" he said.

"*Oui.* A little sad."

"Why?"

"When you get older, you realise you have to say goodbye to the things you love. It's not easy." She smiled wistfully.

"When you are little, you have to say goodbye to things too," he said wisely and Nuala pulled him closer.

They sat there just like that, outlined in moonlight. When it got too cold, they made moves to go back to bed.

*"Tu vas mieux?"* Patrick asked.

"Much better," she said and she smiled. "I forgot to tell you, it looks like your mam will be home on Saturday. Isn't that wonderful?"

His eyes lit up. She ruffled his hair. They climbed the stairs to his bedroom. He caught her hand.

"We don't have to say goodbye, just because Maman is coming home," he told her. "We only live across the road."

"That's right, you do," Nuala said and she tucked him in. She paused at the door. "For as long as I'm in this house, Patrick, this room will always be yours. You can stay whenever you want."

"Really?"

"Yes."

# Chapter 16

When it was certain that Tessa was going to be discharged the following Saturday, relief stirred and settled. They were more than tired of each other now. Fiona was fit to strangle Nuala, Nuala wanted to bang Fiona's head against Tom's, and Saskia couldn't wait to see the back of Tom. Since they had words, he hadn't spoken to her and she fantasised about beating him and his oversized ego to a pulp.

Patrick counted down the days, the hours and the minutes. The week dragged even though in school they made a "Welcome Home" banner and Miss Hennessy chose Patrick and Emma to play Joseph and Mary in the Nativity play. Each child was given a part: angels, shepherds, wise men, innkeepers and animals. Brad Flanagan was given the part of the back end of the donkey. The other children laughed a lot over this and that was when Brad Flanagan decided he was through being nice to Patrick no matter what Miss Hennessy had told them. By Friday, he was back to his old nasty self.

The day didn't start well. Nuala woke Patrick earlier than usual. She was already dressed and all business, no chats or dressing-gown cuddles. She found him hanging out the window and was cross about it. Did he think that money grew on trees? All the heat would escape out the window. He got dressed quickly and quietly.

Over breakfast she didn't speak and he was careful not to slurp his chocolate milk. She sighed when she saw the cereal box was empty. She had black bags under her eyes and she caught him looking at her.

"I'm just tired, pet, that's all, and I have a busy day ahead of me."

Patrick had a feeling the day was only going to get worse. He was right.

At lunchtime he and Emma were in their usual place, under the tree, examining a conker. It was shiny like polished wood. A shadow fell across them. It was Brad. Chad with the too-close eyes was nearby, looking on.

"It's Mary and Joseph," he sneered.

"Go away, Brad," Emma warned.

"No," he said, grabbing Patrick's football.

"Hey, give that back!"

"Why? It's only a piece of crap ball anyway!" and he removed a drawing compass from his pocket and stabbed a hole in the ball. "Look, it's burst already!" He flung the burst ball back at them and ran away laughing.

Chad smirked and walked away.


Saskia rang Nuala. A new barista had managed to give herself third-degree burns. Saskia would have to work late. She couldn't collect Patrick.

"Well, I can't either, Saskia. I've a meeting with a solicitor," Nuala said. "You'll have to ask Tom to do it."

"He's not speaking to me."

"Jesus Christ, can't you sort it out? One more day and we'll all be shut of each other?"

Saskia didn't probe. The teacher's voice was tight.

She dialled Tom's number. He was short. She heard hairdryers whirring in the background. He was at a hair salon. It was probably white-walled and minimalist with non-minimalist prices where an impossibly svelte girl was fussing over him administering a head massage.

"What?" he said.

"You need to collect Patrick from school."

"I'm busy."

"I can hear that."

"Why can't you do it?"

"I'm working late. There's a crisis."

"What, don't tell me, the global coffee market's on the verge of collapse?"

"Forget it."

She hung up.

Saskia waited at the school gate. Her manager had not been understanding. If a member of staff had third-degree burns it was up to all of them to row in. Saskia wondered if this expectation to "row in" was written into their contracts.

The bell rang. Just as the children spilled out of the building, someone stepped up and stood beside her. It was Tom.

"What happened to the coffee-shop crisis?" he said.

"Nice hair," she smirked.

They scowled at each other then watched children bob through the gates, all giggles and shrieks and bellows.

Patrick was last. He dragged his heels and he hung his head. He came over and stood at their feet. Something was wrong. They both crouched down to his eye level.

"What's up, mate?" Tom asked.

Patrick held out his burst ball.

"Brad Flanagan burst my football with a compass," he said.

"Who's this Brad Flanagan?" Tom asked.

"His mam is the lollipop lady. He's always mean to me. Well, he stopped for a while but he's mean again now."

Patrick dug his fist into his eye. Tom put his hands on the boy's shoulders, looked him square in the eye and Patrick's face crumpled. Tom pulled him into a bear hug. The boy's body felt so vulnerable – he was like a little bird with a broken wing.

"It's all right, little man, we'll sort this," he said and Saskia thought she heard a catch in his voice. "Let's go for a burger and ice cream and you can tell us all about this Brad Flanagan fellow before I rearrange his face."

Saskia took one hand and Tom the other and, on the way, they threw the burst blue ball into a skip.

They stopped off at one the bigger sports shops where the assistants were all labels and fake tan. Tom told Patrick to pick out the ball he wanted and the little boy was so excited and shiny-eyed over such a small gift it spurred Tom into a spending spree. He bought him two tracksuits, a pair of football shorts, two pairs of football socks, a kit bag and an Ireland kit.

Then they stopped at the rail of Premier League jerseys and a barelegged shop assistant hovered. She recognised a spender when she saw one. She wore a tennis dress that just about covered her butt-cheeks and hopped from one foot to the other, giving the impression she was about to serve for match point at Wimbledon.

"Which jersey would you like?" Tom asked.

Patrick got so flustered he couldn't remember who Laurent Deschamps had played for. He stuffed his hands into his duffel pockets self-consciously and his nose ran.

Saskia reached down and wiped it with a hankie.

"Who did Laurent Deschamps play for?" Patrick asked the floor shyly.

"Innskeep," the shop assistant and Tom said simultaneously, and the shop assistant beamed at Tom as though they were fellow physicists versed in the same complex vocabulary.

Saskia rolled her eyes.

After the items were bagged and paid for they went to McDonald's for a Happy Meal. It only seemed right for the day that was in it. Patrick was reluctant to talk about the bully Brad Flanagan and his friend Chad who apparently had eyes that were very close together.

"But what if we promised to sort out the situation?" Saskia asked Tom. "Couldn't you beat him around a bit?"

"I'm not sure that's altogether legal," Tom surmised, sucking Coke through a straw.

"So?"

"I'll think of something," Tom said.

Patrick seemed happier. Tom wasn't sure why. For some reason, only known to the boy himself, Patrick seemed to have faith in him, and Tom thought there was a good chance he was the only person who did.

They went home.

Saskia found Nuala at home sitting at her kitchen table. It was dark save for the light from the votive lamp. Tears glistened on the teacher's cheeks. Saskia sat opposite her.

"What's wrong, Nuala?"

The teacher blew her nose. She nodded at the Sacred Heart. "I never noticed how sinister that picture was before until this evening. It's essentially a man with his chest cavity ripped open."

"It's never been a favourite of mine," Saskia shuddered. "It's like a medieval medical journal."

The teacher wiped her eyes.

"You know, all week I've been looking forward to getting back to my old life. Now I'm wondering what life I'm looking forward to getting back to."

Fresh tears rolled off her face and onto the oilcloth, creating pools on the picture-assortment of teapots.

"I must be menopausal," she said and she half laughed. "Where's Patrick?"

"Fiona dragged him in off the street for orange and biscuits."

"That would be Fiona. In for the last hurrah." Nuala sighed. "I had intended on cleaning their little flat, giving it an airing before Tessa came home but I haven't the heart."

"Come on, we'll do it together," Saskia said.

They crossed the street and let themselves into the Kimbas' flat. They polished, dusted, scoured, scrubbed and shone. Afterwards they sat on the couch and let the scent of winter steal in the through the open window.

They locked up and climbed the stairs to the dimness of the upstairs hall. Grey light made a crescent in the fan window above the front door. Saskia felt along the wall for the switch, flicked on the light and a blinking man was illuminated before them. It was the recluse. He squinted and attempted to sidle past. Nuala's eyes narrowed in recognition. She pointed at him.

"It's you," she said quietly. "You had the dog, the one that chased my cat under a car."

Joe Delaney bolted. Nuala chased after him. Anger possessed her and propelled her up the stairs, Saskia in her wake. Nuala caught up with him as he tried to close the door and wedged her foot in it.

"*Let me in this instant!*" she shouted and she forced her way in.

The smell of smoke and dog was overpowering and sickening.

Saskia peered over Nuala's shoulder. The flat was bare except for a few bits of furniture.

The man retreated to a corner and sank to the floor.

"All you had to do that day was apologise for your dog but you ran off like a big coward. And there you are living across the road from me all this time," Nuala said tearfully. "I had to scrape my poor cat off the road."

She shook her head and turned to leave and that was when she spotted the yellow sticky notes and green pen. He was in the process of writing another note. She blinked several times in order to process the evidence. Then she turned, folded her arms and gave the man the look that had struck fear into the hearts of many a student.

"And you're the mystery note-writer too – aren't you just the real charmer altogether?"

She turned on her heel and pulled Saskia down the stairs after her. At the front door she put her hands on her hips.

"The landlord's number, Saskia please, right now," she ordered. "Don't even try and talk me out of it or so help me God I'll beat it out of you."

Saskia was too tired and too scared to argue.

# Chapter 17

In the early hours of Saturday morning, Saskia lay awake.

Nuala had managed to get a hold of the landlord to report the note-writer. He had been surprised.

"Joe Delaney wouldn't have struck me as that sort of person – harmless enough I would have thought, afraid of his own shadow."

"Well, he's not," Nuala had argued, "and his place absolutely stinks to high heaven of dog. I'm surprised you haven't had complaints!"

"I see," said the landlord. "You leave him to me. And while we're on the subject, your friend who received the note, Mrs Kimba, owes me rent. I appreciate she's sick but that won't pay my mortgage."

Saskia had known that Nuala should have kept her nose out it. Tessa had bigger worries than a few nasty words scrawled on a scrap of paper.

She examined the damp spots on the ceiling and the cracks in the plasterwork. Negative thoughts would not let her sleep but she could not help herself. She wanted to scream out the window and shake her fist at the sky.

Tom Winters, the big spender, waltzing in with his credit card to win the boy over. It wasn't fair. She couldn't afford such grand gestures and she felt useless like an unloved rag of a thing, cast aside.

Tessa lay awake too. The night nurse sat down and took her tea break with her. The ward was dark except for the bedside lamp, which enclosed them in a circle of light while the other patients slept. The room resonated with the gentle sound of snores and breathing.

"Can't sleep again?"

Tessa shook her head.

"Do you want to take something?"

"No, thank you."

"You'll sleep when you're ready. So you're leaving us in the morning?"

"Looks like it. I'd prefer if they had some results."

"They may never know how you got those clots but, just as long as you stay on the blood-thinner and come in for regular blood checks, you can go back to living the way you did."

"I don't feel any better."

"It will take some time to adjust to thinner blood."

They sat and chatted companionably. The nurse had three grown-up sons, all soccer-mad. Tessa liked her. She was kind, unassuming.

The nurse drained her tea and lingered at the end of the bed, watching the black woman struggle with her thoughts. She was beautiful but stunted in some way, like a flower that had forgotten to blossom.

The nurse had been around long enough to know doctors were sometimes wrong with their diagnoses and that test results often went missing.


At eight o'clock Saskia awoke to voices on the steps. She felt anxious and wanted the day over with. It was the landlord, having it out with Joe Delaney. She didn't want to listen but it was impossible not to. The landlord was a stocky man who wore T-shirts in winter.

"I know you have a dog up there, Joe – I can smell it from here," he said.

"I don't any more," Joe Delaney said shakily. "She was a stray, got run over by a car a while ago."

Saskia had not heard him speak much before. His voice was surprisingly soft – flat midlands.

"Okay," said the landlord more gently. "But I'm afraid I'm going to have to evict you, Joe. The dog was one thing – it's cruel keeping a dog in a flat that size – but I've heard about these notes you've been leaving around. That's not on at all."

"I called the dog after my wife," Joe said absently.

"And did you like the wife?" the landlord asked cautiously.

"Of course. I loved her."

Saskia peeped out the window. The landlord looked away and towards the mountains. Night had shaken the sycamore of its leaves and now just a few persisted like loose teeth. The air was sharp, winter crisp.

Joe Delaney blinked in sunlight. He was pale and yellowed – a real-life Miss Havisham.

"Please don't throw me out, John," he said to his feet. "I've trouble getting out. I don't like leaving the flat."

"You should have thought about that before you started writing nasty notes," the landlord replied. "I'll call over with your deposit. Good day to you now."

At nine o'clock, Patrick watched Nuala over breakfast as he chewed his Coco Pops.

"You're not talking today, Tata," he observed.

"I'm just thinking," she said and smiled.

"Everything will be fine," he reassured her.

At eleven o'clock a water glass fell to the ward floor and smashed into shards and a puddle of water. The consultant and his team withdrew from Tessa Kimba's bedside and notified the nurse. There had been an accident that would need careful mopping up.

At half eleven, Saskia knocked on Nuala's door. Inside, in the hallway, the phone rang over and over. Nuala and Patrick could not have gone far. She sat on the steps and waited. Tom arrived and sat on the steps a bit down from her and the phone continued to ring in the hall.

Nuala and Patrick were in the back garden picking a bunch of winter roses for Tessa, pink and yellow. When they came inside the phone was still ringing shrilly above them in the hall. Nuala tried to ignore it but its persistence forced her up the stairs. Patrick followed her. She picked up the receiver. Sunlight streamed in through the glass.

"Hello," she said.

Patrick continued on up the stairs to his room and turned to look back at her. She smiled at him and waved him on but he sat down and watched her. He was not used to seeing her on the house phone.

"Nuala Murphy?" asked a voice on the phone.

Nuala recognised it. It was the hospital. She'd given them her landline number, but had forgotten.

"Yes, it is."

"It's Nurse Murray here, from the hospital. I have some bad news, I'm afraid."

"What's happened?" Nuala clutched the receiver until her knuckles turned white.

"It's Mrs Kimba," the nurse said.

Who else would it be, Nuala wanted to ask, but she didn't. Instead she caught Patrick's eye and they studied each other from their different hallway perspectives. She put her hand over the receiver. "Patrick, grab your stuff from your room like a good man – we have to go in a second."

Patrick reluctantly went.

"Sorry about that – you were saying?" Nuala said to the nurse.

"She's had some bad news and is not taking it very well. She asked me to call you," the voice continued but it sounded echoey and disembodied.

"What sort of news?"

The nurse sighed weightily. "I'm afraid Mrs Kimba has been diagnosed with cancer of the uterus."

Nuala sat down on the hall seat.

"But she can't have – we're on our way to collect her, to bring her home," she said and realised she sounded ridiculous.

"I'm sorry, Nuala. I wish the news was better."

"So do I." Nuala spoke quietly now in case Patrick might hear. "How could it have taken this long to diagnose?"

"It seems to have been an administrative error, a fault in our equipment," the nurse said.

"Both?"

"Yes."

"Unbelievable."

"Yes. They plan to carry out a hysterectomy on Monday."

"But she's only a young woman," Nuala whispered.

There was a silence on the other end of the phone.

"Do you have someone to talk to, Nuala, someone there with you?"

"Yes, I do," Nuala said. "I have her son."

"I know," said the voice. "I meant another adult."

"Sure, they're queuing up outside," Nuala said sarcastically.

The doorbell rang then and Nuala stretched the cord to answer the door.

It was Tom and Saskia followed by Fiona and Emma. She motioned them inside. Emma hopped up the stairs to join Patrick who was on his way down. They sat.

"Something's wrong," he whispered to her, not taking his eyes off Nuala. "I always know."

Fiona stepped into the drawing room and shivered. The room closed in around her. It was cold and the décor looked about a century old, all wallpaper and worn rugs and dull brass animal ornaments.

Nuala hung up the phone and stillness settled on the house.

Fiona stepped back into the hall. "Are we ready to roll?" she asked chirpily and then saw by Nuala's face they were rolling nowhere.

"Tessa won't be coming home just yet," Nuala said and she attempted to pull a smile but her lips were stuck to her teeth. She put her hands in her cardigan pockets and bizarrely began to study the pattern the sunlight made on the hall floor.

# Chapter 18

Over the days that followed Patrick retreated into his shell and they couldn't get a word out of him. Each in their own way tried to cajole him: extra Coco Pops, kick-arounds with his new leather ball, jelly babies and jelly beans. He was worried, plain and simple. Of late, he'd watched too many hospital programmes with Emma and knew all about bedside dramas and how people were likely to die or flat-line overnight.

At the hospital his mother sensed his worry and pulled him close to her side. She whispered softly into his ear like she had done when he was a baby and lay gurgling at the ceiling. "You are my angel boy, *ma puce*. I carried you in my belly all the way from Africa. We are survivors. This operation, it will be a piece of cake."

He was not convinced. He sat on the end of his bed and tapped his football from foot to foot: over, back, over, back; rolled it forward, back, forward, back; heel, toe, heel, toe.

From Nuala's windows, he watched winter frost colouring the walled garden white.

Saskia nagged Tom about talking to Brad Flanagan's mother until he caved. On the morning of Tessa's operation he arrived in the café early and watched the lollipop lady over a coffee. Leaves twirled and shoppers scurried.

"What are you doing here?" Saskia asked, pretending to wipe down his table.

"Waiting for Brad Flanagan's mother."

"Okay but I didn't mean for you to skip work."

"Told them I had to see a dog about a man."

"Right. By the way, the other waitress wants to know if you're single," she said, rearranging the sugar-shaker and jug.

"The one behind the counter with the roots showing?" Tom asked without taking his eyes off the lollipop lady.

"Told you you were shallow."

"I might be but at least I'm not blind."

"What'll I tell her?"

"Tell her I'm gay."

"Gladly."

Mrs Flanagan was conscientious. Sewn into her uniform and red-faced from exertion, her expression was serious and she waved down cars with the solemnity of a NASA controller. She was friendly to the children, engaged with them and knew most of them by name. When a tubby boy with red hair, freckles and a face that matched hers joined her side, she left down her lollipop stick to tuck his shirt in and wipe his face with a tissue. He wriggled out of her reach. She wagged her finger at him. He ran.

"Brad Flanagan," Tom muttered.

Once the crowds of children had thinned and Mrs Flanagan was packing up to go, Tom approached her. She looked at him suspiciously and he was half-afraid she might bash his brains in with her lollipop.

"Could I have a word, Mrs Flanagan?"

"Why, who's askin'?" Her accent was very Dublin.

"Tom Winters, I'm a friend, er, guardian, of a boy in your son's class. We have a little problem."

"Oh?"

"Would you like a coffee?"

She shrugged. "Yeah, okay."

Saskia watched them from behind the counter. They made an odd couple. Mrs Flanagan's lollipop lay under the table. Her hair was clipped so short you could see her scalp. She sipped on a latte while Tom told her the story as diplomatically as he could. He told her

114

about Tessa's illness and the fact that Patrick was now staying with a neighbour.

He kept the Brad and the burst football incident until last. This piece of news displeased Mrs Flanagan greatly.

"The little bollox, I'll leather him!" she spat.

"Ah no," Tom said.

"No, forget that. His father will leather him. It's that Chad with the dicky eyes – he's a bad influence, that lad."

"Is a leathering necessary?"

"Ah, we won't really leather him. We'll just shout at him, threaten him. My husband has a shotgun. He hunts – rabbits. He'll wave the gun around a bit to put the frighteners on him."

"I see," Tom said, worried. "It's just I don't want Patrick to bear the brunt of whatever, em, punishment you dole out."

"Leave it with me, love. Before you know it, they'll probably be the best of friends."

"Probably," Tom said sceptically.

When she left Tom sat still for a while. Saskia buttered bread and kept an eye on him. When he was leaving, he brought his empty cup up to the counter.

"What's wrong with you?" Saskia asked.

"Why?"

"It's just you're acting a bit strange – quasi-human almost."

"Thanks," Tom said and he left.

Later Saskia feigned sickness so she could collect Patrick from school. She waited at the school gate with the parents and minders and spotted him amongst the horde: a little brown coffee bean, wrapped up in his duffel and hat and mittens, carrying his new ball. Saskia waved and Patrick waved back and a pulse of happiness went through her.

They went to the playground. It was cold and his mittened hand reached for hers. He was quieter than usual and she pushed him higher and higher on the swing until she got a giggle and a whoop out of him. He had barely said a word all week. She took him to McDonald's for another Happy Meal. It made him happy, momentarily. He examined the chicken nuggets with a kind of wonder and savoured each one of them. Patrick Kimba was a neat little boy. No barbecue sauce moustache or globs down his uniform. She drank a coffee and watched him chewing and thought about Tessa, under the knife, out cold and in a temporary limbo. Then she remembered it was pointless having such dark thoughts, the kind you'd never utter aloud for fear of being instantly incarcerated. Patrick looked out the window and saw a boy riding high on his father's shoulders. His wise eyes met hers.

"Do you have a dad?" he asked.

"Everyone has a dad," she said and he looked at her again.

"But do you see yours?"

"No. He left."

"Oh."

"Yes."

"Why?"

She told him the truth.

"When I was little my brother was killed in a car crash. My father couldn't deal with it. He left."

Patrick rested his chin on his hand for a moment to digest the information, his warm brown eyes watching her sad blue ones. Then he picked up his last chicken nugget and offered it to her.

"You have it," he said.

She swallowed carefully and shook her head. Then she bent down under the table to root in her bag for a hankie.

He took his time eating the last piece of breaded chicken and watched her re-tie her hair into a ponytail. Loose bits stood away from her head. She looked like a sun he had drawn in school with lots of rays coming out of it.

Her phone rang and she watched it ring, waiting for it to stop.

"You don't want to talk right now," he observed.

"No, I don't," she said and she smiled at him.

She was nice when she smiled, less worried-looking. Patrick had heard Tom call her a "mother of swallows" and he didn't know what that meant but he guessed it wasn't good because Nuala said that she'd give him a clip round the ear if he spoke about Saskia like that again.

On their way back to the square, they walked along Clanbrassil Street by the halal stores, markets and kebab houses: all colours and spice and chatter, dark eyes and gestures hammering deals and exchanging news. Men with beards and hats, sandals, thobes and sirwals walked and talked in a rush, "humina, humina, humina".

They gathered at shop counters, and amongst the sacks of rice and jars of spices, watched Arabic soaps and Al Jazeera, and passed the time of day with the shopkeepers. The women wore hijabs and held the hands of small children.

The street was a rush and jostle, a flurry of exoticism, Arab pop music and a constant stream of traffic. Customers pecked at the fruit and vegetable stands like hens and pinched melons, peppers, zucchinis, aubergines, lemons, mangoes and durian.

And it was there, between a stand of watermelons and a kebab house, that Saskia spotted her boss walking their way. It wouldn't do for her to be seen in the whole of her health when she'd cried off sick. She pulled Patrick by the hand into the kebab house where men sat at the tables with glasses of tea and pored over Pakistani papers.

The man behind the counter issued Patrick with a huge white-toothed smile and a green lollipop.

"Green for the footballer, like the Ireland jersey," he said, nodding up and down. "Does your friend want one?" he asked and he nodded over to Saskia whose nose was pressed so close to the glass it made a circle of steam each time she exhaled.

"She's hiding from her boss," Patrick explained. "Her boss is a dragon," he added.

"I understand," the man said. And he handed Patrick a bag of stale bread for the swans on the canal and a red lollipop for Saskia.

They stopped at the canal. Saskia sat on the bench and Patrick fed stale naan bread to the swans. He was quiet. She knew he was worried though there had been no mention of the operation.

The swans gathered gracefully, a white cloud of feathers, and waited for the bread politely, heads bent. The sun dipped and made a pink light on the canal. Patrick held up the last piece of naan and took a moment to choose which swan he would throw it to. An impatient and huge cob swam to the water's edge and made up his mind for him by stepping out onto the bank. They regarded each other, bird and boy. Patrick held out the bread and the swan took it, flapping his huge wings. He slid back into the water and swam away, taking the flock of swans with him and Patrick took off down the bank after them.

"*Come back!*" he shouted into the wind. "*Come back!*"

Saskia, alarmed, ran after him. But he was fast and she couldn't catch him. She cursed herself for smoking and for being an unfit and useless article. But then he tripped and fell down in the frosty mud and the swans floated on, like ghost ships let loose from their anchors. Saskia ran to his side.

"Hey, what's the matter?" she asked but no words came out of his open mouth.

Tears and snot rolled down his face and cheeks.

She helped him up, dusted him down and wiped his nose. They sat on the bench. She cuddled him, rocked him back and forth. Traffic passed over the bridge, horns beeped and people walked their dogs. It was terrifically cold.

"I don't want Maman to die," he said.

Saskia hugged him more tightly. "But your maman said the operation would be a piece of cake. Don't you believe her?"

"She always tells lies so I won't be scared."

"All adults do that," Saskia explained.

"But you don't?"

"No."

"Why?"

"I remember what it's like to be little and lied to. It's hard to swallow."

Patrick nodded. "It's stupid," he agreed. "That day Maman fell in the shop, afterwards we got on the wrong bus and she slept on the grass. She told me the heat was too much for her."

"Maybe it was?" Saskia suggested.

"No," Patrick said. "My maman is from Africa. I'm not a thick."

"I know that."

"It's because she was sick all along."

"Probably."

Saskia handed him a tissue and he blew his nose.

"Is your brother dying a secret?" he asked.

"I don't talk about it," she said.

"Okay."

He took her hand and they walked home along the canal. It was getting dark and the others were expecting them.

They drove out to the hospital in silence, each hoping more than the next that Tessa Kimba would pull through okay.

They bargained with the matron to let them into the High Dependency Unit.

"We're family," Nuala said and the matron gave her a look.

"Are you now?"

"This is her little boy."

"Fine, but just for a few minutes and don't overcrowd her. Make sure you've sanitised your hands."

The room was a jungle of sounds: beeps and ticks and clicks, ventilators, air being sucked and pushed through. The light was low and grey and filtered through curtains, behind which anonymous individuals came to.

They formed a circle around the bed and stared. Tessa was missing her hair. Her sleek pageboy was gone yet she was smiling in a floaty, groggy way, oblivious to the tubes and drips and monitors and bewildered stares.

Patrick leaned in and hugged his mother. Emma stood close by.

"*Salut, Maman.*"

"*Alors* . . . look who we have here . . . two little people." Her words were slow and distanced but her face was relaxed as she took in the concerned faces. "You all came," she said and tittered softly. "You're very kind." She patted Patrick's face. "Good thing I had you when I did," she said tenderly. Then she squeezed Emma's hand. "Pretty girl."

"Where is your hair?" Emma asked seriously. "Did it come off during the operation?"

Tessa smiled. "The wig had to go before they operated."

"Wig?" Emma said curiously and the adults squirmed at her line of questioning.

"African hair is a lot of work," Tessa added, amused yet trying to ease their discomfort. "I go for wig over weave. It's a good thing too as I'm about to lose my real hair anyway."

"Oh, no!" Nuala gasped.

"Yes, they think I'll need chemotherapy and radiotherapy."

"Both?" Fiona asked. Months of hospital visits and check-ups and ferrying and traffic jams stretched out before her.

"They have to make sure they've zapped it all."

"How are you feeling now?" Nuala asked gently, conscious of Fiona's fretful tone.

119

"Good," Tessa smiled. "A little tipsy. I can press this amazing button whenever I feel any pain," she said, indicating a console. "Morphine, wonderful." She sighed. "They say it was successful," she said faintly. "That it was contained."

"That's great," they all chorused like they were in a bizarre hospital musical and then felt stupid in the silence that followed.

"One day at a time, eh?" Saskia said.

They filed out into the corridor and waited by the lifts. Harsh fluorescence reflected on the hospital floor. The doors slid over and back, delivering doctors weighed down by bad news, and visitors harbouring a sense of dread.

A nurse approached.

"Nuala Murphy and Saskia Heffernan?" she said, reading from a clipboard. "Mrs Kimba's consultant would like a word with you both."

The consultant was cold and matter of fact. It was his armour for survival in a world of comas and flat-lines, rogue cells and death.

"Before her operation, Mrs Kimba made you joint guardians of her son Patrick Kimba. It's why I wanted to speak with you."

"Excuse me, doctor?" Nuala said.

"Mister," he corrected her firmly.

Saskia thought it strange that after studying medicine for one hundred years to become a consultant and currying several million favours on top of that, that your title reverted to plain old "mister".

"Mr Hurley, wasn't that just a little dramatic?" Nuala asked.

The "mister" shrugged. "Often, before operations, people want things put in place in case they don't make it. It's always a possibility."

"Thank you, Mr Hurley. That's a thought that will haunt me to my grave."

Mr Hurley peered at her over his glasses. During billable hours, he scheduled no time for sarcasm.

"But she's going to be fine?" Saskia said.

"The prognosis is good. When she has recovered from her operation she will meet an oncologist who will set a programme for her."

He cleared his throat and drummed his fingers. Mr Hurley had something he needed to get off his chest.

"Did Mrs Kimba happen to disclose anything to either of you about her past?" he asked.

Nuala shook her head. Saskia shrugged.

"Anything about her husband – her little boy's father?"

"Only that he's a soldier," Saskia told him. "Tessa is very private but we do know her family died of cholera and that one of her neighbours was eaten by a crocodile."

The "mister" gave her a strange look and exhaled slowly through his nose. He paused then and took a moment to gauge the situation. He looked at his watch and ruminated.

"Did she mention anything about a trauma or violence?" he asked quietly.

"What do you mean?" Nuala asked.

The "mister" twirled his pen and decided he'd already said too much. He shook his head.

"Who knows?" he said in a dismissive tone. "Mrs Kimba is from the Congo. The atrocities committed there were and still are unspeakably bad. Worse than the camps during the Second World War – who knows what she has lived through?"

Nuala and Saskia looked at each other worriedly.

"What I'm trying to say is that Mrs Kimba needs time to recover. She needs to be looked after. She possibly needs counselling. Social services can help."

"Help? We only stepped in as neighbours."

"I understand, Ms Murphy, but Mrs Kimba obviously trusts you, both of you." He shrugged, in the same way you might when discussing plant food.

"She lives in the one-bedroom flat, Mr Hurley."

"Mmm, that's certainly not ideal, particularly undergoing chemotherapy. Mrs Kimba will need some good friends. Take my advice and see what social services can do."

He shook their hands and made moves to go.

"Thank you," Nuala said as they left the room.

"Good luck to you both – I'm sure I will see you around over the next few months."

The women watched him walk away.

"There's something he's not telling us," Nuala said.

"How can you tell?"

"I'm a teacher," Nuala reminded her prissily. "I always know when something's being held back, especially with boys – useless liars. If he was thirteen, I would have shaken it out of him," and Saskia didn't doubt it for a second.

That night, after Patrick was put to bed, Nuala called a meeting.

"I'm going to suggest Tessa move in with me here. She cannot stay in that bedsit, not undergoing chemotherapy and radiotherapy. It would be hell – she needs comfort."

"That's kind of you," Saskia said and she looked at Nuala suspiciously.

"Well, she would just pay rent to me rather than her landlord. In effect, she would be a tenant."

"So she'd have to give up her flat?" Tom asked. "Can't see her agreeing to that."

"It's for her own good. She'll have to see it that way. And I'll still be relying on all of you for support over the next few months."

Fiona folded her arms and sat back in her chair. "I'm sorry," she said, "but I'm out. I cannot provide a taxi service any more. You'll have to come up with another arrangement. One more week and that's it. I've put everything on hold for long enough. I've got a life to get back to."

"Well, that's just great," Nuala snapped. "This is not exactly ideal for me either, you know?"

"Oh, come on, don't give me that! At least you'll get rent out of her!"

They bickered back and forth until Saskia banged the table with her fist and they jumped.

She stood up and pointed at Fiona and then at the door.

"You can leave," she said with gritted teeth. "We don't need you. All you've done is moan and roll your eyes from the start. Isn't it lucky for you that fate allowed you to have a big ignorant jeep under you and that you weren't born in Africa?"

Fiona laughed. "Fate? I've made my own luck. I'll be glad to be see the back of the lot of you." She got up and left.

The table went quiet.

"What did you do that for?" Nuala asked. "We needed that big

122

ignorant jeep you mentioned. It's going to cost us a fortune in taxis."

"We'll work something out," Saskia said coldly.

As it transpired, they didn't have to.

They were all to get their lives back. It was the way Tessa wanted it.

She thanked Nuala for the offer but they were happy where they were and Nuala or any of them were welcome to call over any time. They had done more than enough. It was time for them all to get on with things and for her to get back on her feet, back to work. She would manage from here – make her own way out for treatment. There were buses.

"Buses, of course," Nuala said, bewildered, as though they were a new invention. "If you change your mind, you know where I am."

Patrick was a little doleful packing up. Nuala helped him put his few things into a bag.

"Can this still be my room? Maybe I can stay over sometimes?"

"Yes," Nuala said. "As I said, as long as I'm here this will always be your room."

He looked up at her and she turned away.

"You are sad again, Tata Nuala?"

"Don't be silly, I'm no such thing."

"Okay. It's just if you were, I could give you a cuddle." He shrugged. "It helps."

"If I was, yes you could, but I'm not," she said with a laugh. "Hurry up now, the taxi will be here in a minute and we'll go to collect your mam."

"What about Emma's car?"

"They're busy."

"Oh."

Patrick took one last look around his room and stood on the bed to look out the window. A man walked by with his head down. He wore a baseball cap and sunglasses even though it was wintry and grey. He carried a battered suitcase and appeared to be leaving, going away but not on holiday. He did not look back.

# Chapter 19

The lives, from which they had been torn, resumed – slightly adjusted, like ornaments lifted and returned to a freshly polished mantelpiece. And, for a time, they hardly saw each other. It was as if the Kimbas had never happened, that the solemn black woman and her son were just a figment of their imaginations.

The square sank into deep winter. Rain turned to sleet and covered the walled garden in a delicate light silver. Mornings were dark, the mountains inky black, lights flickered in the hills. Evenings were darker still and gales howled around the houses, under the doors and screamed through the telegraph poles.

Saskia missed Patrick with an ache and she missed the activity. Suddenly the hours were an eternity to fill and all the watching and the listening from her window perch could not satisfy her need for company.

She called down to the Kimbas' flat a handful of times but visits were not encouraged. Tessa only ever opened the door a crack and waited for you to announce your business and then leave. There would be no cosy chats or invites for tea and scones any time soon. If she wanted to see Patrick on a regular basis, she would need to think of an excuse, and it would need to be a good one.

Patrick missed the poster of Pelé and his own room, the outlines of aeroplanes in the dark. He missed Nuala and Coco Pops and the kitchen table, the picture with the lamp and the heat from the range. The flat was freezing, really cold. In the mornings he could see his breath in the dark. Sometimes his mother shook with the cold. Once, when he suggested they go and stay with Nuala for a while, she got cross. It was not to be mentioned again. She wanted things back to normal.

But nothing was normal, really. His mother was losing her hair. Clumps of it were on her pillow in the morning when she woke. She made a joke of it, said it would save time not having to clip it, before scooping it up and putting it into the bin. She was tired all the time too, and she talked in her sleep, in a strange babble of African food: *tilapia, bitekuteku, kwanga, makayabu*, maize, maboke, plantain, and cassava, always cassava, cassava, cassava.

"Maman, what is cassava?" he asked her.

"Something I hope you'll never have to eat, *ma puce*," was all she said.

There was no one to talk to about it. His mother sent Saskia away when she called, Tom was always working and Emma was never allowed out. Her mother had organised a whole pile of "extracurricular" activities for her. Emma had told him she hated all of them but her mother said they would keep her out of trouble and, besides, she had no choice in the matter.

Even Nuala was different. For a while he continued to play football in her back garden and afterwards she made him milky tea or a hot blackcurrant drink but then she stopped watching him play and after that she stopped talking. She didn't ask him questions about school or about how his mam was doing. She preferred to sit like a zombie watching the telly. And one evening when he asked if he could see his room again she said it was best not to, that it might not always be there after all and he went home puzzled. He stopped calling after that.

One good thing was that Brad Flanagan and the horrible Chad with the close-together eyes left him alone. The boys were no longer pals. Someone said Mr Flanagan had threatened to shoot Brad with his shotgun if he didn't find better friends for himself but that was only a story. And, anyway, news like that didn't mean much when your mother was getting sick into a basin or sleeping for so long she forgot to wake up and you were late for school.

He went back to playing football on his own again, out front on the patch of earth, because it was too cold for his mother to go outside. Sometimes, when he kicked the ball ferociously against the wall, he wished she were back in hospital and then he felt bad. Especially when he went back inside and his mother had found the strength to bake a coconut cake with raspberry jam and cut him a big fat slice to have with a glass of milk. Then he lay awake and prayed that she would be okay and that if anyone had to be sick or die that it would be Mrs Fox or Chad with the too-close eyes who no one liked anyway.

Saskia watched Tessa deteriorate. She became thin and frail and aged, hunching wearily against the elements, laden down with bags of yesterday's vegetables. She sometimes wondered if pride would actually kill the woman in the end. Saskia had worn a trail from her flat to the basement offering to help – to do homework, shopping or cooking. It was always refused.

She thought long and hard, trying to come up with some scheme that would loosen the tight grasp Tessa had on Patrick and ensure he could see her and the others again on a regular basis. It was when he started playing out front on his own again that she at last had a light-bulb moment.

She bought an Ireland jersey and a coaching manual and knocked on the Kimbas' door. She knew she would have to be firm, state rather than ask, so there would be no room for argument. To her immense surprise, there was none. Tessa seemed relieved. If Saskia wanted to be Patrick's football coach that was fine by her as long as it didn't interfere with homework.

After that, every evening, Saskia smoked cigarettes under a large umbrella that said "Fair Trade Coffee" and read drill exercises from a book. Then they attempted to practise them together and it was very Laurel and Hardy. She had the co-ordination of a brontosaurus. She kicked the ball with the wrong part of the foot, right on the toe and it was anyone's guess where it would land: on the street, in the bins, in someone's flowerbeds or in an old lady's shopping cart. She couldn't dribble or tackle or block and she coughed and sweated profusely, shuffling back to reference the book for answers. Patrick would sit patiently beside her while she tried to decipher the tips, drills and techniques, cursing under her breath.

The cigarettes made her lungs hurt. Patrick suggested she give them up. So she did and she persisted with the football. Because she loved the boy it became a labour of love and she grew to love the game. She learned the rules and found that once you knew the rules, the game was enjoyable. She read everything she could from the library: Pelé, McGrath, Best, Beckham, Clough and Ferguson. She devoured the sports sections of the leftover café-stained newspapers, books on tactics and books that criticised tactics and she trawled websites with the thirst of a student eager to learn. She learned that she admired Arsène Wenger, Roy Keane, Alex Ferguson and Brian Clough and admired Ronaldo, John Terry and José Mourinho a little less.

She and Patrick watched matches together: Champion's League, the FA Cup, friendlies and international qualifiers. They turned down the volume and pretended to be commentators: "*Duff drives a beautiful cross-field pass on the chest*" – "*A fine challenge by McShane*" – "*Chances are really coming now for Innskeep*" – "*Couldn't get his first touch*" – "*Good distribution from the back*" – "*Oh, nicely placed!*". Neither of them had digital so there was nowhere to watch the Premier League live and this posed a problem. She wouldn't feel right bringing an eight-year-old to the pub. They made do by reading post-match analysis and watching highlights, and together they learned the language of football and how to read the game. Innskeep was their team and Jacques Biet their favourite manager.

The more Saskia's knowledge increased, the more hooked she became. She shouted at the telly, at the ref and at the players, and every time someone made a wrong move she said things like: "He should have cleared his lines quicker" or "Should have passed the ball instead of going for glory like that, the gobshite!" or "When you play professionally you won't be caught dead doing anything as stupid as that!" And Patrick was happy that there was one person who truly believed in him.

It got colder; Tessa got sicker. Some days it took every ounce of energy she could muster to go to work. In the mornings, Patrick made the porridge. In the evenings, he peeled the vegetables.

When he began to cry off football, Saskia started to cook for them both. This time Tessa didn't protest; she didn't eat much anyway. Saskia wasn't a particularly good cook and she called to Nuala to ask for a cookbook and some basic tips. Nuala seemed marginally pleased to see her although the sniff was back. She made a pot of tea and dug out an ancient tome from the fifties. The photography was supersaturated, the women looked pure and had their hair set. Saskia wasn't sure she wanted it. There was every chance some of the ingredients were obsolete.

"Don't you have something from this century?" she asked.

"It's old but it's got all the basics," Nuala sniffed. "There are recipes online, you know."

"I know but I prefer the feel of a book."

Nuala sniffed again and threw a couple of logs into the range; sparks rose.

"I had forgotten how cosy this kitchen is," Saskia said.

Nuala sighed. "So they're not doing so well over beyond?"

"No, they're not. I seriously think Tessa is on the way out. She's eating like a bird."

"Chemotherapy does that. She will recover. There are some good soup recipes in that book."

"She should have taken you up on your offer and stayed with you for a while. Their flat is freezing."

Nuala sniffed again. "Well, the offer still stands," she said. "I've seen you out with Patrick, kicking the ball around. You're well able."

"I'm getting there."

"How come you play out front? It's too small. Isn't there a back garden over there, at your place?"

"It's full of rusted junk."

"Well, you're welcome to play out the back here, you know," Nuala suggested guardedly. "Like, you'd have more room. It's up to you, naturally."

She topped up their cups.

"How is Patrick getting on in school?"

"Good. He's such a bright boy."

"He is. One of the brightest I've come across. How's that little shitehawk Brad Flanagan behaving?"

"Like an angel. Patrick and Emma have even been asked to Flanagans' for tea, imagine? Patrick told me they said yes because they were both scared not to."

Nuala snorted. "If Fiona Fox allows her daughter next nigh or near that estate for tea or anything else, I'll eat my hat."

"I know." Saskia smiled. "She's keeping Emma busy with all sorts of 'extracurricular activities' this weather. Patrick hardly sees her."

Nuala shook her head. "Always such a snob, that one. It eats her alive sharing her middle-class space with immigrants. Lord only knows where she gets her notions. Her father delivered coal. Speaking of notions, where's that Tom Winters?"

Saskia shrugged. "In fairness to him, he did try call to Patrick a few times. Tessa wasn't exactly hospitable."

"Sure, look, isn't that the way?"

Nuala walked her to the door. The teacher pursed her lips and pulled her cardigan tighter. She picked at a piece of loose paintwork and looked across the street.

"You'll tell them I was asking for them, now won't you?" she said and her expression was unsure.

Saskia recognised loneliness when she saw it. "Won't we be over to you," she said, "to play football?" and the teacher smiled then but just a little.

On the Saturday of tea at Flanagans', Tessa could barely sit up. She watched Patrick get ready and he brought her some water. She took a sip and gagged a little. He sat on the bed and they looked at each other. She smiled weakly.

"I can stay and look after you," Patrick told her and she shook her head and told him to head on.

Saskia was taking him to Flanagans' and would collect him later.

Tea at Flanagans' was a mad affair. Brad was the youngest of five boys so there was a lot of teasing and shouting and belching. Mr Flanagan was a mechanic and smelt of grease and oil. Mrs Flanagan roared a lot. She shouted things like "You have my heart broken!" and "I'll murder the whole lot of you if you don't come to the table right now!" and "Shut up this minute or I'm leaving for England, forever!" She didn't mean it, Brad explained, she just had to roar to be heard.

She had pet names for all her children. There was Sauce, Twig, Sambo and Juckie and they all called Brad 'Tot'. It was because he was the smallest. No one used anyone's real names and it was very confusing.

Mrs Flanagan called Patrick 'pet'.

"Hello, pet," she said when she answered the door. "Welcome to the madhouse."

The living room was all legs and arms and was filled with little treasures. China ornaments: dogs, bunnies, birds, boys, girls and milkmaids. There was also a ship in a bottle, a tiny bronze spinning wheel, a Spanish dancer and there were snow globes from all sorts of exotic places like Paris, Rome, Marbella and Killarney.

All of the Flanagans had red hair so when they were sitting at the kitchen table it looked like it was on fire. They ate quickly without speaking, drank huge glasses of milk and then went back into the living room to watch football. Patrick was left alone with Mrs Flanagan. She sighed and lit up a cigarette.

"How's your mammy?" she asked, blowing smoke out the window.

"She's lost all her hair," Patrick said.

"Aw, has she? God help her. They do great wigs these days though."

"I know. She already has one."

"Good for her. Your other little friend, Emma, couldn't come today, could she not? Tot says she goes hip-hop dancing. Isn't that gas?"

Patrick nodded. He didn't tell Mrs Flanagan that the real reason Emma couldn't come was because Mrs Fox said, "Over my dead broken body are you setting foot in that estate".

Mrs Flanagan stubbed out her cigarette.

"Did you have half enough to eat, pet?" she asked. "Those savages would leave you nothing."

"Yes, thank you," Patrick replied and he started clearing the table.

Mrs Flanagan said he was a great chap and that a large bomb under her brood wouldn't see them lift a finger but she'd take care of it, thank you, and to hop along now and watch the football with the rest of them.

They shoved over and made room for him on the couch without taking their eyes off the telly. Manchester United was playing Manchester City. It was called a derby, Mr Flanagan explained, but Patrick already knew that. The Flanagans were all massive Manchester United fans. They all wore jerseys and roared at the screen every time a player did something wrong.

"*Are yizzer blind, ref?*" Twig shouted.

"Yellow card," Sambo said in disbelief. "Where's he goin' with a yellow card?"

"*Useless!*" Sauce roared. "*Me ma coulda scored that!*"

"*You're shite!*" Mr Flanagan yelled and shook his fist at the screen.

"*No swearing, Jim!*" Mrs Flanagan roared from the kitchen.

"Bring back Bobby Charlton is all I say," Mr Flanagan muttered.

"Where's Roy Keane when you need him?" Brad said.

They all said, "Shut up, Tot, yeh gobshite!"

Afterwards the older boys trooped out of the room and Mr Flanagan put up his feet and shook out the paper.

"Tot here tells me you want to play for Ireland? Jaysus, you could play for them now and you'd be better than most of the muppets on the team. Do you play?"

"Yes."

"Well, you'd want to pull your socks up – never too young to take it seriously. You need a good club and a better coach."

"I have one."

"Who's that now?"

"Saskia."

"A girl?"

"She's good."

"Ah Jaysus, lad, you need someone who's played professional. Someone who knows the score, has the feel of the game."

Patrick and Brad went outside and kicked the ball around. It was very cold and the ground was hard. Brad was slow on his feet because he was fat. Mrs Flanagan called it puppy fat but his brothers didn't think so. They said he was just fat.

"Could we have tea at your house sometime?" Brad asked. He was curious to see the inside of a real African's house and a woman with no hair.

"When Maman is better, maybe," Patrick said.

Brad hesitated. "You know, it would be better if you called your ma 'Ma', or 'Mam', not 'Maman'. The lads will only be teasing yeh."

"Okay," Patrick agreed, "but then I'd better call you Tot."

They went back inside then. Mr Flanagan was watching his wife clean out a cupboard in the kitchen while he drank tea. Tot pulled Patrick into the living room and they earwigged through the wall, each using a glass. Mr Flanagan was telling Mrs Flanagan about the man living in one of the lock-ups behind the square. Tot's eyes widened and he dropped his glass and Mrs Flanagan burst out of the kitchen and chased them out the door, lashing them with a tea towel which made them laugh.

But the prospect of a man in a lock-up had stirred their sense of adventure. They made plans to investigate.

When Patrick got home his mother was lying on the couch, shivering. The heater had broken. Patrick made her a hot-water bottle and sat beside her. A single tear ran down her face.

"*Il est temps d'aller chez Nuala, Maman,*" Patrick said.

She nodded.

Patrick rang the doorbell. Tessa steadied herself against the doorjamb. A wind whipped around her skirt. Patrick rapped the knocker sharply.

Nuala answered. When she saw his mother her eyes widened in shock. She brought them into the kitchen and put the kettle to boil on the range. His mother held her hands near the heat and warmed them greedily and then she asked to use the bathroom.

Ten minutes later, Patrick and Nuala found her with her head resting against the toilet bowl.

"Why don't you let me help you?" Nuala asked.

Tessa said nothing at all. She shifted her weight on the floor and patted her mouth dry with a single square of toilet paper.

"Why don't you stay here for a while, just until you are better?" Nuala suggested gently.

Sunlight made squares on the floorboards.

"This is a pretty bathroom," Tessa said. "Rosebud wallpaper and a bath with feet."

"I could run a bath for you now," Nuala said, helping her to her feet. "There's nothing like it to warm you up."

Tessa looked at Patrick. He nodded and looked outside. Leaves blew into red funnels in the wind.

"We would pay rent," she said.

Nuala nodded. "A little," she said. "I will have a lease drawn up, just to keep it professional. And you would have your own space, your own rooms. I wouldn't be in on top of you or under your feet."

Tessa nodded. A ray of sunlight lit up the room.

"Welcome home," Nuala said and she offered her hand.

Tessa took it and squeezed it.

Nuala took care of things. The landlord was understanding. Tessa's deposit would cover most of the overdue rent and she was not to worry about giving a month's notice.

"Tell her I wish her all the best," he said. "My wife had the cancer. Oh, by the way, I evicted that man you complained about."

"I heard," Nuala said. "It was for the best, I suppose."

"I know, though I felt a bit sorry for the aul so-and-so. He told me he had trouble getting out. I think he was a bit of a hermit."

Nuala contacted social services and organised sickness benefit even though Tessa was against it.

"You're entitled to it and, besides, where else are you going to get money? You can't work at the minute."

Tessa couldn't argue with that, and for the first time in her thirty-two years, she let someone else take care of things.

# Chapter 20

Everything got better after that. Life went from being quiet back to being noisy again with everyone around. Nuala got bossy and busy organising. She gave Tessa the bedroom overlooking the walled garden and had the chimney swept so she could light a fire in the tiny hearth. She tried to organise for their stuff to be brought over but Tessa insisted they do it themselves. Patrick knew his mother didn't want anyone to see their *cachette*. His mother would find a new one now in Nuala's. She had a knack for finding them. She said it was a Congolese necessity.

He overheard Nuala on the phone to Tom, saying it was time he dragged his arse out of retirement.

"You could bring Tessa to the hospital," she said. "It's only once a week."

Tom later told Patrick it was useless trying to argue with Nuala. It was like having a conversation with a barrister where words were thrown at you in such a way that you could never win.

Although Saskia was glad the Kimbas had somewhere nice to stay, something niggled her. She wondered if the house was technically Nuala's to let. There had been no sign of the brother with the American accent since, but she was pretty sure the problem hadn't gone away. She hoped Nuala hadn't set herself up for a fall. She had a feeling Tessa Kimba wouldn't welcome any more upset in her life, let alone deceit.

Patrick was back in his old room and he liked that. He watched the Christmas decorations go up around the square. Wreaths were hung on front doors. Christmas trees were placed in drawing rooms with curtains left open so passers-by could admire the lights. Nuala said it looked very Victorian; Patrick thought it looked very boring. Emma agreed. Tot's estate was way better, like Las Vegas. Strings of flashing icicles hung from the guttering; jolly Santas hopped up and down ladders; whole fleets of reindeer galloped past front doors and there were billions of happy dazzling snowmen. But this was not cool apparently, because when Emma asked her mother for just one flashing Santa and a string of icicles, there was a long silence and she was told to go and clean her room.

Tessa rested. On her good days she sat up and helped out with the costumes for the famous Nativity play. Nuala had Tom resurrect the old Singer sewing machine from the attic.

"Is it from the Ark?" he wanted to know. "It looks like it might have stitched together the outfits for the original Nativity, what do you reckon?"

"Aren't you hilarious altogether?" Nuala said.

Nuala discovered that Tessa was quite an expert on the machine. On her bad days, Patrick climbed into bed beside his mother after school. He liked the room. It smelt of lavender, the fire crackled, and it held all the things from their old home: books, plants, pictures and china. His mother even had her own little kettle so they could have a cup of tea and their own chat by the fire.

Later, if she was up to it, she might sit in a chair by the range downstairs and listen to tables or spellings or reading while Nuala prepared the dinner or made bread. Afterwards, while Patrick and Saskia played football out back, she and Nuala drank tea companionably and watched telly.

Tessa began to relax a little and, while she largely kept her thoughts to herself, she sometimes confided in Nuala. She told her that chemotherapy was a desolate place: needles and trolleys and smells and forced normality. Not something you would wish on your worst enemy. She also told her she missed being a teacher.

Nuala told her being a teacher was grand until people said, "Grand job being a teacher, well for you with all those holidays".

Granted, three months off during the summer was pleasant, but without them she would have been put away years ago, locked up in a high security asylum, all the strings removed from her clothing in case she tried to hang herself.

Tessa also told her she worried a little about Patrick's obsession with football. Nuala said she'd always puzzled over the game until she met Patrick. All the talk about World Cup qualifiers and the ugliness that came with it: inflatable green crocodiles, leprechauns, hammers and drunkenness. But Tessa didn't know what she was talking about.

Nuala asked her about her family. Tessa told her they'd died of cholera.

"Yes, I know that," Nuala said, "but what were they like, your people?" and she thought Tessa appeared startled by the question.

For once, she did not have a well-rehearsed answer.

"They were good people," she said quietly. "They did not deserve to die from such an undignified disease. I was fortunate, I survived."

"And you feel guilty about this somehow," Nuala said but Tessa got up to stir a pot and the subject was dropped.

Another time Nuala asked how she'd ended up on Lavender Square.

"When I arrived in Ireland, I considered the African communities with the food stores, the barbers, bars and braiding shops. I observed from a distance: all colourful and bustling, sweet potatoes and papaya, gossiping about the old days and rummaging for news about home and updates on where you could get garri, egusi, yam, palm oil and cassava flour. Nigerians mostly. Nothing to do with me but there was a tug all the same. Still, I turned my back on them."

"You were looking for somewhere different?"

"I found the square by accident. The smell of lavender hit me straight away. That, and the smell of success."

Nuala laughed. "Middle-class snobbery, you mean?"

Tessa shrugged. "I knew I would never be Irish but I wanted my child to be. The Vincent de Paul and the nuns helped me make the flat ready for a baby."

"When's Patrick's birthday?"

"The 17th of March."

"Saint Patrick's Day. I didn't know."

"It was almost impossible to get a taxi that day. Between contractions I remember seeing a lot of leprechauns drinking beer." Tessa smiled. "I knew he was special, right from the start. He hardly cried. I used to wake him up sometimes to make sure he was still breathing. It was as if he knew I was trying to manage on my own."

"Well, he is a very special boy," Nuala said.

Tessa loved the house and lovingly explored the rooms. Nuala found her in the drawing room one day.

"Such a beautiful room," Tessa said. "You don't use it and it has such happy memories – how could it not with a fireplace like that?"

Nuala didn't reply.

Tessa looked out across the street to the walled garden. The gardener kept it reasonably well: cutting, raking, pruning, clipping and shearing even though there didn't seem to be a single soul to appreciate it.

"How about a little walk?" Nuala said.

"It's cold." Tessa shivered.

"Just a round of the square – it will warm you up."

They wrapped up and strolled: north face, west face, south face and back to east. First past the numbers with the overflowing bins, rusting wrought iron and odd-coloured curtains, then into smarter territory, tiled pathways, soft lighting, insured paintings and climbing roses.

Tessa walked tall but slowly. From the outside she appeared in control, proud and haughty, arrogant even, a Parisian academic perhaps, with a PhD in Belgian colonialism.

Right from the start Saskia had guessed a traumatised past even before the consultant spoke to them. She was perceptive like that. Nuala could see it now, clearly. You didn't share a home with someone and fail to pick up on the cracks, and she believed Tessa's fear of the dark papered over a bubbling, troubling cauldron of terrors and a rage that simmered silently beneath a cool veneer. She hoped that, with time, Tessa might feel comfortable enough to confide in her completely.

They rounded the corner and came to the door to the walled

garden. Nuala stopped and removed a large key from her pocket.

"I don't even know if it will work any more," she said. "It's been a while."

The key turned easily in the lock. Inside was a landscape of perfect green grass, beds of winter flowers, leafless shrubs and trees. They sat on a bench and a mist rose from the grass. They breathed it in.

"It is just as I imagined," Tessa whispered.

"My father loved this garden," Nuala said. "I'd forgotten how beautiful it was."

"Why does no one come here?"

"Some people say it's haunted, that a child was killed here once, fell out of a tree. Personally, I think it was a story told by parents to keep their children out of the place and safe under their noses in their own gardens."

The walled garden held a silence and tranquillity. The distant hum of traffic seemed far away.

Tessa exhaled slowly. Her breath was white-silver.

"This is why I left the Congo," she said so softly it was barely audible. "For this sort of place, for peace, beauty. It would have been impossible to rear a child in that madness." She looked about her, present but distant, lost in memory.

"I'm always ready to listen if you ever want to talk, I hope you know that," Nuala said.

But Tessa didn't get to reply.

A twig snapped behind them. It was Patrick.

"Well, if it isn't the man himself!" Nuala said.

"There was no one at home and I saw the garden door open."

*"C'est trés jolie, non?"* Tessa said and smiled at her son.

Patrick surveyed the garden and nodded.

"Well, it's all yours," Nuala said and she handed Tessa the key. "It will be nice for walks during the day when you're able. Come on, let's get home. It's cold."

# Chapter 21

On Saturday afternoons, Patrick was given two euro and allowed take the short walk down the road to the café where Saskia worked. On her suggestion, and as part of a devious plan to find a suitable venue to watch the Premier League matches for free, the café had installed a plasma screen and signed up for the sports channels. Though initially dubious, the manager came around.

"Coffee and football, aren't you mixing it up with beer?" she asked.

"Coffee is the new beer," Saskia told her.

The football drew a crowd: fathers and sons and football fans who wanted to steer clear of the pub in case they were tempted by early pints. The manager was pleased and gave Saskia a raise. It was still a pittance but it meant she got to watch the match while she worked, and Patrick was delighted with her. She always reserved a high stool for him near the counter and gave him a slice of carrot cake with his hot chocolate. Afterwards, they discussed the matches: tactics, passes, manoeuvres and defence and how it all should have been done differently. Those afternoons became precious, a weekend treat immersed in his favourite topic. No one tried to change the subject when there was a match on the telly or tried to make him do homework.

SUSAN RYAN

Some Saturdays Tot and Emma came to the café with him and he shared his cake. It was handy that the café was near the library, Emma explained, because that was where her mother dropped her off on a Saturday afternoon for the children's book club and she could slip away for a few minutes, pretending she was going to the loo. Saskia pretended not to hear her. Having the likes of Fiona Fox breathing fire and looking for her daughter was something she could do without.

One Saturday, Tom came along too.

"What are you doing here?" Saskia asked bossily and her co-workers looked at her sideways.

"I was in the mood for a coffee and I heard about this great café that shows matches," he smiled.

"It was my idea," she said.

"I know. But you could watch matches in my flat with the kids, you know. I have the channels."

"And why would we do that?" she asked indignantly.

He shrugged. "I'll have a coffee, please."

"What sort?"

"Black."

"I always envisioned you as more of a decaf skinny latte type."

"Well, I'm not," he said and he sat down to watch the match with Patrick, Emma and Tot.

Saskia watched him and a thought struck her. It was strange but she could swear he was being nicer, sheepish, and she wondered why that was.

Nuala was equally suspicious. She had agreed to one large dancing Santa for the front of the house and asked him to put it up. Tom thought she was mad and told her so.

"It's awful-looking. Won't it make you look like trailer trash?"

"I'm not interested in your opinion. I just want your help putting it up."

"You're doing this to annoy Fiona Fox, aren't you?"

"Don't be ludicrous."

"You are!" Tom laughed. "Just tell me where you want it and I'll sort it."

Afterwards, she quizzed him.

"You're awful co-operative lately," she said. "I haven't heard a

140

moan or a peep out of you for ages. You even remember to take
Tessa to the hospital without me having to send out a search party.
Are you unwell yourself?"

Tom smiled secretly. Nuala's brow darkened.

"Jesus, you don't have any designs on her, do you? I've seen the
way you look at her. I mean, that would be preposterous."

Tom sighed and shook his head. "No, I don't, Nuala," he said,
followed by, "You watch way too much shite TV."

Tom did like Tessa but not in that way. He didn't quite
understand it. The woman said so little. Their drives to the hospital
were quiet. Initially he was happy about this. In his experience
women spoke far too much and were all too eager to fill every gap
in the conversation with a jibe. There was a calmness to this
beautiful woman who looked straight ahead and was gracious. But
her silences left him wanting to know more.

"You're very quiet," he said one day. "Are you okay?"

She looked at him and it was some time before she answered.

"When you are ill, you do not feel the need to fill silences or do
anything unnecessary," she said. "You are too tired to think about
things like that."

"I get the impression you never thought about things like that."

He smiled and she smiled back but only slightly.

He didn't push her and their journeys continued in relative
silence. Once the boundaries were established, she began to relax
and sometimes she spoke. She was always economic with her
information.

She told him about chemotherapy. "You are attached to a drip.
The liquid is clear. It could be water but it's poison really. You have
to trust them to know what they are doing, the doctors."

"My father was a doctor."

"You did not want to become one, to follow in his footsteps?"

"No, although he wanted me to. Any male doctors I've met seem
unhappy yet all of them want their sons to be doctors too – isn't
that strange?"

"That's because they are men," she said and smiled back.

"So you're a man-hater too, like Saskia?" Tom said and he
smiled sportingly.

"Saskia doesn't hate men," Tessa replied. "You just think she does because she's the first girl who hasn't fallen at your feet. It unnerves you."

Tom sighed. "Where would we be without you women?" he muttered. "I mean you know absolutely *everything*!"

One day when she was particularly weak he accompanied her to the ward. There were already several people hooked up to their stations. They all looked horrendous. Tom felt dizzy. He sat down and watched a cheerful nurse set Tessa up. She had difficulty trying to get a vein. It looked painful. His heart flipped. Tessa bit her lip – tears welled in her eyes – she blinked them away and her bravery made him feel very small indeed.

"Are you okay?" he asked when the nurse was finished.

She nodded.

He looked around. "You still look beautiful even though you're ill," he whispered. "All of the rest of them look awful."

She looked at him strangely and he knew straight away it had been the wrong thing to say – inappropriate, too familiar. He left, mumbling something about being back in a few hours.

Later, on the way home, they sat in traffic. She looked straight ahead. He twiddled with the radio dial.

"I didn't mean to freak you out earlier," he said. "But surely you're used to being admired?"

She looked at him and her expression seemed to indicate pity.

"You hold beauty in such high regard," she said. "You think beauty matters a fig when you're on your deathbed crying for Jesus?"

"I don't believe in Jesus," he informed her.

She laughed. "You mightn't now, but you will. Everybody does in the end."

He was unconvinced.

"You're a good-looking boy," she added, "and you know it. You're used to getting away with things: beauty allows that. But it has its disadvantages. People think beautiful people have nothing to worry about, that everything works out for them. But they are mistaken, aren't they?"

For the rest of the way, they drove in silence.

When he left her off, she stalled.

"I didn't mean to be hard on you," she said. "I know everyone else is. You've been good to Patrick, and to me. We appreciate it."

As he was parking, a finger of guilt poked Tom and he realised something: being around Tessa Kimba made him want to be nicer, to do right by her and her son.

# Chapter 22

On rainy Saturday mornings, if it was too miserable to go out, Patrick explored the big house in the hope of finding a secret passage. The house was old enough for one surely. He tapped along the walls, looked behind the shutters and felt his way into each nook in the wainscot that curved down the stairs from the top of the house all the way down to the very last step. There was no passage or, if there was one, it was so secret he couldn't find it.

On dry Saturdays, after breakfast, he and his mother took the key from the hook in the hall and let themselves into the walled garden. It was bigger than he'd imagined but just as magical. A gigantic horse-chestnut tree, branches outstretched, welcomed you warmly and pointed you towards the pebbled path, which led you along by the redbrick wall past the perfectly shaped hedges, alcoves, crannies, to halt at the edge of a velvet lawn. They sat on the bench and talked about their week, exchanging news and stories in French and Swahili.

Afterwards, there was football. Tot called over and Emma sneaked out to play when she could. But Tot wasn't keen on that. He said girls were trouble and he called her Rapunzel because she was always looking down from her bedroom window like an imprisoned princess with a big cross face. Patrick thought this was funny because Tot often had a cross face himself just like his father.

Mr Flanagan shouted a lot and always said things like, "You'll have me in the poorhouse" or "I'll be dug out of you" and was only completely silent when Patrick's mother called to the door to collect him. Mr Flanagan's cheeks went red then and he opened and closed his mouth like a goldfish. Tot had heard him say to Sauce once that Mrs Kimba was the most beautiful woman he'd ever laid eyes on. And Sauce said, "Wouldn't Mammy be just thrilled to hear that?"

Tot and Emma were always snapping at each other which was a pain because it would have been nice if they all just got along. Tot once made Emma cry. He said, "Your dad is hardly ever around, is he?" And Emma told him to shut up and ran home and Tot wasn't sure why – it was only a question. Tot was more careful around her then. He was as scared of Mrs Fox as anyone.

One Saturday morning, Tot arrived at Nuala's house bursting with news. He had heard his da talking to his ma again about the man in the lock-up.

"Da's friend Mick saw him one night when he was taking a shortcut home from the pub. He said he's got furniture in there and a cooker and everything. Want to go find him?"

"Why?" Patrick shrugged. He was keen to practise the stepovers he and Saskia had been perfecting during the week.

"I dunno – an adventure?"

When Nuala was busy, they slipped out the gate and set off down the lane in search of the mysterious man.

Emma caught up with them.

"God almighty," Tot muttered.

"Where you going?" she asked.

"Nowhere," Tot said.

She looked at Patrick. "Can I come?"

He nodded and put his finger to his lips.

"She's a girl and will be scared," Tot said scornfully.

"No, she won't," Patrick assured him.

The lane, enclosed by a wall of doors on one side and rows of lock-ups on the other, was shadowy with overgrown trees and littered with piles of leaves and twigs and the inner workings of fridges and mattresses. It was a gloomy place, brightened slightly by the multicoloured doors embedded in the redbrick wall, each painted to match the front door of the houses they belonged to.

And if not nailed shut or held in place by a tangle of ivy, they opened into the back gardens of Lavender Square.

The lock-ups were padlocked and covered in graffiti and it was a grim sort of place where hooded teenagers might gather or shady characters like Jim Flanagan's friend Mick might linger looking for mischief.

"This is creepy," Emma whispered.

"*Shhhh!*" Tot hissed. "Follow me."

They crept like a gang of thieves past each battered lock-up which fuelled imaginations already filled with wizards-turned-bad and murderers. The wind blew dust and stony debris against the steel doors, the dark branches of trees sighed heavily and every padlock was rusty as though they hadn't been touched in years. There was no sign of life whatsoever and Tot surmised that the Mick might have had too much whiskey on him. Again.

When they returned to the square, Fiona Fox was waiting for them with a tapping foot and a smile. She invited them in for blueberry smoothies. Patrick sensed a trap but didn't know how to say no.

Tot curled his nose up and sniffed the smoothie, suspecting vitamin content.

"What is it?" he asked.

"It's good for you," Mrs Fox said and gave him a look like she wanted to shake him very hard indeed.

She questioned them and Tot made up a story about a missing football. Patrick knew she wasn't buying it.

"Okay," she said, "but I'd stay away from those lock-ups if I were you. They're not safe, haven't been used in years."

"But there's a man living in one!" Emma blurted out.

Mrs Fox smiled. "I don't think so, Emma, but if there is he will have to be reported to the council. It's not a legal dwelling."

When Mrs Fox turned her back, Tot gave Emma a look and she blushed.

Regardless of Mrs Fox's warnings, they patrolled the lane but saw no traces of occupancy. Patrick was secretly relieved: football was better fun than sneaking down lanes but Tot drove a hard bargain. He thought it was very cool to have the chance of a real adventure on your own doorstep.

But still they saw nothing, until one morning they noticed one of the rusty padlocks was missing. It had been removed. On closer examination they saw that the shutter was raised a few inches. They hardly dared to breathe and huddled together, nearly jumping out of their skins when a hand emerged from under the door to leave out a saucer of milk followed by another hand which contained the tiniest white kitten. When it had finished lapping the milk, a hand emerged once more to retract the kitten and the saucer and the shutter went down. They clutched each other and ran home. The man was real. They had found him.

They did not see the kitten or the man for several weeks after that but found the perfect hiding place from which to spy on him behind an ancient tree, and took turns looking through Emma's mother's opera glasses.

On another fruitless afternoon, when a freezing wind had them thinking of home and the telly, a chink of light appeared under the shutter and classical music floated out, only to be carried away by the breeze. The kitten and saucer emerged once more and Emma trained the glasses on the kitten and door. Inside, someone made '*puss-puss-puss*' sounds calling for the kitten and the shutter was pushed up.

Tot picked up a stone and aimed.

"Don't!" Patrick whispered and he caught his arm but not soon enough.

The stone sailed through the air just as a man crawled out under the shutter and it hit him right on the forehead. He looked stunned and reached up to touch the wound. There was blood.

They dropped the glasses and ran.

Later, when he was meant to be doing homework, Patrick thought about the man. He had looked familiar. He felt bad about the stone and hoped he wasn't bleeding to death. That would technically make Tot a murderer.

That night he couldn't sleep thinking about it, so when Nuala and his mother had gone to bed he put the door on the latch and crept down the lane and left a bundle of food with a strip of bandages outside the lock-up. He knocked gently on the steel door and ran home.

He delivered more food the next night and the next.

Nuala noticed the night-time food disappearances and put them down to Tessa who often didn't feel like eating during the day but probably made up for it at night. Nuala didn't mention it or question her. Instead she made up a plate for her every evening before bed and told Patrick to let his mother know it was there in the fridge for her if she needed it. It was this plate that Patrick pilfered. And every night he tapped gently on the shutter door to indicate the delivery, and collected the empty plate from the night before which would be there waiting for him.

He did not discuss the food plates with anyone. Neither Tot nor Emma was interested in venturing down the lane again. Emma was certain the man they'd seen was a ghost and Tot wasn't taking any chances. Ghost or no ghost, he'd thrown a stone at it and it would be angry.

Patrick wondered why Tot had thrown the stone at all. It seemed a strange and cruel thing to do. If it had hit the kitten he would have killed it. It could have killed the man too – the stone had hit him on the head and the cut could have been a deeper one. But Patrick knew the man wasn't dead. Every night the food disappeared and the lane was so dark and empty no one else could have known about the food except the man.

He often thought about him and the kitten, especially when the wind howled and the frost crept along the rooftops like icy fingers and Nuala told him to say a prayer for anyone who was out in that terrible night. Then one night, when the moon made his room a moonlit blue, he pictured the tiny white kitten trying to keep warm in the cold and he remembered something. He pulled on his dressing gown and runners, sneaked down the stairs and back to the lock-up.

He tapped on the door. The radio was switched off and there wasn't a sound. Patrick knocked again and then again. "It's me," he whispered. "The boy who leaves you food." The shutter opened slowly and the man, a quaking, shaking, wrinkled man with a bandage on his forehead was kneeling in the light of a lamp.

"I remember you," Patrick said to the man. "You used to have a dog. I saw you bury it the day it died."

# Chapter 23

The lock-up wasn't as bad as he thought it would be. There was an armchair and a coffee table and a bookshelf and a camp bed made up on the floor. The radio played, the gas heater gave a little warmth, and a kettle boiled on a gas hob. But there was no window and no telly, only the radio and the kitten for company. There were boxes stacked high and unknown objects covered in sheets so that they looked like oddly shaped ghosts.

The man made a pot of tea and poured Patrick a cup.

"What's that?" Patrick asked, pointing to a large covered mound that spanned the back wall.

"Just an old car, a crock of a thing," the man answered.

"Can I look?"

"No."

"Where did the kitten come from?"

"It's a stray."

"What's its name?"

"Snowy," the man said gently and he picked up the kitten to place it on Patrick's knee.

It was as light as a cotton ball.

"It's a good name," Patrick said. "What's yours?"

"Joe."

"I'm Patrick."

They shook hands formally.

"A good name too," the man said.

"I was born on St Patrick's Day."

"Lots of Patricks are."

The man watched Patrick stroking the kitten. Patrick looked up and met his gaze – the man was very thin and wrinkled but his eyes were shiny and kind.

"Nuala used to have a cat too," Patrick said, "but he was knocked down the same day as your dog. We live with Nuala now, me and my mam, so she doesn't need a cat so much."

"Oh," said the man who was called Joe.

"She makes the dinners I bring you but she doesn't know about you."

"Good."

"You like the food?"

"Yes, but don't tell her or anyone about me, that I'm here."

"Why do you live here?"

"It's only temporary and it's a long story," the man said and he picked up his mug and that's when Patrick noticed the dusty framed photo.

"Is that you in the football kit?" he pointed.

"A long time ago."

"You don't look like that now."

"Thanks."

"Were you good?" Patrick asked.

"Handy enough."

"I'm a footballer too."

"Yes."

"I want to play for Ireland."

"Good for you," said Joe. "You're nothing without a dream."

"Do you have a dream?"

"I'm too old for dreams," he said and looked into his tea.

They sat for a while and drained their mugs. The gas heater made a hissing sound and the kitten played with the tassel on Patrick's dressing gown. Then Patrick said he'd better go or there would be trouble and that he would be back.

Sneaking out of the house every night, without having Nuala on top of you, took practice. She wasn't a great sleeper and still sometimes wandered the house at night. This posed a problem, particularly in an old house with creaks that jumped out at you without warning. He located all of them through meticulous detective work and could hop and trot left and right, avoiding each of them except for four-in-a-row at the curve of the stairs by the arched window. He sat on the steps and pondered. Four steps were too many for his short legs and it was a risky business. It was Nuala who solved the conundrum one day when she was passing him with an armload of ironing.

"When we were small we used to slide down the banister and drive our poor mother mad," she said.

Sliding was easier in a dressing gown than in normal clothes but for a little extra acceleration he carefully polished the banister anyway. So each night, when the house was still, he gently opened his door, hopped on and slid down to the hallway by the drawing room. He had to resist shouting gleefully as he whizzed round the bend to land softly on the floor in his slippers. Once landed, he slunk past the dresser with the mirror and then down another flight, left, right, hop, hop and out the door, which he left on the latch. Then out the gate, keeping in by the shadows and away from the street lamps to the lane where Joe was waiting for him with a cup of tea.

He liked the man, Joe, who could smell a bit but was kind and he always seemed pleased to see him. He wore all of his clothes and a pair of strange striped wool things around his legs which looked like the arms of a lady's jumper. And he ate the food like a starving dog, shovelling it into his mouth so fast Patrick thought he might bite off his fingers by mistake. He watched him with a quiet fascination and wondered what it might be like to live with no rules and no table manners. Nuala was as particular as his mother. She would slap Patrick's hand away from his mouth and tell him to "eat slowly" and "not like a piglet". And then she would ask him if he'd been "born in a byre" like she once asked Tot when he shoved a whole slice of tart into his mouth and washed it down with a glass of milk.

Sometimes Joe poured whiskey into his tea and his hand shook.

They talked about football and school, the upcoming Nativity play and the Morse code which Miss Hennessy had taught them, until it was time for Patrick to hand the kitten back and go home.

When he was not with Joe he often thought about the photograph of him as a young man, once a footballer, but now old and living in a lock-up that was as cold as a cave. There was also a picture of Joe's children, a son and a daughter. In the photo, they were small. Now they were grown up and lived far away. That's all Joe would tell him and then he put the photo away. He said he didn't want to talk about them again.

The night-time excursions continued without Nuala or his mother suspecting. They were busy thinking about costumes for the play and Christmas Day – what they would cook and whom they should invite. If they asked Saskia, who was all alone, then would they be obliged to invite Tom? Presumably he would have Christmas dinner with his parents but should they invite him over that evening? That might not work out as, even though they were miles better than they used to be, he and Saskia had a tendency to snipe at one another. There was a good chance he would stick with his parents though. It was hard to know.

Preparations for the Nativity became frenzied and Emma told Patrick she was sure Miss Hennessy was having a nervous breakdown. She knew all about nervous breakdowns because her mother was always talking about having them. Her parents didn't shout any more. Now they said nothing, and that was much worse. It would be better if fists were banged on tables or plates thrown like in the movies. Silence was like a bomb waiting to go off. You just couldn't be sure when it was going to happen and the worry gave her horrible pains in her stomach.

At night, she and Patrick started sending Morse Code signals to each other from their bedroom windows with a couple of cheap torches Saskia bought for them – silly stuff like "GOOD NIGHT", and "NO ROOM AT THE INN" and "HAPPY XMAS FART FACE", but Emma said it made her feel better.

Patrick told her about Joe and said not to tell Tot and this made her feel better still.

"What's he like?" she asked curiously.

"He can be a bit smelly but he's nice," Patrick told her. "He doesn't have a shower. He has to wash at a basin."

"Oh," Emma said and she wrinkled her nose.

"He was a footballer."

"Was he good?"

"He said he was semi-professional."

"He could be your coach," Emma suggested. "Saskia could be his assistant."

"Nah, sure he hardly ever leaves the lock-up."

Emma shrugged.

On the night of the play, Miss Hennessy was tense and shrieky. Emma noticed her hands shook when she was clipping her veil on with a hundred hairclips. She muttered under her breath, things like "Valium" and "Uppity yuppies". A few moments before that she had roared at Patrick when he asked if he could wear his football boots.

Saskia looked around the hall with interest. It was a dizzying concoction of sights and smells: expensively spun cloth, hair polish, shoe polish, Botox, extremely white teeth, gel-infused nails and a potion of perfumes.

The curtains were drawn and she noticed there was a slight intake of breath and more than one perfectly manicured raised eyebrow when a little black Joseph ambled on stage holding the hand of a blonde, blue-eyed Mary. Fiona Fox's expression indicated vague disturbance while her husband shook with silent laughter. Saskia smiled.

It was clear the story of the Nativity was lost on the children. Because although not a single innkeeper had a room to spare and all was looking pretty bleak in Bethlehem, Emma and Patrick found it fitting to grin from ear to ear. The chorus of angels poked at each other's wings and halos, a shepherd tripped over one of his sheep, a pig fluffed her lines and a wise man's tinfoil crown fell off only to be trampled under the feet of the charging donkey. It was the best Nativity play Saskia had ever seen.

Afterwards, they went for ice cream and Tom told Patrick he made a great Joseph and Patrick thought of Joe in the cold with his kitten.

In the early hours of the morning, Patrick woke up thinking about what Emma had said. Excited, he pulled on his clothes, slid down the banister and removed the key from the hook on the hallstand.

The wind had blown into a gale and it took a few knocks at the lock-up door before Joe heard him. The radio was turned down.

"It's me, Joe – Patrick!" he shouted.

Joe unlocked the padlock inside and raised the shutter. He looked a little wild. The lock-up smelt of gas.

"Christ almighty, lad, you'll have me arrested! It's the middle of the night."

Patrick shifted from one foot to the other impatiently.

"What's wrong with you?" Joe asked. "You're like a frog in a box."

"I'll need a proper coach and a real team if I'm going to play for Ireland," Patrick said.

"Patrick, you're only eight. There's plenty of time. The school will teach you when the time is right."

"I know, but you're never too young to start training properly."

"You want to start now, in the middle of the bloody night?"

"No, I just want to show you something."

It took some convincing but he managed to drag Joe to the door of the walled garden. He took out the key and unlocked it.

"Where did you get that?"

"Nuala gave it to Mam."

They stepped inside and a slight breeze whistled through the trees. The moon had coated everything pewter: the rosebushes, the bare trees, the benches and the grass.

"Very nice," said Joe. "Now can we go? I'm freezing."

Patrick pulled on his sleeve.

"You could train me here."

"Who, what, me? I will in my eye!" Joe stuttered.

"You used to play."

"A thousand years ago."

"But you never forget. It's like riding a bike. And, you know what, you owe me."

"I do?"

"You called me a dirty brat one day," Patrick said. "You thought I'd forgotten. You said that you'd bury me too."

"I didn't mean it."

"But you still said it and that's not good because I'm only a child."

"Course you are," Joe said. "Well, I'm an adult and I live in a lock-up and I can't leave it for love or money."

"You're not there now."

"That's right, I'm not, and I want to go home."

He turned to go and that's when he saw the ghost, a white luminous vision by the door.

"*Jesus, Mary and Joseph!*" Joe yelped.

The ghost batted and flapped about wildly in the wind. It was Nuala in her dressing gown and she was not happy.

"Patrick Kimba, get over here right this instant or God help me I'll string you up! Creeping out in the middle of the night leaving the door blowing in the wind so any passing lunatic could come in and murder us! And you –" she said looking at Joe, but then she recognised him. "It's you," she said faintly. "Jesus Christ, this is just preposterous. Do I even want to know what's going on here?"

The man looked down at his feet. "The boy just wanted to show me the garden – he's looking for a football coach."

"In the middle of the night?"

"I have trouble getting out during the day – it's a bit of a phobia."

"So how, may I ask, would you expect to coach him in the confines of your home?"

"Well, that's what I was just telling him." The man's voice was shaky and his accent was flat, somewhere midlands. He looked tired and ancient and haggard.

"Patrick, why are you bothering this man?" Nuala sighed.

"Because he was a good footballer and he could teach me. We can train here. It's big and no one ever uses it."

"Jesus wept! You have us worn out with this talk of football!" Nuala barked. She pulled her dressing gown around her.

The three of them looked at each other in the moonlight.

"Were you any good at it?" Nuala asked Joe.

Joe lowered his head.

"Fairly handy. I was scouted for England but I was injured."

"And could you train Patrick – give us five minutes' peace?"

"I don't know. I'll think about it," he said.

"Think about it? I think you owe Patrick a promise."

"Maybe if we trained in here, I could. It feels safe. You know, the walls and all."

Nuala looked around the beautiful moonlit garden and back to Joe. He looked a sight, a crumpled-up old newspaper, pathetic more than a threat.

"You'd have your work cut out for you getting the go-ahead from all the other permanent residents. Like me, they all have keys to the door. It would be up to them."

"I wouldn't be much use at that," Joe said and he shook his head violently.

"Well, I'll help you."

"Right."

"Are you still writing those lovely notes as a matter of interest?" she asked through pursed lips.

"No."

"Doesn't the Lord move in mysterious ways?" she said and she sniffed loudly.

They made moves towards the door.

"What's your name?" she asked.

"Joe Delaney," the man said.

"Nuala Murphy," she said and offered her hand. "You owe me a cat."

She closed the garden door behind them.

"Where do you live now?" she asked, wondering where the man had moved to.

"Nearby," was all he said.

"I have your glasses back at the house. I'll give them to Patrick to give to you."

He nodded and went on his way, shuffling along by the walls and away from the light.

The next morning Nuala heard a knock on her door and found a box on her doorstep. It contained a tiny white kitten on an old blanket with a saucer of milk.

# Chapter 24

The evenings were black and ice lined the grey fogs. On the first night of training it was December-bitter and Joe's nerves were shattered. He'd been practising his training style in front of Patrick in the lock-up, pacing the floor, over and back, around the covered mounds of furniture and bric-a-brac, pace, pace, pace. Patrick and Tot had managed to gather a few football hopefuls together for training. You couldn't be a proper footballer without a team. But it made Joe nervous.

He told Patrick it was his first sentence that would matter. It would need to lay down the law and show them all who was boss. Otherwise they'd mess around and make mincemeat of him because that's what eight-year-olds did.

Joe stopped and examined himself in a shard of mirror. His tracksuit was moth-eaten and wrinkled.

"This gear looks like something I collected porridge tokens for three decades ago," he said to his reflection.

Patrick looked at him solemnly and wondered if all adults were a bit mad. Emma was absolutely certain they were. Her mother had been on the warpath ever since football coaching had been mentioned. Suddenly, finding the Foxs' key to the walled garden became important. It was missing and this was a problem, which was confusing because her mum had never set foot in the garden in

157

her entire life. Now it seemed finding the key was the most important thing on earth, like finding the ring in *The Lord of the Rings*. No matter how much Emma explained it didn't matter, that Nuala already had a key, her mother wouldn't listen. This wasn't the point apparently. And then just like that, the key turned up. It was in her father's pocket all along and he slammed it down on the table without any explanation.

Frost formed on the roofs of cars and painted the railings crystallised white. Nuala and Saskia watched the assortment of local children kick through the fallen leaves and assemble in the walled garden. There were six of them – six brave little footballers including Patrick, Tot and Emma. It was dark and the garden lights illuminated them in a soft glow.

Nuala hoped the football would be worth all the fuss because there had been an almighty fuss. Most of the residents had been co-operative. As long as the children were supervised and the door was locked after them when they were finished, then they didn't mind. It would be good to see the space put to use.

The gardener was not so accommodating. So used had he become to trimming, pruning and mowing a garden that knew no footprints, worn patches or flattened rosebushes, he didn't relish the prospect now. He waved his clipping shears threateningly and the words "sacrilegious" and "villainy" were used more than once. Nuala had thought gardeners were meant to be mellow types. She was patient at first and then grew impatient. It wasn't his garden, the residents owned the garden, and could he kindly stop pointing that hedge-strimmer at her, please? Gardening hoes at dawn ensued and it ended with him packing up his accoutrements, swearing he wouldn't be back.

The assembled company saw Joe step gingerly into the garden. He closed the door behind him and trudged to meet his crew. He had made his conditions clear: no adults. "The last thing I need," he said, "is a pack of south-side gobshites standing at the sidelines and glaring at me every time I correct one of their little darlings." He was nervous enough as it was, thank you very much.

After some wrangling, he agreed that Saskia and Nuala could attend the first night at least.

"Are you sure about this guy?" Saskia asked, squinting.

His emerald-green tracksuit made him look like a malign leprechaun.

"Pretty sure," Nuala said.

"Does Tessa know he's the creep who used to live above her?"

Nuala didn't reply.

"Because I'm sure she'd be very interested," Saskia added.

"There's no need to say anything to Tessa," Nuala said firmly. "The man's a bag of nerves, Saskia, that's all. Harmless."

"The question is, why is he a bag of nerves? Maybe he's nervous about the Guards stumbling across his prized collection of dead bodies."

Nuala sighed. "You sound as bad as Fiona Fox. She wanted to know where the strange smelly little man claiming to be some sort of a football coach had materialised from."

"In this instance, she has a point."

Nuala rubbed her arms. Saskia faced her.

"You feel guilty for getting him evicted, don't you?" she said.

"It must be terrible to lose your home," Nuala said distantly and Saskia watched her carefully.

"But he deserved it."

"No one deserves to lose their home. He deserves a second chance, everyone does."

There were six children: one Polish, one American, one Ukrainian and three Irish, all from the square, except for Tot. They looked at Joe and waited. He cleared his throat.

"I'm the Gaffer," he said. "From now on, that's how you'll refer to me. Is that clear?"

They nodded in unison.

"Now, there are no shortcuts to becoming a good team or a good footballer – it's about graft and hard work," he said and he looked at each of them sternly. "Some of you will be natural players. You'll discover you're lucky enough to have a football brain and an instinct for the game. You'll be the Paul Scholes, the Kakas, the Thierry Henrys, the Roy Keanes and the Paul McGraths. Others may not be so lucky – you may have to work harder to acquire these skills, but let me tell you this," he said, and wagged his finger at them all, "you will all have to work hard. Some of you have ambitions for greatness. I want all of you to have ambitions for greatness, even you," he said, singling out Emma.

He chuckled to himself and paced and Tot, Emma and Patrick looked at each other and shrugged.

"Now, it's winter and it's going to get colder. Some nights you'll wish you'd stayed in to watch telly. Other nights you'll wish you'd never been born but if you want to be on this team, you turn up. Is that understood?"

They nodded vigorously.

"And I don't want any half-hearted nonsense. As far as I'm concerned you all want to play in the World Cup and that's the end of it. This is a professional outfit."

He paced the grass again – up, down, up, down.

"Football is a game of skill for the brave-hearted and, to be played properly at all, it has to be taken seriously. That goes for any game – except hockey. Right! This isn't exactly the Neu Camp but it will do for the moment. Let's get this show on the road."

Patrick stepped close to him, touched his elbow and felt the man shaking.

"You're doing great, Joe," he whispered and the man blinked at him.

"In here, I'm the Gaffer to you too," he said and he blew into his whistle.

First they did stretches then laps mixed in with a few sprints. Over, back, over, back from the bench to the ivy-covered wall.

Joe scrutinised them carefully. He let them rest for a moment to catch their breaths before arranging them in a circle with Patrick at its centre.

"*Right!*" he roared. "This is called 'Keep Football'! We're going to practise two-touch. You lot," he pointed at the circle, "are to pass the ball to each other. You receive the ball, stop it, then pass. Use the side of your foot, not the toe. The aim is to keep the ball away from the man in the middle and it's his job to try and intercept every pass. When he stops it, whoever's pass he's stopped goes in to the middle, clear?"

As they passed the ball, he circled them and bellowed into their ears.

"*This is good practice for passing and receiving and, as you know, football is about passing. It's not about soul glory. It's about*

160

TEAM! *When you receive a ball, you must always be thinking one step ahead. ALWAYS! No fannying about. Instinctively, you're looking, feeling out for your next man, who you can pass to without giving it away and making a pig's ear of it, right?"*

Saskia and Nuala went back to the house for water, wedges of orange and a flask of tea. The children were wrung out and sweaty. Tot's head was an orb of red like the planet Mars.

"Aren't you a bit hard on them?" Nuala asked. "You sound like a hangman. They're only babies, they look beat."

"Eight-year-olds have tons of energy. Their parents will be thrilled – they'll sleep like logs tonight."

"But should you be using words like 'fannying'? You'll get into trouble. Fiona Fox would have your head in a vice over something like that."

Joe sipped tea from the beaker. "This is football, Nuala, not tea-sets. If they want to play house, then they're on the wrong playing field."

"How did you get so brave and shoutie all of a sudden?" Nuala was cross.

Joe smiled and his face transformed. "Kids at this age don't want to be treated like kids. They want to be taken seriously. I'm treating them like professionals and I'll get the best out of them."

"Fine, just limit the language, will you, or you'll land us in all sorts of hot water?"

"Aye, I'll try. Thank you for the tea." He wiped his mouth with the back of his hand. "Hit the spot." He nodded at Saskia. "Patrick told me you've been training him. You know your stuff. His habits are good."

He walked away and Saskia felt pleased and annoyed simultaneously: pleased at the compliment, annoyed at how quick she was to accept it from someone like Joe Delaney.

They played three-a-side with real positions: a defender, a midfielder and a forward with closest man dropping back into goal. The play was a spectacle. Skin and fur flying. The dribbling was woeful, the control of the ball awkward and the concept of rules absent, but there was determination and one thing was absolutely certain beyond a shadow of a doubt: the African boy had something.

By the time Christmas arrived, they had a training routine

established and Joe's nerves had calmed a little. There were still days when he couldn't move and his whole body glistened in sweat and Patrick had to coax him out of the lock-up and down to the garden.

"It will be grand, Gaffer," he'd reason through the lock-up door.

"I'm unwell."

"You're grand."

"I'm not."

"Sure we're only kids. We can't do anything to you."

The bad days grew fewer and far between and Patrick hoped that by summer Joe would be brave enough to train during daylight. The lights in the garden weren't bright enough and sometimes they couldn't see the ball at all and ran into each other, which made Joe laugh – and this wasn't a bad thing because when his nerves were at him he looked like he might just lie down and die.

Nuala and Saskia watched the young footballers progress from the sidelines. Joe was like a small autocrat. He blustered like Hitler, paced like Stalin and waved his arms about like Mussolini. But the children respected him.

When Tessa finished chemotherapy, Tom brought over a bottle of champagne. They toasted her good health and Tessa toasted Nuala for everything she'd done for them. Saskia thought Nuala looked decidedly uneasy and it worried her. It would be just typical for everything to go arse over tit just when things were going so well.

On Christmas morning the square gleamed in sunshine. In the farthest distance, the mountains shimmered, white tips down to darkest forest greens, to the fields and patchwork tumbling into suburbia with its glinting windows and curling smoke. Roads and inroads and lanes and alleyways all the way to Lavender Square, and to Patrick who watched it all from his little room. Beneath him, frost covered everything, even the fallen leaves, which were brown now and lay in crumpled heaps.

It had all the makings of a great day. When he woke up, there were parcels at the end of his bed: a brand-new Innskeep top (he put it on immediately) and football socks and football DVDs and football books and a tracksuit. There were Coco Pops for breakfast and for dinner there would be turkey and ham and stuffing and sweet potatoes as well as ordinary spuds. And they'd invited Miss Hennessy and Tom might come over that evening. Saskia was gone home to Galway.

Joe passed by on the street below and Patrick knocked on the window. He waved at Joe, who waved back.

"Colour suits you," Joe called up to him. "You might wear it for real yet." And he was gone off walking.

When Joe returned to the square, Nuala was waiting for him at her gate in her apron.

"Nuala," he said, "the compliments of the season to you. Are you hoping a turkey will pass by?"

"Funny you should say that," she said dryly. "I saw you out walking and thought about asking you over for some dinner. It would be a real favour. If I've to have one more football conversation with Patrick I will throw myself under a lorry. At least you know what you're talking about. His teacher, Miss Hennessy, is coming too and we have more than enough food."

He hesitated.

"Ah now," he said, "what would you be wanting an old curmudgeon like me around for?"

"Just to eat the leftovers."

"Do you think I could have a bath?" he asked, embarrassed. "It's just my shower's on the blink. And maybe wash my clothes? I'm having a white goods crisis."

"Of course," she said lightly as though offering baths to smelly old coaches was a normal thing to do. "Come over a bit earlier then, say three."

She went inside.

Tom rang Saskia to wish her a Happy Christmas. She was less prickly these days, less likely to take the head off you for being a man and he liked to talk about football with her. She knew her stuff. Who played for whom, who managed whom, who cost what and what team was where in the Premier League: mid-table mediocrity, relegation zone or top of the table. She had mentioned something about hating Christmas and not wanting to go home to Galway at all. He wanted to see how she was getting on.

"Well, how is it?" he asked.

"Great," she said flatly. "My mother still hates my father. Pity he's not around so he could be bearing the brunt of it instead of me."

"She must have liked him once upon a time: only two romantics would have called their daughter Saskia."

"I'm sure you're right. Anyway, how is yours?"

"Fine. Lots of questions though about where I'm going with my life."

"And where are you going with your life?"

"I have absolutely no idea," he said, and for some reason this tickled them both and they laughed down the phone for a long time.

In Nuala's house, it was a perfect extended family day. After dinner they lazed and examined their stomachs. They pulled armchairs in by the range, drank mulled wine, half-dozed and half-watched an *Indiana Jones* film. Patrick curled up beside his mother and played with Snowy the kitten who was bigger now and less likely to pee on the floor.

Tom called over that evening. Patrick let him in.

"It's the main man," Tom said. "Happy Christmas! Wouldn't it make Jacques Biet's day to see a man of your calibre in his club's jersey? Here's your present." He handed him an envelope. It was a Innskeep ticket.

"No way," Patrick said.

"Way. Got one for Saskia too. We'll take you there if your mother lets us off."

They played cards and board games and chatted, ate more chocolates and switched to hot whiskeys and the adults got a bit tipsy. Joe dozed into and out of sleep and couldn't get close enough to the heat. Nuala watched him. He had the look of a man who hadn't had a decent sleep in a long time.

Tessa went to bed and Miss Hennessy, whose name was Brigit, got silly.

Nuala decided it was time for Patrick to go to bed before his teacher said something she might regret.

"It was a good Christmas, wasn't it, Tata?" Patrick said when she was tucking him in.

"Yes, it was," Nuala said. "How was Emma? Did you chat to her after Mass?"

"She's okay," he shrugged. "She said her mam and dad aren't talking."

"Oh, well, that's their business so leave them to it."

"I know."

She leaned down to kiss him on the forehead.

"Patrick?"

"Yes, Tata," he said drowsily.

"Where does Joe live?"

"In a lock-up down the lane," he said without thinking and he sat up quickly with a gasp.

"It's okay, pet," she said. "I won't say a word. I was just worried about him. You get some sleep now."

She left the door slightly ajar and the hall light on and she went back downstairs knowing she'd just solved the mystery of the disappearing food.

# Chapter 25

Spring was welcome in Lavender Square. The long dark days and nights of winter had taken their toll. Grey leached skies and lifelessness leaned heavily, so when the light began to linger for a few minutes longer each evening, it was like a beacon of hope. And it was on a spring day that Nuala broached Joe about taking a room in her house.

"The downstairs scullery was converted into a storeroom years ago and later into a bedroom for my father," she explained, "and now I want to rent it out. You know, with a proper lease and everything? I'd prefer if it was to someone I knew."

"And what would make you think I'd want a room?"

"Nothing. I was just putting it out there. Your current accommodation seems unsatisfactory, what with the shower always breaking down and all."

Saskia thought she was mad.

"What are you doing renting out rooms all over the place?"

"I have the space, why not?" Nuala was defensive.

"Okay, but don't come running to me if Joe Delaney turns around and goes postal on you."

In the end it was a visit from the council that made Joe decide. A man in a bad suit with a clipboard knocked on the shutter and explained that someone had reported him. It wasn't classified as a

166

proper dwelling and it was best he move on or things could get sticky.

"Well, we wouldn't want that now, would we?" Joe said and the man with the clipboard scuttled away.

Tom helped him move. Joe didn't want any women tutting over his belongings or untidy habits. Women also had a tendency to throw everything out, things you might think important like football annuals or newspaper clippings or ancient match tickets.

They opened up the lock-up shutter wide, so that sunlight got into even the darkest corners, and started to sort and pile what he needed into a trailer: quilt, clothes, blankets, wardrobe, chairs and shoes until Joe realised everything he owned was junk. They binned the contents of the trailer and transported only the few personal trinkets and memories he wanted to keep: candlesticks, photographs, paintings and books and a Waterford crystal decanter which had been a wedding present.

"My children were left most of our things," Joe explained.

"I didn't realise you had children," Tom said, wondering how a man's children could let him live in a shed.

"We don't talk," Joe said and he didn't elaborate.

"How did you end up with this lock-up anyway?" Tom asked.

"I started renting it years ago to store this aul crock," Joe said and he pulled off the dust sheet which had been covering the car.

"Nice!" Tom said and he stood back to take a good look at it. "We could fix it up. Tot Flanagan's old man is a mechanic and good with old cars. He fixes mine from time to time."

"We could," Joe said. "It can stay here and maybe we could try to keep the fixing up of it to ourselves. I don't want everyone tramping over here to see it."

"I understand," Tom said and he did.

The trees blossomed and Patrick and Emma both turned nine in March. Their birthdays were only a few days apart so they had a joint party.

Spring passed into early summer and it was warm again. Without the gardener the garden grew wild. It was a problem. No one wanted to weed or mow the large area of grass but Joe insisted. Tufts of grass meant footballs bouncing all over the place and even worse, injuries, broken ankles and the like. No one had a decent-sized lawnmower.

Saskia suggested to Tom that he ask his parents. He was hanging a swing from a sturdy branch of the horse-chestnut at the time, and sweating from exertion. Emma had nagged him into putting it up. Saskia noticed that hard work suited Tom. It was May and the pitch looked like a meadow.

"Are you mad?" he said. "They're old."

"I think they'd like to be asked. Who wouldn't like to work in this beautiful place? I know I would if I wasn't making coffee for imbeciles all day."

"Why don't you try the swing out for size instead of doing all that thinking?" Tom frowned, tying the final knot.

"The branch might break under the weight of me," she said.

"I've used reinforced rope. You know the type that keeps the Brooklyn Bridge suspended? Now get on and I'll give you a push."

The swing was a big attraction. Everyone had a go, even Tom's father who felt a bit ridiculous.

"Shame about the state of this place," he said, swinging gently over the dandelions and overgrown grass.

"I wanted to talk to you about that," Tom said. "Would you and Mum be on for maintaining it?"

"Us?"

"You're great gardeners, the best."

"Oh? And what would you know about gardening?"

"Not much except that I know you're good at it. Everyone admires your garden, even the postman and he has a ponytail and no taste."

"It's a big job."

"I know – I'd help you with the heavy work at the weekends," Tom said tentatively, "like with the lawn mowing maybe – sometimes."

"No need," his father said. "I'll get a ride-on lawnmower. I've been waiting for an excuse to buy one and I know a man who can get them wholesale."

As the First Holy Communion day approached, the Rhododendron bloomed into a cerise explosion against blue skies and the children practised their hymns until their dreams were littered with hosannas.

In the mornings, Saskia watched Nuala from her window. She was back to her old tricks: letter-reading on the doorstep, cat on her lap. She looked worried. Saskia didn't blame her. If she was faced with the prospect of having to tell a house full of tenants they had to up sticks, she'd be worried too.

Nuala was scared. She roamed the house with her rosary beads and hid the fresh flurry of solicitor's letters between the out-of-date encyclopaedias in the drawing room.

It was Joe who caught her.

"What are you doing?" he asked, spying her furtively shoving letters into the bookcase. "You look like you're skulking."

"Aren't I allowed skulk in my own home?" she snapped and he exhaled, making a whistle sound.

He followed her downstairs and she put on the kettle. They sat down and she told him about the house and her brother Frank.

"My solicitor says my father intended the house to be left to me, but it's not on paper – or if there is a will I can't find it. I've searched every inch of this house."

"That's a pity," Joe said philosophically and he slurped his tea. "Is that why you're offering leases and tenancy to every Tom, Dick and Harry, hoping to delay the case? You didn't by any chance report me to the council, did you?"

"Don't be a fool, Joe. Don't you think I've enough to think about without having council people sniffing around?"

Joe shrugged.

"Okay," Nuala sighed. "I did think that tenants and leases might delay legal proceedings, but it doesn't seem to be working."

"Does Tessa know?"

Nuala shook her head.

"She would go mad," Joe said. "She strikes me as a very principled woman."

"Well, what in the name of God can I do?" Nuala pleaded.

"Pray," he said.

"I am."

"Pray harder."

So she did. She prayed Patrick's Communion Day would pass without incident and that they'd have a house to celebrate it in.

Tessa finished her radiotherapy and began to put on a little weight. She didn't go back cleaning. With Nuala's encouragement, she

169

started a small dressmaking and alterations service and supplemented this by giving French lessons. She told Saskia it was good to teach again and earn money in a way that didn't leave your hands chaffed and body weary. Saskia wondered why someone with her talents and abilities had ever chosen to clean houses. She didn't ask – she knew Tessa wouldn't respond.

Saskia took her shopping and got her to try on her first pair of jeans.

"Now you look your age – young. You have legs. Who knew?"

"No, I don't look young," Tessa said but she gazed at her reflection in the mirror all the same.

"Yes, you do. Your dresses are lovely but they hide your legs. Now, do you want to pick up a dress or something for the Communion Day while we're at it?"

Tessa shook her head. "I already found a dress in the charity shop."

"Is it a tent of a thing that's going to hide your figure?"

"It's very nice, actually, hardly worn – cream silk with a belt. I'll have to make alterations of course."

"Good for you."


Once the evenings lengthened, the attendance at training grew. Encouraged by Tot and Emma and Patrick, youngsters crawled out from under rocks, crossed estates and skipped down alleyways to the walled garden of Lavender Square until there was the makings of a decent-sized team.

Saskia started to help Joe, whose behaviour was a little more normal now. Training was regimented and he didn't stand for any slacking off. The children liked and respected him though he was particularly hard on Tot.

"*What in the name of God was that, Tot Flanagan?*" he roared one evening.

"A sliding tackle."

"A what?"

"A sliding tackle," Tot mumbled.

"A sliding tackle, my arse!" Joe said, but he lowered his voice. "I've seen herds of buffalo do a job more gracefully than that. You've after giving Emma a right old shiner and if her mother

170

comes banging on your door baying for blood, don't blame me. Have you ever seen a Premier League player with a black eye?"

"No," Tot said.

"Exactly," Joe hissed.

Nuala still thought Joe pushed them too hard.

"They're only babies, Joe. You treat them as if they played for Chelsea."

"Don't be ridiculous, woman. Aren't these the kids who won't be taking drugs and drinking under a canal bridge when they get a bit older? They'll have something to occupy their minds and keep them out of trouble."

Nuala asked if he would take Patrick shopping for his Communion suit. Joe was horrified.

"Me in a department store, are you mad?"

"It's just I know Patrick isn't too keen about having two women fuss over him."

"Imagine," Joe muttered.

In the end Joe agreed. He was briefed rigorously and warned not to come back with something overly jazzy like a white suit or a chequered shiny rag of a thing.

"I'm not stupid," Joe grumbled, wondering how he'd been talked into the job. Shopping was akin to hoovering. He'd have preferred to have stayed working on his car.

They avoided town and walked to Thomas Street market, stopping off for coffee and a cream bun. Patrick licked the cream out of the doughnut, watching the street traders in their smocks ordering breakfast rolls and scones and white coffees. Outside, the stalls were filled with everything imaginable: giant boxes of washing powder, gallons of washing-up liquid, hundreds and hundreds of toilet rolls along with lighters, cardigans, dresses, tracksuits, trainers, towels, watches, batteries, balls of wool, pet food, plant food and teabags.

The traders looked cross and smoked and drank tea and stared at you if you looked for too long and didn't buy anything.

"I know they look like they'd eat you alive," Joe explained, "but they're the best Dubliners you'll ever meet."

In a menswear shop nearby, the man was patient. He was old

like a granddad and wore a tape measure around his neck.

"Gentlemen," he said and bowed his head. He winked at Patrick. "How can I help you today? Do we have a young footballer here about to receive his First Holy Communion?" He tilted his head to one side as if it was a very serious business.

The changing room was hot and stuffy and each outfit was more awful than the last. Patrick tried on a navy pinstripe suit with a red dickey-bow.

"Come out here now and give us a twirl!" Joe called in.

He sat on a chair supplied by the shop assistant and Patrick stood awkwardly, while Joe scrutinised him.

"I'm not sure about the dickey-bow," he said. "I wouldn't be so sure about that at all. You look like a bus boy in some awful Deep South movie," and he laughed as though this was the funniest thing in the world. "Sorry, son." Then he got serious.

Next Patrick tried on a chocolate-brown suit and he looked a little too disco, like a member of the Jackson Five, and that didn't do either. Then there was a black suit and he looked like a hit man. Then a beige, a white, a grey and a kind of plaid that screamed Rupert the Bear.

Patrick sweated and Joe felt sorry for the boy.

"What would you recommend, sir?" Joe asked the man with the tape measure. "What would a future international footballer look good in, do you think?"

The man scratched his head.

"Have you ever seen Laurent Deschamps in a suit or Pelé?" he asked Patrick.

Patrick shook his head.

"They look pretty good, I can tell you. Deschamps has got real style. He wears Prada. Us, we're out of Prada, but this colour here, charcoal," he pointed to a grey suit, "is always good. How about you give it a go?"

It was a winner.

"Do I look as good as Laurent Deschamps?"

"Better," Joe said.

"Have a sweet, while I wrap this up for you," said the man.

Joe winked and Patrick felt good. He took a bull's eye from the jar the man kept behind the counter for young men who survived

172

the ordeal of Communion shopping.

Two weeks before the Communion, Nuala began to breathe easy. She prayed and bargained as she prayed. If she was in the clear at the end of the big day, she'd give €50 to charity, okay €100, and she would come clean with Tessa. She would go to Mass every day for the rest of her life and she would stop nagging Joe about the state of his room. She blessed herself with holy water. She lit so many candles in the church the sacristan came out to make sure she was paying for them. She avoided walking under ladders, she kept clear of the cracks in the pavement, she lay awake at night pleading, apologising and praying until the moon faded and the sun rose. She looked terrible. She didn't care.

A week before the big day, Tom and Saskia and Patrick went to see Innskeep play Chelsea at home. They took an early-morning flight to London and it was rowdy with boisterous red-faced fans drinking Guinness and addled-looking air hostesses.

Patrick could hardly sit still. Everything was new: the way the plane took off at an impossible speed and roared up in the air over the city and the fields and the sea until the islands off Dublin Bay looked tiny and then they were in the clouds. He smudged his face against the window, taking it all in and then they were descending over the English coast and over the countryside. His ears popped.

They took the train into the city and then the Tube to the grounds and it seemed like the whole world had come to see the match. The Innskeep stadium was impossibly huge – brand sparkly new – and when they climbed the steps to their seats and looked down to the pitch, it was like a perfect green sea.

"What do you think?" Tom asked.

"It's the most beautiful place I've ever seen," Patrick said and not once did his eyes leave the pitch or the players. They seemed to dance, not really play football at all: *Thomas, Parr, Deschamps, Paget, Solomon.* They dribbled as though they were gliding, tackled skilfully and passed the ball to the right people without even having to look for them.

The atmosphere was electric. It hummed, carried you, rang through you and drank you in. Huge pie-eating men with huge pie-eating wives and children roared abuse at the Chelsea players. They booed every time they got the ball, whistled and howled. Tom wasn't so sure a London derby so close to the end of the season had been such a great idea. It felt like they were in a pressure cooker that might explode any minute, flinging entrails and jerseys and meat pies all over Innskeep's pristine stadium.

Just before half time, a penalty put Innskeep ahead and Chelsea were down to ten men.

"*Down to ten men! You're well and truly donald-ducked!*" a man the size of a house sang tunefully.

But Chelsea weren't. They dug in and pulled out an amazing second-half performance and equalised for a draw which left the Innskeep fans relatively happy because the draw meant the cup was out of Chelsea's reach.

On the way home that evening, Patrick was silent, overcome by it all: the colours, the skill, the dance, the curling shots and the power, the sheer volume of the crowd and the thunderous noise level. All through the match, he'd sneaked glances at Jacques Biet who spoke French just like him and paced the line but remained composed. He stood tall and straight with his hands in his pockets and frowned deep in concentration, reading every move, anticipating the next. He was the type of manager you'd want to play well for, one you'd want to please so you could put a smile on his face.

Somewhere over the Irish Sea Patrick looked away from the window and stated half to himself and to no one in particular: "I want to play for Jacques Biet."

"You could do worse," a man said before going back to sleep under his Innskeep scarf.

Patrick daydreamed, filling his head with cheering crowds that chanted his name and happy thoughts but these dissipated the moment he arrived home.

It was obvious there had been a huge row. The house was strangely quiet and full of closed doors and the air fizzled with electricity. His mother was locked in her room, Nuala was crying and Joe was drinking large whiskeys. Patrick knew something really terrible had happened but no one would tell him anything. Joe shook his head and turned up the telly, Nuala hid in the bathroom and his mother said she'd be out to him in a minute. He went out the back to kick the ball against the wall.

The sky was streaked gold and pink and the air smelt of fresh-cut grass. The ball made a rhythmical thud against the wall, *badump badump, badump*, and Patrick thought it was typical that such a great day could be kicked down just like that and he was struck by a horrible thought: that all the good things in his life were about to disappear. He thought about the way things used to be, before Nuala and Snowy and Coco Pops and Joe. Before football and the walled garden, Emma and Tot and Morse code, Tom and Saskia and Saturdays in the café with carrot cake and hot chocolate. Back to before his own room with the aeroplane wallpaper when he and his mother were by themselves and cold, and his mother was scared of the dark and the stairs, when he had played with his crummy old blue ball without a soul to kick it to.

He kicked the ball harder and harder until his feet hurt, hoping everything would be back to normal by the time he went back inside, that whatever had happened in the space of an afternoon and changed everything would have changed back.

He sneaked out through the gate and asked Saskia to come over. There was some sort of crisis. He was sure Nuala would talk to her.

Nuala was sitting at the kitchen table. Her eyes were red. Patrick went back outside.

"We're going to have to leave here," Nuala said and she put her head in her hands.

"Your brother?"

"Yes. How do you know?"

"I overheard him talking to you that night I let him in."

Nuala shook her head and wiped her eyes.

"Did Tessa find out?" Saskia asked.

Nuala nodded dolefully.

"I was in town – she answered the phone. It was bloody Frank. She found the solicitor's letters too. She was so angry."

"What did she say?"

"All she said was, 'It seems it was not your house to let'. She was icy."

"I can imagine."

"She wouldn't look at me, kept looking out the window across at the garden. She said, 'I thought you'd taken us in out of the kindness of your heart.'"

"*Ouch*. What happens now?"

"She said they'll stay until this "bloody Communion Day is over and done with", then they'll leave and move far away from Lavender Square. "She thinks we were all in on it."

"How terrible."

"Yes, it is."

For Emma, she would always remember her Communion Day as the worst day of her life. For Patrick, it would be one of the best. The row seemed to have been sorted or at least swept tidily away like all the dust in the drawing room, which sparkled now since Nuala had decided to use it again. There was a white tablecloth on the table and the chimney had been swept. The house was bustling with preparations and Nuala spent the week cooking and baking. She kept saying they were going to make a real celebration out of it, before wiping tears away with her apron, and Joe kept disappearing and acting like a spy. It was all very weird.

From early morning, the sky was painted in clouds of pink that moved and billowed like silk with folds of purple. The early summer air smelt of lavender and old sunshine.

Nuala sat on the window seat in her room and drank tea knowing that at the end of the day, like Cinderella, her life would revert to the way it had been before, except it would be worse because she had more to lose. She hoped it would go slowly and that it would be a memorable one for Patrick. Joe had been acting strangely all week, furtive and non-committal, and she prayed he wasn't having some sort of meltdown. It would be terrible for the boy if he let him down or made a show of him on top of everything.

Patrick woke early and listened to the seagulls and then fell back to sleep. When Nuala woke him, she ran a bath and told him to have a good wash. Sunlight made freckles on the floorboards and the bubbles made a mountain that spilled over the edge. He dunked his head like a baby seal and imagined he was swimming in the tropics. He got dressed and found Nuala in the drawing room, ferociously polishing a knife.

"Tata, is everything all right?"

"Of course, Patrick, why?"

"It's just it looks as if you're going to kill someone with that knife."

"Come here to me, you! You look so good I could eat you up."

"Do I look like Laurent Deschamps?"

"A hundred times better. Here's a little present for you. It's from me and I hope you'll always keep it close."

She handed him a tiny box. It contained a silver cross on a sturdy chain.

"Do you like it?" she asked. "I made sure the jeweller gave me something that wasn't girly."

"I really like it," Patrick said and he got Nuala to fasten it around his neck immediately.

"Good man. Now let's get cracking."

She picked up the knife, repolished it and caught her reflection. She looked sad. She would have to smarten up and make the best of the day even though Tessa wasn't speaking to her and Joe was dawdling. She felt like she might snap. She tried to breathe deeply but it didn't work and an almighty crash from downstairs didn't help.

Joe shouted up to her.

*"Nuala! I could use a bit of help here, please!"*

She swore and raced down to his room, knife in hand, only to find him pinned to the floor by the ancient chest of drawers. A cloud of dust caught the sunlight.

"How on earth did that happen?" Nuala asked impatiently. "That thing weighs a ton. It hasn't been moved in years."

"Just help me up and stop giving out! I'm already late."

"For what?"

"Never you mind."

Together they managed to get the chest of drawers off him.

"But what were you *doing*?" she asked as he staggered to his feet.

"I was trying to look behind it – it looked as if there was something jammed behind it and I wondered ..." He pointed. "Look!"

Nuala's eyes widened. A pile of moth-eaten documents lay at her feet. She picked them up. There were birth certificates and marriage certificates and piano certificates, there was even a blessing from the Pope.

And there was also an envelope with her name on it. She recognised the writing as her father's.

She looked at Joe. They raised their eyebrows simultaneously.

She handed it to him; he sneezed.

"Open it," she said.

He opened it. The single sheet of paper was so old it had almost disintegrated. He scanned it and then started to whistle infuriatingly.

"Joe!" Nuala said and she took a swipe for the paper but Joe dodged her.

"Patience, patience," he said and he smiled.

He perused the page once more before handing it to Nuala.

It was a will. She took off and up the stairs two at a time to Tessa's room.

"*I told you praying harder would work!*" Joe called after her with a chuckle.


At midday, Nuala and Tessa and Patrick sat and waited for Joe, to set out for the church. He had told them to wait. It was important; he didn't specify why. The clock ticked and the house seemed to sigh with relief, the tensions dissolved.

The doorbell rang. Nuala opened it and stood there staring. Then she stepped outside and beckoned to the others to follow her.

They moved outside: sunlight hit their faces, a faint waft of roses drifted their way and cherry blossoms drifted to earth.

There was a car at the gate, blue and white with fins – something American, perhaps.

Joe was sitting in the front seat. He waved.

"Did you steal it?" Nuala asked.

"No."

The engine purred and the interior was huge and comfortable, with blue leather. They climbed in and did a lap of honour before going to the church.

"Where did this materialise from?" Nuala demanded.

"It's my old Austin Cambridge. We've given it a bit of a

makeover. It's not every day you get to ferry a future World Cup star to his First Holy Communion."

Fiona Fox marvelled at the tastelessness of the whole affair. For every well-cut suit and simple cotton communion dress, there were a million tiaras, white umbrellas, meringues and artificial flowers. And though the scent of lilies, incense and candle wax permeated the church, the stench of hairspray, fake tan and Brylcream beat it down with a rally cry of victory. And then there was Nuala and that Joe arriving in that ostentatious blue-and-white spectacle, cheapening the whole affair. It was a Communion, not a hillbilly agricultural show. Joe Delaney looked like a Mullingar cattle dealer – all he was missing was a strand of baling twine to keep his jacket closed – Nuala grinned idiotically and Patrick was so excited he could hardly stand still. The only one of them with any elegance was the boy's mother. She looked sophisticated in a delicate cream dress. Fiona walked over to compliment her but stalled. She recognised the outfit as her own. It was one she'd donated to a charity shop. It had cost an absolute fortune. She itched to know what Tessa Kimba had paid for it – twenty euro at most – and the thought enraged her. She gritted her teeth and squeezed Tessa's arm.

"You look very well, Tessa," she said and she gave the outfit a quick scan – from neck to knee and back – down, up, down. Tessa had obviously made alterations – it fitted her willowy frame perfectly, not a bulge or a flaw, except for the tiny ink mark on the right cuff, almost invisible, the result of an indelible marker which had slipped from her grasp during a fraught transatlantic conference call with a client.

"Thank you," Tessa said. She watched Fiona examine the miniscule ink stain and somehow knew the dress had once been hers.

Their eyes met. Tessa's gaze was unflinching. Fiona looked away but not before Tessa saw something new. It was pure resentment.

Nuala thought the day had a dream-like quality. The church was colourful and brimmed with excitement, song and smiles. The flowers were beautifully arranged, the candles burned brightly and Patrick got to carry his football in the Offertory procession. Afterwards, there were hundreds of photos against brilliant

Rhododendron bushes. The sun was high and toasted everyone warm in the good-humoured air.

At home, they wore party hats. Saskia and Tom came for lunch, Miss Hennessy too and Tom's parents. After eating, they lounged in the back garden over wine and coffee. Then they played football in their bare feet and had races up and down the garden until they could no longer run and had to lie on the grass to recuperate. Later, the fire was lit in the drawing room and the adults played cards. Outside, the sky was navy-clear with stars, and the streetlights came on around the square.

When it was time for Patrick to go to bed, Nuala took him upstairs. She sat on the end of the bath and watched him wash his teeth. She felt light-hearted with relief. She exhaled long and slowly.

Patrick climbed into bed and examined the silver cross. It glinted in the moonlight.

"Thank you for the cross, Tata," he said. "I will always wear it."

He sounded older then, like someone who had seen it all before and Nuala realised the little boy had become the most precious thing in her world. She did not say this. Instead she said, "It will keep you safe on the pitch."

She looked around the room and examined the aeroplane wallpaper.

"Would you like to change the wallpaper?" she asked. "It's very old and could do with a bit of freshening up? Maybe you might like something to do with football on your wall and we could sort that out. Those aeroplanes are ancient."

"I like them."

"Well, we'll see," she said with a smile.

"You look so happy now," he said.

"I am."

"But what about the row?" he said warily.

"Well, I kept something from your mam that I shouldn't have – but that's all over now."

"Mam likes to know where she stands."

"I know. No more hiding things from her. I've made a promise."

"Does that mean we're going to stay with you?" he asked, and he hardly dared to hope.

"Yes, it does, now get some sleep," Nuala said and she got up to leave.

She was at the door when he called after her in the dark. "Tata?"

"Yes, pet."

"I love you," he said.

"I love you too, Patrick," she said calmly.

When she had gone, he took out his torch and opened the window. He was later than usual and Emma was already signalling but it wasn't her normal "GOODNIGHT FART PANTS".

This was different. She was spelling S-O-S-S-O-S-S-O-S-S-O-S, over and over.

There was some kind of trouble.

D-O-O-R, he spelt out.

When he opened the door she was standing there, carrying a stuffed rucksack. He put his finger on his lips and led her up the stairs. One squeak and Nuala would be out on top of them and there would be questions. In his room, she left down the rucksack and they sat opposite each other on the beds.

"What's the SOS?" asked Patrick.

"My father is leaving my mother and I've run away from home."

# PART 2

# Chapter 26

On his tenth birthday, Patrick started writing to Jacques Biet. The idea came to him at the St Patrick's Day parade as the Colombian majorettes were passing. They were beautiful, mesmerising, sparkling, and also looked like they were freezing to death. Tom had turned and winked at him, mouthing "Colombia", and Patrick's next thought was the World Cup in Colombia and how he wanted to be there. He decided it was time to get the ball rolling.

That night, he wrote his first letter to Jacques Biet. Ten was an age to be reckoned with, he figured, the right age to start writing to the manager he intended to play for. Besides, his teacher at the time, a Mr Butler with leather patches where his elbows should be, told him he had a nice turn of phrase. He also told Patrick he had all the makings of an English teacher or a French teacher. Patrick did not feel the need to mention his intention to play football for Ireland or for Innskeep, even though Mr Butler was a massive football fan. Teachers and grown-ups in general, he discovered, just looked through you when you said things like that, or smiled like they felt sorry for you or thought you were a dreamer.

Even his own mother didn't tolerate much talk of professional football. She was far more interested in spellings, tables, maths and essays. And as for talk of his father, this was encouraged even less these days. She looked sad and distant if ever Patrick mentioned him so he asked less often and then he stopped asking altogether. His mother might have given up on ever finding him but he hadn't. If talking about him made her unhappy then he would keep his plan to find him a secret. That way when he did eventually turn up, it would be an even bigger surprise for her. It all made perfect sense to him.

He spent ages crafting his first letter, carefully wording it and then rewriting it over and over. He didn't want any inky mistakes, blobs of Tipp-Ex or misspellings. He used a dictionary to be absolutely sure. Carelessness in writing would suggest sloppiness in play and Patrick was not a sloppy footballer.

He decided to come clean with the Frenchman and tell him about his father as well as his football ability. He felt it might help his case and that Mr Biet, with his calm nature, intelligent face and fatherly approach to his young teams, would sympathise. Once the father business was out of the way, he could tell him about all the other stuff. About Lavender Square FC with its unusual pitch in the middle of a square in Dublin and its flowery name, which no one liked much because it was sissy, more suitable for a girls' team even though they'd had no girls since Emma had stopped playing. About Joe, their coach, who was strict but fair and didn't treat them like babies, and Saskia, their assistant coach and manager, who had the best knowledge of football in Ireland (for a girl). And about the "Dublin Youth League" which was a real league with serious matches which scouts from England sometimes attended in order to find potential Premier League players. Patrick felt it was important to point this out to the manager because Innskeep hadn't had any Irish players in a long time.

In the end, despite all the things he wanted to say, he kept the letter to a single page, front and back. The manager was a busy man with a lot on his plate, and a long essay of a letter might frighten him off. He wrote it in polite French.

*Dear Monsieur Biet,*

*I hope you are well and not working too hard. My name is Patrick Kimba and I am from Ireland. I am ten years old since today and I am black. Some people say I look like Laurent Deschamps. My mam says that's because Irish people think all black people look the same. My mam is African and gets very cross with Irish people sometimes. She is very beautiful. My friend Tot thinks she is the most beautiful person he has ever seen and even more beautiful when she is cross. Nuala says Tot can be too smart for his own good sometimes.*

*I do not know my father. He lives in the Democratic Republic of Congo and my mam does not know where he is. He is a soldier and a hero and she does not know how to find him. I want to find him because she needs someone to look after her. She got sick a few years ago and that is why we are living with Nuala and Joe in one big house.*

*I am a handy striker and I would like to play for Innskeep. I want to play for Ireland too in the World Cup in Colombia. At the moment, I play for Lavender Square FC and Joe Delaney is our coach. He trains us like Premier League players because he thinks treating us like babies is no good for anyone. We play the offside rule and everything. We won the cup in the League last year and even beat St Joseph's. No one ever beats St Joseph's. Last season, I scored twenty goals.*

*Maybe you could come over and see us play sometime so you can see us for yourself. With your help I could be the next Laurent Deschamps. Joe says I have his pace. I have sent you a photograph of me on my Communion Day so you know what I look like. I hope to hear from you soon.*

*Yours sincerely*
*Patrick Kimba*
*PS Good luck with the rest of the season.*

The Frenchman's London address was not listed and this posed a problem. He could always send it to the Innskeep stadium but that was too big and a letter could easily be lost in the piles of fan mail and player contracts. It was also too stressful a place to read a letter. Patrick mulled, ball-tapped and swung, over and back, on the swing in the walled garden until the answer came to him. He would send the letter to the Innskeep training ground. He jumped off the swing, ran home, looked up the address online and then he posted his first letter to Jacques Biet c/o The Innskeep Training Ground in Barbury, Surrey.

That was the first letter. By the age of thirteen, he had written twenty-five letters and received no reply. He continued writing anyway. He did, however, stop waiting by the letterbox in anticipation of an envelope with a stamp of the Queen's head. He was disappointed but did not hold it against Monsieur Biet. He understood he was a very busy man, what with Manchester United fans singing horrible songs at matches and journalists making up rumours about him being fired. Patrick thought he had a kind face, and it was the first he saw every morning when he woke up and the last before he switched off his bedside lamp at night. Sometimes the moonlight bounced off the poster Saskia had bought for him and made the football manager look like a god. Nuala thought he was handsome, because when he hung up the picture she asked, "Who is that handsome chap?"

Often Patrick daydreamed about the Frenchman arriving in Lavender Square, stepping out of a black chauffeur-driven car and telling the driver to switch off the engine because he had some football business to conduct with a young man and he would be a while. Then he would push through the gate, admire Nuala's roses and pause briefly at the steps, speculating which door he should knock on. Should he climb the steps to the big front door or stay at ground level and rap on the door under the steps? Jacques Biet was a clever man. Patrick decided he would gauge the visit as a formal one, worthy of the big front door, and would climb the granite steps to press gently on the doorbell.

Sometimes the daydreaming seemed so real he was dismayed when he snapped out of it only to find himself sitting at the drawing-room table over a shitty old maths problem and not at the Innskeep training ground in Barbury. Writing to the manager helped to make the daydream more real and that was why he continued to write to him.

It became part of a routine just like push-ups, sit-ups, ball-tapping and training. He did not think about it. Every minute spent practising or writing or building his strength was one step closer to greatness.

The dream of finding his father became part of that, bound into the game until he no longer thought about it. Both ambitions were interwoven; one did not exist without the other. Both relied on results: on winning and winning was everything – it was the burning pinprick of white light that appeared every time he closed his eyes.

# Chapter 27

*The Bugle* was the first paper to pick up on the mutterings of Patrick Kimba's fledgling football career. One of their schoolboy league reporters, a Richard Watts, found the square named after the lavender that grew in every garden. Ambitious and eager to spot a future star, he wrote a short piece for a corner of the sports section. He headlined it "AG IMIRT PELÉ", in what he considered a clever pun on the name of the football legend, the Gaelic for "playing football" being *"ag imirt peile"*. He described Patrick as a natural with a feel for the game and a cool head and reported that Lavender Square FC were a pleasure to watch. The article generated a murmur of excitement among supporters and match attendance rose.

This infectious fuss was helped along by Pim Van Hartenstein. His appointment as Ireland manager had created a fresh buzz about the game, and his talk of needing to find and nurture young talent had every club in the country bursting to wheel out the next Brady, Keane, Doyle or Duff. It was rumoured that the Dutchman intended to show up at matches unannounced, and this news had necks craned to full capacity at all matches – from under 7s to League of Ireland. Anyone who was old enough to remember the heady days of Italia '90 anticipated a new age in Irish football. Inflatable green crocodiles were rooted out and inflated, moth-eaten jerseys and leprechaun hats shaken out and pulled on. Some said it was like waiting for the Second Coming; for Patrick it was proof he was going in the right direction. His mother didn't agree, and this was the beginning of his troubles.

For a few years, things had been good. Lavender Square, tucked away from the traffic, was lulled in the musk of lavender. Pink moons floated through navy skies and the seasons passed, weaving their way around each of them. Falling leaves, budding blossoms. In Nuala's, life was simple, settled and pleasant. Nuala cooked, Tessa cultivated an impressive and productive vegetable garden, Joe trained the team, the rest of them dropped in. They all loved the house. It had a sagging comfort: baking smells, well-worn armchairs and a fire in the hearth. And things could have gone on like that forever, only for the boy and his dream.

Patrick sprouted and lost his French accent. He went to school, played matches and watched matches. At thirteen, his ambition to play professional football was no less certain than it had been when he was eight. The problem was it was slightly obsessive and it was an obsession his mother didn't care for. Joe didn't care much for it either. Joe, who had signed up for a simple training arrangement, hadn't bargained for what he referred to as a "Copa América Extravaganza".

It had all started with the need for a bigger pitch. They needed a full-size pitch for the eleven-a-side game which meant a move out of Lavender Square to Bushy Park and this didn't suit Joe at all. When the team registered as Lavender Square FC and joined the League, he pushed Saskia forward, with Tom as her back-up, for all the form-filling and League meetings and formalities like Garda vetting. He would still coach but he didn't want any attention. Fixture sheets were posted, calls came in from League people and referees and other coaches and then, just before their first League match, the lavender-coloured kits arrived. Tom found a sponsor in the form of a tea client who wanted to promote their new herbal range. The colour didn't impress Joe.

"They're going to get awful hardship wearing a kit that colour," he said.

"The colour makes sense once you hear the name of the club," Saskia reasoned.

"People will get used to it," Tom added.

"No, they won't." Joe was adamant. "Call it lavender all you want, but it still looks pink to me. Poor little feckers."

The team emerged from glorious obscurity, stepping into the limelight wearing a girly kit and, just like that, everyone knew about Lavender Square FC.

Shortly afterwards, Joe started to fall apart. He was suspicious of Richard Watts from the outset. The reporter attended every match, even when he wasn't working. At first his articles had a minimal effect. Only a scattering of parents showed up at their matches. They weren't interested in a wrinkly man with a collection of questionable tracksuits. But then word got around about the black kid with the magic touch and supporters started to make their way to matches, home and away. With them, came a small group of Africans. They peppered the crowd and were silent at first, but once settled regulars, they made themselves heard by humming a low drone that sounded all at once mesmerising and eerie. It was rumoured they were from the Congo. They attended every match and slipped away as quietly and as quickly as they arrived, not keen to linger. While recession had seen other immigrants pack up and leave, Africans had nowhere else to go and football, which was free to watch and played well by one of their own, even if it was a young kid, added a bit of colour to their lives. If the boy was accepted, then there was a chance they might be too.

It was this sort of fuss that made Joe nervous. He told Saskia that crowds or journalists or humming Africans had never been part of the deal. Patrick had pestered him into training the team and somewhere along the way it had got out of hand. He blamed himself for ever agreeing to get involved, and then shifted the blame to Pim Van Hartenstein, cursing the Dutchman for fanning the flame of football hysteria. Joe wasn't interested in the born-again interest in football. He didn't want attention of any sort and resented analysis, and with the League came analysis. Lavender Square FC was criticised for taking the game too seriously. The small-sided game was meant to be fun, a League secretary explained to Saskia, a way of preparing the children for the eleven-a-side game. There was no use forcing them onto a full-size pitch before their time or insisting on the offside rule when they didn't need it yet. There was already enough trouble from fame-obsessed parents shouting abuse from the sidelines.

They failed to see that under Joe's gruff exterior there was huge kindness, that for every bellow there was encouragement and for every bark there was praise and high hopes. He was a like a skilled doctor with no bedside manner, his spikiness an armour against a world he was still uncertain of. Shouting gave him strength and whistle-blowing the courage to go on because the truth was every training session was still a personal struggle and every match a cliff-face to be climbed. Saskia could see this; Patrick too.

Patrick told her that for days before a match Joe did not sleep. He tossed and turned and roamed the house to cool down, his breath rasping and jagged. He would sit on the step by the arched window and look out across the rooftops, watching the night pass by in lights and jet streams, sirens and chimes, dozing in and out of sleep.

Sometimes Patrick might sit with him for a while or bring him a cup of tea, and together they would watch lights blinking from city to sea like a cloth of shimmering diamonds, without ever saying a word. They understood each other. Patrick didn't speak, not unless Joe did. Patrick knew that sometimes words were no use, not in describing something beautiful, nor in giving comfort. It was this instinctive sense of how the world worked that made him a great footballer, and it was why Joe soldiered on.

When Saskia and Joe were alone before training, to mark out a course, or afterwards when tidying up, she tried to get to the root of his paranoia. But what came out was only a worry without a root cause. He felt like he was being watched, plain and simple, and his instinct was to run and hide. Saskia didn't point out that being watched was par for the course when you were a football coach. She felt this might send him over the edge. She was no psychotherapist but she believed Joe's baggage had something to do with his wife's death and that he'd never properly dealt with it. He had once hinted to Nuala that his children in some way blamed him for it. It seemed unreasonable since she had died of cancer not a bullet wound but Joe didn't condemn them. If anything, he agreed with them and there was no more said about it. They lived abroad now and were no longer in touch.

Joe's instinct might have been to run but Saskia knew he would not. He would never leave Patrick and she was pretty sure he wouldn't leave Nuala either. They fought like cats and dogs but were close really. Joe said it was impossible not to respect a woman who turned a blind eye to clumps of muck on her newly washed tiles and tolerated strings of young footballers traipsing through her kitchen looking for Coke and crisps. This was as affectionate as Joe got.

Richard Watts started bringing along a photographer, and it was rare when Lavender Square FC didn't feature in the paper. Anyone with an interest in football was keen to see what all the fuss was about. They wanted to check out the curious African drone for themselves and see if they could spot the scouts who were said to be making regular checks. Those who did come to see the young team play weren't disappointed. They had talent. Patrick Kimba, who could score from anywhere and was a class apart for his age, was part of it certainly, but there was more to it than that. On the pitch, each of the players had a sense of place. They were disciplined, hardworking, unified and intelligent and they won games: Cherry Orchard, Portmarnock, Home Farm and Bosco's.

Readers were keen to put a face to the coach behind the impressive team but Joe always stepped aside, mumbling excuses, pushing Saskia forward. But his wish for obscurity made him all the more sought after. It was obvious to anyone who knew about football that Lavender Square FC had a first-class coach.

Richard Watts persisted, keen to be the first to get an interview with him and Joe resented him even more for it.

As a youth side, the team thrived. They played matches: lost some, won more. They collected cups and medals.

Patrick grew taller, into a confident young man and a fine footballer. Long-limbed, lean and athletic, he cut a presence on the pitch. There was an effortless grace about him. He seemed to move slower than the others did, yet he moved faster. He could change pace without bluster and frustrate the opposition who found him impossible to mark. It was difficult not to notice Patrick Kimba and, because of this, supporters could be cruel. Sometimes, in the heat of a match, someone might yell "*Monkey Boy!*" He always laughed it off. Patrick was too hungry to let names drag him down. He tackled, scored, passed and was as good in the air as he was on the ground. He was a leader and up for every game because every match was a step closer to where he wanted to be. The boys listened to him, even Tot. His desire to succeed had affected them all, and now each of them had their own dreams: Everton, Spurs, Derby, Sunderland and Leeds United. There were new teams in the Premier League each season which brought fresh new hopes.

They climbed League tables: under 9, under 10, under 11, under 12, under 13. Week after week, their team photo appeared in *The Bugle* and often the junior soccer supplement of *The Star*. The profile of the club continued to rise and it terrified Joe. There was talk of scouts and he prayed for a scout to take the young boy off his hands. Once that happened, he could step back and fade out, his promise fulfilled, his dues paid.

Before the Under-13 League kicked off they were already tipped to win it. Patrick revelled in the build-up and, despite Joe's constant mutterings and witterings, he relished the season. When coaches yelled "*Mark Number 10!*" from the sidelines, the thrill was electrifying. Winning was another high altogether. It lifted him out of his boots and had him floating over the pitch. Nothing could match it. It was giddying. By the time they got to the last game of the season, Patrick knew he had become a force to be reckoned with. His name and number had been noted. Everything was going smoothly, as planned. In the not-too-distant future, he would be right where he wanted to be – at Innskeep.

Years later he would tell a journalist that if he had known what was around the corner, he would have given up there and then. Just walked off the pitch and kept on walking, plain and simple. Sometimes the pursuit of a dream was not worth the heartache that came with it.

# Chapter 28

A few days before the final game of the Under-13 League, Saskia inspected the gear in the kit shed and afterwards sat on the swing. She often did this when she wanted to think. It cleared her mind. When it started to drizzle she went home and, from her window, she watched over Lavender Square. Flecks of rain hit the window. A breeze angrily swept up debris from the night before, busying it into temporary neat piles.

The green door at Number 5 opened and Fiona Fox stepped outside. She looked dishevelled and pulled on a cigarette as she paced. The wind scattered the ash. She was rarely seen any more. The separation had left her rattled. Saskia believed the woman was embarrassed more than sad. Mark Fox's new relationship wasn't exactly suitable dinner-party conversation.

A car pulled up at the kerb and the pacing stopped. A pale Emma Fox got out and waved at the driver as the car drove away. Fiona Fox stubbed out her cigarette and they went inside.

Emma had said she would call over. She often did. Something in the younger girl had caused her to gravitate towards Saskia. Saskia believed it was their common lack of place. Emma's pale face and apologetic expression suggested she wasn't quite sure where she belonged. Saskia had always hoped that she herself was destined for some place better than a mock-Italian café. She just wasn't sure how to get there. Still she made coffee and coached football and she wondered if that's how her life would pan out, how her story would end: everyone else's tied up in a neat bow, she a childless barista with an encyclopaedic knowledge of football and an impressive collection of tracksuits.

Sometimes Emma sketched or painted – she showed artistic promise – or they watched TV and ate beans on toast. It was relaxing which was an accomplishment in itself because Emma wasn't an easy-going thirteen-year-old. Patrick said it was difficult to be laid back or happy-go-lucky when your mother was the Antichrist and your father had a girlfriend who couldn't cook. Saskia understood all this. What she didn't understand was why Fiona Fox allowed her daughter over to her flat at all. Tom said Fiona Fox was okay with Saskia because she was the best of a bad lot. If the choice was between Tot and Patrick or Saskia, Saskia was going to win out. She was reliable and not a potentially corrupting influence – which he meant as a compliment. But it made Saskia feel old and boring. Patrick said the Foxs' house was grubby now that Emma's father wasn't around. It also stank of smoke. He didn't like being there but it was more than grubbiness, it was the atmosphere. He was absolutely certain Fiona Fox hated him. He wasn't sure how he knew this but he did, and it didn't overly trouble him – he didn't like her much either. It just made it more difficult to see Emma.

Nuala said it was impossible to hate a young boy but Patrick didn't agree. He said some people hated everything around them, particularly those whose husbands had taken up with Ukrainian girls.

Tom emerged from his flat and waved up. Saskia waved back. They would go for a pint later. No doubt there would be a new woman to discuss. Tom's love life was a constant source of amusement to her. There were several girls, and they were all the same: svelte and beautiful, so impossibly cool it was as if they spoke a different language. They all held onto him for as long as they could by pretending not to be interested in him.

"Aren't you just the proper little ladykiller?" she observed once.

"They all start out fine and then turn into stalkers," he grumbled.

"That's because they're pretending to be something they're not."

"Which is?"

"Not all that interested."

"And when did you get to be such an expert?"

"I have a pair of eyes."

He laughed.

"You're a gas woman."

"Well, you have to have a sense of humour with a body like mine."

"You wear tracksuits. No one has a clue what sort of a body you have."

"Well, I do, and that is why I wear tracksuits."

"With all the running you do up and down the pitch, it can't be that bad."

They often met for a pint. Tom said it was good to sit and talk to someone who didn't twirl her hair or trip to the bathroom every five minutes to check her eyeliner. Saskia wasn't sure what sort of praise that was. It probably meant he saw her as one of the lads which made her feel like crap. She liked him, a little too much. She couldn't help it even if there was no point thinking beyond friendship. She liked being around him. By now their conversations were easy, fluid. They talked about everything: the state of the world, the weird rise of white supremacy, Patrick, Joe's weirdness and football. Sometimes, when Saskia talked about football, Tom gave her a strange look. She wasn't sure whether it was admiration or pity, but she might not see him for days afterwards. There was a chance her superior knowledge of the game put him out. Tom could be odd like that. She put it down to flakiness. As a human, he had vastly improved over time, but flaky relapses were to be expected. He was too good-looking not to fall foul every so often.

When he came into the café, the other girls swooned. They asked how she could possibly hang out with "that guy", the one who looked like he belonged in a Ralph Lauren photoshoot, and not be "like totally in love with him"? He was *gorgeous*. Saskia knew there was no point in being totally in love with him. Girls like Saskia Heffernan could not afford to entertain thoughts about guys like Tom Winters.

She poured a cup of tea and watched Joe's old Austin Cambridge return to the square. Tessa drove now. The car made a pleasant purring noise and it was comfortable although the blue-leather seats burnt the legs off you in summer and froze you solid in winter. If Joe drove Patrick to school the other kids stared. It was difficult to ignore a big blue car with white fins.

Tessa parked expertly. She, Nuala and Patrick got out, no Joe. Tessa was a better driver than Nuala. Joe had taught both of them, and while he and Nuala rowed relentlessly over clutch, gear and mirror co-ordination, Joe and Tessa hadn't fought, not once. Tessa didn't waste energy blustering. She just listened. That's what Tessa did best. Even when you asked her a question she had a habit of redirecting it back to you. She and Nuala were good friends but, even after four years of living under one roof, Nuala knew she didn't know the half of what went on in her head. Sometimes she thought she was actually regressing. She seemed weighed down by a burden that only shifted when she was in the back garden at her vegetable patch or busy at the sewing machine where the whirr of the Singer in the solitude of the drawing room worked as a kind of meditation.

Tessa's interests were carefully measured, her emotions kept in check and most of the time it was impossible to know what she was thinking. If she was bothered by something, she might blink a little faster, inhale sharply through her nostrils or turn and stare into the fire as if hoping for an answer from the flames.

She liked to keep busy. She gave her French lessons and took orders for debutante dresses. Girls arrived armed with patterns and yards of silk from Thailand – and chequebooks. They stood in the drawing room in their underwear and giggled and found Tessa cool, almost silent, but they didn't care as long as she knew how to cut on the bias and got the job done. It was known that the beautiful Mrs Kimba was not only good value, but also an exceptional seamstress.

She and Nuala had taken up bridge together. They joined a club with a mix of age groups and liked the way the game kept the mind ticking over. Several eligible men had approached Tessa but she refused each of them in the same cool unreadable manner. Patrick understood her best and often stepped in as translator. Like the day her biometric card arrived in the post with an accompanying letter making it clear the ID card was to be carried at all times. That day she didn't leave her room.

"I think she feels like a tagged heifer," he explained gravely to Joe and Nuala. Patrick had a tendency to pick up Joe's sayings.

They knew the matter would not be mentioned. Tessa would not speak about it for weeks, not until she had mentally dealt with it herself.

The silences frustrated Nuala. It was difficult to share a home with someone who wouldn't let you in, and Saskia knew the teacher would not be so tolerant but for Patrick who she loved like a son. After one glass of wine too many, Nuala had once told her she believed he was an angel who'd been sent down to rescue them from their once hopeless existences. She had a point. For Saskia, life was better than it had once been. True, she was still making coffee but her involvement in the League helped make up for it. She had never understood what people meant by the term "beautiful game" until she got under its skin. Now she watched every game with the reverence of an art connoisseur and chewed over every touch, turn, flick, pass and tactic like a food critic. She loved when the rhythm of a game flowed – when players moved with the ease and poise of dancers, so skilled and accurate that she could read the game like a much-loved story that revealed something new every time you read it.

Of course, League meetings were male-dominated and, as a result, there was lots of talking and parading of egos before getting down to decision-making. Sometimes she said things like, "Could we wrap this meeting up, gentlemen? I've a wash to put on," just to rattle their cages. Sometimes they told her to shut up; mostly they listened to her. They respected the girl with the nice voice who knew her football and managed so successful a youth side.

Emma called over when it was getting dark.

"Well, how are they?" Saskia asked and Emma shrugged miserably. "That bad?"

Emma shrugged again. She was a pretty girl but unaware of it, with peachy skin and long blonde hair which she wore in a shiny plait when she wasn't obsessing about her ears. She was convinced they stuck out. They didn't.

"We played gin rummy and ate cake."

"That was nice."

"Sure."

She knew Emma puzzled over Valentina Bazik who had long pink nails and couldn't cook to save her life. She added yoghurt-covered peanuts to everything because she loved them and Emma's father didn't mind. Nor did he mind that she smoked mint cigarettes and wore very tight jeans. Mark Fox had met her in the bank and then in the square when she was living in a flat just a few doors away from Saskia.

"Are you sure you never saw my father with Valentina?" Emma had asked her once. "I'm not meant to know but I heard them shouting about it, my mother and him. It's where they met up sometimes, in the football club when it was just a walled garden and you have a good view from here of the garden gate."

Saskia had suspected goings-on in the walled garden when she'd been stalking Joe at night and thought no more of it. It wasn't until she heard the rumours about where Mark Fox had been meeting Valentina Bazik that she put two and two together. She shook her head. There was no point in going into details about Mark Fox's romantic trysts. It wouldn't do Emma any good. Valentina was always happy and chatty and their tiny apartment was spotless. You were asked to take off your shoes at the door. Her father said she had grown up in poverty. She was grateful to be in Ireland and proud of her beautiful home.

They had made up a room for Emma. It was pink – pink walls, pink curtains, pink duvet and pink carpet. On the dressing table, there was a pink hairbrush and mirror set. It had been Valentina's as a young girl but now it was Emma's.

Valentina talked a lot and spoke like a KGB commandant in a *James Bond* film. If there was something bothering Emma, it was dealt with straight up around the table. Her father seemed to like this; Emma liked it too. What she didn't like was the way her mother quizzed her inside and out after her visits.

Emma took off her coat and took a box out of her bag. It was a jigsaw.

"Valentina gave me this. It's a Ukrainian country scene and it looks difficult," she said anxiously.

"We'll handle it," Saskia said. "I'll make us some tea."

"Okay."

They laid the pieces out on the table and got to work. They spoke sporadically. The necessity to concentrate helped Emma relax and she momentarily lost the pinched expression. But just as they finished the jigsaw they discovered there was a piece of sky missing. Saskia said it made the jigsaw unique. Emma didn't agree.

"There will always be a hole in the sky now," she observed and she broke up the jigsaw and put it away.

Emma went home and Saskia switched on the news. It was unpleasant but, like a car crash, impossible to turn away from: rallies, marches, racist incidents, road deaths and job losses. The reports had been initially hushed about the rise of the right. People were hopeful that cautious tones might keep it appeased like an unpredictable animal. It hadn't worked. The intolerance of immigrants rose. No jobs for teenagers; that was the start of it. Immigrants had filled all the mushroom-picking, rubbish-tipping, floor-sweeping and greasy-spoon positions – working for nothing, bowing and scraping, no complaining. Then there was the question of schools. Waiting lists as long as your arm for Irish children. Saskia had once heard a discussion on late-night radio about schoolgirls wearing the hijab. It made way for a deluge of grievances and fears of terrorist cells and potential terrorist attacks which bubbled up from under the surface. Generalisations burned up phone lines and fuelled the fire. Fear sparked paranoia and exaggeration. African men and their attitudes towards women were debated. A crackdown on immigrants who'd been claiming welfare under false pretences did nothing to calm a frenzied situation. Nor did a flushing out of immigrants who were suspected Islamic fundamentalists. Neighbours reported neighbours, arrests and deportations were being carried out swiftly and with little protest. The dark and dusty immigrant corners of the cities, new suburbs and towns were now in the spotlight and the finger of blame was close behind. No one had any idea of how many there were. There were thousands of them, they were here to stay, and they were not welcome. It was chilling.

A hint of intolerance began to creep into the game but Joe told her it had always been part of the game. Paul McGrath had got terrible grief as a young fella. If you were black and good on the ball, you were picked on, that was that. This didn't give Saskia any comfort and she thought it was rich coming from Joe the former note-writer. Even if Patrick laughed off the jibes, she couldn't.

Her phone rang. She answered.

"Mam."

"Eight road deaths in two days."

"I saw."

"I'm beside myself."

"I know, Mam. I know."

Her mother sighed.

"How was work?"

"Busy."

"Any chance of you leaving that café this summer and getting a real job?"

"I was thinking of joining *Interpol*."

"No need to be cheeky – the neighbours are always asking, that's all."

Saskia yawned.

"Well, I won't keep you," her mother said with her trademark tone of disappointment, and she hung up.

Reports of road deaths bothered Saskia too. There were so many of them. She thought of those left behind to pick up the pieces and the enormity of the sadness haunted her. Sometimes it made sleeping impossible. Nothing worked except Valium – not yoga, meditation or visualisation, although she liked the idea of visualisation, the notion of picturing something and it appearing on your doorstep. She had explained how it worked to Patrick and had given him a poster of Jacques Biet for his room.

"Visualise him as your manager," she told him, "and he will be."

When Tom heard this, he laughed so hard he had to sit down but Patrick had hung the picture of Biet up anyway. It wouldn't do any harm. Besides, she knew more about football and most things than Tom did.

Saskia switched off the TV and looked out over the square and into the walled garden. The last game of another great season was coming up. For some reason she didn't feel good about it and she wasn't sure why. She hoped she wasn't turning into another Joe. One paranoid crazy was enough for any team.

# Chapter 29

Patrick called for Emma the night before the final. They sat on her front doorsteps and she threw the ball repetitively so Patrick could practise his headers. He neatly headed the ball back into her hands every time. She no longer played on the team but knew the drill.

"Any news from the Ukrainian jury?" he asked.

"This time she gave me a jigsaw."

"Oh?"

"It's missing a piece of sky."

"Maybe it's a hidden message about the hole in the ozone layer. Does it matter?"

"No," she said and they both giggled at this.

Patrick went to sit down. The curtains twitched and then Mrs Fox was looking out and straight at him. He smiled and waved.

"It really annoys her when you do that," Emma said.

"I know." Patrick grinned.

At first he thought he had been imagining Mrs Fox's dislike of him. There was a chance she was just upset at the world for taking her husband away. But after a while he knew he wasn't. She had a way of looking at him, sideways, as though talking to him was a huge effort and she'd prefer to be doing something else like sluicing out a sewage tank. Also she had never once said, "Call me Fiona" like she did to lots of other kids and he realised that Mrs Fox only ever said this to people who mattered.

When Patrick asked why her mother didn't like him, Emma didn't try to soften the blow. They had always been honest with each other. She said her mother described all of them at Nuala's as a band of tinkers, all noise and raucousness. She called Joe "the tramp", Tessa "the clever one with her cash-in-hand businesses" and Nuala "a gullible fool".

"With you it's different," she said. "She thinks you're unsuitable but also cheeky."

Patrick didn't agree. "No," he said. "She doesn't like me because I'm not afraid of her."

When Emma confided in him about her ears, he was equally truthful.

"They stick out," she said and she pulled back her hair to show him.

"You're soft in the head," Patrick said and she brushed her hair back self-consciously.

"Mum says I'll always have to wear my hair long."

"Well, I think you're very pretty," Patrick said and he blushed then though thankfully Emma couldn't tell. There was one advantage to having dark skin.

His mother had told him to stay away from Emma's. Mrs Fox had made it clear she didn't want him around. So why push it? Emma was his best friend, that was why. His mother sighed and said the world didn't work that way. But Saskia told him nothing should come between friends, not even bad eggs like Fiona Fox. Friends were there for each other through thick and thin and Emma needed a good friend like Patrick.

Patrick persevered. He ignored the looks, the upturned nose and cold reception – for Emma.

Emma told him he was the only one, apart from Saskia, who didn't tiptoe around her in case she fell apart. All the others looked at her with pity. They squeezed her hand and patted her head. Nuala often made cherry scones and gave her some in a paper bag to take home. Joe gave her the odd fiver to buy sweets. Tessa made her silk purses out of material ends and Tom brought her extra-large hot chocolates when they watched matches. Even Tot was nice.

Patrick knew what it was like to not have a father around and wasn't afraid to remind her that her father only lived down the road and not in a country that was at war and thousands of miles away. When her mother was screaming the house down and slamming doors, this thought gave Emma some comfort.

Patrick also understood things. He understood why she chose to stay with her mother, even when her father said he could probably fix it for her to come and live with him and Valentina. Emma would not leave her mother alone. Despite all her roaring and shouting, she knew that somewhere deep inside her mother was just sad. That was the thing about growing up, she told him, you noticed how lots of people were just sad or lonely or scared. Shouting was just a way of hiding it.

As friends, they told each other everything. Patrick had told Emma about his letters to Jacques Biet. It had sounded silly when he said it aloud – childish – but she didn't think so. "Why not? He seems like a nice man, kind," she had said.

Now at last he told her about his plan to find his own father.

"Oh?" Emma was confused. Had this something to do with Jacques Biet? Was he also in the business of finding fathers – a private investigator as well as a manager?

"When I play for a big club like Innskeep," Patrick explained, "everyone will know my name and my father will find me then without any hassle. It's what the dentist, Mr Singh, told me years ago."

"I see, that's clever," Emma said and she smiled even though that seemed like a very long shot indeed.

Patrick made her swear solemnly she wouldn't tell anyone. Emma made him swear he would never stop being her friend no matter how much her mother tried to keep him away.

When Emma was sad, Patrick made her laugh. When her mother was sleeping off a hangover, he pushed her on the swing until she was soaring high above her troubles. He taught her some French; she taught him chess. They still sent each other messages in Morse code even though both of them had phones now.

He told her he sometimes heard his mother crying softly in her room. Emma told him she often heard her father and Valentina having sex in their room and this made her feel weird.

"At least it means they like each other," he said wisely.

"Sometimes it doesn't sound like it. Sometimes it sounds like they're hurting each other."

Mrs Fox wanted to send Emma to a private boarding school. Emma refused. A private school would mean no more Patrick. Emma knew this and her mother knew she knew this. Emma also knew her mother would keep trying until she got her way.

Patrick got up and tapped the ball, kicked it up in the air and kept it there: head, chest, knee, foot. He was always fidgety the night before a match.

"Are you okay about tomorrow?" Emma asked.

"Naw."

"Is Joe?"

"Joe is always worried."

"I know."

The front door opened slightly and Mrs Fox poked her head out. "Teatime, Emma," she said before closing the door again.

Emma got up; Patrick dribbled the ball home.

Mrs Fox was one problem; his own mother was another. His summer report had been poor, he hadn't reached scholarship standard, and now she was on the warpath. She knew football was to blame. His head was in the clouds and this would not do at all. Football or no football, her son was going to college. It was why she'd come to Ireland.

Patrick thought it unfair he should get such a hard time for daydreaming when his mother was well able to daydream herself, especially when she spoke about the Congo. Only a dreamer would talk about the Congo as a nice warm place with mangoes growing on the side of the road and exotic birds and friendly people while skimming over the fact that in parts the ground was covered in human bones. Now she listened to a Congolese radio station at night and read the Congolese newspapers online searching for good news from the place she still called home. She had started writing letters herself, to a schoolteacher friend who had moved to Brazzaville in the French Congo. His mother was always in a good mood when the envelopes with the coloured stamps arrived.

Saskia said his mother's nostalgia was probably a kind of homesickness. It was normal to miss the place where you grew up, especially as you got older, and nostalgia wasn't always logical. But Patrick knew it was more than this. The letters from Brazzaville had started arriving in the post shortly after the biometric card had. Tessa wasn't an Irish citizen like he was. The racial unrest scared her. She felt she was no longer welcome in the country that had once welcomed her. He hoped she hadn't any ideas about returning to the Congo just yet. It would play havoc with his plans. It didn't sound like a place where football thrived. He wanted to find his father for sure, but to come and live with them in Ireland. Not the other way round.

Joe was another worry altogether. He'd been good for a long time but now he was bockety again like an old banger of a car. He often threatened to step down as coach. He'd been saying it for ages, ever since the first night of training and Patrick had never believed he would. But lately Joe was getting worse. Even though the Africans with their presence and humming were never threatening and the journalist from *The Bugle* only wrote nice things about them, Joe was convinced they were all out to get him. He was behaving strangely and drinking more whiskey. He was also back on the smokes. Tot said he smelt like a hoor's handbag.

When Nuala asked Joe if he was okay, he hid behind the paper; when Patrick asked him why he drank whiskey, he said it calmed the demons – but Patrick didn't think it was doing a very good job of it. At times Joe's nerves were so bad his cheeks developed a jittery tick and his T-shirt stuck to his back. Patrick hoped he would be okay. He needed Joe. Even in his doddery state, Joe knew how to get the best out of him as a player. He told Patrick he had the intelligence to read a game and take instruction. The hours of practice had given him a real feel for the ball and now it was part of him. He knew how to receive it, how to pass it and where to send it. He could stop it dead at his feet and hold onto it until he put it in the back of the net. He was a natural goal-scorer but had the intelligence for midfield. Joe switched him between front and middle to strengthen his game. Joe knew how the game worked. He also understood the importance of winning and that to Patrick it was everything.

Before going inside he sat on the steps and thought about the following day's game. St Killian's were known as "The Killers" because they were very good at getting away with playing dirty. It would be a tough match because it was away, and it would probably be nasty because their supporters were as rough as guts. But none of that mattered. What did was a win. Lavender Square had to win the match in order to win the League; Killian's only needed a draw.

# Chapter 30

Next day, on the way to the grounds, Saskia was quiet and Joe was restless. While the boys got ready, he waited outside and chain-smoked. Lavender Square's supporters assembled at one end and Killian's at the other. Joe didn't like the look of them. They had a rough element. He pulled his cap down over his forehead. The day was grey and muggy. It would be heavy work on the pitch.

The teams came out and warmed up.

Before kick-off, Saskia called them together and they trotted over. Joe swallowed. When he spoke, his voice sounded far away, not like his own at all. Fourteen pairs of eyes followed him, over, back, over, back. They were relying on him for some choice words, encouragement, something to set them on their way and put them in winning mode. He was at a loss so he stole something Brian Clough, the legendary manager, used to tell his first team.

"Right, gentlemen, this is just another game so let's go out there and play it like that."

Then he went through the formation. "Four-four-one, Josh up front with Patrick, Tot on the right, Mark on the left, Luke and Kristian centre and you four, Tommy, Gary, Jack and Craig at the back. Subs on the bench and you'll all get your game. Mark up and keep the ball rolling. And remember do *not* argue with the referee or swear. I know him. He's a bollocks and he'll red-card you if you so much as fart in his direction."

They lined up and the referee walked the line. They lifted their feet, one and then the other, so he could examine their studs. He checked their fingers for rings and ears for earrings. Patrick pushed his silver cross safely under his shirt, out of sight. The game kicked off.

The first half was a disaster. The pace was fast from the off and Saskia could see nerves were getting the better of the Lavender team. They couldn't settle and their play was jumpy. Killian's were nippy and went for the ankles like terriers. They meant business and, shortly into the game, they were the first to attack. A midfielder broke down the right and fired over a cross which their striker just failed to get his head to. A few minutes later, a magnificent through-ball sailed past Lavender Square's back four setting up Killian's for a clear shot, but just as their forward was about to shoot, the ball bounced awkwardly and the shot went the wrong side of the post. Joe shouted at the defenders to smarten themselves up.

Then just before half time, a Killian's forward broke into the Lavender Square box. Tot dived in, taking him down in a bumbling tackle and the referee had no hesitation in pointing to the spot. Killian's scored their first goal from a penalty. They scored a second from a corner and would have scored a third only for a great save.

At half time, the boys trooped off and into a huddle. They were quiet. The horrible dragging feeling of being 2-0 down weighed on them.

Joe spoke quickly as he circled them.

"Okay lads, take a breather," he said.

The boys guzzled water and looked at their feet.

"You look like you're scared of them and they know it. You can beat these boys, fair and square. Stick to that Number 8 like a fly to shite, Kristian – he looks like he wrestles bullocks before breakfast."

The Polish boy blinked at Joe incomprehensibly; Saskia explained what Joe meant in plain English.

Joe surveyed the sidelines. There was a good crowd now, and they were a rowdy ugly-looking bunch. It bothered him that Nuala and Tessa were in the crowd. The atmosphere was volatile and he didn't like it. It didn't feel safe. He adjusted his cap, pulling the peak even further over his face. One half down, one to go; he could do this.

He looked at Saskia; she nodded. He looked back at the boys. They looked dispirited.

"Lads," he said more gently, "you know you're better than this lot. So just get out there and keep passing. That's all you have to do. Keep it simple. No fancy crap. Our two strikers haven't even got a look in yet. Score one goal, another will follow and then another. Go on now. Good boys."

It did the trick. The team lined up for kick-off and, from the centre of the pitch, Patrick scanned the support. He saw his mother and Nuala and a sprinkling of Africans. Joe was right. If they scored one, another would follow. His mind cleared; the sidelines and the crowd disappeared then and the game appeared before him. His opponents became obstacles that just needed to be dribbled past and run around. They could still win.

Ten minutes into the second half he intercepted a pass, dribbled around his markers and belted it past the goalkeeper. Then, ten minutes after that, Luke Lamerski scored from a corner taken by Tot and they were level.

Killian's fought back. Determined not to be outdone, they forged ahead and took their chances, egged on by their supporters who screamed from the sidelines but Lavender Square defended fiercely. In order to win they needed a moment of magic. That moment came just before full time. The goal originated in the Lavender Square box. It started with a kick from goalkeeper to defender and they never lost possession. Passing beautifully from boy to boy, short and precise like Joe had told them to, they worked their way down the field as a neatly choreographed flight unit. The ball landed at Patrick's feet. He tapped it from left to right, right to left, tipped the ball past a defender, ran around him to collect it and hoofed it past the keeper. It was a lovely goal. Not one you'd expect from a thirteen-year-old. The mouths of the crowd made O's in astonishment. The whistle blew and the boys jumped on Patrick. He could feel the grass on his cheek. It smelt good. He whooped. But when he was dragged back up to his feet he noticed a shift in the atmosphere. There was an edge to it now and an object whizzed past his ear. Things were being thrown. It was so dumb. He laughed. They would have to make a run for it. But as he reached to shake hands with Killian's captain, something struck him on the head. It was a bottle. It didn't shatter but it stunned him. He touched the spot. In the distance he could see the Africans filing out. There was an urgency to their step.

Saskia was signalling to him wildly and he moved towards her. He started to run and that's when he heard the shout. It came from the sidelines, as precise and as clear as though through a megaphone.

"*Dirty nigger!*" said the shout. And then, "*Go home!*"

Patrick stopped dead. The ref blew the whistle but the shouting continued. It turned into a chant. Saskia hurried the others off the pitch and into the bus. More bottle missiles sailed through the air. Joe yelled at him but Patrick wouldn't move. He seemed utterly mesmerised by the chant as though it were some mystical harmony. Joe ducked and belted into the centre of the pitch to haul him away but as he reached Patrick a man approached with a smirk on his face. Joe recognised him and turned away. The man put his hand firmly on Joe's shoulder and spun him around.

"I remember you," he said. "So this is where you've been hiding. Still hanging out with little boys, Joe Delaney. Don't worry, I won't breathe a word to a soul."

The drive home was hushed. No one knew what to say. It was a horrible situation. The silver cup sat between them but it was tarnished now.

Back in the square, Patrick got out of the bus. He went straight to Emma's. She knew there was something wrong. They walked wordlessly to the walled garden and sat under the tree. Patrick told her what had happened, how the words had stabbed like a knife, and she listened. He plucked angrily at the grass as he spoke; Emma stayed quiet. When he finished, they sat there just like that. She moved closer.

"There will be lots more where that came from," she said.

"Why?"

"That's the why. That's the way the world seems to work now."

"Great answer."

"There is no answer. These people don't care about you. If you

212

were fat, they'd call you fatso. You're black, so they call you nigger."

He shrugged. "Nigger, go home. That's what they were shouting. But I am home. This is my home," he said angrily. "I was born here. I want to play for Ireland, for fuck's sake."

"I know that, Patrick," Emma said. "But if you do you will have to toughen up. This is just the start of it. The higher you go, the worse it's going to get. Secondary school won't be a walk in the park either."

"You think so?"

"I know so. That's the price you pay."

"For wanting to play football?"

"For putting yourself out there and wanting to be the best."

"How did you get to be so mammyish?"

"My parents broke up so I grew up before my time," she recited and smiled. "That's what the counsellor told me anyway."

He put his head on her shoulder, she put her arm around him and they sat there, just so, until the door opened and Mrs Fox was there standing before them. She looked horrified, as though she'd caught them doing something vile and she gave Patrick such a look of disgust it scared him.

Emma was marched home and he was left alone, wondering what he'd done wrong.

# Chapter 31

By putting on a brave face, Patrick gave the appearance of a quick recovery. He knew if he showed any hint of trauma, his mother would be on his case with a banning order. He was already in enough trouble with his exam results as it was and it would work as a final excuse. But the truth was the incident at the match had affected him. He could not get the image of the flying bottle out of his head and how he'd made a lucky escape because so many things could have gone wrong. The bottle could have shattered and split his head open, cut his eye or worst of all, a bit lower and it could have severed a ligament in his leg. Then that would be it, no more football. Without a fully functioning pair of legs with all the ligaments, tendons and muscles in perfect working order, you were done for. And the realisation of just how thin the line between making it in the game and having to leave it behind forever kept him awake. Not making it was not an option. He prayed, bargained and begged for a scout to appear so he could be magicked away to a safe place where there were no flying bottles and security was paid for and tight.

The others were equally shaken by the bottle-throwing incident. Days afterwards, Patrick caught Nuala crying at the sink.

"What's wrong?" he asked.

"Onions," she said and she dabbed her eyes with her apron.

He stood next to her. He was taller than her now.

"It doesn't bother me, what they say," he said. "Sticks and stones, I don't even hear them when they call me the N word or a 'jungle boy'." He smiled when he said this. It sounded stupid, harmless, in the safety of Nuala's kitchen.

"Well, I hear them," Nuala said and her voice wobbled. She leaned over the sink and tears fell into the dirty dishes. "You're my precious boy."

He put his head on her shoulder. "I'm grown up. I can handle it," he said.

"I know you can, love. It's just that I can't."

With his mother, it was different. She was harder. She didn't stand crying into the dirty dishes. She stiffened with rage. She asked him to stop playing football. He shook his head. Her anger over the episode forced her to do something she had deliberately avoided since coming to Ireland – she went and sought out other immigrants. Tessa needed to be in the company of people who knew exactly what she was going through. She joined a local support group where she met other Africans, some eastern Europeans and several Muslims from war-torn everywhere.

Fiona Fox used it as another excuse to keep Emma and Patrick apart. She expressed concern for her daughter's safety. Emma could see right through her.

"Staying away from Patrick would make me as bad as the scumbags on the sidelines," she said. "Anyway, I wasn't even at the match. You said I had to tidy my room, remember?"

Her mother didn't like her using the word *scumbags*. She also didn't like her tone, and said so.

Emma shrugged. "Maybe you should talk to Dad about it all, see what he thinks about the danger of being with Patrick," she suggested innocently, knowing her mother wouldn't do anything of the sort.

Richard Watts wrote a report on the match and made a point of condemning the incident and its racial overtones. Nuala was pleased he'd brought the issue to people's attention but Joe was sceptical of the journalist's motives. In the midst of the chaos his picture had been snapped without his realising. Seeing his face in print, fuzzy though it was, spooked him so badly he hardly left his room for a week and, over the summer break, he regressed alarmingly. He told them he would not be returning as coach.

Up until that point, apart from wearing his silver cross during matches, Patrick hadn't been a superstitious player. Superstition normally set in at professional level, when there was more to lose. Still, there was no harm in getting an early start. Anything that might ward off flying bottles was good and, if Joe really wasn't coming back, they would need all the luck they could get.

He found an old pair of his underpants which Nuala now used as a polishing cloth and decided they would be his lucky underpants, he swopped the laces from his new football boots for the ones from his old boots and he dug out an ancient pair of smelly shin pads which had once absorbed the impact of a particularly enormous defender. Patrick also decided he would say a prayer to the picture of the Sacred Heart before every match as well as bless himself at the holy water font every morning.

He told Nuala who said confusing luck and religion was blasphemous. He pretended not to hear her. Instead he went outside to practise headers where he was cornered by his mother.

She was on her knees at the vegetable patch. It ran along the back wall and she kept it perfectly neat with everything carefully labelled: lettuce, rocket, radishes, potatoes, courgettes, pumpkins and cabbage. She'd even had the door in the back wall reinstated so that seeds, compost and fertiliser no longer needed to be dragged through the house. Nuala said Tessa's green fingers saved them a fortune.

When she saw him, she called to him in Swahili. This was not a good start. Swahili was their secret language. His mother used it when she wanted absolutely no one else ear-wigging.

He stood beside her and tapped the ball from foot to foot.

"Stop that!" she ordered in Swahili and he stopped tapping.

She pointed to a spot and he sat down on the grass beside her. She picked at a weed.

"So, soon a new season," she said, and she didn't sound very happy about that. "And a new school in September. You were scholarship potential but of course you frittered all that away. Your teacher said you spent the whole year daydreaming about football.

That is about to end, I won't tolerate it," she said and she started stabbing the soil with the trowel. "Do you know what else he said, your teacher? He said your ability to write a formal letter is remarkable. He described your turn of phrase as 'sophisticated'." Tessa shrugged. "This does not impress me. Who writes letters any more? I want to hear about sums and spellings."

"Joe says I have a football brain," Patrick muttered. But that was the wrong thing to say.

His mother's eyes narrowed and she spoke very slowly in case he missed anything. He had heard it all before but it always had the same effect: a hard fist of guilt.

"Joe is not your father. I am your mother and you will listen to me. You only have a football brain because football is the only thing you put into it. You also have a brain for essays, long division and the mountain ranges of France."

"How do you know?"

"I know because you are my son."

"But maybe I'm more like my father, like when it comes to schoolwork."

His mother savaged a thistle. Patrick plucked at the grass. He knew he was walking on thin ice. She left down the trowel and spoke through gritted teeth.

"When your father was called up to do his duty, he trusted me to make the right decisions for you and that is why I came to Ireland. He wanted the best for you. He knew that going to school in the Congo would always be a struggle. That trying to make ends meet would come first. Patrick, you may be the image of your father, but he did not want you to end up like him. He never wanted you to be a soldier."

She downed the trowel, shifted her weight off her knees and sat, pulling her knees into her chest.

"It was difficult moving here, away from my home, so you would have opportunities. I arrived with nothing. I stayed in a boarding house with dozens of others, waiting, hoping, praying that some person somewhere in a grey building at a computer would find it in his heart to grant us refugee status and not turn us away."

Patrick had heard the "person in a grey building at a computer" speech many times before but not the bit about him being the image of his father who didn't want his child to end up like him. That was new and it was rare for his mother to mention his father at all any more.

"But all fathers like their sons to be good at football," he reasoned.

"Yes, they do, but not if they're thickos who can't recite their twelve times tables!" his mother replied viciously. "This dream of yours to play for Innskeep or whoever, that's fine. It's good to have a dream, but it is just that, a dream. You cannot sacrifice everything else for it, because it just might not work out."

"I just want him to be proud of me," Patrick said.

"Then do well in school," she said wearily.

This was all very well but how could his father be proud of him if he didn't know where to find him? His mother didn't understand that school wouldn't get him anywhere. He'd be just the same as everyone else, blending into the background. Football was his ticket. His shoulders slumped.

"Patrick?"

"Yes."

"How about wanting your mother to be proud of you? You are a very good footballer and I think this is a good thing but school is far more important to me. Primary school is over – this year is the real thing. You have a brain: now use it, please."

She picked up the trowel again and pointed it at him.

"Here's the deal, if you don't, football will be banned *forever*. Am I making myself clear?"

"Yes."

"Yes, what?"

"Yes, Mam."

Tessa pulled herself up.

"Patrick?"

"Yes, Mam."

"You'll be doing some extra tuition for the rest of the summer."

"Oh, with whom?"

"With me. Go inside now and take out your English book. I'll be in shortly."

Patrick put his football under his arm and went inside with a leaden heart. In the drawing room, he placed the ball under his chair and took out his English book, opening it to "A Famine Scene" by Walter Macken.

His mother came in after a while and spent some time discussing Walter Macken and the Great Famine with him. Then she left him alone, with instructions to continue reading, while she helped Nuala in the kitchen.

As he read, he tapped the ball from foot to foot, left right, left right, left right, until he did not notice he was doing it any more. It would become the norm for all his hours of homework. He would not realise until years later that his mother's insistence on schoolwork over football would be partly responsible for the control of the ball he was to become famous for. Had he realised it then, he might have gone to her and thanked her instead of hating her for not believing in him.

Later, when it was time for bed, he went looking for her so he could say goodnight but she was already in bed and her door was locked. She was pretending to be asleep but he could hear her crying softly under the covers. The guilt was overpowering.

He sat on the stairs until it was dark and then he went down to Nuala. When she saw him, she switched off the telly.

"What's up?" she asked.

"Nothing."

"Tell me another one."

"How do you know?"

"I always do."

"That's a bit scary."

"It will be a lot scarier when you turn fourteen," she smiled and she put on the kettle.

"It's Mam," Patrick said and he felt bad talking about her in her absence. She had warned him about blabber-mouthing.

"Yes," Nuala said gently.

Patrick swallowed and chewed his lip.

The kettle boiled and clicked off.

"She's crying. What does she cry about?"

Nuala got up to make tea. She stirred the tea-leaves in the pot, poured two cups and sat down again.

"Honestly? I don't know, Patrick. Your mother is like Joe in many ways. They are both trying to deal with things that happened a long time ago, painful things. Sometimes the thought of letting go of the past is so painful people choose to hold onto it."

"That doesn't make any sense."

Nuala shrugged. "Not to you and me it doesn't but it seems to be the way it works. Your mother lost her whole family to disease and her home too. It takes years to come to terms with things like that, if not a lifetime."

Patrick looked up and studied her over his mug of tea.

"I like that you don't treat me like a child. You tell me things, not like Mam."

Nuala smiled and topped up his cup.

"You always seemed to be able for the truth," she said affectionately.

"And what did Joe lose to have him jumping out of his skin and acting all weird and fidgety all the time?" he asked.

Nuala sighed. "His wife died and his son and daughter moved away."

"Why did they do that?"

"He doesn't talk about it, Patrick. I've always found that people tell you things when they're ready, not a second before. If you try and force their hand they keep things secret forever."

"Secrets are stupid," Patrick said and he realised he sounded just like a child as he finished his tea. He got up, rinsed his mug and reached down to kiss Nuala goodnight.

He paused at the door and turned.

"Did she ever tell you that I'm the image of my father?"

"She didn't," Nuala said with a smile.

"Is it a good thing, do you think?"

"I'd say so, pet – why?"

"It's just she never talks about him and she did this evening and I wondered if that's what was making her cry."

He shrugged and closed the door and Nuala was glad, because she had no answer for that.


The next morning Nuala found Tessa in the garden tackling a cluster of weeds with vigour.

"You're up bright and early," Nuala said and she handed her a mug of tea.

Nuala sat on the grass.

"You'll get wet," Tessa said.

"I'll dry off," Nuala replied.

Tessa looked up and squinted in the sun. She sensed Nuala was on a mission.

"You're on a mission," she said and her face closed over.

Before Tessa shut down completely, Nuala came straight out with what she wanted to say.

"I've never pushed you for answers, Tessa. I know you have your own way of dealing with things but Patrick asked me last night why you sometimes cry. I thought it was important you know."

Tessa swallowed and her lip quivered and for two seconds her face was raw, youthful and open. Then she put down her mug and started attacking the weeds again. Her expression tightened.

"I'm always here for you, Tessa, you know that," Nuala said. "When you told me you wanted no more secrets I made you a promise and I've stuck to it. I cannot recommend it highly enough. It sets you free."

Tessa stopped weeding. Without looking up, she spoke. Her voice was steady but steely.

"Nuala, you're a good woman, I'm very fond of you, so I'd hate you to take this the wrong way. But your cut-and-dried psychology doesn't provide all the answers for the enormity of third-world problems or war zones or indeed anything of what I've had to go through."

Nuala nodded and was calm in her response. "I understand that, Tessa, completely, but your son lives in Ireland, not in the Congo, and your past is not his to deal with."

Tessa sat perfectly still.

"You're right, of course," she said. "I carry that, all alone."

"You don't have to."

"Really, and what platitudes would you have for brutality? That everything happens for a reason?" Tessa laughed bitterly.

"I don't know what you mean," Nuala said.

Tessa pointed the trowel at her.

"My family did not die of cholera, Nuala. They died violently, for no other reason except they were in the wrong place at the wrong time. I survived, I escaped and I must live with that. Now, as you pointed out, I have my own way of dealing with things, and I am trying to do just that, so I would ask that you just let me get on with it. Some day I will feel strong enough to talk to you about it but not now, not today."

For a while Nuala sat in a semi-dazed state then she got to her feet. She put her hand on Tessa's shoulder and squeezed it before going back inside.

# Chapter 32

The next season was different. Patrick could tell straight away. Up until then the team had been lucky. Now came the test. It felt like the first rung in the long ladder to professional football and the real deal. The boys all wore the same expression he did, the one he saw in the mirror every morning before school and at night when he brushed his teeth: steely determination and eyes that flashed with hopes of glory.

In their first match of the season, they were trounced so brutally by Mel's that the opposition's supporters actually laughed from the sidelines.

Saskia was on her own; no Joe. Mel's were grown-up, assured and comfortable on the pitch. They kept their positions, their defence looked impenetrable and they took advantage of sloppy play and mistakes to score goals. Next to them, Lavender Square looked like a fast-forwarded comedy show: ten men chasing one ball. Saskia couldn't understand it. They were a good team, an interesting mix of talent and personality, and they had a regular eleven with some to spare. They'd grown into the game together and were comfortable around each other. There was a solid back four, the keeper was lanky and saved goals with ninja stealth, the midfielders were grafters particularly the Polish boys, Luke Lamerski and Kristian Kubovy. Tot wasn't bad on the right, as long as he didn't lose his temper. Up front there was Josh Reynolds, who was generally considered an imaginative player, and then there was Patrick. Joe had always thought he had something. Saskia could see that but, for her, what set him apart was courage. Patrick Kimba was brave and not afraid to take chances. The boy had guts.

But now, it was as if they'd all forgotten everything they'd been taught and they were eight-year-olds all over again. Afterwards they were quiet. Defeat stung and the humiliation of being laughed at rang in their ears. They were simply not used to losing and they didn't like it. Saskia scavenged for words of encouragement but could find none. Joe would have known what to say.

Joe continued to fail to show for training; Saskia took them instead and Tom helped. He said she was good, excellent in fact. Her read of a game was impeccable and she spoke football language with ease, but Joe's absence unsettled the team. They were used to the Gaffer and missed his shouting and his insults. Saskia could raise her voice impressively but was no match for Joe when it came to telling Tot to get up off his fat backside or the goalkeeper to stop handling the ball like a girl. In their second match, they were thoroughly hammered once more and in their third too. Suddenly goals were harder to come by, keeping possession was sometimes impossible and defences were more difficult to break down. Every match was like stepping up to a force, one that was fearless, unafraid and smug, more comfortable in a kit than in its skin. Supporters were hardcore. They spoke football and only understood people who spoke football back. Fathers with their own hopes and dreams roared from the sidelines for their sons who'd been born into and grown up in households and neighbourhoods steeped in football for so long it was an essential part of them. It was as far removed from mollycoddled middle-class suburbia as you could get. Every boy who pulled on his shin pads and socks and laced up for a match knew that hard work was the only way to getting to where you wanted to be. That illusions of grandeur on a muddy bumpy football pitch, all sweat and snot and spit and blood, would never get you to Old Trafford. It was graft not notions that would get you there.

They were up against clubs that had been established for years:

Kevin's, St. Joseph's, Crumlin, St. Francis and Lourdes. Clubs with whole communities behind them that were used to crowds and having the corners knocked off them by senior players and coaches and managers and brothers who'd been around the block more than once and knew all about the harsh reality of the world of football. Lavender Square's team was a babe in the woods in comparison and there was an edge to some of the crowds that wasn't altogether pleasant.

The next few games were no better and Saskia knew they'd lost their confidence.

She went to see Joe.

"They've lost their confidence," she told him, "and they think you've lost confidence in them."

"A win will get it back."

Saskia sat back in her chair. He looked exhausted.

"What is it, Joe? Where is this paranoia coming from? Would it help to see someone?"

"A shrink?"

She shrugged.

"Don't be daft. I know exactly what's wrong with me. I just don't like crowds."

"Have you ever thought you might have agoraphobia?"

"What now?" he spluttered.

"Joe, when you lived in the flat across the way, you never left the house."

"I had my reasons."

Saskia asked Nuala what she thought. Nuala was protective.

"It's just one of his spells, he'll get over it."

"But what if he needs psychiatric help?"

"Isn't that a little dramatic?"

"No, Nuala. The man is falling apart."

Nuala sat down and looked thoughtful. "I found his daughter's email address once on the back of an old envelope when I was rooting around. Maybe I should try and get in touch with her."

Lavender Square continued to lose badly. After a loss to Stella Maris and another silent drive home, Patrick kicked his way through the house and stayed out back juggling the ball until it grew dark: left foot, right foot, knee, knee, chest, right foot, left foot. There were sirens in the city and streaks of moonlight in the sky and he could just about make out the ball. But he could sense it, feel it. He kicked the ball high up towards the moon and tears of fury stung his eyes.

For the first time since his visit to Mr Singh's surgery, he doubted himself. He could feel his future slipping away and he raged against it. He kicked the ball in frustration against the back wall of the house, cursing his passing, heading, timing and his teammates. All dreams of victory were being washed down the drain. He had to win and he had to make it work. There was no other option. But they weren't winning, not even close. They were going nowhere and there was a reason for it. He slammed the ball against the wall, a bird stirred in a tree and then Patrick realised exactly where the blame lay.

Joe sat in his room and drank a beer. His room was out of bounds to the cleaning roster and therefore messier than the rest of the house. It was also filled with football paraphernalia: old *Roy of the Rovers* annuals, framed team photographs, sticker albums, scrapbooks, medals, books, signed autobiographies, jerseys and footballs. The news flickered on the telly. Some president was speaking out against some racist incident. Joe cleared a space on the couch and Patrick sat down, tapping his football from foot to foot. The windows were open, a moth fluttered in the lamplight. The TV's volume was low, muffled and urgent.

"You want us to lose, don't you?" Patrick said without taking his eyes off the screen. His tone was angry.

"What are you on about, yeh little bollocks?" Joe spluttered. "Haven't I been out breaking my neck training you since you hunted me down as an eight-year-old? I've been under the weather of late. That's all."

Patrick tapped the ball faster and then stopped. He turned to look at Joe.

"What are you so scared of?" he asked and he started tapping again, left right, right left, *doof, doof, doof*. "We need you on the sidelines giving us direction and instructions. We're losing our matches. Don't you care?"

"You're in a different league altogether. Maybe you're just not good enough. Maybe that's why you're not winning games," Joe said. He drained his beer and then scrunched up the can.

"Bullshit."

"Don't use language like that or your mother will go mad."

"I'm angry."

"Well, I'll be angry in a minute if you don't show some respect."

"*You're the Gaffer*," Patrick whispered ferociously. "*You used to act like one.*"

"Haven't you got Saskia?"

"Saskia's brilliant. She knows every single thing about football but she is not a player, not like you used to be. She does not have the feel of the game. Why are you acting like a big chicken-shit hiding away in your room?"

Joe's face turned purple with rage. "Where did you learn to speak like that? I'll murder you, you little shitehawk!"

"*I'll murder you back, you old shitehawk!*" Patrick hissed and he looked so serious and determined that Joe laughed and the bubble of anger dissipated.

Joe switched off the telly. He folded his arms across his stomach and looked thoughtful.

"Fuck it," he said. "I'm scared."

"So what? So am I. All the time. What have you got to be scared of?"

"I feel people watching me."

"They might be. You're a good coach."

"I don't like people watching me, talking about me."

"Neither does Jacques Biet. He just pretends they're not there."

"How the fuck would you know what Jacques Biet thinks?" Joe said.

"I know plenty," Patrick said sullenly.

Joe opened another beer.

"You drink more than Brian Clough ever did," Patrick grumbled.

"I do in my hole."

They looked at each other.

"I used to be a very different man," Joe said softly. "Then

227

something happened and it changed everything. I became scared of people so I stayed inside. Once you do that for a while it's difficult to go outside again. It kind of creeps up on you."

"But you've been fine for the last few years," Patrick pleaded.

"I've a bad feeling about something," Joe added. "I'm afraid of being recognised and meeting someone from my past. Things happened a long time ago that are best not spoken about."

"Things like what? Like those horrible notes you used to write?" Patrick said smartly. "I know it was you."

"I apologised for that," Joe said and he looked at the ground, embarrassed.

"Not to my mam. She still doesn't know it was you."

Joe looked at the boy and wondered if he was trying to cut some sort of a deal.

"Are you trying to cut some sort of a deal? This is the real world, you know, not some class of a spy film where everyone blackmails everyone else."

"You made a promise to train me and now you're chickening out. I don't care about the things you've done before. I just want to win. I *have* to win," he said.

He got up and stood at the door.

Joe washed down a huge surge of guilt with a swig of beer.

"You may have a bad feeling now," Patrick said, "but it will be a hell of a lot worse if we lose again on Saturday. We need you there. We can't afford to lose another match. If we do we can kiss the League goodbye."

He closed the door and went back outside where he practised until it was bedtime.

Joe sat in his room with the light switched off, mulling over what Patrick had said. He was an astute boy. One day he could make a fine captain on a great side and he owed it to him to help him get there even if it meant facing up to things he did not want to, even if it meant the death of him. He needed to ignore the foreboding that nagged him. The boy was right. He had made a promise. He put his tracksuit into the wash. Then he took out his emergency bottle of whiskey from wardrobe and went in search of Nuala. He knew he would not be able to cope unless he talked to someone.

They sat up until the small hours. At first she looked at him suspiciously; he was used to this. She asked questions, quizzed him inside and out and then she got upset. Joe did not. He was taciturn. He poured them several whiskeys. They talked until the bottle was nearly drained and Nuala promised to keep what he had told her secret, although she couldn't understand the need for secrecy if he hadn't done anything wrong. He told her that wasn't the issue – the issue was that most people believed there was no smoke without fire. That was the way the world worked. Nuala said that was most unfair. Joe said that was the way the world worked too.

Joe's return to the club made a difference. Their teamwork improved. They talked to each other, called for the ball, encouraged each other and trusted each other. During every session Joe drummed the basics into them: keep it simple, keep the ball and play it forward, nice simple passes, score and win the ball back. He told them the game was about graft, not glory-hunting or fancy tricks or bicycle kicks, that it was about running your bollocks off, chasing the ball down and getting it back – organisation and unity, not running around like headless chickens.

They grew up and into the game and a new energy clicked into gear, an unspoken language, a taut connection and a rhythm. They wanted to win and they knew they could. When they were under pressure, they piled on the pressure and turned the flow of a game, and their season turned, slowly at first, but then they got better and then they started winning.

Their winning streak attracted racist remarks from the sidelines. Most of them were harmless enough, not really anything that could be penalised. It was hoped ignoring the matter would make it go away.

But football matches got uglier and it became a problem. Supporters could be ferocious. Tot was sent off more than once for protecting his friend. He once boxed a talented centre-half square in the nose because his father kept shouting "Rag Head!" at Patrick. The father threatened to sue. The referee told him that bigoted remarks were not looked upon kindly in courts. He withdrew his complaint. Lavender Square had a point deducted. Patrick told Tot he could fight his own battles.

"He called you 'Rag Head'," Tot said and his face glistened at the unfairness of it all.

"It doesn't matter."

"But you're not even fucking Muslim!"

"So what? Those guys who yell that stuff think we're all the same."

Clubs were quick to voice their outrage over racist slurs. Red cards, point deductions, fines, suspensions and expulsions helped to curb the problem but it didn't go away. Tessa and Nuala stopped attending matches. Tessa could not bear it and Nuala said something broke inside her every time Patrick was singled out. For Joe the whole unpleasant matter signified doom and the black cloud gathered mass and refused to shift. For the first time in a long time, he was afraid for someone other than himself; he was afraid for the young boy.

The night before Patrick started secondary school he took him for a drive up into the Dublin Mountains. The car drove smoothly, the interior smelt of leather and the dashboard was a pleasing vintage of dials and buttons and lights. It was sparkling clean.

"You love this car?" Patrick said.

"I do."

They parked and got out and sat on the bonnet. The mountain air smelt of heather.

Joe sighed with pleasure.

"My wife and I used to come for drives up here."

"Do you miss her?"

"I do."

"The car makes you feel close to her."

"Gor, I suppose it does, son."

They sat there, just like that, in the cool mountain air. Beneath them, the city was a pool of twinkling lights.

"How do you feel about tomorrow?" Joe asked.

"Grand."

Joe took off his cap and scratched his head.

"Teenagers can be awful cruel to anyone who's a bit different."

"I know well."

"Even if you're scared, let on you're not."

Patrick shrugged. "I always do."

"I know you do, son, I just thought I'd say it again, just in case. Bullies have a tendency to clear off when they see they're not getting anywhere."

# Chapter 33

Secondary school was like stepping onto a battlefield without being informed which side you were fighting for. At first everyone looked the same and seemed the same, but after a few short weeks the teenage classifications emerged.

The bratz were pretty girls who wore lip gloss. The boggers were the boys who played Gaelic football and hurling and had spitting competitions. The tools played rugby and gave each other wedgies – they were like the bratz except boys. The boogers came from wealthy south-side suburbs, ate quinoa and wore organic cotton. They earned their pocket money by carrying their parents' empty wine bottles to the bottle bank. The fatsas were fat kids who were always good for a snack. The heads wore headphones and black eyeliner and the nerds were just plain old-fashioned nerds.

The unclassified floated. They were made up of an assortment of immigrants, weirdos with strange ticks and the super-brainy.

Emma, Tot and Patrick had each other. Patrick and Tot joined the soccer team and, for a while, Patrick's talent on the pitch meant that the two black marks against him – the fact that he shared a house with Nuala Murphy, a teacher widely feared, and that he was fluent in French and therefore a complete lick-arse – were handicaps which could be overlooked. This reprieve did not last long, however. A group of second-year boys who beat up younger kids after school and filmed it on their phones started to pick on him. The ringleader was a blonde dude called "Spider". The web tattoo on this neck was just visible above his shirt collar and he smoked in a way that suggested it was some great talent. He had filled out since Patrick last encountered him, highlighted his hair and given himself a nickname, but Chad with the too-close eyes was just the same as he'd been in primary school. He still had it in for Patrick, only this time Patrick wasn't scared of him. He was bigger than him for a start. He refused to call him Spider and was the only person in the school (apart from the teachers) who called him Chad. In hindsight, this was a mistake. There was something unhinged about the boy whose father dropped him to school in his Jaguar and made a big show of beeping the horn as he drove away. Tot told Patrick that he'd heard Spider's mother had run off with a black man.

"Oh right, so I'm to blame for that, am I?" Patrick said. "Like voodooing me from the sidelines will bring her back?"

"I dunno, I'm only sayin'." Tot shrugged. "It was some Nigerian lad."

"With a big mickey, I suppose."

"Well, I didn't get to check," Tot said and they both laughed at this long and hard.

Nuala said Spider's father was some big-shot developer and a crook to boot and that Spider was destined to follow in his footsteps. His mother had done the sensible thing and upped and left when the coast was clear and the bank account balanced. Patrick didn't care about any of that. What he did care about was the way Spider kept hanging around. He was a creep. He fancied Emma and let her know through one of his gang who said "Spider wants to go with you".

"Why would I go with someone who can't even ask me himself?" she said.

Spider took this response as encouragement and tried to approach her himself but Patrick always seemed to be in the picture. When Emma couldn't shake him off politely, she told him she wasn't interested. Other kids overheard and laughed. Patrick was one of them. Spider didn't like this and got nasty. He took it out on Patrick. He began shoving him in the corridors and making snide racist remarks in his presence. He referred to Joe's Austin Cambridge as "the jiloppy" and to Joe as "the kiddy-fiddler". Emma said it was jealousy. He should ignore him.

Patrick tried to and discovered the secret to secondary school was juggling. Between homework and his mother forever breathing down his neck about essays and grammar, writing letters to Barbury, Surrey, grief from the sidelines, raging hormones and the standard of football they needed to play to stay up as League contenders, he felt like a circus dog. Trying to ignore Spider and his stupid gang was just another thing to add to the list.

But ignoring him didn't seem to work. Spider had it in for him now and that was that. He and his friends started showing up at matches. It was unnerving. They didn't taunt. They just watched silently and it was sinister. It was difficult to know what they were up to. Someone said they had some sort of betting thing going.

The racist slights at matches didn't go away either but Patrick learned to deal with them by absorbing himself in the game. He tuned out anything he didn't need. He could hear his teammates calling for the ball, Joe's instructions and the referee's whistle. Somewhere in his subconscious he could hear the Africans' low-drone hum but that was it. The remarks did not reach him so they did not get to him but they did bother other people.

Richard Watts took up the baton on the racist element of the game and wrote about it in his articles. He asked Joe for an interview and, when Joe refused again, he asked Saskia. He wanted to know more about the team to get a more personal insight. He suggested they meet in a city-centre hotel. She was surprised but agreed. Football interviews were usually less formal: outside dressing rooms, in draughty corridors, on the sidelines or between two cars in the car park. Because it was in a hotel, she made an effort. That is, she cast off her tracksuit and wore a pair of jeans.

The hotel was minimalist, male, with its greys and varying tones of white. Outside the city bustled with Friday-night expectation and sodium-yellow oozed into the foyer making patterns on the plain carpet.

Richard Watts was friendlier in person; he was also better looking than she remembered. He offered her a cocktail; she asked for a glass of wine. She talked about her love of football and Richard Watts was charmed. They discussed the Premier League, batting their knowledge and analysis back and forth until she realised they'd finished their drinks. He offered her another and told her she reminded him of Birmingham's Managing Director, Karen Brady, a real woman who knew her football inside and out without feeling the need to throw her femininity to the wolves. Saskia's eyes sparkled and she switched to talking about her young team and went through the season in detail, wondering if Richard Watts was interested or bored to death.

"You have a soft spot for him, Patrick Kimba?" the journalist said when she eventually stopped talking.

"He's like a little brother."

"Joe Delaney sounds like an interesting man."

"He's an exceptional coach. I would think he's like Bill Shankly, smart, or Brian Clough, rough around the edges but brilliant."

"Does he swear as much as Mr Clough did?"

"No. But I think Clough had a lot more to swear about," she said with a smile.

He smiled back.

When they finished up they walked to the foyer and talked about the next match. They shook hands. He looked at his shoes.

"Would you go out with me sometime?" he asked.

"Really?" Saskia thought she'd misheard him but he smiled at her, waiting for an answer. "Why on earth would you want to go out with me?"

"Are you joking me? You've got the best voice since Elkie Brooks and you can talk about football without asking for the offside rule to be explained. You're the hottest date in town."

Saskia's heart turned and her whole body gravitated towards the compliment. She realised she'd been lonely. Perhaps her life was about to change direction.

She told Joe about the date. Joe thought it sounded fishy. Although used to Joe's gruffness, she was upset.

"And why is that? Because I look like the back of a bus and the likes of Richard Watts wouldn't be caught dead with me?'

"Jesus, love, don't you know I think you're a topper? It's just he's a tabloid journalist. What the hell is he interested in a kids' team for?"

"He has an angle."

"Don't they all?"

"His angle is racism."

Joe wasn't convinced. Richard Watts worried him. He still hadn't forgiven him for putting his photo in the paper.

Disheartened, Saskia decided to keep the date with Richard Watts to herself but then let it slip to Emma by accident that evening when she was over.

Emma was intrigued by the contents of Saskia's chest of drawers and sometimes Saskia let her look through her things. The younger girl liked the Balinese jewellery box in particular.

"When are you going to get to use all this stuff?" she asked.

"If I ever get married," Saskia told her. "The bottom drawer is a country thing, a tradition."

"Who would you like to marry?"

"Someone nice."

"I think Tom's nice," Emma said.

"He is, and he's got a girlfriend. Several of them in fact, and they're all very pretty and model-like." Saskia was firm.

"I think Tom likes you – he just doesn't know it yet."

"You're mad in the head. Believe me, I am not Tom's type."

"Well, I don't like his type," Emma said with disapproval. "None of them eat cake."

"Yeah, well, I eat plenty of cake and guess what – I'm single."

"Well, I think you're pretty," Emma said, "and cool too. You should wear your hair down. It's gone fair in the sun."

"I'm fat."

"No, you used to be. It's just your clothes are wrong." Emma wasn't quite sure what that meant but it was something she'd heard on a TV makeover show.

She insisted they go shopping.

"You can't go on a date in your tracksuit – or those old jeans."

"I know that," Saskia said, hurt. "I'm not dumb."

She agreed to go shopping anyway. It turned out Emma had a good eye and was alarmingly persuasive. She was also very comfortable with the concept of the credit card. After an exhaustive session of clothes-shopping, she convinced Saskia to get cooler glasses. The ones she had were scratched and bent out of shape from running up and down a pitch in every weather. Then she brought her to the only make-up counter where the shop assistant's face wasn't orange. The make-up girl was patient in demonstrating how the right eye make-up could transform her and Saskia discovered that with money (or a maxed-out credit card) anyone could look semi-decent.

For their first date, Richard took her to a tapas bar. Everything Saskia wore was new: jeans, high-heeled sandals, wraparound top, glasses, even her knickers, and Emma had bossed her into wearing her hair down. She felt ridiculous, like a fake and certainly too glamorous to be any use on a pitch.

But Richard was visibly impressed. He ordered everything on the menu and a bottle of wine that wasn't the house red. He kept stealing glances at her. The lighting was kind and the music was soft and Cuban.

He was open. He told her he was from Blackrock, from a moneyed family with a fondness for stiff traditions like sherry before dinner and marrying well. For as long as he could remember, he'd wanted to escape suburbia and become a journalist.

"My parents didn't approve of tabloid journalism until they heard how much it pays. Also, there's a certain craft to it. I enjoy it, especially now that I'm getting somewhere. One half-decent scoop and I'll be on the pig's back."

She told him she was from Galway, from a family with no money, and that for as long as she could remember she had wanted to escape too but not to serve coffee. That was never in the plan.

He laughed and asked about her name. "It's beautiful, the name of a Russian princess. Your parents had imagination."

"They were romantics once, I suppose."

"Not now?"

"No."

"That generation. They all ended up hating each other in the end."

He dragged her out to dance. He could salsa, she couldn't. It didn't matter – he led. He liked that she knew her neighbours.

Dubliners normally didn't care whether their neighbours rotted or not.

She told him it was nothing to do with being from the country, that none of them had known each other until Tessa Kimba fell ill and they were forced together to look after her son.

"We felt responsible," she explained. "He had no one else."

She told him how Joe had once been a recluse and ended up living in a lock-up.

"Had he something to hide?" Richard asked. "Was he on the run from the Mafia?"

"Not Joe," Saskia smiled.

Richard Watts smiled back.

She knew it wasn't wise to invite someone back to your place on a first date but she didn't care. It had been years since there'd been anyone worth mentioning and she trusted Richard Watts. He made her feel like she was brimming with life. She ached to kiss him, feel those lips, his stubble against her cheek, see those legs, all taut male muscle.

They went back to her flat. He admired it, he touched her face, he whispered her name and then he pulled her towards him and kissed her. He was gentle and they melted into each other. He closed his eyes and in the moonlight he was god-like, and a thousand white butterflies fluttered through her. They climbed the stairs to her bed and stripped each other slowly in the dark and he ran his hands along her body, shaping every curve. He said her name and kissed her and looked into her eyes and she was his.

# Chapter 34

The season continued and the year slipped by and Tom realised he was missing Saskia. Having a weekly pint had become part of their routine; now it was gone. She was always with Richard Watts. He sometimes watched them together in the evenings from his flat. They strolled casually and held hands, teased each other and laughed. The moonlight outlined them in a silvery magical light and they were beautiful, perfect, and their laughter chimed like bells. He watched them linger at the foot of the steps to her flat before going inside. Richard touched her face. Tom leaned forward. He wanted to steal their bubbling new-love excitement and wrap it around himself.

"Go home," Tom said aloud and he realised he did not like Richard Watts. He wasn't sure whether it was because he rode around on a dinky red moped or because of his schoolboy enthusiasm and questions and eagerness to be part of their lives.

Joe didn't like him either.

"I don't like him," he told Nuala. "I think he's sly."

"You think everyone's sly."

"He's a journalist."

"So what? He only ever writes good things about the boys."

"He seems to be camped out here from morning till night drinking our tea and dragging crowds into matches."

"Isn't he going out with Saskia? Why wouldn't he be around?"

"He's reeling us in. I'd prefer if he kept his snout out of things and out of my business. I don't need anyone raking through my past."

"Joe, Richard Watts knows nothing about you. He works for a rag of an old tabloid and reports on schoolboy matches. What harm can he do?"

But Joe was plagued by the idea that for some reason the journalist was using Saskia to get to him. The season could not be over soon enough. When it was, he was going to get away for a bit, drive away in the Austin Cambridge to the Cliffs of Moher maybe where he could breathe, feel like there was an escape. Maybe he would be able to convince Nuala to come with him.

Patrick kept his part of the deal and did his homework as diligently as he could. His teachers were pleased with the results of his Christmas tests. He also kept up his letters to Jacques Biet. He wasn't sure why. In ways, it was like a diary. It made him think about each game, examine their achievements and scrutinise their disappointments. Now, he enclosed newspaper clippings. Every night after washing his teeth, he wrote a few lines in a copybook about training or, if there had been a match, he summarised the goals. *Doyle rolled a free kick to Flanagan who took off down the right wing and crossed to Kimba who sent it home to score the only goal of the match.*

He was careful not to sound overly cocky and included summaries of the not-so-great games as well as the great games in his letters to the Frenchman, just to show he understood that football was about taking the good with the bad.

On Christmas Day they walked the beach. Spring was a different matter. It was raw-bone cold. A bitter wind came in from the Atlantic and the country assumed a white layer of permafrost. Pipes froze and burst, fans dressed like Eskimos, and when they shouted, their breath made an icy fog.

Saskia and Joe still trained the team. Although the club played their home games at Bushy Park, they still trained for the most part in the square.

Joe was tough. He roared instructions. "*Right, only when I say*

240

*'Keano says', do you do what I say, otherwise it's down and three press-ups if any of ye mess up. Do you hear me, Tot Flanagan? Keep jogging! Right, 'Keano says' hit your right foot!"*

The line would all bend to tip their right foot except Tot who tipped his left and Joe would shout at him.

*"RIGHT foot! Keano says bloody right foot! If you don't know your left from your right, we're at nothing here!"*

"Terrorist," Tot muttered. It was his favourite insult for teachers, coaches and parents.

After stretches they did ball work: dribbling, headers, ten-yard passing, one-touch passing, left foot then right, juggling, shooting and cushioning. Then they played a seven-a-side.

*"Right!"* Joe bellowed, always pacing. "I want clean play. I want you to keep passing the ball. That means you too, Patrick, by the way. Try and play a more midfield role, set up goals, give the others a chance to score. Closest defenders pull back to play keeper when threatened. And bloody talk to each other! If you don't communicate then you won't know who's behind you or what to do with the ball. Ask for the ball then move forward and pass before you're tackled. *Right, let's go!"*

As the season wore on, games became more heated. Referees, fed-up with fouls, racial run-ins, feigned injuries and screeching parents, blew their whistles and issued yellow cards and warnings to parents who got out of hand.

Sometimes after matches, fans would turn up at Lavender Square. They'd heard about the curious square and wanted to see where the team had got its name. But the private residents complained. They didn't like strangers hanging around snooping and dropping cigarette butts. Giving the walled garden to Joe Delaney and his football club had been fine when the boys were boys but now that they were older and in a League, it was different.

Several times, Tessa asked Patrick to leave the League. She'd find somewhere else for him to play. Somewhere he wouldn't have to listen to such abuse. Patrick shook his head. His grades were good so he'd be staying put. That had been the deal.

She tried Joe instead. Joe was no help.

"He has his own notions about playing for Innskeep and for Ireland," he told her.

"*Merde!* Eejitty notions," Tessa snapped.

"Well, it's not me putting the ideas into his head. I'm not quite in Innskeep's League."

"If you aren't, then who is?"

"I don't know but he's obsessed and if that's where he wants to be then he needs to stay in the League. He realises that himself so you'll have a devil of a job trying to get him out of it."

Nuala tried to allay Tessa's fears by being light-hearted.

"He is obsessed but at least it's a healthy obsession. I think football makes him feel part of something, Tessa, more Irish."

"For God's sake, he *is* Irish," Tessa said.

"I know that," she said gently, "but not everyone knows it. Joe says other coaches still ask where he's from, if he's from Nigeria."

"And what does Joe say?"

"That he's from Dublin, of course, from Lavender Square. What else would he say?"

Tessa shook her head bitterly. "What do you have to do to fit in? In this bloody country?"

"Playing football well is a good start."

Tessa wondered where that left her in the scheme of things.

Spider and his gang continued to shove, push and snicker in the corridors and also attend matches. Sometimes they followed Patrick. They kept their distance but he knew they were there just the same. They knew his route to school, where he lived and his routine. The strain took its toll. The only person he could talk to about it was Emma. Anyone else would have had the thugs reported. That's what adults did. Even cool ones like Saskia. They thought they were doing good but all it would lead to was a beating.

Emma asked if he was ever scared. He told her he often was but he let on not to be. She asked if he ever thought about running away. Sometimes he was tempted. She was too.

She removed the cover from her phone and took out the postcard and unfolded it. Worn now but still Mont-Saint-Michel, the perfect French village on a hill where there were no parents or mothers with vendettas. They studied it.

"It's good to know it's there if we need it," Patrick said and he smiled.

Emma refolded it and put it back into its hiding place.

"You keep it hidden," Patrick said.

Emma nodded. "I don't want to lose it and I like to keep it close. They're fighting over the house now as well as me."

"Great craic."

"It is. And Mum is mentioning private schools again."

"She knows what she's doing," Patrick concluded grimly. "African boys don't go to private schools unless their father is a despot."

"It won't work," Emma insisted. "You're my friend and that's that. She'll just have to get used to it."

"She might wear you down. She convinces people for a living."

"It will never happen."

"Your mother will try anything."

Emma knew it. She didn't tell Patrick that her mother was now rallying the private residents to have the club closed and the keys returned.

When Nuala was approached by the residents' committee, she was appalled and immediately guessed Fiona had something to do with it. Fiona Fox knew Patrick liked her daughter but he utterly adored football. Closing the walled garden off to the team was one sure-fire way of getting at him and ensuring Emma and Patrick saw less of each other.

She marched to the green door and knocked on it.

Fiona raised her eyebrows in greeting when she answered. They rarely spoke.

The house was cold and smelt of smoke. Fiona looked weathered, tired and embittered.

"Cup of coffee?" she said without enthusiasm.

"No, thank you, trying to stay off it."

"Everyone's going healthy these days," Fiona sighed.

She filled the kettle anyway. Nuala sat at the table and looked around the shabby kitchen and out into the garden. It was unkempt and choked in weeds.

Fiona saw her looking. "I'll get round to it. Never seems to be time for anything these days."

"How are you keeping?"

"Toing and froing with lawyers is not how I'd envisaged my life turning out."

"I hear you're trying to have the football club shut down," Nuala said. She had decided a statement would work better on Fiona Fox than a question. She studied the dark grain on the table. There were flecks of cigarette ash. She blended them into the wood and looked up.

Fiona blinked rapidly. "The residents are bothered by the rough element hanging around," she said, lighting a cigarette.

"I see," Nuala exhaled. "Naturally though, you're helping them along."

"They don't need helping along. They've minds of their own."

"Really? It wasn't the impression I got when they called to my door. Patrick is Emma's friend. Football is his life and the team still trains there. Why would you try to take it away from them?"

Fiona stabbed out her cigarette. "Spare me the teacherly lecture, Nuala," she said. They spend far too much time together to be healthy. I caught them wrapped up in each other a while back in that cursed walled garden."

"Yes, Patrick told me about that. He said it was Emma had her arm around him. It was innocent but you turned it into something with the look you gave them."

Fiona curled her lips in disgust and shivered.

Nuala laughed and stood up. "Patrick and Emma are friends. Patrick is far more interested in football than girls, believe me."

"I see, you think you're an expert now because you've a few years of rearing someone else's child under your belt. How great for the rest of us to have your expertise to hand!"

Her tone was caustic but left Nuala unperturbed.

"You always had a twisted mind, Fiona, even in school. Do you think I don't remember all the horrible things you used to say about me? I have a long memory. Why don't you give Patrick a break? He's just a boy and he's not having an easy time of it."

Nuala left then, knowing it was pointless trying to reason with the woman who'd bullied her so horribly in school.

# Chapter 35

Patrick thought it was funny that the more Mrs Fox tried to keep him away from Emma, the more he wanted to be around her. They spent every spare moment they could in the walled garden, playing on the swing or kicking around a football. Sometimes Patrick wanted to kiss her but was shy about it. They'd always been friends and it didn't seem quite right. Instead, they giggled a lot and practised the bicycle kick over and over even though Joe didn't approve of such fancy-pants moves.

The weeks passed by in a blur of drills, meals, matches and study and, despite a billion problems like the threatened closure of the walled garden, sideline swipes, Joe's nuttiness, and the likes of Spider and his stupid gang, the Lavender Square Under-14 team managed to work their way from bottom of the table, to mid, to the top.

Both the top teams needed to win and had similar records. It would be a tough game but Lavender Square had the home advantage.

Patrick was fired up and ecstatic. He believed he was on the cusp of something huge.

A week before the final he wrote to Jacques Biet. Right after he posted the letter, everything started to go wrong.

Joe's sixth sense went into sensory overdrive and his nerve-endings tuned to a high-pitched scream like tree frogs sensing the advance of a snake. He didn't sleep and Nuala found him one night dozing on the stairs. She stood over him and saw he was in a bad way. There were hollow shadows under his cheeks that she'd never noticed before. She gently shook him awake. They went downstairs and she made tea.

"After this match, I want you to walk away, Joe," Nuala said.

He rubbed his worried and wrinkled forehead. "I've got a really bad feeling about something," he said.

"You always have a bad feeling about something."

"I know."

The clock ticked and the dawn chorus started with the *tat-tat-tat* of a robin.

"My wife used to say that a robin was the spirit of someone passed," Joe said wistfully.

Nuala looked out the window. Dawn streaked across the sky.

"Do you ever think about getting in touch with your children?" she asked.

"I used to," he said and he got out of his chair.

He stopped at the door and turned to her.

"Did I ever tell you that you're a fine woman, Nuala," he said, "a real gem? Thank you for everything." He closed the door and went to bed.

Joe's bad feeling seemed to make way for a whole load of other things going wrong. It began with Patrick's lucky underpants going missing in the wash. He cross-examined Nuala who was puzzled about his distress.

"But aren't they full of holes?" she asked.

"They're lucky."

"Not with your bare backside hanging out, they wouldn't be. Can't you pick another pair?"

"It won't be the same."

A simple pair of missing underpants seemed to upset the balance of the household.

Nuala had written an email to Joe's daughter, but couldn't find her email address. Tessa caught her rooting through Joe's things.

"Did you find what you were looking for?" she asked coolly.

Nuala started. "Yes," she said.

"Do you root through all of our drawers?"

"You know I don't."

"Do I? Remember what we agreed: no secrets."

Tessa received a letter herself. It was another one from Brazzaville. The sight of the Congo Française stamp excited her; the letter not so much. It was warm and friendly but the subtext urged Tessa to stay where she was, that no matter how unwelcoming Ireland might seem at times, at least they had a home, Patrick had a school and they were safe.

Then the household's upset balance acted as catalyst for more things going wrong beyond it.

Richard, who up to that point had been the epitome of dedication, cooled and began to withdraw. He told Saskia he was busy working on a scoop but that he would definitely make the match. They'd been living in each other's pockets and the change sounded alarm bells immediately. She sensed there was something up and was unnerved.

Tessa found out before Saskia did. One of her early-morning customers, a debutante with a questionable taste for salmon-coloured silk, informed her without meaning to. She spotted Richard Watts leaving Saskia's from Nuala's drawing-room window while Tessa was pinning the seams around her ample waist. The girl made an excited call on her phone and told whoever was on the other end that she'd just seen some other girl's boyfriend snogging some chick on a doorstep in Lavender Square. The language was so convoluted Tessa had trouble deciphering it but she got the drift of the conversation. She mulled over whether she should tell Saskia. She was inclined to let others look after their own affairs but Saskia had been good to her. She decided she would tell her when she got the opportunity. But she didn't have to: providence got there before her and, by the time it did, Tessa's mind was as far from Saskia's worries as it ever could be.

Meanwhile, Tom debated whether he would go to the match or not. Richard Watts irked him immensely. He hated his over-familiarity with Patrick and with all of them, and his cheery beak which was rarely shut. He seemed to have reeled everyone in but Joe who always left the room or slipped out of the picture when

Richard was in it. It was as if he feared him in some way. Tom feared him too but in a different way. He feared being landed with him in a corner where Richard would be doing most of the talking and engaging in that tiresome habit of private-school backslapping. But much as the bollocks annoyed him, Tom knew he would go to the match. He wouldn't let Patrick down.

Tot was having difficulties too. The difficulties were with his father who had informed him that he, Tot, would be helping him out in the garage that summer. When Tot asked if this could possibly be viewed as child labour, his father went so mental Tot thought he was going to have a heart attack on the spot. Tot knew it was a device to keep him out of trouble and away from Patrick. His father didn't like the look of those older lads who were following them around. By keeping him off the streets, they'd lose the trail.

Then Emma's father sprang it on her that she would be going to the Ukraine for a fortnight's holiday with him and Valentina, and from there to Paris on a student exchange. He sold the idea with enthusiasm but Emma knew her mother had got to him somehow, and she was disappointed in him. It meant she would miss the final.

The day before she left, Fiona weakened and let her off to the café with Patrick for a final jaunt. Feeling a little reckless, they hopped on the tram and sneaked off into town instead. It pulled away silently. They spoke French and pretended to be foreigners in a strange land. They felt very grown up.

They went to a café on Grafton Street and ordered cappuccinos. They watched shoppers dash and pounce and bump and scowl.

A man was begging. There was a placard by his feet. It read: "The Property Tax Evicted Me."

Emma was in a distant dreamy mood. She hadn't left Ireland but was already feeling nostalgic.

"You remember the day Miss Hennessy taught us Morse code?" she said.

"Course," said Patrick.

Outside, people passed: women in fur coats and spray-frosted hair, skateboarders, teenagers, Goths, Rockers, Punks, Homies, Tree Huggers, Heelers, men in suits and mothers with children. Checkout girls puffed on their smoke break. There were gangs, road sweepers, couriers, gurriers and men delivering bread. A street artist stood still: a Statue of Liberty that moved when you put money in the tin by her feet. A string quartet drew a crowd.

"Just think," Patrick said, "after the summer you will speak French like someone from Paris. No more Congo slang for Emma."

He grinned and she smiled.

"My mother."

"Yesim, Miss Emma," Patrick said doing his slave-boy impression and Emma laughed so hard milk foam came out her nose.

Outside, they gave a few cents to the beggar. Patrick tucked his hands into his jeans and they walked down to Trinity and over the cobbles. It started to drizzle. A wind howled through the arches and pushed people along quickly to their destinations. They crossed the empty cricket pitch and sat on the steps of the Pavilion.

"I remember Miss Hennessy teaching us the Morse code," Patrick said. "Good thing she did too, considering how your Communion Day turned out."

"What a strange day! Do you think that when I become a serial killer I'll be excused because of my parents and their bullshit?"

"Maybe, but I wouldn't risk it. So, do you think your mother hates me more for the black thing or the football thing?"

"Both, I suppose. She'd prefer if you were a barrister's son."

"Right and how many of those do you know?"

"Too many."

They huddled together on the steps and talked easily to each other about parents and their weird ways, Innskeep and football and school.

"So are you going to keep writing those letters to Jacques Biet?" Emma asked playfully.

Patrick shrugged, embarrassed by the question.

"It can't do any harm," Emma said, sorry to have teased him.

Patrick shrugged again. "Doesn't matter anyway, I'll get there one way or the other. It's just around the corner, I can feel it."

They were quiet then and the sun cut a golden line across the cricket pitch. They watched the shaft of light. Tail-lights winked through the railings, horns beeped, a bus advertised a new type of stock cube. A gang of students crossed the grass carrying books and folders and walked towards Lincoln Place to the pub.

"Mum is going absolutely mental over this trip to the Ukraine," Emma said.

"She'll get over it."

"I'm tired of trying to keep everyone happy. I hate all of them."

"No, you don't."

"No, I do," she said, and she looked worried then. "I don't want to go away. I don't want to miss your match. I don't want to be away from you."

"There will be loads and loads of matches, way more important than this."

They watched the sun inch downwards. They looked at each other again and the air changed between them like a teenage whisper. He swallowed and his brown eyes looked into hers. He looked down at his feet and took her hand. His was warm; hers was cold.

She was scared and sad at the same time. Everything was changing.

"So many bad things have happened," she whispered.

"Lots of good things will happen too."

"Do you promise?"

"I promise."

He leaned in then and kissed her softly, right on the lips for the first time and the kiss tasted like chocolate sprinkles.

Emma left the next day and Spider and his friends tracked Patrick down. They cornered him in the lane behind the square and pinned him against the wall. Spider spoke and his voice sounded like gravel.

"Now that your little friend is gone, I just wanted a little word. About this match on Saturday, Kimba, you need to lose it – it's important."

"Forget it," Patrick said, more bravely than he felt.

"You'd better not, Kimba, or your life won't be worth living. Remember, we'll be there, watching. We always are."

# Chapter 36

On the morning of the final Patrick woke up at half five on the button. He pushed up his window. The square sat in perfect stillness and the air was so clear he could see pathways in the mountains, forest, fields and hedgerows. Not another soul awake only the birds. A single magpie fluttered up and out of a tree in the walled garden. He hoped a second would follow. It didn't. It was the first black cloud of the day.

Thoughts of the match gave him butterflies. Jude's were one of the best youth sides and everyone seemed to agree that it was a great thing to have reached the final except his mother. The few days before had been tense. Joe said it was ludicrous. Anyone would think it was the Bernabéu they were heading for and not an Under-14 match in Bushy Park. Lavender Square FC with its almost arseless kit and ramshackle HQ was a million screaming miles from Real Madrid's pristine masterpiece. But Patrick knew Joe's grumpiness was just worry. Saskia was tense too and muttered something about love troubles.

A jet passed overhead. It made him think of Emma. Patrick brushed his fingers across his lips and thought of the kiss. Sometimes he wanted to put his arm around Emma and mind her until the end of time. There was no one in the world who would understand that only Emma. He didn't like it that she wouldn't be at the match. He hadn't texted her to tell her about Spider's threat; he hadn't told anyone. If he got a beating, so be it. He wasn't about to forfeit a season's work.

He grabbed his football and went downstairs in his pyjamas. The grass was cold and wet under his bare feet. He practised his turns until Nuala tapped on the window and signalled it was time for breakfast.

Saskia woke up worried. Her jaw hurt. Lately she'd been grinding her teeth in her sleep. The possibility of Richard's waning interest worried her. She knew she could not return to a life of Valium and inventorying her bottom drawer. She would scrutinise his behaviour at the match and re-evaluate.

Nuala made a ton of sandwiches. This panicked Joe. Big preparations suggested something big was going down.

"Are you planning on selling those sandwiches or are we're making a run for it and going underground? It's not an All-Ireland hurling final, you know?"

Nuala ignored him.

Patrick cleaned his boots on a sheet of newspaper at the table and picked at surplus egg sandwiches.

Joe shook open the paper.

"Don't eat too many of those egg sandwiches," he remarked. "Otherwise you'll poison the whole lot of us with your farts."

"You're very cranky today," Patrick said.

"And you're going to quit while you're ahead if you know what's good for you," Joe barked.

"I'm only saying."

"Talk to the hand," Joe said and raised his paper higher to indicate that the conversation was over.

After lunch, Joe disappeared to his room. The house had turned into a madhouse with the doorbell ringing, Nuala shouting about sandwiches and Patrick still talking about the disappearance of his lucky underpants. There was the stomping of feet and the kitchen filled with the voices of young boys and their laughter and parents trying to shush them. He could hear Tot telling jokes and making smart remarks about Jude's.

Joe lit a cigarette and smoked out the window. His bowels rumbled. In a few hours it would be over. He would take Nuala for a spin to the mountains. The air would be cool there and they could look down over Dublin. From the mountains, the city looked manageable, like sōmething you could handle – a walk in the park.

Early afternoon, a cavalcade of cars set off for Bushy Park. Joe drove Tessa, Nuala and Patrick. Tom drove Saskia and the rest of the team followed, divided between various cars and parents. When they arrived, there was already a crowd there.

Mothers laid out rugs, kids chased one another and fathers exchanged racing tips and talked about the Premier League. The African supporters arrived; an Asian woman circled selling ice creams and bottles of Coke; parents and brothers and sisters and grannies and older footballers, younger footballers and want-to-be footballers skirted the corners of the pitch. There were deckchairs and inflatable chairs and red faces and crying babies and the air smelt of sun cream.

At half three, Joe pulled the boys into a huddle. There were giggles and shoves. They never failed to comment on the colour of their kit.

"I look like a girl," Tot said.

"Yeah, you do," teased Luke Lamerski whose Irish sense of sarcasm had really come along.

"Well, so do you!" Tot blustered back.

"Lads," said Joe, "could we move away from talk of the kit? You sound like a pack of aul' ones. Just be glad you have one. Now, when you're ready, shut up and listen."

He grappled for some words of encouragement.

"Right, lads," he said. "You know what you've got to do."

"*Play ball!*" they choroused.

"And what else?"

"*Look after your patch no matter who comes into it!*" they sang in a well-practised response.

"And what did Bill Shankly always say?"

"*If you're not sure what to do with the ball just pop it in the back of the net!*"

"No bother to ye. Now get out there and play like you did all season! Good lads."

The size of the crowd was intimidating; Jude's had a strong support base. The atmosphere sparked with expectation.

Tessa stayed close to Nuala and Tom. Saskia trailed behind looking out for Richard Watts. There was no sign of him until just before kick-off when she saw him squeeze through the crowd with a photographer. He waved to her. The whistle blew. Relief made her breathe easier.

It was warm. Spectators fanned themselves. Patrick kissed the silver cross around his neck. Lavender Square won the toss and the teams took up their positions.

Jude's came roaring out of the traps and took the lead after just nine minutes. Their approach play was slick, they were tight and they passed the ball accurately. Their back line was steely and Patrick knew they were up against it. Lavender Square were already defending wildly, not getting a chance to move up front and they would have been several goals down only for a string of heroic saves by the keeper. As good as he was, after twenty minutes Jude's went ahead 2-0 when a defender skipped past Luke Lamerski in midfield and delivered the ball into the striker's path who finished with ease.

*"Pull your socks up, Luke, for the love of Jaysus!"* Joe shouted.

He did and seconds before the half-time whistle he pulled back a precious goal for Lavender Square, robbing the ball with a spot-on tackle to finish past their keeper who was left stranded.

At half time, they lay out on the grass. They were wrecked; the heat was too much. Joe squinted in the sun and spied the photographer. He pulled the peak of his cap forward until it almost touched his nose. The African drone sawed through his skull. There were so many people and people were still arriving: strange people with unfamiliar faces. It was hard to breathe.

Only thirty-five minutes left then he was out of there, into the car – gone. This would be his last match, promise or no promise. He was done.

Saskia poked him in the back.

"Say something," she hissed.

Joe brushed the sweat off his upper lip and, without thinking, removed his cap to fan himself.

The photographer focused and clicked, focused and clicked. He had been instructed to take photos of the manager but to be subtle about it.

Joe pulled his cap back on. "Right, lads, they're tough, but you can take them. Get the ball, keep it and pass it forward. That's all you've got to do, nothing fancy or exotic. Good lads."

The boys got to their feet and lined up. The Africans started up a low hum and its harmony floated high over the pitch. Patrick felt a connection to them. The whistle blew.

Lavender Square fought hard for the ball and began to create some genuine chances but it didn't stop Jude's extending their lead to 3-1 five minutes after the restart. Half the crowd groaned, the other half cheered and Patrick's heart sank.

In the heat, the crowd shimmered like a mirage around the edges. Somewhere amongst those faces, Spider was watching and was pleased. Patrick took a deep breath and felt calm. The pitch rose before him, the world slowed, the picture adjusted to crystal clear. Tot's red face loomed before his.

"We're fucked," he whispered.

"No," Patrick said calmly, "we're not. Keep your arse in gear. Just don't let them have the ball again. All you have to do is set up a few shots."

"Don't I feckin' know that?"

"*Just feckin' do it then!*" Patrick hissed.

They found a way back into the match. They kept battling for the ball and never let their opponents dominate possession. Then Mark Kelly intercepted a pass and chipped it to Tot who dribbled it down the right wing with all the grace of a charging rhino. Patrick timed the run perfectly, Tot hoofed a cross and Patrick volleyed it home. On the sidelines blurs of supporters jumped up and down.

Joe's words echoed in his ears.

"*That's it, lads! Don't be afraid to take your chances. Keep talking to each other and listen to each other. One more and you'll get another one!*"

Jude's stepped up a gear. But when the ball was cleared, it landed neatly at the feet of Kristian Berlowska who hammered home another goal. The crowd roared. They were equal. The tension dial turned up a notch. Patrick shouted at his teammates and made hand signals. Sweat ran into his eyes. Five minutes passed, then four, three, two, one, then two minutes of extra time. Still no score but then in the deadening heat with only a moment to go came a flash of brilliance, the type any football supporter lives to see.

The photographer captured it on film. A supporter recorded it on his phone. Had he known the significance of those few seconds of footage, that it would be replayed over and over in slow motion for years to come, commented on, analysed and paused – he might have caved under pressure and not captured it so well.

A high kick, long and powerful and Patrick sprang up to meet it majestically and the world seemed to push away beneath him. He met the ball with his head, beating the midfielder in the air. He knocked the ball forward to Josh Reynolds and then made a run for it. Josh brought it on to just outside the box. Patrick was ahead of him.

In the distance, Joe yelled: "*Take a shot, Josh, take a shot!*"

He took a shot. It wasn't powerful enough. Patrick turned and watched the ball float towards him, slowly, slowly, slowly like a star falling to earth. He flew, he soared, one leg up and then the other to connect in a perfect bicycle kick. He turned to see the ball hit the back of the net. The whistle blew. He dropped to the ground. He smelt the grass, the soil, the daisies and the sun. He thought of Emma and of his mother and Joe and Nuala. He thought of Jacques Biet and he thought of his father, deep in the heart of the Congo.

They had won. Another season down.

With one ear to the ground the noise was distorted: crowd-cheer, backs patted and hands clapped – hugs given and commiseration. All was sunshine and smiles and happy chatter. He stayed on the ground. His back was thumped and slapped. He could feel the vibration of footsteps on the ground, people passing. There was a slight breeze through the leaves in the trees. Just a few seconds for eternity to pass through. He smiled and tasted grass in his mouth. He wanted to rest.

The pitch cleared of supporters; the team lingered. Their photo was taken with the cup. Patrick kissed it and held it high. Someone passed around ice-cold cans of fizzy orange. There was excited chatter and they sat around going through the match kick by kick until it was time to drive home.

When they got back to the square it was dusk. Patrick went straight to the walled garden. He sat on the swing and sailed high, laughing out loud. When he slowed and came to land, the door had shut and Spider stood before him. It took a second for him to realise he was trapped. It was dark now and no one could see him. Two boys caught his arms and held him firm. He struggled against them but they were bigger. Then a boy stepped out from the shadows and pointed his phone at Patrick. He was recording. That's when Patrick knew he was done for.

"I told you to lose, Kimba," Spider said. "You didn't listen."

"Screw you," Patrick said more bravely than he felt.

Spider smiled. As quick as a flash he leaned in, wrenched Patrick's cross and chain off his neck and threw it aside.

"You're still not listening," he said. "And for that, you don't get to play again." Spider drew back his foot and jammed his boot heel into Patrick's right knee with such force that both boys fell to the ground. Spider got up and delivered two more heel kicks to the knee before making a run for it.

Patrick felt the vibration of disappearing footsteps and he smelt smoke and heard sirens. Smoke billowed into the night, muddying the air, its acridity destroying the aroma of lavender. Something was burning. There were shouts and voices. It was a car. Someone had set fire to a car. Before he passed out, two videos had been posted on social media and were doing the rounds. The first was of his beautiful bicycle kick; the second was of the cruel battering to his knee. Patrick knew his life, as it had been before, was over – his dream shattered in the place where it had all begun.

# Chapter 37

They sat in the hospital and made a white-faced row. Nuala blew her nose and sighed tearfully. Joe took her hand. Saskia was inconsolable. Tom stared straight ahead at the wall, glancing now and then at the TV. The news flicked from story to story with the volume turned low: hate rallies in the US, a banking enquiry, a political scandal, freak storms, a mother pleading for a reprieve on a deportation order.

Tessa sat separately to them. She watched the woman on the telly begging and beseeching and she wondered why she would want to stay in a country where there were no niceties left. She got up and went outside. The air was thundery and it began to rain – large penny-sized drops. She let them fall, roll down her face to wash away the day. She walked past the smokers and the ambulance area down the avenue of trees and into the dark to a bench where she sat in the twilight. City lights sparkled and glinted and shimmered, oranges and reds and whites and yellows and greens. The traffic made a constant hum and splashes through new puddles. Overhead a jet roared into ascent: over the city with its hem of coast, over Ireland's Eye and away, far, far away. She went back inside.

The consultant was gentle. He had sons of his own.

"Mrs Kimba, your son's head is fine, just minor concussion from the fall. His knee though, it's trickier. The kneecap was dislocated. He will have trouble with it and football will be a problem. It's certainly out of the question for the time being. I am sorry about that for him."

"Thank you, doctor. I'm just glad his head is okay. Football I don't care for."

She shook his hand.

After the Gardaí left, they took turns going in to see him.

Tom stood over him. Patrick, who had looked like the happiest man in the world just a few hours before, now looked like a boy lost. Tom touched his shoulder.

"All right, mate? Did you tell the Gardaí what you won't tell us?"

Patrick shook his head.

"I told you, it was dark, I couldn't see."

"A likely story," Tom said. "Think it over when you feel up to it. Whoever did this to you should be locked up somewhere and wearing a jumpsuit with his name on it. Look it, we're only allowed a minute or two each. I'll go get Saskia." He lingered at the door. "Think about what I said."

Patrick shook his head again. The painkillers were making him groggy and stupid. His voice came out in a croak.

"She's not to come in," he said. "She hates hospitals."

"No one likes hospitals, mate."

"I know but her brother died in hospital, years ago. She's not to come in. I'll see her afterwards."

Tom went to look for her and found Saskia sitting on a bench, in from the rain under the ambulance canopy. The air smelt of sea. She was crying softly. Tom put his arm around her. The muscles in her back tightened. He retrieved his arm.

"Patrick will be fine," he said.

"Everybody dies," she said dully.

"Yes, everybody does die, but Patrick is not going to die, not today."

"Joe's car, he loved that car. What a hateful species we are."

"It's only a car. He'll get another one."

Lights flickered across their faces as ambulances arrived and offloaded. Relatives stepped down and into the light, scared and numb, wondering what came next.

Saskia couldn't bear it.

"God, I love that boy!" she said angrily.

"I know."

"If anything happened to him I would die, no question."

"I know."

She buried her head in her hands. Tom put his arm around her again. This time she let him and she folded into him.

"What happened to your brother?" he asked.

"He was killed when I was twelve," she said into her knees. She sat up and wiped her eyes and face with her sleeves. "I was late collecting him from school and he crossed the road himself. A car ran him over, a fast driver. My mother has always blamed me."

"You were twelve, Saskia, a child yourself." Tom gently took one of her hands in both of his.

She didn't notice. She looked straight ahead at a spot in the distance as though trying to reason with it.

"My father left in the end. A marriage just crumbles when a child dies. The grief is too much."

"Why didn't you ever say anything?" he asked.

"What's to say, except it's why I hate dangerous drivers."

She leaned back into him then and felt safe.

"Remember the time Fiona Fox's car was trashed?" she said dreamily. "I did that. She's always been a total dick on the road."

"Nice work," Tom said. "I suspected as much." He was wondering where the great Richard Watts was in the scheme of things. He had disappeared after the match. There had been no sign of him since. "Have you spoken to Richard?"

"Can't get him on the phone. It's ringing out."

"Oh."

"He has a deadline."

"What's it about?"

"He wouldn't say."


Nuala stayed up with Joe that night. His car had been one of the last links with this wife. Now it was burnt to a cinder. He could not sleep.

"I knew it was going to be a shite day."

"No, you didn't."

"I did, and the worst is yet to come."

"And how would you know that?"

"I just do."

As it turned out, Joe was right.

The next morning Saskia opened the café and arranged the papers. Her face was blotched and she looked wretched. She still had not heard from Richard but his headline did catch her eye. She let the papers fall to the floor and ran. She was out of breath by the time she got to Nuala's.

Fiona Fox got a tip-off from one of her journalist contacts.

"You live on Lavender Square, don't you?"

"Yes."

"Didn't your daughter play football there?"

"A few years ago – why?"

"It's just one of our boys got a scoop on a children's football coach there. It's big."

Fiona hung up and clicked on the online edition. She smiled and lit a cigarette.

When Nuala brought Saskia into the kitchen, Joe and Tessa could see she'd been crying. Saskia laid the paper out on the table. Nuala sat down, Joe stood up and Tessa flinched violently. The headline read:

**PAEDOPHILE COACH INVOLVED IN RACIST INCIDENT**

For a moment no one said anything and then Joe spoke so quietly he was barely audible.

"I told you that hack would only bring us trouble," he said and he seemed to crumple into himself.

"What is this, Joe?" Tessa said and she looked wild-eyed.

"I was accused of something a long time ago."

"Child abuse?" she said and the words sounded alien, dirty in the homely kitchen.

"A young boy with no father showed promise on the field and I took him under my wing. I paid for it. His mother had primed him. She was looking for a pay-out."

"Couldn't you have told us before now?" Tessa asked. Her hands shook. She wanted to go away somewhere quiet where there was no ugliness, no talk of abuse or interviews with police about schoolboy thugs.

"You would have questioned me, looked at me differently, the way you're looking at me now."

"*How the hell would you know that?*" she screamed.

"Because my wife did," he said softly.

He rubbed his forehead violently in an effort to scrub out the past and they all sat in the glow of the votive light, the clock ticking as if nothing had changed at all.

"I was innocent," Joe said, "and I was proved innocent but people were strange around us. My wife took it very badly. We moved away from our hometown, up here, but she got sick and when she died the children blamed me for it." He said this without any emotion. Joe Delaney had accepted his fate years before. "I am sorry for what this will bring on this house. The reporters, they will camp outside like crocodiles around a watering hole."

Nuala put her hand on Joe's.

Tessa looked from Nuala to Joe, from Joe to Nuala.

"You knew about this, didn't you?" she said and her eyes flashed. "Damn you all to hell with your secrets!" She got up and left the room.

Nuala narrowed her eyes at Saskia and slammed her fists down on the table so hard that Saskia jumped.

"*That bollocks, Richard Watts!*" she shouted. "*I knew he was trouble from the minute I laid eyes on him!*"

This wasn't technically true but Joe thought it best not to correct her.

"I am sorry for ever bringing him near you," Saskia said miserably. She felt sick. She also felt stupid.

"*Don't whitter!*" Nuala shouted. "*Go and find him so I can kill him!*"

There was a knock at the door. It was Tom. He had seen the paper at work and left in a hurry. He was carrying a bottle of brandy.

"Hoped you'd be here," he said.

Nuala fetched some glasses and poured them a stiff measure each. And then, in the early morning sunlight around the table with its jolly teapot tablecloth and so many happy memories, they drank hard liquor. Hard liquor would be required to actually read at the article aloud.

Tom picked it up. He swallowed.

"Are you sure you want me to do this?"

Joe nodded.

"Don't leave anything out," Nuala said. "I want to know exactly how much we can sue that gobshite for."

"You can't sue someone for speculation, Nuala," Joe said gently.

Nuala's eyes flashed. "I can do what I bloody well like if the person in question sat in our house and drank our tea under false pretences."

Tom picked up the paper again. He looked at Saskia and felt awful for her. She looked ashen. He would deal with Richard Watts later. The main photograph was of the team and there was an inset picture of Joe without his baseball cap looking villainous. The article was typical tabloid. Richard Watts had dragged up old facts and re-examined them and gleaned information from every conversation he'd had with Saskia to add to them. He wrote about a talented immigrant boy with a knack for scoring goals and a sick mother. He described the square, its eclectic pocket of residents, its abundance of lavender and its garden, once private, but now opened up to the square's young footballers and home of Lavender FC. He went into the match against Jude's in detail: the accurate passes, the magnificent goals, the African supporters and finally the attack that followed, leaving the talented footballer injured, possibly never to play again.

He wrote about the house with the white door, home to Patrick Kimba and his mother, where they'd been taken in by former footballer, Joe Delaney, when she'd become ill. Then he dug into Joe Delaney, the youth coach and once-suspected paedophile, renowned for grooming young boys who'd somehow managed to avoid Garda vetting. He made no direct accusations but the implications were heavily leaned on and the article was damning, highlighting the plight of immigrants and their vulnerability to racist extremists and preying opportunists.

"I'll wipe my arse with that rag of a newspaper," Joe said and he pushed his chair back.

Joe went to the hospital to see Patrick. The Gardaí had been to question him, the reporters wouldn't be far behind. It was only a matter of time before they assembled outside the house.

Joe mistook Patrick's expressionless face for suspicion.

"I didn't do anything wrong, lad," he said.

"I know that, Gaffer. I believe you. Sure you've never laid a hand on us – only ever shouted. It's just Richard wrote that I might never play again – is that true?"

"What would that eejit know about knees? The only people you're to listen to are your doctors and your physiotherapists." He sounded more positive than he felt. He had a feeling that Patrick would never be the footballer he wanted to be now. Not with a banjaxed knee like that.

He walked home by the coast and let the breeze brush against his face. His life felt like a minute feather on the wind, thrown and flung and vulnerable. He would have to leave now, go away. There had been enough people hurt already.

In the middle the night, Saskia woke suddenly.

She called Tom's mobile.

"Can you come and talk?"

"Sure," he said sleepily. He pulled on his coat over his pyjamas. They sat outside on the steps of Saskia's. She handed him a mug of tea.

"I hate him and I hate myself. I told him about Joe living in the lock-up. He was suspicious. All he'd to do was a bit of digging."

Tom slurped his tea. He could see their breath. It made a silver mist. A stray cat prowled for mice.

"Are you okay?" he asked.

"I feel exceptionally stupid. Imagine not being suspicious of the man asking me out on a date in the first place? He was just biding his time, mining away until he'd pieced together all the evidence he needed. I don't even know where he lives. He always stayed over with me and now he won't answer his phone."

Tom laughed.

"It's not funny," she said.

"It will be one day."

They cursed Richard Watts and stayed up talking until the sky lightened.

Then Tom stood up and pulled her to her feet.

"Leave Richard Watts to me," he said, kissing the top of her head. Her hair smelt good, clean like baby shampoo.

They parted and he went home.

He didn't go to bed. Instead, he rang the girlfriend of a colleague who worked the graveyard shift at a mobile-phone company.

"I hear you're a genius, that if I give you a mobile number you could tell me where the owner is? I need to track a man down and he's not at home."

The girl was hesitant.

"That sort of information is only usually given in criminal investigations."

"This is a criminal investigation," Tom said. "Besides I've heard you all read text messages and listen into calls when you're bored."

The girl laughed flirtatiously and tapped some keys.

"At the moment, that mobile phone is in the city, on the river," she said.

"Is that as close as you can get?"

"What does the mobile owner do?" she asked.

"He's a journalist."

"Then try the early houses along the docks. It's where they go to celebrate a scoop."

"How do you know that?"

"As you mentioned," she said coyly, "I listen to conversations."

Tom got into his car and went in search of Richard Watts. He felt empowered, like warrior seeking the head of an enemy on a spike.

He found him in Captain Bligh's, sitting at the bar, triumphantly reading his article over a pint of lager.

Tom pulled a stool up beside him.

"Hello, Richard," he said.

Richard looked mildly alarmed.

"Nice article."

"Thanks."

"I was being sarcastic. You really put the ass in class, don't you? It's slanderous."

"That's tabloid journalism. It's a particular style – you wouldn't understand." Richard smiled infuriatingly. "Anyway, I got my facts from a good friend of yours. I'll think you'll find they're correct."

"She confided in you, told you about her friends."

"I'm a journalist."

"I know your type. You're a pretend journalist with no imagination. You can only find stories in other people's pain."

"Right," Richard sneered. "Grow up, would you?"

Tom ordered a coffee. The bartender put a mug in front of him and poured silt from a coffee pot that smelt like it had been brewing for days. It would need sugar. Tom took his time, tore and poured in three sachets of sugar and stirred.

"You're right," he said in agreement when the bartender was off serving someone else. "I am childish. I can't help it. It's probably why I work in advertising-slash-sales promotion. But what I said still stands. You're a talentless hack looking for the big time and this is probably as far as you'll go. If you write another word about any of us, I'll put a big ol' photograph of you on Twitter with a big ol' headline about how 'Little Dick Watts' sleeps with people to get his stories. Turns out I've a pretty decent Twitter following. You'll never work in this town again." He took a sip of his coffee and grimaced. It tasted like silage effluent.

Richard laughed. "You're full of shit."

"I'm not."

"You don't even have a photo of me except the one for my by-line."

"Saskia has one."

"She doesn't."

"She does. She took one of you while you were sleeping one night, as naked as the day you were born," Tom lied. "She's weird like that. You backed the wrong horse, comrade."

He slid his money across the counter, left and drove out of the city with the zeal of a medieval mercenary.

He stopped at Foxs' and leaned on the doorbell. He knew Fiona was home because her jeep was outside. A shape appeared in the doorway.

"Tom Winters," she said.

"Fiona Fox," he said.

"How's Patrick?"

"Fine. I'll tell him you were asking for him," he said dryly.

"And how can I help you?"

"Well, it's not help me exactly, it's more help a friend of ours."

"Yes?"

"Yes."

Fiona did not ask him in.

"Couldn't you give Joe a dig-out? Do a bit of trouble-shooting for him, go on the radio maybe or do some cartwheels outside government buildings? It's what you do best, and he's innocent."

"How do we know that?"

Tom looked at Fiona with her drawn face.

"We know that, Fiona, because we believe what Joe tells us. He was also proved innocent."

"Why do you people think I owe you anything? I have my own problems."

"You don't owe us but I just thought I'd ask anyway in case you'd reconsidered joining the human race."


Patrick was discharged and returned home to the square, to the house with the white door where he and Joe and Nuala and his mother became hostages in their own home. Reporters camped outside and waited for someone to emerge, anyone to show their face so they could file a report. Inside, they switched off the news, took the phone off the hook and took peeks outside through the curtains.

Patrick noticed his mother was cool towards Nuala and he overheard them having an argument one night in the kitchen. His mother seemed to think Nuala knew about Joe all along.

"You allowed a suspected paedophile to live under the same roof as my son. How dare you!"

"But he was innocent," Nuala protested.

"How were you so sure of that? Patrick is my son. It's up to me to make decisions about his welfare."

"I believe in giving people second chances," Nuala reasoned. "Joe had mended his ways since his days of writing nasty notes."

"*What did you just say?*" his mother said ferociously. "You mean to tell me that Joe Delaney is the same man who used to terrorise us with those evil little notes? You have *got* to be joking me!"

Nuala said nothing.

"We agreed, no secrets," his mother said calmly, "remember? But you just can't help yourself. It's the way you're wired."

Nuala lost her temper.

"*You're a fine one to talk!*" she shouted. "*You've got more secrets than Fatima!*"

"What are you talking about?"

"Oh, for heaven's sake, Tessa! Your life is a list of unexplained bullet points. Your family, your home, your husband – they're all off limits. Even the consultant after your operation hinted that something wasn't right."

"And none of it is any of your business," his mother said quietly. "It doesn't concern or affect you."

"I am your friend."

"No, Nuala. You are not my friend. Friends do not withhold information that could affect a child's wellbeing. Once those vultures outside leave, we'll leave."

Patrick dragged himself back upstairs and lay on his back in bed. His heart beat loudly. Everything was falling apart.

Joe sat in his room like a shrinking shadow and turned things over in his mind. Tessa doubted him and he didn't blame her. She had her son's interests at heart. She and Nuala had had an argument and now she and Patrick were leaving. It was awful.

After a few days of no contact, Tom asked the postman to deliver a message to the household under siege. Their mobile phones were switched off and he wouldn't call to the door in case it attracted even more attention.

The postman parked his Raleigh Chopper at the edge of the kerb and waded through the reporters. He shoved Tom's note in through the letterbox and whistled as he cycled away to continue on his round.

That night, Tom borrowed his father's car and collected Saskia. They drove past the reporters at the front of Nuala's and parked down the lane by the door in the back wall. Joe, Nuala and Patrick slipped out and piled into the car. Tessa refused to come. They drove out to the south wall and walked to the red lighthouse.

Dublin Bay curved around them, ferries sat on the horizon and made reflections on the water like lit-up hotels, the air smelt and tasted of salt and delicious freedom. They walked; Patrick limped. He told Joe his knee was no good and he knew it. Joe told Patrick physiotherapists could work miracles.

"Remember Roy Keane's cruciate ligament? He didn't push his recovery."

"I won't be playing again," Patrick said emphatically.

"See how things pan out, son." Joe took a drag on his cigarette. "Give it time. You're still only a boy."

Patrick stopped and lagged behind. Joe turned to look back at him.

"I don't want to talk about it any more."

They walked on without speaking, aware that a dream had been swept out to sea.

Tom and Saskia walked ahead. He asked her how she was feeling.

"I still feel like an idiot and, to top it all off, I'm heartbroken over that bastard too."

"I spoke to Richard."

"Oh? When you say 'spoke', did you use a blunt instrument?"

"I have my methods. He won't be bothering you again."

"You sound like a Mafia don!" she laughed.

"Fugetaboudit."

They walked, inhaled and exhaled.

"I've been thinking," Tom mused, "about a project we could work on together. It's an idea for road safety."

"Oh?"

"It's a bit cheesy, but it could work. You know those 'Baby on Board' stickers? I'm suggesting 'Human on Board' versions. The idea is to get people thinking about how everyone's life is worth driving safely for."

"Sounds interesting."

"It might have an impact."

"Anything's worth a shot."

They stopped at the end of the pier. The waves crashed and the wind swirled around them, pushing them closer.

"I'm really sorry about your little brother," he said.

"I know you are."

The others caught up and the five of them huddled together and looked out across the bay.

"We could get on a boat," Joe said.

"That would be running away," Nuala said into the wind.

"So?"

"This will blow over."

In the end, Fiona Fox made it blow over. A few days before her daughter left the country again, this time for Paris, she cut a deal with her.

"I've been thinking," Emma said.

"Oh."

"With all your high connections you could help Joe Delaney. That's your job, helping people in trouble."

"I do that for paying clients, Emma, not two-bit coaches."

"He's not a two-bit coach and Patrick needs him. Patrick is my friend."

Fiona sighed and lit up a cigarette.

Emma pulled her nightdress over her knees.

"If you help Joe I'll go to one of the private schools you want me to go to," she bargained. "But it has to be one with art classes."

Fiona eventually agreed and used her pull to get a prime-slot exclusive. Evidence was corroborated and Saskia was interviewed. Fiona said she was the best choice as she was his assistant coach. She was nervous but she did it for Joe, and she did it for Patrick. Fiona was mildly impressed by her. Once Saskia got onto the subject of football, she was at ease in front of the cameras, eloquent almost. It worked. The story petered out and the camera crews packed up.

Emma left for Paris to learn proper French, without telling anyone about her deal with her mother. And the residents of the house with the white door emerged once more but to a world adjusted.

The incident after the match had changed everything. The media attention had interrupted a cosy existence and let in nastiness. The video of the attack put Lavender Square on the map and the Garda presence increased. The private residents weren't happy. They gathered once more to discuss the future of the walled garden and reconsidered a decision they had made when Patrick Kimba was eight years old and wanted to learn how to play football. It was a different matter now.

Fiona Fox was the first to lay her key on the table. The others followed suit. Lavender Square FC would have to train somewhere else.

# Chapter 38

Tessa and Patrick found a new home in an apartment in the city where there was no lavender. Even though Nuala apologised a million times over and begged them to stay, they packed up and left anyway. And although Patrick missed his friends and his bedroom, part of him was relieved not to have to look out over the walled garden on which he could no longer play.

For several weeks he did little except stare into space: at the ceiling, the telly or the wall. Thoughts bounced around in his head and he refused to let them settle. He did not want to think or to talk, just to be left alone. There would be no more letters to Jacques Biet.

The apartment was quiet. In school they'd learnt the term "deafening silence" – now he knew what it meant. The thump of a football against the back wall, the *tap-tap-tap* of studs on the tiles, the clamour of young voices, the squeak of the gate, the low purr of the Austin Cambridge, no more, all gone.

He picked at his food. He never felt like eating. Sitting still for hours on end didn't give you an appetite. It just made your feet itch to kick a ball, kick anything.

His mother insisted he go to Mass.

"It won't do you any harm. You can pray that your knee gets better."

The homily went on for over an hour, the priest droning on about forgiveness. Patrick was unforgiving.

Afterwards the priest approached them.

"How's the footballer?" he beamed. "Saw that bicycle kick of yours online. You're a celebrity."

Patrick looked down and said nothing.

Tessa scolded him afterwards.

"He was only politely enquiring about your knee."

"I'll kick him in the knee," Patrick muttered.

His mother begged him to talk. He had suffered a trauma. Keeping his feelings to himself wouldn't do him any good. They would eat him up. He skirted her questions and pushed her concerns away. He'd done enough talking. There was nothing left to say. The Gardaí had quizzed him enough.

Patrick was sticking with the line that it had been dark, he could not recall. He wanted to forget Spider, but Spider followed him into his dreams. His boots made an echo on the pavement, the same line whispered over and over, again and again: "*You'll never play football again, you'll never play football again.*"

When he woke up in the middle of the night he couldn't get back to sleep, not until dawn creased the sky pink and the first bird sang. No amount of turning over for a cool part of the pillow could shake the line out of his head. Thoughts and memories stirred momentarily, then drifted, billowed and settled once more. Talking would do no good, nor would turning Spider in. How could it? His knee was either a useless lump of damaged flesh and bone or it wasn't – a few square inches of his body that marked the difference between one future over another. To talk and recall details would only spell out what he already knew. That up until that point his whole life had been about just one thing, one ambition half-realised, now dead, which meant the hope of finding his father was too. Although something nagged him now about that too. It was something Nuala had said during that argument with his mother. He tried to quash it but it hung like a big question mark to an unanswered question. He had too much time on his hands now. He looked up the Congo online and read nothing good or heroic about Congolese soldiers on any website and it spooked him.

He questioned his mother but she was stone-faced.

"Are you sure you've told me everything about my father?" he asked.

"You know as much as I do," she replied.

"And you're sure he was a good man?"

"Of course. Where are these questions coming from?"

"I have a right to ask."

"And I am answering."

He left it at that but his heart felt as empty and as hollow as a cave.

He went for physio twice a week. The physiotherapist asked questions and took notes and told him that his knee would be fine. It just needed time. But Patrick knew "fine" wouldn't cut it at professional level. He knew with absolute certainty his knee wasn't right. It didn't feel like it belonged to him any more; it felt like it was detached. The blow was just too much to digest.

At first everyone asked how it was. They were keen for an update on his progress, eager to see him back kicking a ball, and they kept positive. But after a while the queries started to dry up and then they stopped altogether. No one was saying anything and he knew this was not good.

He knew Joe would be honest. He phoned him one day when his mother was out.

"The physio is telling me my knee should be fine in time but it doesn't feel right to me."

"But the X-ray came up good, didn't it?" Joe said.

"I know but that doesn't mean I'll be match-fit for professional level."

"Well, why not wait and see? Give your knee the time the physio says it needs."

But Patrick couldn't bear to wait only to hear bad news at the end of it.

"Please don't bullshit me, Joe. Is there a chance that I'm fucked altogether?"

"There is," Joe said, "but I wouldn't give up just yet."

"Thank you for being honest," Patrick said. "What am I going to do now?"

He stopped going for physio. He also took down the framed poster of Jacques Biet that he'd hung in his new room with its new

274

white walls and smashed the glass with his good foot. He shoved the broken frame under his bed.

The summer lazed by. No Tot. He was being kept busy at his father's garage. He would see him at school in the autumn but then Patrick got news from the school that he'd sat the scholarship exam for. They were trying to encourage diversity and had read about the racist incident in the paper. The video of his attack had also been brought to their attention. They would be pleased to have him on board. He would start at the new school in September. He could see his mother was quietly pleased about this.

Patrick got one postcard from Emma. It was in an envelope. Mont-Saint-Michel at sunset. Her message was sunny, not heavyhearted like she had been before she left.

> *Dear Patrick*
> *I hope your knee is getting better. I thought this postcard might cheer you up. We took a trip here last weekend. It is as beautiful as I always thought it would be. I loved it. We will visit it together some day. Sometimes I think about our kiss. This is why this postcard is in an envelope! I will write a proper letter soon. No email here and my phone is locked in a vault in case I'm tempted to text in English!!*
> *Love Emma*
> x♥ x♥x

He studied the picture of Mont-Saint-Michel: sea to spire a triangle of medieval magic, narrow streets, nooks and crannies. Emma had made it there after all. He wanted to run away there too to be with her. He trimmed the postcard down to size until it fit comfortably in his wallet and waited for a letter to follow. But Emma didn't write again and he had no address for her.

He called to the house with the green door. He knocked and waited. Mrs Fox always took her sweet time. The garden was overgrown: roses choked by yellowed grass, burnt dandelions fighting with parched daisies and wallflowers shrinking back to the sidelines.

Fiona finally opened the door. She looked terrible.

"Patrick," she said flatly.

"Hello, Mrs Fox," he said and he left a pause.

"How is your leg?"

"Knee."

"How is your knee?"

"Fine, thank you. I came to ask for Emma's address in Paris. She doesn't have her phone much."

"Sure, but I doubt she'll have time to write." Fiona smiled. "François is keeping her busy. That's the boy she's staying with. François is French for Francis."

She tapped her foot. He watched it tap. It halted, and the ash on her cigarette grew long and fell to earth.

Patrick felt a swell of hatred and turned to leave.

Then he said something that surprised even him.

"I know François is French for Francis, Mrs Fox," he said steadily. "I speak French, remember? But I doubt French-for-Francis has kissed Emma yet – not like I have."

He regretted saying it the moment he said it because her face contorted with rage. She flung her cigarette butt aside and lunged at him. He skipped away out of reach.

"Get off my property, you filthy brat!" she spat. "And don't ever come near my daughter again or I'll ring the Guards."

Patrick smirked. Fiona slammed the door. He knew he'd made an enemy for life.

# Chapter 39

Emma started in her new school; Patrick started in his. For a brief spell, he was famous because of the two videos on social media: one great kick; another horrible kicking. The video of the attack had received thousands of viewings, some from people as far away as Texas. Several posted comments. Someone in the US said it was a victory for white supremacists; a football supporter in Liverpool said it was a football travesty; a Garda in Kevin Street said it would help identify the perpetrator which it did. Spider was subsequently brought down town and afterwards Patrick heard he was sent to some sort of special school. It did not make him feel any better. Chad with the too-close eyes was being punished but it would not change anything. It would not bring back his dream or his future.

Without football, Patrick felt like he no longer belonged. At lunchtime he walked the perimeter of the hockey pitch or stayed in the library and read: *Great Expectations, Catcher in the Rye, Brother in the Land* and *Sophie's World*. The library smelt good. Maybe he would become a scholar after all just as his mother had always dreamed.

Lavender Square FC became defunct. The team scattered. Secondary school played a part but without Patrick they were missing their heart. The boys joined other clubs and Joe retired.

Patrick's life fell into a routine removed from football: school, homework, reading, computer games and films. Up until then, teenage horribleness had alluded him. Football had distracted him magnificently. Now it arrived like a crusade of headless horsemen. He snapped, shrugged, rolled his eyes and answered questions in a monosyllabic grunt. His mother left him be.

Joe bought him a trampoline and erected it in Nuala's back garden. It was an excuse to get him over to the square more often. Tessa didn't mind him visiting the odd time as long as she wasn't expected to. Anything that appeased the teenage beast was welcome. And Patrick spent as long as he could on the trampoline each time until he could no longer take the ache in his knee. It helped to shake out bad thoughts from his head.

He grew his hair. Joe started calling him "Michael Jackson – The Early Years". Nuala thought this was inappropriate but it made Patrick laugh so she stopped chastising. Some Saturdays, he and Joe met in town and went to the cinema to watch westerns which had made a comeback. Life went on.

Tot had made new friends. There was no word from Emma. Patrick assumed she had settled into her private school, mingling with girls who talked about rugby and not soccer.

Emma's mother cleaned out her room. She bagged the tokens of a spent childhood: an incomplete tea-set, battered teddies, broken dolls, soccer boots, jerseys, shorts and shin guards, and a torch that needed a new battery. She dropped the bags to the charity shop: tidied away, dispensed of, done and dusted.

Saskia put Richard Watts behind her and stopped making coffee. Tom told her it was time to grab life by the balls so she did. A new sports channel had seen her on TV during the whole affair with Joe and had been impressed. They needed a female football pundit to balance out the male abundance and offered her a trial. She was trained up and started on a morning show: post-match analysis of League of Ireland games, signings and transfer dealings pre-Premier League. Her fellow pundits, all male and hardy ex-professionals, were initially dubious. But she remained patient and in time it paid off. She earned the respect of most of them.

She grew to love the buzz of the studio and realised she had a natural rapport with footballers, managers and pundits alike.

People tuned in. They liked the girl who kept the men on their toes. The ratings went up and the show moved to an evening slot. That was when she began to believe she would never have to make coffee for a living again. She moved to a renovated garden flat a few doors up from her old flat.

She and Tom approached the Road Safety Authority with the "Human on Board" car sticker idea. The authority bought it. They were willing to try anything that might help to reduce road deaths. It was launched in conjunction with radio stations nationwide. The stickers were handed out by young people who had sustained injuries from car accidents, at traffic lights, traffic islands and toll booths. Some people were incensed; most were moved, and the campaign took off.

Joe, set free from his past and its demons, became more relaxed in himself. He shed the baseball cap, got new glasses and took long walks with Nuala along the canal, by the sea and in the Phoenix Park. He told her he would be forever grateful to her, for believing in him. She was touched.


Months passed. In early spring, the following year, winds rushed the clouds across the sky and the sun made fleeting appearances through wispy clouds, making pleasing puddle reflections. The squalls stirred the lavender, perfuming the air in a dreamy wash nostalgia. The garden lay untouched, unused. It grew leafy and green, budding, blossoming and blooming.

It was almost a year since Patrick had kicked a ball. They all thought he had coped remarkably well, that he'd adjusted but he hadn't really. He was lonely: for the game and for his friends.

The game came back to him in dreams: turns, kicks and tricks; volleys, chips and passes. He felt the pitch under his feet, the soil, the muck, the dirt and the grass. He saw the game: every player, opponent, referee and opportunity and the quiver of the net as the ball hit the back of it. He heard the crowd, the clapping, the cheering, and the hum, and then he heard the voice in his head: "*You'll never play football again.*"

Changes were being made within the various League structures to tackle racism. Local community groups and national integration organisations worked to change attitudes and reduce racial incidents but it was too late for Patrick.

Everyone made an effort not to talk about football around him. This was difficult because talking about football was what Saskia did for a living. Tom said he watched her, that it was funny seeing the-girl-next-door interview Mark Lawrenson and refer to him casually as Lawro. Patrick could not watch the show. He knew he would never be a guest on it, that he would never be an ex-professional, just a boy who once had a dream.

Some mornings he woke up and did not want to live. Other days were better – not much, but better. Like the day he got an A+ in his abstract English essay, "My Life as a Bird", and his mother actually wept she was so happy. That was a good day. Or the day he and Tom went to the sea and swam for hours off the rocks in deep water and they saw harbour porpoises. That was a good day too.

There were several really bad days. Like the day Paul McGrath came to the school and asked whoever played football to raise their hands. A flock of hands shot up. His was not among them.

Or the day Tom handed him back his cross and chain. "Dad found it in the walled garden and wondered if it might be yours. I got it fixed," he said.

Patrick reached for it, examined it and put it on. "Thanks," he said without enthusiasm.

His footballer's instinct for superstition still believed that the cross and chain was some sort of talisman. The fact that Spider had whipped it off from around his neck before giving him a whooping had left him wide open, unprotected and primed to receive the mother of all injuries from which he believed he would never recover.

But the worst day was the day he came across the torch in the charity shop. He found it on a shelf between a teddy with one eye and a pair of rollerblades. He picked it up and twisted it open and found the initials he expected, E.F., scratched on the inside. There was a piece of paper curled around the old battery. He pulled it out and unfolded it. On one side, the Morse code alphabet was written out in his distinctive scrawl. On the other, there was a birthday message. It read:

*Dear Emma,*

*I've written the code out for you now so you've no excuse not to stay in touch! Morse out. Patrick Kimba, Future Football Legend x.*

A wave of loneliness washed through him. He paid for the torch and walked out. He walked the canal for miles, west to where the sun was setting. He sat on a bench until it got dark and he was shivering with the cold. He knew Emma would not be coming back, at least not to him.

The walk did him good and he took to walking, feigning organised study as the reason for his long after-school absences. He walked for as long and as far as he could get away with, and sometimes into areas he knew he shouldn't, where kids played football on the street and threw stones at him. He walked and walked, thrashing ideas and memories around his head and sometimes he thought his head would burst. Other times he thought he would die without a friend and then, quite by accident, he made a new one, one lunchtime.

He was walking and kicked a Coke can into some trees. He heard a yelp and a girl emerged from the conifers.

She was partially deaf and spoke funny and therefore was the equivalent of teenage poison.

"What did you do that for?" she asked crossly.

She wasn't in his class so he had not heard her speak before, just people imitating her. Her words weren't pronounced properly.

"I didn't do it on purpose. What are you doing hiding in there anyway?"

"What else can you do when you're an outcast except hide and dream of being somewhere else?"

He shrugged.

"Why the shrug?" she said. "You must know what I mean or else you wouldn't be wandering around here on your own."

He laughed.

"What's so funny?"

"Nothing."

They sat on the grass.

Her name was Siobhán. She was pretty: dark-haired with pale skin. There was a hearing aid in her ear. She caught him taking a look.

"It's called a hearing aid," she said, and she sounded pissed off about it.

"Sorry," he said.

In the distance gangs walked the perimeter of the all-weather pitch, others smoked under the trees and older pupils coupled up and snogged in the bushes. He wished he hadn't invited her to sit down. She would cling to him now and he wouldn't be able to shake her off. But it wasn't so bad. She was funny and smart. They met at lunchtimes and sat on the grass to eat their sandwiches. Afterwards they shared a bottle of Coke, played cards, watched videos on their phones or chatted about music or telly. They understood one another and found they shared a similar sense of humour and mindset.

"Why is it that we don't fit the bill?" he asked her.

Siobhán always gave her answers thought. She picked a daisy and rolled its stem between her fingers.

"Well, the others are scared of me," she said sensibly. "They think that because I don't pronounce my words properly I'm retarded. With you, on the other hand, it's a number of things. You're African and everyone knows Africans would rob your kidneys clean out of your body if you turned your back. At the same time you've taken all our jobs and our school places and you're all on welfare, and to add insult to injury, you're probably a terrorist to boot – sure don't you all look the same, you Muslims?"

He smiled and then he giggled and he lay down on the ground and laughed up at the sky. No one had ever been so frank about his place in the world. For the most part, people either tiptoed around his colour by being super-nice or were outright racist.

"People really think like that, don't they?" he said.

"Too right they do though to be honest with you, here in school, I think it's more a school-kid jealousy thing. You think those fuckheads who wear lip gloss even know what a terrorist is? You've just broken all the rules of being a teenager. You're the tallest in our year. You have smooth black velvet skin, cool hair and no spots. You're the best at French in the whole school, even better than our teachers are, plus you're gifted at English."

"Why do you think that?"

"I overheard Miss Farrell telling Tornado Thighs in the staff room. I was changing the vase water and she read out this paragraph from an essay you wrote. Tornado was so moved she even stopped eating for two seconds. Sometimes they forget that I'm only partially deaf, not totes deaf."

He told her about his once-dream to become a professional footballer. "It was all I wanted my whole life."

"And now?"

"Now I'm scared. I'm not sure where I go from here."

"Aren't we all? I am scared every day," she admitted. "Scared of being teased or being made a show of in the classroom. I'm always waiting for one of those blonde bitches to flush my hearing-aid down the toilet."

Patrick looked at his new friend.

"You're brave," he said.

"Meh!" Siobhán shrugged. It was a habit of hers. She constantly shrugged at the world as if to remind it she didn't care.

Patrick decided that if Siobhán could get on with things with a set of imperfect ears, then he could too with his dicky knee.

He still walked but football stopped dominating his thoughts. Finding his father did too, which was just as well as his mother had started dating. She introduced Patrick to Tarek, a Syrian man she'd met at her support group, as her friend. He seemed fine. Quiet. Possibly troubled. Patrick shrugged it off. He shrugged off Emma too. She was folded neatly away and Tot was pushed aside.

He reached some sort of peace; the desperation dissipated. He took the picture of Biet out from under his bed and rehung it without the glass. The picture was no longer threatening – it was comforting because Saskia had given it to him. So once more Jacques Biet's face became the first he saw each morning and last thing at night. Without the constant longing and ache to succeed, his head cleared and he saw the world from a different perspective. It was a big place with possibilities. Without the football, there was space for other thoughts. He was embarrassed about his letters to the Innskeep manager. It seemed like a childish idea now.

For the first time he took a close look at his mother and saw she was lacking in some way. She was not like Nuala who was open with her feelings, or Joe who joked when he was sad or angry or scared, or Saskia who blamed herself when things went wrong. His mother was a mine of secrets: neither happy nor sad. When he was in the mood he asked her about the Congo and he noticed she tended to become jumpy and guarded. The teenager in him liked seeing her squirm and he pushed for answers though he always felt guilty afterwards, especially when he heard her sniffing away tears in her room.

"What do you cry about?"

She started slightly. "I am lonely," she said.

"You didn't have to leave Nuala's," Patrick reminded her.

"I did. I was tired of the secrecy. Nuala broke a promise. She just couldn't help herself."

"You are hard," Patrick said. "If you're so lonely, then maybe that Tarek guy is not the right one for you. Go and find someone else, someone who might make you laugh for a change. And as for secrets, you're the most secretive person in the universe."

When she looked up he saw he'd gone too far. Something changed in his mother's expression and she seemed to deflate right there in front of him. He sat down opposite her.

"What is it, Mam?"

For ages she said nothing and she looked different, very young, not like his mother at all, and her voice was quiet, like a whisper.

"You think I want to relive that horror over and over, talk it through?"

"What horror, Mam?"

"My family, Patrick. Your family."

"I know they died, Mam and it's terrible but cholera is deadly."

His mother shook her head. "No, Patrick. They all died before their time and it wasn't from cholera."

They sat there for a long time in silence and his heart felt like a stone.

"What happened?" he asked.

"Rebels," she said in a choked-up voice, and she got up and left the room.

Patrick wondered if he'd understood correctly. The prospect that his grandparents had been murdered was too much for him to get his head around. He was sorry he'd asked.

He didn't enquire further and his mother didn't say anything more about it. He would ask again when the moment was right. There were too many other things to deal with. His mother's mild relief, for one, that football had disappeared out of his life. It seemed unfair. It was as if the world had shaped itself around her to fulfil her wishes, not his, and it took a lot of walking to get that conclusion out of his head.

He walked to the Phoenix Park and lay on the grass. For miles around him in the green fields, amongst the copses and along the tree-lined avenues, families picnicked, cyclists cycled, runners ran and people walked their dogs. He watched the deer grazing and remembered the day he and his mother had taken the wrong bus and ended up in the park.

In the distance a team played a match. He heard the referee's whistle and felt a tug. It was still there, the longing, though gentler now. He wondered if it always would be. He decided it wouldn't. A butterfly fluttered in front of him and flew away. It took his dream with it and he decided to let it go right then. And he did, which, when he looked back years later, was interesting. Because since he was a boy Saskia had always told him that it was when you let go of something you wanted really really badly, that was when you got it. It was to do with the order of the universe. Tom told her it was faux-Buddhist claptrap, forgetting that all his job offers in advertising had flooded in when he no longer yearned for them.

Patrick had never really believed her or given much thought to it. So weeks later, when he was taking the long way home along the canal, he wasn't thinking about it then either. What he was thinking about was the sudden cloudburst and how there would be words about his damp clothes when he got home. He decided to go to the square instead. There were a few missed calls from Nuala. He would surprise her and could also dry his clothes on the range. Nuala wouldn't say a word.

But when he arrived, there was a strange car parked at the gate, a sleek black Mercedes. He sneaked inside and heard voices in the kitchen. Not in the mood for visitors, he took the key from the hook in the hall and crossed the street to the walled garden. He hadn't been in it in over a year.

He circled the goalpost and leaves rustled in the breeze. He sat on the swing and raindrops rolled off the seat to the ground. He swung high then higher and higher until the branch sighed. He felt better. A dog barked, doors opened and closed, and windows made orange squares of light in Lavender Square. A red harvest moon sailed high. He swung and he swung and it felt good, drifting slowly back to earth, down, down, down to stop.

He left the swing swaying in the breeze and crossed the street to the house again. The strange car was still there. Whoever it was must be a welcome guest. Nuala was not keen on people outstaying their welcome. He had no choice but to go in – he was cold now.

He opened the door and wiped his feet on the mat. There were voices in the kitchen and there was laughter, the tinkle of glassware. He opened the kitchen door. It was warm and bright. The smell of tea and cake and whiskey was welcoming. The room went quiet. There was a sea of faces and they were all smiling up at him.

"*Bon soir, Monsieur Kimba,*" said a voice.

The voice belonged to Jacques Biet.

# Chapter 40

Patrick didn't know what to do, so he sat down. His legs were shaking and he wasn't sure if he was dreaming or not.

The Frenchman looked bizarrely at home in Nuala's kitchen. He drank from a mug of tea and helped himself to fruitcake.

Joe was looking at him in awe. His jaw kept dropping, almost skimming the table. Saskia bombarded him with questions and begged for an interview on her show. He spoke French beautifully and he was polite.

The scene had all the elements of a dream and Patrick had dreamed the scene so often he didn't know what to say, so he asked the most stupid question anyone could ever ask their hero.

*"De quelle porte êtes vous entré?"*

The manager didn't twitch. He didn't slam his fist on the table and yell, *"I fly all the way from London to see you and all you can think to ask is what door I came in?"* Jacques Biet was accustomed to journalists and club directors and stupid questions.

He smiled. "The big front door, naturally. An important visit always merits the big front door, doesn't it? And I am here on business."

"Business?"

"Yes. Maybe we should take a walk?"

They stepped outside into the square and walked under the

streetlights. It was getting dark and his mother would be worried. The shadows pushed the decaying buildings and overflowing bins out of sight and eclipsed the peeling paintwork. All that was left was pure outline, a Victorian square of symmetry. Windows of light, fanlights of latticed diamonds, silhouettes of steps and arches, and the musky scent of lavender pounded by the earlier rainfall.

The square was quiet. People were indoors, eating dinner and watching the news.

"What a beautiful place to grow up in!" said the Frenchman.

Patrick remained mute. There was still the danger of waking up and he didn't want to.

They walked: past Numbers 11, 12 and 13. At Number 14 Patrick found the words for his second question.

"Why did you come here?"

"You stopped writing," the Frenchman replied matter-of-factly.

"You got my letters?"

"*Bien sûr*, your letters, newspaper clippings, photos and the bits of dried lavender, nice touch. Then, after years of receiving them, they stopped." He clicked his fingers. "Just like that!"

They walked on, past Numbers 15, 16 and 17.

"I wondered why. I thought to myself, where is this boy gone, perhaps he has lost interest in the game? Then a short while ago I see this video on the internet: a young boy scoring from a perfect bicycle kick and then afterwards, his leg in pieces, the handiwork of some brainless piece of work. I recognised your name and I said to myself, 'That's the boy, my old friend Monsieur Kimba'."

Patrick looked up. Jacques Biet shrugged.

"Football is the only thing I watch, and I watch as much as my wife allows. Then I read about your coach, Joe. What a nasty business, and what an accusation."

They kept walking and Patrick wished the walk could last forever, that they could just walk in circles until he got old. The disappointment of not being able to play football for the greatest man on earth might have eased by then.

"That is why I'm here," the manager said.

Patrick stopped walking. The Frenchman stopped a few yards ahead of him and looked back.

"I've not played football in over a year," Patrick said. When he heard the words aloud, it felt like all his insides had shattered. "You've come a year too late, Monsieur Biet," he added dolefully.

The manager shoved his hands deeper into his coat pockets and looked up at the moon.

"It's cold, let's walk again," he said.

They did.

The older man scratched his face and was thoughtful.

"It was a nasty injury for sure but you didn't tear the cruciate."

Patrick shook his head.

"And the X-rays were fine?"

Patrick nodded.

"So why did you give up physio?"

"I just thought that at the end of it all the news would not be good and I couldn't hang around to hear that. My knee felt like it was broken in two."

"Knee injuries are excruciating, even the smallest knock, and they can be tricky to get right for sure – but you should be fine. It sounds like the real injury was psychological, to your head." Jacques Biet knocked gently on Patrick's head like it was a door to make his point. "It was very traumatic what happened to you."

He stopped walking. He looked down and drew pictures on the path with a foot. His shoes were shiny and he was dressed impeccably.

"I have a proposal for you. We have some of the best physiotherapists in the world at our Youth Academy. Come over and they will have another look at the knee and we'll take it from there." He looked up. "I spotted a trampoline in the back garden – do you use it?"

"All the time."

"And how is your knee now?"

"Okay mostly, I think."

"Look, I'm not making promises – there are no promises in football. But what I can give you is some time at our Youth Academy. The boys start back in July. After the physiotherapists check you over you'll meet the other boys, maybe play some football again if you want. It may lead to nothing but it will be an experience."

Patrick swallowed. He stopped and leaned against the bonnet of a parked car. He thought his legs might give from under him.

"Why are you doing this for me?"

"Between you and me, being a manager is not easy. Most of the time the letters you get are from disappointed fans or from fans from other clubs who are plotting your downfall, sometimes your death." He laughed. "Your letters were a pleasant change. I liked the sound of Lavender Square. In France, down in Provence, we have fields of lavender. It is a very nostalgic plant, isn't it?" He inhaled deeply.

They continued walking until they came to the walled garden. Patrick took the key from his pocket, turned it in the lock and opened the door.

The manager whistled. "Now that is the prettiest football pitch I've ever seen. There is a walled garden in Barbury too, though without the pitch."

"There is no pitch here now either. It is closed."

"Maybe it will reopen when you return after the summer. People like fame, a bit of sparkle about the place."

Patrick shook his head.

"This cruel boy, he broke your spirit," Jacques Biet observed. "Now we must mend it."

He walked over to the swing and sat on it.

Patrick watched him swing gently over and back, over and back, and grinned. It would have been something to tell Emma. Jacques Biet sitting on their old rope swing and no one was there to see it only him.

"This is like the strangest dream," he said.

"Every footballer says that when a manager turns up on their doorstep but you are different. You have two dreams, don't you? The second to find your father? Maybe you will find him but I wouldn't bank on it. There is every chance he does not want to be found."

"He doesn't know where to find me, to find us."

"*Mmm*," said the Frenchman dubiously. "I'd keep the whole thing to myself for the moment if I were you."

"I always have."

"Good. One dream at a time, eh?"

# Chapter 41

The English countryside in July was golden with sunny cornfields. It was a welcome change from London which was exciting but stuffy and hectic with its underground which was unbearable – a suffocating mix of tourists with suitcases and office workers with briefcases.

Before getting on the train to Surrey, Tessa and Patrick visited Covent Garden and had lunch on the cobblestones at a table with an umbrella. The summer air buzzed with excitement and exoticism and all sorts of English accents. A crowd watched a juggler on a unicycle. Patrick sipped a juice and picked at pasta. Nervousness filled his stomach and kept hunger at bay.

For Tessa, London was overpowering, a chasm of memory and emotions. When she'd passed through before on her way to Dublin there had been no money for burgers or coffees. Patrick had been an unnamed bump. She had wandered the streets filling in time until it was time to board the train at Liverpool Street for Stansted. Now the bump was a man on his way to a football academy somewhere outside London and her emotions were mixed. The results of his summer exams weren't as good as they could have been. Monsieur Biet with his polite French and excellent manners had distracted him and she wasn't happy.

There had been words. She was steely; he was sullen.

"I told you: bad results no Academy."

"I will do better next year."

"You most certainly will. It's your Junior Cert year."

"Who cares about the bloody Junior Cert?"

"I care about the bloody Junior Cert! And don't use the word 'bloody' or I will belt you."

There was a stand-off.

Tom and Saskia acted as mediators.

Tom took Patrick to a biscuit factory, one of his client accounts. It smelt of raspberry filling. Everyone wore nametags and looked glum. Men in dungarees and hairnets smoked outside.

"Why did you bring me to this dump?" Patrick asked.

"To show you where uneducated footballers, the ones who don't make it on the pitch, end up – shovelling shit."

"I get it. Can we go now? The smell of fake raspberries is something rotten."

Saskia took Tessa to a five-star hotel in the city for afternoon tea. The waiters wore gloves. Their nostrils didn't flare when they saw Tessa, and they referred to each of them as "madam". Saskia ordered two glasses of champagne.

"Why did you bring me here?" Tessa asked. "Not that I'm complaining."

"To give you a taste of the life you could grow accustomed to if Patrick does become a professional footballer." Saskia raised her eyebrows.

Tessa laughed. "And if he doesn't it will be beans on toast, is that it?"

"Don't you worry about that now – just savour the moment."

They sipped their champagne and watched the tanned and wealthy check in. Saskia slipped off a shoe to feel the carpet. It was the type your feet sank into.

"Give him this chance, Tessa. He's been through a lot and deserves it."

"We've all been through a lot."

"We have but he's just a boy."

"I don't want to have raised some dummy who can't sign his name."

"Well, there isn't much chance of that. He's already a bright and educated boy."

"The minute football goes into his head, learning goes out," Tessa said crossly.

Saskia left down her cup. Sometimes Tessa could be very hard. It was unfair.

"Do you know how many doors Jacques Biet puts himself out to knock on? Bugger all, that's how many." Saskia's tone was clipped.

"He is my child, Saskia."

"I know that, Tessa," she sighed. "I really do and I understand how hard it must be to let him go. If he was mine I'd keep him stitched to me."

"I want him to be safe. Football isn't safe, not if you're black."

"Crossing the road isn't either. If we were all to think that way we might as well just lie down and die."

Saskia thought Tessa looked exhausted.

"You seem tired, Tessa. Is everything okay?"

"I'm fine."

"Have you had a check-up recently?"

"I'm not sick," Tessa snapped.

Saskia put down her cup.

"You know, Tessa, a few years ago I tolerated shit from the whole lot of you. Bore the snapping and complaining like a doormat but I'm a different girl now." She was firm.

Tessa nodded. "I'm sorry. It's just I thought life would get easier the older I got." Her voice was raw, tearful.

"Patrick said you're seeing someone. Is he good to you?"

"Tarek – he's just a friend," Tessa said guardedly.

"I'm sure you're missing Nuala," Saskia said gently. "You had a lovely arrangement in that house, the whole lot of you, for those few years."

"Nuala betrayed me," Tessa said snippily.

Saskia sighed again.

"Jesus, Tessa, 'betrayal' is a big word. We're not living in Tudor times. Nuala was trying to protect Joe, protect you all, and at the end of the day, Joe was innocent!"

Tessa put on her coat. Her face was dark and troubled.

"Don't you 'Jesus, Tessa' me, Saskia. None of you have a clue, not one clue."

She left and Saskia didn't try to stop her. Tessa would text and apologise and the subject wouldn't be mentioned again. That's how it worked with Tessa. Any time you thought you were getting anywhere, you were in danger of hitting a raw nerve which you got the blame for before she fled.

Before Patrick left for Barbury, he went to see Nuala and Joe. Nuala couldn't stop crying. Patrick was embarrassed.

"I'll be back in two months, Tata."

"I know. I'm only a fool."

Patrick hugged her into his chest. He felt and smelt like a man to her now and she knew she was losing him.

"I might not even make it," he whispered.

"You'll make it," she whispered back. "I always knew you would. Have you got your cross?"

"*Oui*," he said and he plucked the silver cross out from under his T-shirt to show her.

They looked each other in the eye.

"*Merci pour tout, Tata Nuala*," he said.

"*Bonne chance*," she said back.

He shook Joe's hand.

"See ya, Gaffer."

"Arra now," Joe said awkwardly and he pulled the boy into a hug.

"You taught me everything I know," Patrick said to his shoulder.

"So far, son, so far. Do what they tell you over there now. They know what they're talking about."

Barbury, Surrey, was pretty. It was old. Once upon a time there had been blacksmiths, bailiffs and cordwainers; now there were footballers.

For their first night, they were put up in a country house. Their rooms had washstands and latticed windows. The next morning at ten, a taxi would collect them and take them to the Academy. Patrick didn't expect to sleep but he did, soundly. It was Tessa who didn't.

At breakfast, they pushed eggs around their plates. Both felt like fish out of water. Patrick's stomach was a knot of anxiety. Unconsciously he kept checking his knee under the tablecloth to make sure it was still there. His mother watched him fidgeting.

"You have your whole life ahead of you."

"People always say that when something bad has happened or is about to happen."

"Whatever is about to happen, you'll deal with it. You've been through far worse than this."

"I suppose."

"You suppose right."

The taxi driver was enormous and jolly. His Innskeep jersey strained to accommodate his ample frame.

"Another young hopeful, eh? What's your name, lad?"

"Patrick Kimba," said Patrick Kimba.

"Position?"

"Striker or midfield."

"Handy. Well, Patrick Kimba, I'll be looking out for you," said the taxi driver. "I've been a Innskeep fan my whole life."

The driveway was long and sweeping and the building large, modern and shiny and professional-looking. It was a long way from Lavender Square FC and it was daunting. It was also quiet: no shouts from a drill, echo of young voices or pips of a whistle. Their footsteps made a hollow sound on the floor and the building seemed to be empty until an athletic man in pristine tracksuit pants appeared through a door labelled *Medical Rooms*. A tag on his T-shirt read, "*Physio*".

Patrick swallowed. The man smiled.

"Patrick?" he said and he stretched out his hand. "Mr Biet asked me to meet you."

The man introduced himself as Andy. He was friendly and his accent was warm. He referred to Tessa as "love". He sat them down and explained that Patrick's first day would be spent in Medical.

"Mr Biet told us about your injury, Patrick, so we're going to give you a bit of an MOT, to see how things are ticking over."

If the man called Andy was sceptical about the outcome, he gave no hint of it. Tessa was told she was free to go after a bit of form-filling. She was also welcome to stay and have a nose around, drink coffee, eat cake, whatever she fancied.

"Most mums are only too happy to take the train into London

to go shopping." Andy winked.

Tessa didn't tell him that she wasn't like most mums.

"I'll stay put," she said. "In case Patrick needs me."

"I'll be fine, Mam."

"I know you will but I'll be nearby all the same."

The medical rooms were a cross between a gym and a doctor's surgery. They were white and bright and vast and smelt of antiseptic. There were tables, curtains, shiny instruments and utensils, machinery with knobs and dials, weights, benches, lockers and footballs. Everyone wore tracksuit pants and T-shirts, many carried clipboards. They all smiled and nodded. It was impossible to tell if they were used to informing footballers about the end of their careers. Patrick's palms sweated. He wanted the day over with and to be back on the train to London, far away from the possibility of any bad news. It would be too hard to give up on a dream twice. Yet after just half an hour at the Academy and just the tiniest sliver of a taste of a professional set-up, he knew he never ever wanted to leave.

"Right, lad, let's get you fully checked out, shall we?"

He was asked to remove his trainers and socks and led to a table, the first of many.

As Patrick was unlacing his shoes, Nuala was busy lighting two dozen candles in the church. The flames made a warm glow on her face. Joe told her she looked like an amateur pyromaniac. He waited in a pew and pretended to pray.

A door opened and shut and the priest's footsteps made a *tip, tap, tip, tap* down the aisle. He smelt of incense.

"Have we a special intention, Nuala?" he asked with a wink. It was his attempt at ecumenical humour.

"Patrick is getting his knee checked out today," Nuala said. "By sports specialists in England. There's a slim chance he'll be okay."

"Oh?"

"He's over at Innskeep Youth Academy as we speak."

"Is that so? God Almighty."

"I wonder could you say a prayer for him, Father?"

"Of course – I'll give him a special mention at eleven o'clock Mass. You'll stay for it?"

"We will."

They all prayed – Saskia, Nuala and Joe – even Tom who hadn't prayed since he was ten when he had set fire to a vase of dried rushes in his father's surgery.

At lunchtime Tessa rang Saskia.

"Well?"

"Not a word."

"That's a good sign."

"Is it?"

"No news is good news. We'll keep up the praying this end."

Tessa walked the grounds. The July air smelt of warm grass. She sat down at the centre of a perfectly manicured football pitch. The grounds man didn't say anything. They were used to having all sorts of people at the Academy.

The pitch felt warm underneath her and it seemed vast, impossibly huge, one goal miles away from the other. Patrick had once described it to her.

"Being on the pitch is like being in a world where every blade of grass is precious, every second essential and the thump of the ball the most glorious sound in the world."

At the time, Tessa thought that a boy who could describe something so ordinary so beautifully was wasted on a pitch. She still did.

To her, the football had always been a boyish fantasy like wanting to be an astronaut or a cowboy. She thought of her son and his father, and she thought of the Congo. A place at Innskeep Youth Academy would change everything. It would mean a move to England and she wasn't sure she was ready for that. The breeze tickled her face and she started to pray too. She just wasn't sure what she was praying for: a football pro or a ticket home. Part of her prayed he would be sent packing; the other half wanted her smiling laughing son back, the one with spark and ambition and joy.

For Patrick, the morning passed in a series of tests: toe-touching, knee-taps, leg raises, questions, furrowed brows, ticked boxes and pens down. He was prodded and poked and pricked, scanned, monitored and re-examined. There were few smiles, no words of encouragement or 'nearly theres'.

He expected grave news and at the end of the day he knew by Andy's face what the outcome was.

"Well, lad, how you feeling now?"

"Weird. No one hardly said two words to me all day."

"They're professionals doing their jobs, Patrick, that's all. They take a lad's career seriously."

They walked outside. He could see his mother in the distance walking in from the pitch he would never get to play on. And for a moment he hated her for making him different, making him African and an easy target.

Andy put his hand on his shoulder and Patrick felt an ocean of pity radiated from it.

"Well, lad," he said. "I'll be saying goodbye to you now."

Patrick nodded miserably, looked down at his useless hateful knee.

"I know."

"Do you?"

Patrick looked up. The man's eyes sparkled.

"Youths train at Old Head, lad, not here."

"You mean I'm all right?"

Andy shrugged. "Medically yes. Sounds like it was mostly in your head like Mr Biet guessed. I'll give you a few exercises for the knee and we'll keep an eye on it. But the real test will be in a few days with the other lads on the pitch. Though if what the boss says is true and he thinks you're a find then you won't have anything to worry about, will you?"

A bolt of pure joy electrified Patrick and he hurled himself at the man he'd never met until that day.

Andy laughed. He was pleased. "Easy, lad, or you'll do me an injury and all."

He shook Patrick's hand. "Good luck, Patrick Kimba."

Patrick thanked him and turned to leave and Tessa knew by his stance, even before she could see his face, exactly how her prayers had been answered.

Patrick reported for duty four days later, ecstatic, excited and ready to roll, but the sight of a hundred boys just like him called a halt to his gallop. That's when he remembered he hadn't kicked a ball in over a year. There were boys as young as nine who looked as though they belonged and he knew immediately that every one of them was just as ambitious as he was. If he wanted to get noticed he would have to try extra hard. There were other black boys just like him, equally athletic and determined, which was a good thing too. It was nice not to stand out a mile for a change.

They were divided into groups according to age. They watched each other warily and mutely like normal teenagers.

The coach for Patrick's group was a no-nonsense Peter who knew that a good workout would force them into talking to each other. His accent was different to Andy's. Instead of 'have' and 'happens', he said 'ave' and 'appens'. He paced in front of them as he spoke and he briefly reminded Patrick of Joe.

"Okay, boys. You're at the Innskeep Youth Academy and you're 'ere because you are good. What 'appens now is 'ard work. Now, I'll expect two things from you. One is punctuality. That means being on time, all of the time. The other is dedication. Once I 'ave those, I'll try my best by you. Play your cards right and you could be picked for bigger things, even at this level."

A tangible wave of excitement rippled through the group, a ripple of determination generated by twenty hopefuls, each deciding it would be him that would be the one to impress.

"Right, let's be 'aving you then – ninety-minute training session. And make the new boys welcome, yeah? Patrick there 'as come all the way from Dublin."

They looked at him, he squirmed and the whistle blew.

They warmed up and did drills. The coach was encouraging and called each of them by name. "Well done, Mark, Majdy, Jamaal, Patrick. Take your touch, Baba, Sisi, David." Afterwards they were handed bibs and divided up for an eight-a-side. That's when Patrick realised that Joe's methods had been truly professional.

"All right," Peter said, "below 'ead 'eight only, keep passing and rotate with subs every five minutes."

The play was fast: dribble, pass, move, volley, drive, pass. Patrick was muddled. His heart beat and his brain worked slowly like glue sliding down a wall. The year out had done him no good.

There was no power in his kick or control in his dribble and the other boys stopped sending the ball his way. He was a striker but scoring no goals. He felt like screaming; *I can do better than this!*

Afterwards, when they were slow-running to cool down, a boy called Ben jogged alongside him. He was black too and from a place called Brixton.

"Only your first day, mate," he said and panted. "Chill out, yeah? You'll be all right. Jacques Biet won't be calling over to check up on you any time soon." He laughed then and ran ahead towards the showers. Ben had an easy laugh and powerful legs. "See you tomorrow, Paddy," he shouted back over his shoulder. From then on that's how Patrick Kimba would be known there – as Paddy. And Ben-from-Brixton would become one of his closest friends: Ben-from-Brixton, future Innskeep centre half, future centre half for England.

# Chapter 42

By the end of the first week, Patrick had settled in a little better but his confidence was at a low ebb. He was getting more of a touch on the ball but he still felt like a slow-motion amateur in comparison to the other boys. His knee bothered him a bit too by the end of each day but he didn't mention that to anyone. Instead he fearfully kept doing the exercises Andy had given him.

He rang Saskia. She was in an editing suite looking over old footage of Wayne Rooney.

"Patrick!"

"Hi, Saskia."

"How are you getting on over there?"

"I think I've lost it."

"Don't be daft."

"I keep making a complete balls of it. My passing is utter shite."

Saskia drummed her fingers and paused on Rooney mid-air.

"I'm just looking at some footage of Rooney."

"What footage?"

"That goal he scored for Everton against Arsenal when he was sixteen."

"And why are you telling me this?"

"I'm telling you because you're as good as him. Not that I'm biased or anything."

Patrick sighed. Saskia's head could be in the clouds sometimes.

"How often were you out with the ball when you were small?" she asked.

"Every second of the day," he said, wondering where she was going. All he'd wanted was a friendly ear.

"Right."

"Right?"

"Well, that's what you've got to do again. You need to work that little bit harder to get back to what you were before: a cocky, sure-footed striker."

He started staying on late after that. When training was over and the rest of the boys had packed up and gone home, back to Luton, Peckham, Brixton, Enfield, East Acton and Finsbury, he stayed on. He dribbled up and down the pitch, sprint, jog, sprint, jog. He took shots at goal and practised whatever they'd covered that day: stepovers, wrong footing, back foot turns, half-volley sweeps or just keeping the ball in the air; one foot to the other, right, left, right, left. He kept up his knee exercises and, as his muscles firmed up, the knee ceased to bother him. Slowly his form began to return. The boys began to trust him and knocked the ball his way. He set up goals and scored goals.

Still he stayed on late, then later still. He practised shooting for hours on end until it was dark. First for accuracy and then for power, back of the net: *bang, bang, bang*. When he'd get back to the guesthouse his dinner would be dried out and his mother would be already asleep. He'd grab an apple and go to bed where he slept soundly, tired out and played out.

The old flutter of excitement started to creep back. First he curbed it, he hardly dared entertain it, and then he let it unfurl and blossom until fresh hopes and dreams of glory rose to the surface and sprang to life, invigorating him. Every cell in his body tingled with energy, his reflexes clicked like clockwork, and his instincts hummed ready and waiting to receive, flick, run, turn, collect and score! He was back and he was in form but still he stayed late – practising, shooting, juggling – alone but not completely alone. He was being watched.

They played and won matches. At a match against the Under-18s, Patrick scored a hat trick. He was hoisted up into the air and nicknamed "Patrick Hatrick" for a day. Everyone thought this was very clever except for the Under-18 team.

For the first time in a long time, the world was a brighter place. Things were looking good. He had good friends again, he felt at home and he knew he never wanted to leave.

Tessa, however, decided it was time for her to leave. She packed her few things. Patrick watched her. She was upset but disguised it by acting all teacherly.

"I'll see you in a few weeks," she said primly, "refreshed and ready for study."

"Yes, Mam."

She hugged him but he was so big now it was like him hugging her.

"I love it here, Mam," he said tentatively. "They don't care what colour I am as long as I can kick a ball."

"I know, Patrick. But I still want you to do your exams. That's the deal."

Patrick was tired of deals brokered by his mother. This time he was sure he was going to be offered a different kind of deal and, if he was, he had no intention of going home, no intention whatsoever.

The weeks slipped by. They trained and played on the scorched earth in the sweltering heat. Mid-August the Premier League kicked off with much excitement.

As Patrick's time drew to a close, there was no sign of any discussions or mention of the option to stay and panic set in. The thought of going back to frenzied discussions about the Junior Cert filled him with dread. Every evening he stayed out later and later. He took shot after shot, pounding the ball at the goal from thirty yards out until his legs ached. No one there to see him only a pale summer moon, or so he thought. Someone watched, took notes and went home.

He played his last few games in full throttle but afterwards his heart was heavy. It was like being given a taste of paradise only for it to be taken back again. On his last day, Ben-from-Brixton shook his hand.

"We'll see you back here someday, mate, I'm sure of it."

The coach was noncommittal.

"Well done, Paddy. Keep up the good work on the pitch and in school."

And that was that, no goodbyes, no promises and no Jacques Biet. Patrick Kimba, known briefly as Paddy, left Old Head bitterly disappointed.

Come September he went back to school and it was hellish.

Going from Old Head to a double-history lesson was too much of a shock to the system to bear.

Patrick, shell-shocked and sullen, quizzed his mother and they fought relentlessly.

"*Did you say something to them over there, did you put them off?*" he shouted.

"Don't be ridiculous and don't you dare talk to me like that!"

"*If I ever hear that you said something about my stupid bloody exams to put them off, I will never, ever speak to you again!*" he roared back and left, slamming the door behind him.

The door-slamming became a regular occurrence and Patrick watched his mother with suspicion. He noticed she'd become more secretive about her letters and emails since his return. She'd changed the password on the computer and had begun keeping the key to the post box hidden. She was cool and business-like when he questioned her.

"I'm waiting for a letter from the Congo, a letter from the government concerning my status."

"Oh yeah?"

"Yes."

"Can I see the stamps?"

"I'll save them for you."

"Why are you being all secretive?"

"I'm not."

Patrick wasn't convinced. When she was out one day he looked through her things but he found nothing of interest only boring old letters from the bank. He would have to do his own detective work.

He tried to talk to Nuala and Joe but they were no help. They were acting strange, lovey-dovey almost, and it was gross.

He met Saskia for coffee. Her eyes sparkled and she looked different. He caught men looking at her.

"Men are looking at you."

"They're not," Saskia said but he could tell she was pleased.

"Do you think Joe and Nuala are at it?"

Saskia laughed. "I haven't a clue. What makes you ask?"

"I called around and they were acting weird – lovey-dovey or something."

"Sure they might as well."

"It's weird – they're old."

"Patrick, they deserve happiness. And by the way, they're not old."

Saskia met up with Tom. Tom was sullen.

"What's wrong with you?"

"Nothing."

Saskia guessed it was something to do with some girlfriend or other. "Patrick thinks Joe and Nuala might be up to something."

"Like what?"

"Like romantic stuff."

"Jesus, no."

"What would be wrong with that?"

"They're past it."

Saskia stood up and put on her coat. She looked upset.

"What did I do?" Tom asked.

"You figure it out," Saskia replied and she left.

She dropped by Nuala's on her way home. Joe answered the door in an apron.

"Don't ask," he said. "She's got me helping her with the cooking. Come in, come in, she'll be delighted to see you."

Nuala was at the kitchen table peeling apples. Joe put on the kettle. Evening sunlight poured in through the window and the scene was of easy domesticity. Saskia sat down. Patrick was right. Nuala had a glow about her. Joe was wearing new clothes. He looked like a proper grown-up, vaguely handsome. His whole manner had changed since his name had been cleared.

He handed Saskia a cup of tea; she smiled.

"What?" he asked.

"Am I sensing romance in the air or am I just imagining it?"

Joe looked shy; Nuala smiled.

305

"You're not," she said. "We're going to make a go of it. We're going to get married."

"I cannot think of two people who deserve happiness more," Saskia said, hugging them both.

When Nuala told Patrick her news, he was unenthusiastic and she got cross.

"*Can't you think of someone else for a change?*" she shouted and her face flushed. She flapped him out of her way to get to the range. He was getting too big for her kitchen. "Shouldn't you be doing something useful like studying?"

"I wish everyone would stop talking about studying," he said through gritted teeth.

Nuala poked him in the arm. It hurt.

"It's time you stopped moping around like a bear with a sore arse!" she snarled. "Complaining about your mother as if she had a say in deciding who stays on at Innskeep. Sometimes you act like you hate her. How do you think that makes her feel?"

"*I'm sick of thinking about how my mother feels!*" he yelled back. "*It's all I've ever thought about. Has she ever stopped to ask what I want?*"

Nuala's eyes narrowed and she let a roar out of her. "*What you want is what we've all been thinking about since we met you! Washing kits and going to matches in the freezing cold and letting complete strangers wander about the house, holding your hand every time you lost or drew or doubted yourself. Get out of my sight before I skin you alive, Patrick Kimba!*"

Nuala was flustered. The thought of marriage to Joe both excited and worried her. Joe was going to be her husband. 'Husband' was an amusing word, funnier the more often you said it. She'd thought the prospect of acquiring one had passed her by. Now it would be Joe. She tried to remember him as he had been – a strange recluse, and she could hardly picture it. But she did know that if someone had pointed him out to her on the street all those years ago and said, "That's the man you're going to marry", she would have run for the nearest bridge and thrown herself off it.

Saskia told her it was only a special type of woman that could have seen past Joe's faults and found hidden qualities. Nuala knew this wasn't true. There was no way on earth Joe would have been entertained for two seconds only for Patrick. It was Patrick who'd looked past the shabby curmudgeon exterior and seen Joe's potential, and it was Patrick she had to thank for the man she loved because she did indeed love him.

She ran out after Patrick and caught up with him down the street.

"I'm sorry," she said.

He said nothing.

"I haven't told you this but I'm trying to get in touch with Joe's son and daughter."

Patrick looked at her.

"They haven't been in touch for years because of that nasty business with the little boy and their mother dying. They blame him."

"That's hardly fair."

"Life isn't always fair."

"No, it isn't."

They looked at each other.

"I would like Joe's children to be at the wedding but I'm having trouble tracking them down. His daughter hasn't responded to my emails. It could be an old address, who knows?"

"Maybe she doesn't want to be tracked down," he said.

"Maybe but I'd like to give it another go."

"I am happy for you and Joe," said Patrick. "I would hate for you to be lonely."

"We miss you and your mam."

"She might come round yet," he said.

"I'm not sure, Patrick. She's a very principled lady. I was wrong to keep secrets from her."

They started walking back to the house. When they reached Nuala's, they sat on the steps. Patrick untied and retied his shoelace and looked up.

"What's up, Patrick?" Nuala asked.

"I think my mam is hiding something," he said.

"Like what?" Nuala asked carefully.

"Emails and letters."

"She gets letters from an old friend in the French Congo. She likes to have that connection with Africa. I forward them to her. The fact that she hasn't informed anyone about her change of address gives me some hope." Nuala was wistful.

"Any other letters?" Patrick asked.

"Nothing that springs to mind."

"Then why is she so careful to hide them from me? She even keeps the key to the post box hidden. I haven't found her new *cachette*."

"*Cachette*?"

"She's always had one for our passports, her credit card, important documents. In the flat the *cachette* was under a loose floorboard – it was a nook behind one of the shutters in her room when we lived with you."

"I suppose she thought she needed one," Nuala said, a little taken aback by the information.

"She said it's the Congolese in her, hiding things, a necessity."

"Well, she won't find any loose floorboards in a new apartment."

"I know. I haven't come across any in my hunt."

Nuala looked at him. "You know letters and emails are private, Patrick," she said, thinking a little guiltily about her own snooping in Joe's affairs.

"I know but … there's something fishy going on, I'm sure of it."

Nuala knocked his shoulder with hers teasingly.

"Were you hoping for a letter or email from England?"

"Yeah. I played my best football."

"They'll be back for you so."

"I don't know."

"Maybe you should keep practising just in case."

He shrugged and looked thoughtful. "You told me before I left for Barbury that you always thought I'd make it. Do you still think that?"

"Yes," she said truthfully and she put her hand on his face.

He smiled a half smile.

"Did my mother ever talk to you about her family? You know they didn't die of cholera at all – they were killed by rebels?"

Nuala nodded.

"Why didn't you tell me?"

"That wouldn't have been my place, love."

"She only let it slip because I caught her at a bad moment. She didn't mean to tell me at all." He shook his head. "No one should have to keep stuff like that to themselves."

"I think she feels her past has no place here. That it's too inconceivable for us to grasp in Ireland."

"But people get murdered here too."

"Not quite as often or as violently and suspicious deaths are investigated at the very least."

"You know what the weirdest thing is, though?" he said.

Nuala shook her head.

"I think she feels guilty for being alive."

"I think you're right, Patrick. Try and be patient with her. She will tell you things in her own time and some day it will all come out in the wash."

"I'll be an old man by the time I know everything about my mother," he said.

"Is she still seeing that Syrian fellow?" Nuala asked.

"Tarek – yeah."

"What's he like?"

"He doesn't say much but Mam seems to like spending time with him."

"I suppose they have similar pasts, both having to leave where they're from. Maybe they're of comfort to each other."

"Oh, I'd say it's a laugh a minute all right." He stood up to leave. "Why don't you just ask Joe about his kids? You don't have to say you're trying to track them down, just ask casually like."

"I'll try but I'm not very good at casual and he always clams up when he thinks you're on the hunt."

"Some things never change then," Patrick said and he pecked her on the cheek and left for home.

# Chapter 43

On Nuala's suggestion Patrick joined the football team at school and he practised everything he'd learned at Old Head: driving, chipping, volleying, passing, controlling, heading, chesting, stepping over, wrong-footing, turning, running and shooting. There was no one on the pitch to match him and no one who could get past him. Siobhán came to watch him play. She overheard the coach say that he hadn't seen anything like it in a long time. But there were no calls from Jacques Biet and there was no word from Old Head or Barbury. It was as if his time there had never happened.

The lead-up to Christmas was busy. A slight upturn in the economy saw an increased placement for dress orders. Patrick studied for his mock exams. Relations between him and his mother remained cold. He tried to do as Nuala said and be patient but he still watched and waited for an opportunity to find her letters or read her emails; none presented themselves.

Joe placed the orders for turkey and ham and, on Nuala's instructions, painted the front door black. It was time for a change.

"Is that what marriage is all about, a list of instructions? I'd forgotten about that end of it," Joe joked.

"There will be no marriage if you keep that up."

"Ah sure, I'm only pulling your leg."

"Go and pull somebody else's."

Nuala said nothing to Joe about trying to contact his children. There was no point in getting his hopes up. But she nearly let it slip once or twice.

"Why did you call your daughter Donna?" she asked.

"How do you know my daughter's name?"

"You must have mentioned it."

Joe squinted at her over his paper.

"We called her after the greatest footballer on earth – Maradona," he said seriously.

"You did not!"

"Course we didn't," he said and he chuckled. He put down his paper and looked out the window. "We just thought it was an interesting alternative to Mary."

"Where does she live?"

"New York now, I believe – runs or owns some neighbourhood bar in Manhattan with her husband."

"What's it called?" Nuala asked as casually as she could.

"Why?" Joe said and he frowned at her.

"Just interested."

"Well, I don't have a bog what it's called," Joe said and he took up his paper again.

Nuala spoke to Tom. Tom was hesitant.

"Maybe Joe is better off not having them around."

"If I want your opinion I'll tell you!" Nuala snapped.

"Okay, calm down! I'll see what I can do."

Tom came up trumps. He located Donna Delaney through his agency's New York office. He spoke to a Marcie there. She was from Queens and sceptical. She chewed gum between sentences.

"Who are you – Columbo?"

"It's a favour."

"You bet it is but you're cute. I've seen your picture in the network directory so I'll cut you some slack."

"You're a dote."

"A what?"

"You're a diamond."

"They all say that. Then they run off with a cheerleader half your age."

Marcie knew a guy in the Irish bar scene who knew Donna

Delaney and her husband. Their bar was called *The Leenane*. It was on Second Avenue. Tom delivered the phone number to Nuala.

"You're a trooper," she said and she kissed him on the cheek.

"I know."

"Now I've an awkward phone call to make."

"Good luck with that."

Tom met Saskia for a pint.

"I hope Nuala knows what she's doing. I'm not sure Joe is all that fond of surprises."

"She knows him best."

Tom looked at his friend who had grown in confidence and now gave definite answers to everything. She walked tall and briskly, smiled more and even spoke faster, as though she had a lot of life to catch up on. He watched her on TV. Not because she was his friend but because she was good. She was captivating and he wasn't the only one who thought that. She was fast-talking, witty and knowledgeable and she was smart. She didn't try too hard or to be one of the lads. Nor was she a starry-eyed Bobette only there to make up the gender ratio. Her match predictions were uncannily accurate, her football language impeccable and she often second-guessed a manager's plan.

"I suspect he'll play a 3-5-2 for this one, use O'Neill as sweeper, midfielders defending and attacking, getting the crosses in."

Sometimes she commentated. Her voice sounded good. It was reassuring, like it knew what it was talking about. "No great power in that flick. A spiky start and Italy playing an awful lot of long balls at the moment – haven't they read the rulebook of Italian football?"

Tom wasn't sure how he felt about guest pundits trying to impress her, flirt with her almost on screen. Sometimes he switched channel.

"Why'd you do that?" Patrick asked him once when they were watching an Ireland match.

"They make fools of themselves, those men flirting with Saskia."

Patrick laughed. "You're jealous."

"Don't be soft."

"You're the one who's soft. You fancy her but you're too chickenshit to admit it."

"No, I don't," Tom said but after that he wasn't sure how he felt about Saskia. He knew he always looked forward to meeting her and liked being with her and talking to her but he couldn't see beyond that.

A few weeks before Christmas, Patrick and Joe went Christmas shopping and Nuala met with a wedding organiser who ran her own catering company. Nuala brought her into the walled garden.

"How beautiful!" the woman said. "Ideal for a summer wedding."

"It's where we actually met."

"That's nice."

"At the time, he thought I was a ghost," Nuala said and she laughed at the memory.

Afterwards she made the phone call she'd been putting off. She sat on the seat in the hall and dialled the number in New York. It was early afternoon in Manhattan.

A woman answered. She sounded Irish with a slight American drawl.

Nuala cleared her throat.

"Hello," she croaked. "Is that Donna, Donna Delaney?"

There was a pause.

"No one has called me that in a while," the woman said.

"My name is Nuala Murphy," Nuala explained. "I'm calling from Dublin, about your father."

"Is he dead?"

"No, he's not. Quite the opposite, in fact."

On Christmas morning there was snow and Patrick realised he hadn't seen Emma or Tot in a year and a half: no emails, calls, texts or anything. Every holiday, Emma was whisked away mysteriously and out of reach; Tot was never around. He hadn't thought about either of them in a while, which was kind of interesting, because that day they both turned up.

After Mass Patrick walked to the square to exchange presents. His mother went to collect Tarek. She had mellowed sufficiently to accept Nuala's invite to Christmas dinner.

Patrick's shoes made footprints in the fresh snow as he passed

Foxs'. There was no sign of life. The jeep was not parked at the gate.

The priest was already at Nuala's. He shook Patrick's hand.

"How's the Innskeep boy?" he asked and Joe sighed.

Patrick wondered how the priest had a knack for always asking the wrong question at the wrong time.

He crossed the street to fetch Saskia. She and Tom were outside her flat, firing snowballs at each other. He felt like he was interrupting something.

"Am I interrupting something?" Patrick asked.

"We figured that being out in the snow would give us a half-decent excuse to drink hot port before lunch," Tom said. "Have you been chatting to Emma?"

Patrick shook his head. "She's away."

"Might have been, mate, but she's back now," he said nodding towards Foxs'. "That's Attila the Mum going in the house there now."

Patrick headed back to Nuala's. He lingered outside. He wasn't sure why. Emma had forgotten about him. He walked the square: north, west, south and east. Robins made dashes of red breast against the pure white, smoke curled up from chimneys and the air smelt of ice and burning wood.

Fiona Fox spotted him from her bedroom window, Emma from the drawing room. Fiona was quick but Emma was quicker. The door shut beneath her and Emma was out in the snow running towards Patrick Kimba just like she always had. He smiled and leaned down to kiss her on the cheek. Fiona watched them stroll down the street arm in arm and stop at the foot of Nuala Murphy's steps.

Emma noticed there was a strangeness between them. He was cross with her. She didn't know what to say.

"I like your overcoat," she said. "It's very smart."

He noticed her accent was posh now, not hers. She pronounced coat like the Dutch player's name – Kuyt. He nodded, looked down at his shoes and then directly at her.

"We haven't seen each other in over a year. A lot has happened. This coat is just one thing."

"It can't be that long."

"Well, it is," he said softly. "Where have you been?"

"School."

"Do they handcuff you in there?"

"Pretty much. Yes."

He didn't smile. She started to reverse out the gate.

"I'm sorry," she stammered, colouring pink. "I tried, I really did. She just made it impossible. You shouldn't have said anything about our kiss."

She blushed. He swallowed.

"I'd better go – she'll be looking for me," Emma said, turning to go.

"I've got something for you," Patrick said.

"Oh."

"Just wait a sec."

He pushed open the door of Nuala's and went inside.

Emma looked up and saw Nuala watching her from the drawing-room window. Emma waved and Nuala turned away. Maybe it had been a long time, too long. There was a tap on her shoulder. It was Tessa with a man. He looked Middle Eastern or North African.

"Hello, Emma," Tessa said and she kissed her on the cheek. She introduced the man as her friend, Tarek.

His handshake was warm but his smile was cautious.

The door of Nuala's opened and jollity escaped. It sounded warm and cosy. Patrick stepped back outside. Tessa and Tarek said goodbye to Emma and went inside.

"He seems nice," Emma said. "Where's he from?"

"Syria."

"Poor man. Do you like him?"

"He's fine, I suppose. Quiet." Patrick reached into his coat pocket then and took out something. It was her old torch. "I found it in the charity shop down the road – thought you might want it back," he said, handing it to her.

Emma remembered their Communion Day and felt sad. She looked at him. He was so tall now and gorgeous. His mouth was serious but his eyes were still kind.

"I replaced the battery," he said. "It needed a new one." He moved back towards the door.

"You've changed the colour of the door to black," she said. "It's always been white."

"Yes. I like it. It's a good colour," he said and smiled. "You should tell your mother that sometime."

They looked at each other and were friends again for a moment.

"I see you wear lip gloss now," he said.

"Yes," she said, distracted, and bit her bottom lip.

"Seems to be all the rage," he said. "Lip gloss."

And she couldn't tell if he was being sarcastic or not.

"I'd better go," she said.

He turned back and walked her to her door.

"Happy Christmas, Patrick."

"Happy Christmas, Emma."

He looked up and saw Fiona Fox watching them from an upstairs window. He waved and blew a kiss and she gave him a look of pure hatred.

Emma frowned at him. "Why do you deliberately annoy her like that?" she said and she was cross.

"Aw, Emma, it's just too hard not to," he said and he laughed.

"Right, well, I hope it doesn't come back to haunt you," she said and she walked away.

She let herself in. Her mother was waiting for her and she was smiling.

"How's Patrick?" she asked.

"Good," Emma said guardedly.

"Good."

"And who was that man with Tessa?" her mother asked casually while helping Emma out of her coat.

"His name is Tarek."

"Tarek?"

"He's Syrian, poor man," Emma said and she turned and saw that her mother's smile had changed. She didn't like the look of it. The smile was what Tot had always referred to as her "cat who got the cream" smile.

"Well, now," her mother said and Emma didn't like her tone either.

Later on, she heard her mother on the phone.

"Revenue," she said up close to the receiver.

There was a silence then until her mother recited her number clearly as though for a voice message but not her name, and it seemed strange to be leaving such an odd voice message on Christmas Day. Emma tiptoed back downstairs and into the kitchen. She'd a feeling her mother didn't want to be heard and it was best not to strain an already difficult day. The house was cold. She would light a fire.

Tot called to the door as Patrick, Tessa and Tarek were getting ready to leave.

"Hiya," he said. He was fatter now, clearly not playing football.

"What do you want?" Patrick asked.

"Some lads said you spent the summer at Innskeep."

"What about it?"

Tot's face flushed. "Look it, I'm sorry I haven't seen much of you."

"You haven't seen any of me."

"You're in a different school and you've moved from the square. I didn't cop on until recently."

"Well, you always were a bit slow," Patrick said and he shut the door.

# Chapter 44

Patrick turned sixteen. He studied and was moody. However hard he tried to push football and Old Head out of his brain and force the American War of Independence in, he couldn't. His mother still guarded the letterbox like the Kremlin and she seemed more worried than usual. Her behaviour put his curiosity on overdrive. He was determined to get to the bottom of it and he conducted a thorough search of the apartment one morning when she was at the dentist and he was meant to be studying. The apartment was perfectly neat, tidy and symmetrical. He would have to be careful to put things back exactly as he found them. He didn't rummage or rifle or frantically open drawers like people did in the movies. Instead, he scanned: the chests of drawers, wardrobes, pictures, ornaments and plants. The letters wouldn't be where you'd expect to find them, in a drawer or locker or a filing box. They would be somewhere less obvious: behind a picture or in a jewellery box with a false bottom. He scanned again, every room, and his eye fell on the mirror in his mother's bedroom. It was a few centimetres off centre. He lifted it off the wall. There was a slit in the paper on the back. He reached in and pulled out several slim bundles bound in elastic: their passports, post-office books, a bundle of cash and a pile of neatly folded letters. All Congolese postmarks and stamps save for three which were from the revenue commissioners looking for money. No letters from London.

Disappointed, he returned to his desk. Back to Irish grammar, theorems, the Wall Street crash, eskers, drumlins and photosynthesis, and he concluded that this was how it was going to be: tied to a desk learning, revising and reciting until the end of time. The thought filled him with a sorrow so deep he almost choked on it.

Nuala was anxious. The wedding was meant to be a simple affair but simplicity had somehow mutated into a multi-layered Hollywood production. There were lists upon lists and so many things to think about: the weather, the music, the priest, the guests, the garden, the gifts, the caterers, the canapés, the flowers and the food, not to mention the question of long-lost relatives. There had been countless phone calls and emails to Joe's children and she regretted having ever got in touch. She was now bearing the brunt of old grievances which had bubbled to the surface and it was more than she was able for but she couldn't tell Joe. She'd opened a can of worms and now had to deal with it herself.

Joe thought she was just stressed over the wedding and worried about her. She took his concern as criticism.

"Aren't we a bit long in the tooth for all this codology? Couldn't we just hit the registry office and be done with it?"

"*Aren't you a bit brave to be asking questions like that?*" she screeched at him.

Joe met Tom and Saskia down the pub.

"She's like a madwoman," he grumbled. "It was easier the first time round."

Glances were exchanged. Saskia raised an eyebrow. He would be sorry for moaning when he found out what Nuala was trying to engineer for him.

She met her for coffee and they ordered wine instead.

Nuala looked worn out and upset.

"How are things on the Western Front?"

"Patrick is like a bull and Joe is uncooperative. I don't know why anyone bothers getting married at all."

"It will be worth it."

"It will in its arse."

"What about the Americans?"

"They're not coming."

"You did your best and maybe it's for the best."

Nuala blew her nose. "You know, I realised last night that neither of us will have any family there. That's just sad and we're not even bad people. I bet when that hoor Fiona Fox got married every member of her family was wheeled out, even the dead ones."

"And look how well that turned out."

"True."

"You've got your friends, all of us, better than family any day. Family are just a large pain in the backside. Now how about another glass of wine?"

"How about another five glasses of wine?"

The weather dried up, list items were ticked and the exams loomed. Patrick wanted them over with. He was tired of being cooped up inside. He wondered how Tot and Emma were fixed for them. Sometimes he thought he should have been more civil to them at Christmas but he had felt let down. They'd fecked off when he'd needed them most. But other times he thought how nice it would be to chat to them again. They were his oldest friends. He longed to tell them about the two months he spent at Old Head but at the same time he didn't really want to talk about it at all. Emma would understand that. No one had understood him like she did, not even Siobhán. Thoughts spun round and round in his head. The exams would start and then they would be over and then what? There was nothing to look forward to, only Nuala and Joe's wedding and that was just for a day. After that the summer stretched out like an empty canvas. It would be just him and his mother sniping at each other. He sighed and opened *Othello* and started to make notes, notes about another black man who'd made an absolute balls of his life.

With Joe's family not coming, Nuala relaxed a little and a few nights before the wedding the house had an almost laid-back air to it. Joe read the paper and Nuala painted her nails while quizzing Patrick on The Treaty of Versailles. At nine o'clock they switched on the News and upstairs the doorbell rang. No one moved.

"Hop up there now like a good chap," Joe said and he poked Patrick with his rolled-up newspaper.

"I'm a visitor now too so why should I have to answer the door?" Patrick mumbled, sloping out of the room.

"That's because you're young and we're old and decrepit."

Patrick answered the door.

A man and woman stood waiting.

"Is Nuala home?" they both asked at exactly the same time.

Patrick thought they might be religious types so he didn't let them in. He went back downstairs to the kitchen.

"There's a man and a woman at the door looking for you, Tata," he said, sitting down.

"Did you not bring them in?"

"I thought they might be Scientologists or something."

"That's all I need," Nuala said, removing her apron.

"They're very tanned," Patrick added.

"Tanned as in like yourself?" Joe joked without looking away from the telly.

"Funny for an old man, aren't you?" Patrick joked back. With only one more exam to go, he'd begun to unwind.

But the couple at the door weren't Scientologists. They were Joe's children. Nuala could tell straight away. She brought them into the drawing room and wasn't sure what to do with them. The three of them looked at each other.

"I thought you weren't able to make it," Nuala said and she realised she sounded harried. "I mean, I'm delighted you're here – it's just I've said nothing to him and I'm afraid he might have a heart attack."

"Oh," said the girl who was pretty and pleasant but her eyes were sad.

The boy was handsome and looked like Joe. Nuala felt a wave of tenderness towards them. They were Joe's children and they'd turned up. She settled them and went downstairs.

"Joe?"

"*Mmm.*"

"I've a surprise for you. I need you to remain calm. This could be a bit of a shock. There's someone here to see you. They're upstairs in the drawing room."

"Is it Sebastián Fernández and his entourage? Tell them they can have your man here for twenty million."

"Joe," Nuala said, pausing. "Your son and daughter are here to see you."

It took a moment to register. His eyes widened and he swallowed. "How?"

"I got in touch with them. They're here for our wedding."

Patrick looked from Nuala to Joe and from Joe to Nuala.

"Aren't you going to go up and say hello?" Nuala was gentle.

Joe sat glued to his seat. Then he stood up obediently, looking scared and a little shaky. Then he sat down again. "How do I look?"

"Great."

Nuala kissed him on the cheek, helped him to his feet and pushed him gently out the door.

They climbed the stairs and Joe pushed open the drawing-room door.

"Hello, Daddy," the girl said and Nuala knew everything would be okay.

# Chapter 45

Early on the morning of the wedding the caterers let themselves into the walled garden and started to set up. They hung lanterns, arranged chairs for the ceremony by the oak tree and covered tables in snow-white tablecloths. By the time the dew was burnt off, they had set up a trestle table under the shade of the horse-chestnut tree and lined it with polished silver, plates and glassware. A pile of crisp linen napkins made a neat white mountain and rugs were laid out on the grass to encourage guests to loll.

A few hours later, the band set up a small stage and tuned their instruments and Tom's parents clipped and snipped, making last-minute inspections before going home to get ready themselves.

The wedding organiser surveyed the finished product with a practised eye. The lawn was manicured and a lush green – the lines of the once football pitch now almost completely faded – the shrubs were pruned, the beds of flowers weeded and the rose bushes were in bloom. Even the butterflies fluttered in a celestial choreography. It was peaceful and still, a scene awaiting the director to yell, "*Action!*" It would be a perfect day and it was.

Patrick gave Nuala away. He walked her through the door of the garden and across the pitch to the foot of the oak tree.

Emma watched from her bedroom window. Patrick looked so good in his suit. It would have been nice to talk to him, to see how he got on in the exams, to dance with him, to be close to him. She wanted to touch him, to kiss him, properly this time, to feel his hand in hers and she regretted not standing up to her mother and insisting on going to the wedding. She turned away from the window. She would write him a long email of apology for not being the friend she always thought she would be. Or maybe she would send him a good old-fashioned love letter. She knew her mother had asked Nuala for the Kimbas' new address.

Nuala beamed and looked beautiful in a simple long-sleeved ivory dress. She carried a bouquet of her own roses. Her make-up was understated and her hair styled. The organiser nodded in approval and checked to make sure her young staff weren't slouching, nudging or poking each other as they were inclined to do at an older couple's wedding.

It was an emotional occasion and Joe made an amusing yet poignant speech about how he and Nuala had first met, explaining how it certainly hadn't been love at first sight. He spoke of Nuala's love for Patrick and his mother Tessa, of her generosity with her home with its kitchen table where the chairs were pulled out and the kettle put on for anyone who called. He spoke about his first wife Eileen and the wonderful years they had together, and his children and how thrilled he was to have them there with him today.

"I am a lucky man," he said, ending the speech, and he kissed Nuala tenderly.

After the food, the lanterns were lit and there was dancing. The sunset made a pink sky, the moon hung high over the gardens and the music drifted up and over the walls, curling into the night infused with the smell of lavender.

"Do you want to dance?"

"Sure."

Patrick led Saskia out to a Dean Martin number.

"You look hot," he remarked.

Saskia wore a strapless midnight-blue dress that his mother had made for her.

"Thank you," she said. "You look very handsome."

They people-watched as they danced. Tessa swayed in time to

the music and looked happy, Joe and his children chatted eagerly, Nuala beamed and looked radiant and Tom danced with his date for the evening but looked morose.

"When is he going to get it over with and dump her?" Patrick asked.

"You're very young for that talk," Saskia said and smiled.

"I'm sixteen."

"Ancient."

"Fuck's sake," Patrick said. "If he was a real man and had any sense he'd hunt you down and sweep you off your feet."

Saskia frowned. "We're friends," she said defensively, "and maybe I don't want to be hunted down."

He twirled her. Joe had told him that twirling was a good way of changing the subject. It worked.

A breeze rustled through the leaves and the notes danced in the air.

"So no Emma today?"

"No."

"What has got into her at all?"

"Her mother, I'm guessing."

"Don't be too hard on her."

"Why?"

"She's had a lot to deal with and she's a brave little thing. You know, I shouldn't really say as she swore me to secrecy, but during that whole nasty business with Joe she made a deal with her mother. It's why Fiona Fox helped to clear his name and Emma went off to that posh school."

Patrick stopped dancing. He was stunned.

"You look stunned," Saskia said.

"I am," he said. "She never told me."

"Probably because she was whisked off to that posh school before she got a chance."

"But I didn't hear from her again – the odd text, nothing more."

"Well, it's a strict school by all accounts," Saskia sighed. "What are you going to do for the summer?"

"Haven't a clue," he said, still thinking about Emma and wishing she was there with him. "Something will turn up," he said without conviction.

And quite unexpectedly something did.

After midnight, when everyone was getting squiffy and silly, he left the garden, pausing to gaze up at Emma's window. Tomorrow, he thought. Then he went back to Nuala's. She had made up his old room for the night. He made tea and channel-flicked before climbing the stairs to bed. He paused at the hall table and examined himself in the mirror. He undid his bow-tie.

"*The name is Bond, James Bond*," he said to his reflection and he laughed.

And that's when he spotted the letter. His heart almost stopped. It was addressed to his mother and the stamp had a picture of the queen's head. He picked it up as calmly as he could and went downstairs to put the kettle on. While he waited for it to boil, he wondered if the letter would provide any clues to his mother's secrecy. By the time he'd steamed open the envelope, he'd burnt himself several times. The first thing he noticed was the Innskeep letterhead; the second was the signature – Jacques Biet. Patrick's hands shook and his heart beat as he read it.

> Dear Madame Kimba,
>
> Thank you for your email in response to our phone conversations and my offer made on behalf of Innskeep United. I appreciate your concern for Patrick's welfare and understand your desire for him to continue his education through the Irish education system.
>
> I reiterate when I say that Patrick's joining the Youth Academy would not impinge on his education – quite the opposite, in fact. An educated footballer is a better footballer. As I already mentioned, I myself have a degree in Business and a Masters in Economics and am a true advocate of formal education.
>
> However, having observed Patrick from a distance during his stay at our facility, I must impress upon you once more our enthusiasm to have him on board. He showed real promise and displayed skills that no coach can ever put into a boy. He is also an intelligent lad and showed an uncanny sense of anticipation. Having vision and a sense of what is about to happen on a pitch before it does is the greatest skill

in football. I thought it was important to mention that. It is rare to see world-class potential in someone so young.

Having said all of that, I respect your decision and will also do as you ask and not get in touch with Patrick directly until he is eighteen. If you wish to speak to me at any stage, you can reach me on my mobile, detailed above, or at the club.

I wish you well, Mrs Kimba.

Yours sincerely

*Jacques Biet*

Patrick went up to his room and reread the letter several times then he saved the manager's mobile number in his phone.

He turned out the light and sat at the window until at last he saw Nuala and Joe, arm in arm, unsteadily approach the house. He heard them enter and their footsteps climb the stairs. The door of Nuala's bedroom opened and then closed.

After that, he was gone. There was a six-thirty flight to London in the morning. He planned to be on it but needed a credit card to make a booking.

When the house was still, he tiptoed out of his room and slid down the banister, landing softly on the hall floor. He left a note for Nuala on the hall table and let himself out of the house and ran through the darkened streets and alleyways, back to the apartment.

His mother was dozing in front of the television and the kitchen smelt of relatively recent toast. He would need to be quiet.

He tiptoed into her room and waited. No sound. Then, in a fluid movement he took down the mirror, took out the bundles through the slit in the paper and removed his passport, his mother's emergency credit card and a wad of notes from the elasticated stash.

Back in his own room, he changed into his jeans, packed a small bag and left, the door clicking softly behind him.

# Chapter 46

They didn't notice he was gone until mid-morning and even then they weren't overly concerned. The house was chaotic. There were suitcases lined up in the hallway and wedding presents and wedding-present wrapping paper scattered all over the place, half-eaten breakfasts on the kitchen table, half-drunk cups of tea on every surface and a taxi driver waiting impatiently at the gate. Nuala ran up and down the stairs for their passports, then their tickets and then her sunglasses. Joe read the paper and waited. She was in one of those moods. If he offered to help, she would scalp him.

"Where is he?" Nuala demanded in a teary fluster. She was wearing her hundred-year-old sunhat and he hadn't the heart to tell her it looked awful. "I'm not going until I see him."

Outside the taxi driver honked the horn once more.

Joe handed her Patrick's note.

*Dear Joe and Nuala*
*Congratulations again and have a great time. I left early as I don't like goodbyes.*
*Love, Patrick*

Nuala frowned. "How odd," she said.

"You'll see him in a few weeks, love," Joe said gently. "Come on now or we'll miss our flight."

Patrick's day had got off to a bad start. He hadn't booked in time to catch the early flight which gave him a few hours to kill while hoping his mother didn't catch up with him before he got the chance to leave.

He rode the elevator: up and down, up and down. He played video games, drank tea and watched the planes take off and land, take off and land. He people-watched and people watched him. He reread the letter several times over and dialled Jacques Biet's mobile number, no answer. He left a message.

At ten thirty he went through security: trainers, belt and hoodie off, mobile, keys, headphones and silver cross on a chain in the tray.

He drank a smoothie and then perused duty-free, testing the lotions and balms. A woman with an orange face followed him closely like a shadow. She wanted to make sure he wasn't pilfering or pocketing something or planning to use a sample bottle of Eau de Parfum to conjure up an explosive device in the name of Jihad.

He turned and stared at her. She looked away.

"I'm not going to steal anything," he said plainly.

"It's my job to keep an eye on people," she said snottily.

"What about that guy over there with the tracksuit and moustache carrying the empty sports bag?" He pointed.

She didn't look over.

Patrick put down the cologne and left and nearly walked straight into Joe and Nuala. They didn't see him. He ducked out of sight. They were going on honeymoon and looked happy despite their bickering. As they walked towards their gate he felt a wash of loneliness. He hadn't had a chance to say goodbye in person.

He boarded and tried the manager's number again before switching off his phone. Still no answer. He would try again in London. He ignored the missed calls from his mother and pushed thoughts of her out of his head. He was furious with her. He'd kept his part of the deal, studied for and sat his exams; she'd broken hers.

The plane landed in Stansted. He dialled and redialled, left message after message to no avail. He wandered through the vast white airport for ages, checking and rechecking his phone, and felt stupid. His departure had been rash and a mistake. Now he was stuck in London with nowhere to go. There was every chance the manager had changed his mind about him. Things happened fast in football and perhaps he'd grown weary of trying to convince his mother. He clenched his fists, cursed his mother and boarded the train to the city anyway. He redialled and left a message, citing the date, time and train before going underground and losing coverage.

Tessa was surprised when Patrick hadn't shown up by lunchtime. She dialled his mobile number. It rang but there was no answer She pulled on her gardening gloves and stepped out onto the balcony. She missed her vegetable patch in Lavender Square. Now she only had window boxes and a bin for growing potatoes. The air was soupy and the sky darkened. She worked until clouds, thick and navy and heavy, joined forces and the first crack of thunder jolted her. Rain began to fall as thick and heavy as silver dollars.

She went inside. She dialled Patrick's number again. Still no answer and a tiny flutter of worry ran through her.

She cleaned the kitchen. Outside the rain fell in a continuous stream and worry gnawed at her. He never normally stayed away this long. Patrick liked his food and his meagre pocket money did not stretch to cover chips or crisps or wraps. She sat at the kitchen table and tried to hem a dress but couldn't concentrate. She went downstairs and checked the post. There was just one letter, no stamp. It was another official-looking one and she didn't like the look of it. This time it had not been forwarded from Nuala's.

She went back upstairs and redialled Patrick's number. It rang out. Where on earth was he?

She made tea, sat down and opened the envelope. It was another letter from Revenue and it said the same thing. She looked up and out through the window into the teeming rain. A date had been set for an audit. Someone had reported her for tax evasion and she was advised to get her accounts in order. They were looking for four years of accounts. Immigration had been informed as a matter of course.

Tessa's hand shook and she put down the letter. Now they knew where she lived. She got up and paced the living room and sifted through all the people she knew. Someone had taken it upon themselves to report her and she wondered who she could possibly have aggravated to such an extent that they felt the need to do such a thing.

She had no accounts to speak of. Her savings were modest; not enough for a four-year tax bill. She took down the mirror in her room and lifted out the bundle from her *cachette* to get her post-office book. She knew immediately it had been meddled with. She went through it carefully. Her money was short, her credit card gone and Patrick's passport was missing. She dialled his number. It went to voicemail.

She dialled Saskia's number; she answered.

"Tessa?"

"Saskia, have you been talking to Patrick?"

"Not since last night, why?"

"His passport is missing."

"Maybe he just needed ID for something," Saskia suggested. She didn't add, 'For a six-pack of lager for example'.

"No, I think he's gone somewhere."

"How can you be so sure?"

"He's taken some of the housekeeping money."

"Would that be enough to run away on?"

"He's taken my credit card too." Tessa hung up.

She knew exactly where Patrick had run to. She was about to dial another number when the doorbell rang.

It was a man and woman. She knew they were from Immigration straight away. It was the way they were dressed. A memory hit her with a jolt: grey building, take a ticket, wait in line. Her heart thumped against her ribcage. She was in trouble.

The train was full of tourists: bags, rucksacks and maps. Patrick watched them enviously. Somehow he was different and he always had been. Whether "smelly" or "jungle boy", it made no difference. He was different and that was that, and the only time he'd ever felt part of something was in the heat of a match when nothing else mattered and winning was everything. Now that prospect was probably gone too. His mother, so determined to keep him off the field and at a desk, had allowed the dream to be waved under his nose only to have it taken off him.

He got angrier. The train stopped at Tottenham Hale. People got on and avoided sitting next to him. A tall and angry black youth in a hoodie spelt trouble. By the time he emerged at Liverpool Street he was so angry he wanted to kick something hard. Only thing was there was someone already waiting there for him on the platform.

It was Jacques Biet wearing sunglasses and he didn't look one bit pleased.

# Chapter 47

He nodded at Patrick and they walked swiftly without speaking through the busy station. The Frenchman's legs were long and Patrick had to run to keep up. Commuters stopped and stared, elbowed and double-took. Jacques Biet striding through Liverpool Street tube station wearing sunglasses with his coat flying behind him – he looked like that bloke from *The Matrix*. He was fast too. Because by the time phones were switched on to document the evidence, he was gone. Outside, there was a car waiting.

They got in and it pulled away, smoothly gliding into London traffic. The Frenchman breathed deep through his nose and closed his eyes.

Patrick bit his lip and waited for a bollocking but when Jacques spoke his voice was kind if a little drained.

"It is not often I wander through tube stations looking for runaways," he said and then he sighed deeply.

"I'm sorry," Patrick replied. "It's just I found your letter and I ran."

"So I gather."

"What do you mean?"

"Your mother called me."

"Oh?"

"Oh yes. You're not too old for a kick in the pants, you know?

I wrote the letter to her, not to you." The manager shook his head.

Pedestrians wove through red buses and cyclists and cars oblivious of the great manager and his young protégé. For a moment Patrick wanted to be among them. He felt very small indeed. The manager turned to look at him. His expression was serious, unblinking and intimidating.

"But we've got bigger problems, young man," he said. "Your mother is being questioned by Immigration."

"For what?" Patrick said and he thought about all the forms his mother had filled out over the years. Maybe she'd forgotten to dot an i and he smiled at the thought of it.

But Mr Biet was not laughing.

"Tax evasion is a crime, Patrick. But it's her association with Tarek Raslan that's the bigger problem. Someone has reported him for suspected involvement with Islamic State."

"*Tarek!*" Patrick shrieked. "He's no terrorist. He hardly says two words."

"Well, that doesn't seem to be the case," Jacques Biet said dryly.

Tessa sat in a small grey room and counted the holes in the lino. Counting would help to keep her sane as she filed through all the people she knew. Someone had reported her, someone who knew all her affairs and every aspect of her business: the French lessons and the dressmaking, where she was from and how she had come to be there. They knew her new address and about her son who was Irish, unlike her, this was made clear. She was just another African immigrant who had broken the law. The interrogators were cold; their questions invasive. She answered their questions but they would not answer hers. No, they could not say who had reported her. It had been done confidentially. They asked about her relationship with Tarek too. Initially it was embarrassing as they poked for potential intimacies but it soon became frightening and then terrifying as the questioningly steered in a new direction – that of terrorist sympathies.

Memories rushed back to nip at her heels. It was the smell of disinfectant mixed with fearful hope, sweat and worry. The years peeled back and left her exactly as she had been – a mother alone and desperate, heaving with morning sickness, waiting in line in that room full of burkahs, thobes, caftans, kohl, beads, bangles, braids, gele and turbans. Every desperate nationality, each suspicious of the other, clutching their papers and passports, all at the mercy of a man behind a glass pane.

They had eyed her small bump with suspicion and pursed lips. At the time, Tessa herself was not sure about how she herself felt about her bump. It was the bump that had forced her to leave, quickly, without thinking or telling many. Ireland was considered receptive. She put things in order and left: Kinshasa, Brussels, London, Dublin. Now, she was not so sure about Ireland's receptiveness. She never really had been. Irish people stuck together. No matter how long you were around, you were never quite part of the clique. But she had loved Lavender Square. Nuala's fine kitchen with its warm range and the quiet drawing room with its high ceilings and a view for each season: autumn golds, squally skies, purple lavender, winter snow and silver frosts. The drawing room, where Nuala had set her up for French lessons and sewing. Nuala her once-friend and confidante, who knew everything about her and at the same time nothing at all, had betrayed her twice. With a jolt, Tessa realised there was really only one person who fit the whistle-blower bill and that was Nuala – Nuala who had taken them in off the street so she could hold onto her home and then married a once-suspected criminal. Suddenly it all seemed like a bizarre conspiracy.

It was late afternoon by the time they reached Surrey. Patrick was to stay at a boarding house run by a lady called Shirley who looked after several young Innskeep footballers. She was kind and wore an apron like Nuala and Patrick felt lonely for her then. His mother, he could not think about, not yet. The mixture of anger and guilt was overpowering. For the first night he would have a room on his own, after that he would share with a French boy called Arnaud.

"Am I staying?" Patrick asked. He was confused. "What about my mam?"

Mr Biet put his hands in his pockets and raised his left eyebrow. "Isn't this where you want to be?"

"Yes, but not without my mam."

"*Mais oui*, but didn't you leave her this morning without saying a word?"

"I didn't think."

"No, you didn't," the Frenchman said and Patrick knew he was being taught a lesson.

"Shirley is a good lady. She will look after you. Tomorrow you should play football with the boys at Old Head. It will keep your mind off things. In the meantime I'm going to see if we can bring your maman over here. I'm trying to arrange a meeting with the Home Office and I'll see what we can do."

Before the manager left, he advised Patrick not to make any phone calls.

"Someone you know reported your mother to the authorities. So it's probably best not to speak to anyone until you've spoken to your maman."

"No one at all?"

"No one."

Patrick didn't sleep. He tossed and turned in the heat and thought about his mother. What if she was transported to the deepest darkest heart of Africa in the middle of the night? Mr Biet promised that this would not happen but Patrick had heard of things like it. He had also just sat a history paper. It was possible for a whole race of people to disappear overnight and for your neighbours not to know a thing about it. His imagination spun out of control and haunted him. He wanted to ring Nuala or Saskia or Tom but had promised not to. The fact that they were like family and none of them fit to harm a fly didn't matter. It was best to wait, the manager told him. The priority was to sort his mother's affairs. There was nothing Patrick could do except try to keep his mind off things. But that was next to impossible and, in the early hours of a new day, he knew his mother had tried to crush his dream but he would never forgive himself for deserting her. He would spend a lifetime making it up to her.

He was tired next morning at breakfast and knew he would be useless on the pitch. But Mr Biet was right. Football took his mind off things. The sprints and ball work, kicks and tricks worked to shake the worry out of his head. The lads were friendly and Ben-from-Brixton shook his hand.

"Good to have you back, Paddy," he said. "Maybe you'll stay this time."

For five days, Patrick kept the same routine: breakfast, ballpark, back to Shirley's then bed. He was fine when he was on the pitch but, once off, his heart was heavy and his future looked uncertain. It was a strange sort of limbo and not how he'd ever envisaged the beginning of his professional football career. Joe and Nuala had always featured and Tom and Saskia, Emma even and maybe Tot, standing proudly on the sidelines or in the stands dressed head to foot in the Innskeep colours. Now, it was as if his life before had been erased overnight.

There was no word from his mother and no sign of Mr Biet. There were missed calls from Saskia and text messages from Nuala and Tom. He switched off his phone to avoid temptation. He wasn't going to annoy Jacques Biet twice and put his future in jeopardy.

His roommate was homesick for Marseille and glad to have someone who spoke French. Both missed their mothers and kept the fact to themselves. They played vingt-et-un each evening until it was time for bed and, although neither ever felt like sleeping, all the physical exercise saw them conk out as soon as their heads hit their pillows.

Another three days passed; Patrick began to stay after training. After the other boys left, he stayed behind and practised goal kicks for an hour or more: left foot, right foot, *bang, bang, bang*. He found that once he had a ball at his feet, he could cope, keep focused. He hurled his energy into every ball, powering it into the back of the net. Sometimes he looked over to the sidelines, hoping to see his mother or the manager or someone he knew and sometimes he was certain he could hear Joe calling his name. But there was never anyone there except the grounds men or linesmen and he began to think that's where he would remain forever. Living in that strange transience, a half-baked footballer, half-realised, until he was old and grey and unable to kick a ball a yard in front of himself.

Then one evening, when the sky was turning pink and a segment of moon appeared, he looked over to the sidelines and did see his mother. She was walking towards him and looked as beautiful as ever, a tall, willowy African queen wearing jeans and she was waving. He dropped the ball and ran.

As long as they had each other, everything would be okay.

# Chapter 48

By the time Nuala and Joe returned from their honeymoon, Patrick and Tessa had moved into a pretty house in Croydon with bay windows, wooden floors and lots of light. Once their things were unpacked and arranged, it felt like home. They celebrated by ordering in pizza and Cokes and watching *Match of the Day*. His mother's new interest in the game amused him. He didn't ask but he guessed she felt she owed the game something for saving her skin.

"What's that he's just done there?" she asked, pointing at the screen.

"A half volley."

"And that?"

"A step over."

"And what's that?"

"A back foot turn."

"Okay."

He asked if he could get in touch with them at home in Lavender Square. Tessa asked him not to.

"Not for the time being anyway," she said. "I need to do a little investigating first. Will you let me do that?"

"Okay, but who are you investigating? None of our friends would ever report you."

338

"We don't know that. Ireland has changed. Lots of people want people like us to leave."

"I know but I am Irish, Ireland is my home."

"This is your home now, Patrick," his mother said and her expression indicated the subject was closed.

Patrick didn't push it because he wanted more than anything in the world to stay at Innskeep. He would get in touch with the others when the time was right and tell them everything.

Tessa signed the papers Jacques Biet gave her.

"You got what you wanted in the end, Monsieur Biet," she said. "My son," and she smiled. There was no malice in her voice.

"I would have preferred a little less drama, Madame Kimba," he said. "Your friend, the Syrian man, was cleared?"

"Yes. Thank you for your help with that, with everything …"

"I'm glad I could help. And, Mrs Kimba, I meant what I said: I think Patrick's got a bright future."

"I think so too," she said and she did.

Every day Patrick went training and Tessa set about making their house a home. The size of London, where it seemed every second person was black, gave her a sense of freedom she hadn't felt in a long time. She liked the markets where you could buy anything you wanted at a good price: suits, jeans and shoes or pears, potatoes and mangoes. She walked taller. She ditched her wig for good and decided to let her natural Afro grow with pride. When people stared now, she understood she was being admired. A woman in a café on the banks of the Thames told her she looked like a model and didn't believe Tessa when she told her she had a sixteen-year-old son.

The people at the job centre were helpful and explained that with a little further study she could teach again. In the meantime she took a job as a receptionist in a law firm that needed a French speaker.

In the evenings, they ate dinner together and discussed their day like a normal family. They did not mention the past. They would move on now and get on with things. Patrick would start studying for his A-levels in September, Tessa would take her teaching exams and life would go on.

In Lavender Square, life did not move on quite as smoothly. When

Nuala and Joe returned from honeymoon, Nuala knew there was something wrong when she turned the key in the door. She was not sure how but she did.

She tried to call Patrick only to discover his number was no longer in service. She asked Tom and Saskia over and they sat around the kitchen table just like they always had done. They were worried. None of them had heard from Patrick.

Saskia told them about her bizarre conversation with Tessa.

"She believed he'd run away."

"And why on earth would he do that?"

"Maybe he ran away to join Innskeep," Tom suggested.

"People don't run away to join Innskeep," Saskia snorted. "It's not the circus."

"They do if their mother tries to prevent it," Nuala said. "I'm going over to Tessa's."

Tom drove them over and together they trooped up to the door. But when they rang the buzzer, someone else answered. The Kimbas no longer lived there. They had moved away. It was a mystery.

Nuala cried for weeks. Patrick's absence left an unstoppable void. She missed their chats over pots of tea and ached to hear his voice. She had tried to get through to the Academy but, although polite, the Academy was protective of its young players and not inclined to disclose details to strangers over the phone. When she asked if she could speak to Mr Biet, she was told he was busy.

"But he ate some of my fruitcake once," she explained. Only afterwards, did she realise how like a fruitcake she must have sounded. International football clubs were most certainly accustomed to phone calls from crazy people.

Saskia tried to get in touch through her media connections but to no avail. The Innskeep Academy was for young footballers who were fiercely protected from the media glare.

Every day Nuala climbed the stairs to Patrick's bedroom and lay on the bed with its Innskeep duvet cover, letting the tears roll down her face. She was inconsolable. Sometimes Joe lay beside her and took her hand. He was hurt too but didn't talk about it. He knew it was worse for Nuala. For her, it was like losing a son.

"Where are they, Joe?"

"I don't know, love."

"I miss him so much."

"And am I not enough for you?"

"Of course you are," she protested. "It's just for years I've had a boy and now it's as if he never existed."

No one knew anything, not even the Guards who told her if people packed up and left of their own free will it was no business of theirs to track them down. By all accounts, Patrick and Tessa Kimba seemed to have disappeared in the middle of the night and could not be reached. Both of their mobile numbers had been disconnected.

# Chapter 49

Summer slid into autumn. Geese formations called out, "*south, south, south*" as they flew over the square which turned gold then red then brown. New children walked in pairs to school, giggling and chattering, all bows and brightly coloured schoolbags.

Siobhán returned to school and there was no Patrick. She shrugged in her habitual way. Maybe he'd show to collect his Junior Cert results. In the meantime she just got on with doing what she'd always done before – floating.

Tessa and Patrick left an empty corner in the lives of those they had occupied. One that initially was empty and obvious but, as the months passed, it filled up with the debris of living: scraps and odds and ends, bits and bobs. Their names were mentioned less and memories of them lay dormant. Each of their friends was hurt in their own way and nursed their own private wounds. When Tessa was sick they'd visited her in hospital and looked after her son. Patrick had grown up from boy to man on their watch and had learned how to play ball under their tutelage and with their encouragement. Could two close friends just walk out of a life, close the door and not look back without so much as a thank-you note? It stung.

They saw less of each other. Patrick had been the reason, the glue, and without him there were fewer excuses or reasons to meet, pop over or stop by. Life moved on.

After receiving poor exam results, Tot's parents sent him to the school where Patrick had been. Tubbier and rounder and more crotchety, he was bullied cruelly and cast aside. He took to walking the perimeter fence and that was where he met Siobhán just as Patrick had before him. Even though she spoke funny and was as deaf as a post, having someone was better than having no one at all and they became friends. It didn't take them long to make the Patrick connection.

"He never mentioned you," she said.

"I let him down."

"Oh?"

"I think my parents weren't all that keen for me to be around him, not after he got that beating. I didn't cop on to what they were up to."

"Are you a bit stupid?" Siobhán joked.

"I'm prone to it," Tot said in all seriousness.

"Well, I never let him down and I've not heard anything from him either. I thought he'd be back to collect his results."

"No sign?"

"Nothing."

"I wonder how he got on."

He did very well as it turned out – A's in French, English and History, B's in Maths, Science, Geography and Business, and a D in Irish. Tessa was very pleased.

Emma did well too although not as well as Fiona wanted her to.

Fiona met with the school principal.

"I'm not happy."

The principal arched her eyebrows. She wore last-season designer suits and was surprisingly glamorous for a teaching type.

"Mrs Fox, Emma got the results she was capable of."

"What is that supposed to mean?"

"I mean your daughter is trying her best. Except for her artistic ability, she is not an A student."

Fiona coloured. "You mean to tell me that I've been paying these preposterous fees only to be told this?"

The principal did not flinch. She had met a trillion Fiona Fox types over the years. They were all similar: bland and blustering and forgettable.

"I am removing my daughter from this school."

"As you wish, Mrs Fox," said the principal without putting up a fight.

And so Emma also ended up where Patrick had been, with Tot and with Siobhán. They spent many a lunchtime speculating where Patrick had disappeared to. Perhaps he'd joined a fourth division club in England or returned to Africa. They agreed Africa was the most logical explanation – but why leave without saying anything?

Both Emma and Tot suffered their own private guilt. Patrick might have stayed if they'd been better friends to him. They spoke to each other about it on their walks home.

Tot told her he could call for her in the mornings. Lavender Square was a shortcut for him. Emma asked him not to.

"It's my mother – she'll run you."

"If she didn't want you hanging around with the likes of me then why did she take you out of that mega-posh school?"

"I wasn't worth the fees."

"Parents. My aul' lad said 'I want you under my nose, Tot Flanagan, so I can kick the arse off you if you step out of line'."

They laughed. It was nice being friends again. Around Tot you didn't have to watch what you said or listen to yachting-holiday stories.

When Emma, Siobhán and Tot tired of discussing the whereabouts of Patrick, they started playing football, just the three of them, knocking it around to each other. Others started to join them, other floaters who thought, "Hey, if they let a deaf girl play then surely I can too?".

They played every lunchtime, and Emma realised it was the happiest she'd been in a long time. A gang of them started going to Saskia's old café on Saturdays to watch matches. It was cool seeing Saskia on the big screen. Sometimes Tom stopped by to say hi.

Joe and Nuala bought a dog and fell into a new routine. Every morning they got up early and walked it together. Then Joe continued on to the shop for the papers and Nuala made a pot of tea and cut some bread for breakfast. By the time he returned, the tea was drawn to a perfect tar and they read the papers. At intervals they read bits out to each other, commented and took another sip of tea. Joe learned to cook. Nuala took over in the garden, weeding and harvesting all the vegetables Tessa had so lovingly planted. Sometimes she sat back on her heels and wondered if she would ever see her and Patrick again.

At first, the cooking was messy. Joe found new recipe books convoluted and overly wordy with too much back story. He pulled out Nuala's mother's home economics book from the fifties and mastered the traditionals: roast beef with Yorkshire pudding, steak and kidney pie, stew, shepherd's pie, meatballs and bacon and cabbage. He also made vats of vegetable soup. The cooking took his mind off things.

Joe was sore and had difficulty acknowledging it. The fledging footballer he'd taken under his wing had flown without a promise or a thank-you. When he thought Nuala wasn't around, he took to talking to the Sacred Heart like so many had before him. It was usually when he was doing something like stuffing a chicken or dicing vegetables and mulling over something he needed to turn over in his head. It was through such conversations and reasoning that he came to terms with Patrick's desertion.


Tom saw Saskia on the telly more than in person. She was always busy. But when their road safety campaign was nominated for a number of awards, they attended the ceremony together. She looked magnificent in a figure-hugging black gown and her hair twisted up into a sophisticated-looking roll. Her eyes sparkled and she looked happy. She sat beside the creative director who was uptight and unsubtle but a good man.

The campaign won three golds and, each time she and Tom went up to collect an award, she smiled at him. For some reason it irritated him.

"Well done, us!" she said and smiled afterwards.

"What's with all the smiling?"

She smiled more widely and spoke through her teeth. "It's called being happy."

Tom led Saskia out onto the floor. He held her close and it felt so good, natural almost. She wasn't skinny or macrobiotic; she was athletic and she smelt clean and delicious. He had a sudden and inexplicable urge to reach down and kiss her behind the ear and did so. She looked up at him and his heart turned over. Saskia was beautiful. He couldn't believe he'd never seen it before. It knocked him for six.

"Hey," she said.

"Hey," he croaked.

"You're not going all mushy on me, are you?"

"Me? I might be."

"Don't mess with me, Tom."

"I promise I won't." He pulled her closer.

She looked at him. His expression was intense.

"Are you drunk?" She hoped he wasn't going to make a scene.

"No. But I'd like to take you out on a date."

"Really?"

"Really."

"Okay."

A week later, Tom brought Saskia to a French restaurant where the napkins were linen, the staff professional and the food divine. It was heavenly.

"It is too much?" Tom asked anxiously.

"It's heavenly, thank you," Saskia said and he seemed pleased.

She thought it would be weird being on a date with Tom but it felt right. They chatted away easily, stealing glances at each other over dishes and glasses.

"You look beautiful," he said and she smiled sheepishly.

She put down her napkin and looked straight at him. "Don't get me wrong, Tom, this is really nice, but why a date now?"

"Am I too late?"

"No."

"I've liked you for ages – it just took me a while to see."

"And what made you see?" she teased.

"Seeing you with Richard Watts always annoyed me and I didn't know why. And then when he hurt you I genuinely wanted to injure him. Of late I realised after being out with you for a pint or a coffee that I missed you desperately when you went home."

She was smiling at him.

"What?" he said.

"You're cute when you're in love," she said and she started

when she realised she'd said too much.

He laughed.

"Are you laughing at me?" she asked, worried now in case she'd blown it.

"I'm not. It's just, of course I love you."

They held hands across the table. Couples nearby smiled at them. Saskia felt liked she'd been invited to a party she'd never been invited to before. It felt good.

"Patrick knew how I felt long before I did," Tom said.

"He did?"

"One day I got thick when one of those pundits was flirting with you on the telly and he slagged me about it."

"He was always on the money, that little guy. I miss him."

"Me too. I'd love to be able to tell him that I finally got my act together."

When they got back to the square they went into the walled garden. Saskia sat on the swing. He pushed her gently. After a while he stopped pushing and came around to face her.

"I think I've never moved away from the square because I wanted to be near you," he said.

She looked at her feet, unsure again now in case the bubble was about to burst.

"I love you, Saskia," Tom said. "I have for ages. I want to marry you."

She looked up. "That's cool because I've got a bottom drawer all sorted and everything."

"I heard about that."

He caught the swing and held it still. Her eyes filled with tears.

"Saskia, I'm telling you I can't live without you."

"If you're joking me around, Tom, I will murder you."

"I'm not."

He took her face in his hands and kissed away the tears and found her mouth and it was perfect as though they had been made to kiss each other.

"I wish this had happened years ago – I've wasted so much time," he said.

"We have loads of time, Tom."

"I love you, Saskia."

"I love you, Tom," she said. "I always have. Now let's go to bed."

"Yes, ma'am!"

The leaves fell and the frost came in and they all got on with things. The cracks were papered over and Nuala came to the conclusion that she'd never see the Kimbas again. She counted her blessings and had Tom and Saskia over for dinner. They toasted each other and wished the Kimbas well wherever they were.

# Chapter 50

Jacques Biet had been keeping tabs on Patrick's progress. The boy was focused and possessed an uncannily adult calm and attitude. He also had a great left foot. It was his secret weapon. But most importantly, Patrick Kimba wasn't the type who went for glory. This was unusual for a striker let alone a young kid keen to impress his peers and his coach. It was a desirable trait and it displayed intelligence beyond his years. If the young footballer was clever enough to realise that accurate passing and teamwork was how games were won then he would go places and sooner than he thought.

The coaches at Old Head tried him in various positions on the pitch. Although a natural goal-scorer they felt he was grounded enough and smart enough to slot into an attacking midfield role. It would be unusual for a sixteen-year old to be wheeled out at so young an age but not unheard of. Before Christmas, he was chosen for an Under-18 side, then in January he came on ten minutes before the end of a reserve match against Leeds and made his mark.

The coach made a call to Jacques Biet.

"We have a lad out here you might want to take a look at."

"Oh yes?"

"An old head on young shoulders this one, let alone young legs – Patrick Kimba."

"I found him myself. He's a strong boy, that one, mentally and physically."

"You haven't lost the knack then, Mr Biet."

Patrick took his progress in his stride. He ignored the smart comments and nudges. They were nothing in comparison to being called a "jungle boy" from the sidelines or having your knee kicked in. To Patrick football was uncomplicated. It was life that was complicated and life had prepared him well for the gruelling mental and physical strength of the senior game.

He and Ben-from-Brixton became good friends. It was an easy friendship. They played different positions and therefore weren't competing. Sometimes after training they went to the cinema or to an amusement arcade with a group of the other lads. Some of them were into drinking cans and talking about all the women they'd shagged. Patrick suspected most of them hadn't had as much as a feel-up. He himself wasn't interested in the drinking part. His mother had made him read Paul McGrath's autobiography and it had frightened the crap out of him. Neither was Ben into drink – his father told him he'd be put on a ship back to Africa if there was a whiff of drink off him.

Some evenings they went to Ben's for tea. His mother, a woman with a big smile, fed him rice and dumplings and ackee and her fussing made him lonely for Nuala and for Lavender Square.

Ben and Patrick talked about football and Old Head and Innskeep, picking apart matches, analysing the technique of the first team and it reminded him of how he and Saskia used to analyse matches.

He and Ben rarely spoke about the prospect of making it to the top level. Patrick believed it was because they both assumed it would happen, at the right time and in the most natural way possible. There was no other alternative. That was the way they saw it. You didn't spend your whole life thinking and dreaming only to be sent home in the end. This was not an option.

Being at the Innskeep Stadium, with its felt green pitch, walls of stands rising up to the sky and pulsating emotion, filled Patrick with absolute desire to play there himself.

"Some day, mate," Ben said, "some day."

That some day was just around the corner, the following spring as it so happened, on the eve of his seventeenth birthday.

# Chapter 51

Emma arranged to meet Siobhán and Tot and the other footballers in the café to watch the Innskeep match for her own birthday celebration. Tom would drop by. Saskia would be commentating on the match. All Emma wanted from her mother was some money to pay for coffees and cake. She told her she was meeting some of the girls from her old school. She knew this would nip any potentially awkward questions in the bud about the pedigree of whom she was choosing to spend her seventeenth birthday with.

As their birthdays approached, both Emma and Patrick had briefly wondered what the other was doing.

Emma sat on her bedroom windowsill and looked out over the walled garden. It was a beautiful garden. She had never fully appreciated it before. They had been lucky to have it for a pitch. She wondered would Patrick ever play on it again.

In Croydon, Patrick opened one of the drawers in his bedroom and the slightest waft of dried lavender escaped. Nostalgia hit him and he sat on the end of his bed and thought of the square. Had they all forgotten him at this stage? Very possibly. Some day soon he would see them all again no matter what his mother thought. For the time being there was football to be played and there was no way he was putting that at risk.

Downstairs, the phone started to ring. For a moment he thought it might be someone from home but it wasn't. It was for him, and it was Jacques Biet. He told Patrick to report to the Innskeep stadium the following Saturday kitted out for the QPR game. He wasn't making any promises but if the score was healthy he'd think about putting him on for five minutes near the end. Patrick put down the phone and went for a walk. Croydon was pretty but not Lavender Square. It would have been nice to take a stroll with Joe, north, west, south and east, on the cusp of what was surely the biggest moment of his life.

Saturday was fresh and yellow but bitterly cold. Emma walked to the café with a wad of cash from her mother who was going out for the day so there was no fear of her landing in on them. She pulled her coat tightly around her and felt sorry for anyone playing football that day. It was unusually cold for March.

In the distance, Tot and Siobhán waved. The two of them were awfully chummy these days. There was a chance they were snogging. Tot wouldn't say. He was fiercely protective of the partially deaf girl and glared at anyone who stared at her hearing aid for a second longer than appropriate.

At the Innskeep stadium, thousands of supporters filed in, fathers and sons, whole families and gangs of friends. They were vocal and in high spirits. The season was going well. Queens Park Rangers shouldn't hold any great challenge.

Tessa wasn't sure what to say to Patrick. There was nothing to say.

"*Bon chance, ma puce.*"

"*Merci, Maman.*"

"Play fair."

"*Oui.*"

"No matter what happens, we'll have chips for tea."

"*Bon.*"

The team trooped into the dressing room, all shiny and new and ready to play ball. The other players joked among themselves, slagging and bantering. Patrick pulled on his boots and said nothing. Ben had told him to keep his gob shut among the firsts or they'd tear him a new one.

The manager was soft-spoken and encouraging. He introduced them to Patrick. They nodded and eyed him up and down. If they thought Jacques Biet was losing his marbles for fielding a baby, they didn't say.

They lined up opposite QPR. At the mouth of the tunnel there was a wall of sound waiting, a noise so thick and tangible you could feel it in your toes. Patrick knew he should feel overwhelmed, out of his depth, faint even, but he didn't. Since the age of eight, he'd been conditioning himself for that very moment. The team danced on their toes and jogged out through the tunnel, studs on the cement, *clack, clack, clack*, and the roar of the crowd rose and engulfed him like a warm old friend. Patrick knew he had come home.

In Dublin, Saskia checked through her notes before going on air. She went through the team sheets, looked at the set-ups, scrutinised the formations and looked at the bench.

Her notes fell to the floor in her hurry to find her phone. She made a call to a football colleague in North London.

"There must be a mistake," she said. "There's a Patrick Kimba named on the team sheet."

"No mistake. It's some kid from the Academy."

She rang Tom.

"You might want to watch this QPR game."

"We're just about to, love, why?"

"I've found Patrick. He's on the Innskeep bench."

Tom rang Joe. Joe and Nuala grabbed their coats and ran down to the café. As they arrived in the door, the camera panned over Patrick Kimba. He looked cool-headed, grown-up. Nuala sat down. Tom asked for the volume to be raised. Emma looked at the telly and her heart stopped. Patrick was in the Innskeep dug-out and he was looking straight at her.

Saskia came up on the screen. She remained tight-lipped while her male colleagues criticised Jacques Biet's decision to include another kid in the squad. She took a sip of water. She was addled. Why had Patrick not told her or any of them where he was? She looked up. Her panel were looking at her, waiting for an answer.

"Well?" they enquired. "What do you think, Saskia?"

"I wouldn't underestimate the boy," was all she said.

The match kicked off. By halftime Innskeep were two nil up with two hard-won goals. QPR had no intention of rolling over and fifteen minutes into the second half they got one back because of a stupid mistake. The manager wasn't impressed and shouted a barrage of French expletives. Ten minutes later Innskeep clawed one back and held the score at 3-1.

Patrick was told to warm up.

As he jogged up and down the line he knew he was being watched and commented on. He guessed Jacques Biet was being ripped apart by commentators everywhere.

Five minutes to go, the board was held up to signal the substitution, 16 for 8, and Patrick was sent on, to the centre, the engine room.

"Just get the feel of it," the manager said. "Only a few minutes to go. We're safe."

He ran on. His back was patted, his shoulder squeezed. He did not look up but he could feel the crowd, thousands of eyes all watching him. He inhaled and focused, tuned out the noise of the crowd and tuned into the game. He watched the ball and sensed those around him. All they had to do was keep possession and ride it out. He ran up and down the pitch, watching and listening, eyes darting left and right. Fulltime came and went and then a minute into injury time there was a kick-out. The ball sailed deep into their own half where it was won and dealt with by the right back who neatly passed it forward to the right wing. He back-heeled it to Patrick. Patrick brought it forward. His marker, sensing an amateur, thundered towards him head on. Patrick kept his cool and made to look as if about to take him on, but instead, just seconds before he reached him, he flicked the ball right, with perfect accuracy, to reach the right wing who was already on the run. The crowd roared with approval. A lesser player would have bottled it, lost possession. The winger collected the ball and took off down the line with pace to kick a perfectly weighted cross which was headed home. The whistle blew. The cheering was deafening. He looked up and took in the enormity of the event. He breathed in, out, in, out. The pitch suddenly seemed huge and he felt a wrench as his arm was pulled up into the air. The skipper held up his arm, presenting him to the home crowd, and the reception was thunderous. The team made their way towards the tunnel.

The manager was smiling and nodding. "You helped set up that one nicely, well done," he said. "They'll want to talk to you, you being new and so young and all."

Patrick was jostled along into the tunnel where a reporter was waiting to interview him. His teammates pushed him forward and wolf-whistled. His face came up on screen. In the café in Dublin they all watched in disbelief. After all those months, Patrick had turned up, and at a Innskeep match. He had made it all the way to where he wanted to be but not told them. He looked confident and unafraid as though he belonged.

"Patrick Kimba," the reporter asked, "how does it feel to have made your Premier League debut?"

"It feels as good as I always imagined," he said calmly and he smiled.

"You're very young to be competing at this level. That's an incredible achievement."

"Thank you. It's all I've thought about since the age of eight."

While Patrick was being interviewed, Tessa was making her way through the crowds and was thinking about chips for tea. At intervals, she wiped tears off her cheeks. A man in a Innskeep scarf asked her if she was okay. She nodded.

"I'm happy," she said.

"Me too, love," he said. "You see that young lad the Gaffer sent on – that's the future, that is! Remember the name: Patrick Kimba."

"I will," she said.

# Chapter 52

For a week nothing happened, except for Patrick finishing up at Old Head and moving to the training ground at Barbury where he started training with the reserve team. If he was high on his A-team debut, the reserves brought him back to earth sharply. They were all competing for first team places and a player in his twenties, with a lot less career left than Patrick, was not going to engage in cosy chit-chat and what-ifs.

He was interviewed by *The Guardian* in a hotel near Regent's Park, all marble and mahogany and country-house armchairs. The journalist was impressed by the young boy with the sophisticated turn of phrase and mature attitude. The meeting went on longer than expected and what resulted was a well-written and interesting piece. As a result the article was bumped up and given a bigger spread.

Patrick talked about the square where he grew up, of their quirky pitch in the walled garden in Lavender Square, their coach Joe Delaney, who had always trained them like professionals and how his dream came true to play for Innskeep. When asked about his family, he said it was just him and his mother, as well as a group of people in Ireland who had taken care of him when his mother was ill. They'd become a kind of extended family.

"It sounds like you miss it there?" the interviewer observed.

"Sometimes I do."

When the interviewer asked him about his father, Patrick stalled. It seemed silly now to bring up the father he'd never known but had once dreamed of finding.

"He was a soldier in the Congo, Bartholomew Kimba," Patrick said. "I was born in Ireland. I never knew him."

"So you could actually play for the Republic of Ireland?" he said.

"Yes, I could," Patrick said and he smiled.

The photographer took a shot.

After the interview Patrick realised he was homesick. He considered calling Saskia but then decided against it. He would wait just a while longer. In Dublin, each of them read the article. Nuala wanted to catch the first flight to London and hang outside the Innskeep grounds until he showed up but she stopped herself. She had listened to hours of football conversations, cooked countless dinners, washed kits, checked spellings and tables and shared her home. The interview was pleasant, complimentary even but it didn't explain anything, not why they had upped and left like thieves in the night.

Saskia was hurt too and snappy as a result. Her colleagues noticed and wondered what had the normally chirpy and professional presenter eating the head off everyone around her. They put it down to man trouble and weren't wrong. Saskia read the interview over and over again; she watched Patrick's first team debut and afterwards his brief TV interview, searching for clues. She freeze-framed his face. It was solemn and in control. He was a man now. She chewed on her lip and considered arranging it with work so she had an excuse to go to London. But then she dropped the idea. If the boy who had always considered her a sister couldn't be bothered to lift the phone then she sure as shit couldn't either.

Tom met Joe for a pint. He guessed he might be hurting too. Joe took long draughts from his pint of Guinness.

"A boy lives under your roof for years," said Joe, "in the blink of an eye he's gone and then he shows up on telly and in the paper. I'm gobsmacked."

"Stranger than fiction."

"That it is. Nuala is like a weasel back there taking the house apart. She was worried sick about him, a boy she half reared. What got into them at all, do you think?"

No one had an answer but then one presented itself and everything became clear.

Irish sports journalists, eager for their own interviews, made their way to Lavender Square. They called to the door.

Joe was no longer afraid of them.

"You're on private property," he said.

"We're looking for Patrick Kimba. We understand this is his home."

"Not any more, it isn't. Patrick Kimba and his mother left here several months ago. That's all we have to say about it."

Calls were made, football contacts contacted and the trail led to Saskia. She wouldn't talk to them either.

"Like Joe Delaney said, they packed up and left without a word to any of us. That's all we know."

The standoffishness whet appetites. It sounded like there had been some sort of falling out. Some reporters tried to reach Patrick down in London. The club was polite but uncooperative. No, they didn't hand out contact details of their players; Patrick Kimba would be in touch if he wanted to talk. No contact was made.

Articles were written based on facts already known. Joe's case came up again and once more was held up to the light like a negative. Then they moved on from Joe and, without realising it, one journalist solved the mystery of the Kimbas' disappearance.

The wife of a man who drank in the same pub as a youth-side manager worked in Immigration. One night, after a Chardonnay too many, she let it slip to her husband about Mrs Kimba's run-in with Revenue and friendship with a suspected terrorist sympathiser which turned out to be unfounded. He was overheard telling a friend by a barman who was waiting for a Guinness to settle. The barman mentioned it casually to the youth-side manager who was friends with a sports journalist. The story was written as a filler and printed. Someone who knew Tessa Kimba's affairs very well had reported her for tax evasion and spiced it up with a little suspected fundamentalism. It had been dealt with. No big deal. It was clear the woman wouldn't have to worry about tax bills any more, not with a son who showed the promise he did. Case closed.

Saskia came across the piece first. She read it and handed it over to Tom. After breakfast they called over to Nuala and Joe where they found Emma sitting at the kitchen table feeding bacon fat to the dog.

"What on earth?" Nuala said when she finished reading.

Saskia was looking at her intently.

"She thought it was me," Nuala said. "Tessa thought it was me who reported her."

Saskia nodded.

Emma took the paper and when she read the piece a distant bell started ringing in her head – *ting, ting, ting.* She went home and watched her mother closely. The alarm bells grew louder. She took the key to the garden from its hook and crossed the street to the green door. She sat on the swing and swung until the alarm bells stopped ringing. Afterwards she went to talk to Nuala.

"I think it was my mother who reported Tessa."

Nuala said she would have to be sure, that you couldn't go around accusing people on a hunch, especially not people like her mother who had loads of pull and media connections.

"But it's not a hunch," Emma told her. "She quizzed me last Christmas when she spotted Tarek with Tessa and that evening I heard her on the phone. I thought it was strange. She asked for Revenue and then left a message and her number. It didn't make sense until now. Remember, she also asked you for the Kimba's new address?"

"But why would she do such a thing?" Nuala asked.

"She hates Patrick," Emma replied. "She always has."

Nuala said she would go with her but Emma wanted to talk to her mother alone.

"I just wanted you to know," she said.

"You're a good girl," Nuala said.

"No, I'm not," Emma said miserably. "I lost touch with him. I told him I would never let her get to me, but I did in the end."

While Emma was figuring how she would confront the issue with her mother, Patrick was about to confront a different issue altogether.

Training had finished for the day and he was the last in the dressing room. He tied his shoelaces and sat back to absorb the dressing-room smells: shower gel, spray, antiseptic, disappointments and victories. He inhaled, exhaled and revelled in it.

Then he stuffed his things into his gear bag and went outside where there was a man waiting for him.

He knew it was his father immediately.

# Chapter 53

The man was tall and worn around the edges. He wore an army jacket and jeans and there was solemnity about him. His hands were stuffed deep into his pockets and he looked unsure of himself.

Patrick was dumbstruck. He stepped backwards and leaned back against the changing-room door for support. The metal was cold against his back. His legs were glued to the ground and there seemed to be an ocean between them. Time stood still and he couldn't think of a word to say.

Eventually, the man spoke.

"It's been so long," he said. His accent was French. "You've grown into a fine boy, someone to be very proud of. I saw you play. You are like Pelé, *non?*" He smiled.

Patrick nodded dumbly.

The man walked over and held out his hand.

"Bart Kimba," he said and shook his hand. It was firm, dry and warm.

"Where have you been?"

"Everywhere," his father replied.

"Me too," said his son.

They walked to a local café and got coffees and two buns. His father counted the money out carefully and smiled at him.

They sipped from their mugs and regarded each other shyly.

"How did you find me?"

"I read that interview. You mentioned my name. You have achieved your dream, *non*, to play for Innskeep?"

"When I was small, it was always to find you."

"And now you have."

"Yes."

His father told him about being a soldier in the Congo. The heat and dense forest, roots tangled in roots, trees overshadowing trees, rivers teaming with fish, hippopotamus, crocodiles, the air thick with rifle fire and the smell of blood, death and decay.

Patrick shivered; his father put his hand on his arm.

"Too much detail. I'm sorry. I forget. It's just you strike me as a young man able for anything."

"It sounds like it was hell."

"It was."

"But you're here now and safe."

"I am."

Patrick drained his cup. "We should go home to Mam."

"Mam?"

"Yes."

"It has been so long. I might not recognise her."

"She'll know you. She told me all about you."

They caught the train to Croydon. The journey had a dreamlike quality. People looked at him and smiled, and looked at Bart Kimba with interest. Maybe they saw the likeness.

"Do all Premier League players take the train?" his father asked with a smile.

"Just this one. This one who has a mother who insists on keeping it real because I'm only seventeen and she doesn't want me getting notions."

"A lady who doesn't take any nonsense."

Patrick got up and pressed the Stop button.

"Yes. You see," he said, getting out of his seat, "you remember her well."

Patrick was nervous now. Turning up without warning might give his mother a stroke. He should have called her first. She wasn't fond of surprises.

She was stirring a pot and smiled when he came in. He watched her for a moment from the doorway, grinning.

"What's the cheeky grin for?"

"I've a surprise for you."

"Oh?" Her brow creased slightly.

Patrick fetched Bart Kimba from the porch and led him into the kitchen. His mother started. She stopped stirring. Patrick withdrew from the scene and stood by the fridge. It was getting dusky outside. A dog barked. His mother's face was unreadable.

The man stepped forward, offering his hand. His mother flinched.

"Bartholemew Kimba," he said, introducing himself.

His mother's eyes widened to the size of dinner plates.

"Impossible," she whispered.

"No, it's me all right," the man said.

Whatever was in the saucepan started to burn. No one made a move to take it off the hob.

"How did you know to use that name?" She sounded furious, suspicious.

"That is my name," the man said mildly. He looked to Patrick for support.

"Don't you recognise him?" Patrick asked and his voice was on edge. "My father, he has found us. He was a soldier in the Congo. He just told me all about it."

His mother tottered backwards and leaned against the sink. She gripped the draining board so tightly her knuckles turned white. She looked at Patrick and he didn't like her expression. It seemed to indicate some huge disaster was unfolding.

"This man is an impostor, a fake," she said quietly. "Your father never knew he had a son."

Patrick looked at the man. The man shrugged.

"Tessa," he said. "They were crazy times, a war. There have been so many women. I figured it must be me when I read my name in an interview. I fit the description. I have the name."

"I wonder would you have been so forthcoming if we were still dirt poor and living in a shack?" she said bitterly.

"*Mam!*" Patrick shouted. His mother was ruining everything. She ignored him.

"You were a soldier?" she asked then. And she was really angry now. "One of the Mai-Mai with your poison-tipped arrows? I know all about soldiers. But nothing about you. I made the name up. I made it up to protect my son, to give him a father, something to hold on to."

Patrick gaped at his mother.

"I never knew your father," she said. "And he never knew of your existence." She was shrinking now, disappearing almost, and the kitchen was filling with smoke.

He tried to say something but his words came out as a puff of air. The smoke alarm started to go off and, by the time Tessa had opened the doors and windows, Bart Kimba had slipped away and Patrick was gone.


In the house with the green door, Emma stood on the threshold and batted the door from hand to hand casually. She studied her mother's face and noticed something different. It was a tiny quiver of something foreign. It was fear.

"Are you coming in or going out, Emma?" she asked.

"I'm trying to make up my mind," Emma said.

Her mother gave her a strange look.

"I bet you thought they'd disappeared forever, didn't you?"

"What's got into you? You're talking in code."

"I know it was you that reported Tessa," she said. "I heard you on the phone, months ago, leaving that message for Revenue."

"I haven't a clue what you're talking about."

"Yes, you do. You've always resented them."

"For God's sake, Emma, you're a child. What would you know about how I feel?"

"I'm not a child. And I know spite when I see it."

"*How dare you, Emma Fox!*" her mother screeched.

Emma remained calm. "You always tried to keep me away from him."

"I wanted the best for you."

"He was the best. He *is* the best and I love him."

Her mother laughed. "Love. Right. You're naïve, Emma. It will all make sense when you're older. Mothers know what's best for their children."

"Sure, but they don't know everything. I bet you never reckoned

Patrick would end up playing for Innskeep."

Her mother didn't like that. Her face turned white with rage and Emma ran. She raced up the stairs two at a time to her room where she locked the door and put on her headphones. Her mother chased after her and hammered on the door.

"*Open this door at once!*" she shouted.

Emma raised the volume and drowned out the shouting. She picked up her torch and sat on the windowsill and spelt out "I LOVE YOU, PATRICK KIMBA" over and over before lying back on her bed.

Darkness fell but Patrick didn't come back. Tessa sat up all night. The house was eerily silent, no banging of presses and bowls, opening and closing of the fridge door or thumping down the stairs. His gear bag sat unopened. She lugged it to the washing machine. She would wash his kit to have it ready for him when he returned. His phone sat in a side pocket. Wherever Patrick had gone, he couldn't be contacted.

Morning came; still no Patrick. The club called. It wasn't like him to miss training. The day passed by and still Tessa waited in a paralysed numbness.

Jacques Biet phoned.

"Is something the matter?"

Tessa's breath was raspy. Her voice sounded drugged.

"Patrick has had a bad shock."

"What sort of a shock?"

"The sort that makes you run away," she said.

"*Merde.* Have you called the police?"

"No."

"Well, it's time to call them."

The manager hung up, briefly wondering if Patrick Kimba was worth all the baggage but knew already that he was.

Tessa picked up the phone and called Nuala. Maybe he'd gone back to the place he called home, back to Lavender Square. The conversation was initially cool but the moment Nuala heard about Patrick's disappearance, she said she was coming over.

"You don't need to," Tessa said.

"I'm coming anyway."

"It would be good to see you."

"Sure but let's just work on finding Patrick."

When Tessa hung up the phone rang again. She assumed it was Nuala but it wasn't. The voice belonged to a man. He spoke French badly with a Dutch accent. She told him it wasn't a good time but he persisted. She listened to what he had to say and hung up, wishing Patrick would just come home.

Her mother had tried to bargain with her but Emma didn't leave her room until after she'd gone to bed. She unlocked the door and listened. Silence. She figured her mother was asleep. She tiptoed downstairs to the kitchen. The fridge hummed. She opened it and saw that some dinner had been left for her. She set the microwave and switched on the radio, low. The headlines reported that young Innskeep player, Patrick Kimba, was missing.

Emma took off then, up the stairs as quietly as she could. She packed a rucksack and left, locking her door behind her, pocketing the key. Then she raided the fridge and let herself out the front door. She looked up. Her mother's bedroom light remained off.

Next morning, the doorbell woke Fiona. It was Nuala.

"We were wondering if Emma had heard from Patrick."

"Why don't you ask her yourself? She won't speak to me."

They climbed the stairs and knocked on her door but Nuala had no joy either.

"Emma, love, it's Nuala. We just want to know if you've heard from Patrick. Tessa called early this morning. She's very worried. He's taken his passport."

She looked at Fiona.

"She's not in there."

"How do you know?"

"I just do."

She went home and packed a suitcase.

Joe watched her. "I don't see why you should drop everything the minute Tessa Kimba decides she needs you."

"You're probably right but she sounded desperate. She said there's something she needs to tell me."

"Well, you can count me out. I don't want anything to do with the pair of them."

"I know. That's okay. I'll see you in a few days."

As Nuala's plane took off, Tessa's doorbell rang.

"Who's there?" she asked the shape through the frosted glass.

"It's Emma."

Tessa let her in.

"How did you know where to find me?"

"I rang the club and they put me through to the manager once I told them it was about Patrick."

"I see."

"I heard he was missing. It was on the news."

"You haven't heard from him?"

"No."

Tessa made them tea and toast. She wasn't sure how Emma thought she could help but it was comforting to see someone from the square. They sat and sipped tea. Emma thought Tessa looked terrible. It looked like she hadn't slept in days and her blouse was stained.

"Why did Patrick run away?" she asked.

"Because I lied to him."

"About what?"

"His father."

Tessa looked at Emma. Emma stopped chewing.

"Did Patrick ever talk to you about his father?" Tessa asked.

Emma shrugged.

"Emma?"

"Not for a long time. When you were sick we talked about fathers a lot."

Tessa put her head in her hands. Emma touched her hand.

"He wanted someone to look after you. It's why he played football. He reckoned that if he became a star he would have a better chance of finding him, your husband."

Tessa raised her head and looked utterly bewildered.

"The trouble was, there was never any father," she whispered.

"But there had to be a father," Emma said and she wondered if Tessa was some uber-Catholic who believed in immaculate conceptions.

"There was, a bad one. I made up a good one up to protect him."

She dabbed her eyes with her sleeve.

"So he wasn't a soldier?"

"He was."

"And he was a brave soldier just like you said?"

Tessa shook her head. "In the Congo, soldiers aren't there to protect people – they're either there to protect the Government from the people or out for themselves. They are ruthless and violent and powerful. They rape women and kill families without giving it a second thought. In Africa, you are considered unclean if you are raped . . . you are punished for a crime you didn't commit."

Emma put down her mug. A silence hung in the kitchen. A fly buzzed at the kitchen window. The buzzing sounded like cannon fire.

"Were you raped?" Emma asked tentatively and her voice came out as a squeak.

Tessa nodded slowly and shivered at the same time. "They came to the school."

"You've never told anyone. What about Patrick?"

Tessa shook her head. "When I found out I was pregnant, I knew I had to leave or there would be no future for us, only misery." Tears ran down her face but she didn't seem to notice.

"You could have told Patrick the truth," Emma said. "He's like you. He has guts. He would have handled it."

That evening when Nuala arrived she rang Fiona straight away.

"Emma's here."

There was a pause as Nuala waited for Fiona to stop shouting.

"I'll get her to call you," she said and she hung up.

When she tucked Emma in that night, she sat on the bed. "Do the two of you think running away is the solution to everything? This is real life, you know, not a soap opera." She tried to sound cross but her voice was kind. "Do you have any idea where Patrick might have run off to?"

Emma shook her head.

"Sleep on it. If you think of anything, let us know."

She switched off the light and shut the door.

Emma fell asleep to the sound of muffled voices downstairs. She dreamt of Patrick and the walled garden. In the dream, the garden was dark and overgrown: the grass long, the swing frayed, the door splintered and peeling. She could hear Patrick's voice but couldn't find him. His torch flashed SOS but she couldn't see him.

In the grey dawn she woke to the flashes of torchlight. It took her a moment to realise it was the lights of a street cleaner. She sat up in bed and listened to the sounds of London. She took a sip of water and processed the remnants of her dream.

"Where are you?" she whispered. "Where would you run away to?"

Then she thought of something. She pulled her phone out of its cover and took out the folded postcard. So old now and faded, it was hard to distinguish the sea from the island. She smoothed it out on the bedspread.

"Mont-Saint-Michel," she said and her heart missed a beat.

Then she swung her legs out of bed and got dressed. She knew where to find Patrick.

# Chapter 54

In Paddington, Emma bought a ticket to Paris. The ticket clerk raised an eyebrow.

"On your own, miss?"

"An aunt is meeting me on the other side."

"Righto. Don't talk to any strangers and keep your money on you at all times, deep in your pockets, along with your passport."

On the train, she sat opposite a nun whose nose was deep in a racy romance. At times she pulled out her beads to say a prayer.

As the train pulled out of Paddington and out of London, Emma hoped her hunch was right. Otherwise she would look very silly indeed, and her mother would string her up.

Right about now, Nuala would be finding her note.

When Nuala found Emma's note, she kicked the bed and hurt her toe. She was hung-over. She and Tessa had drunk too much whiskey and she wasn't sure she was quite up to ringing Fiona Fox to inform her about her daughter's second disappearance. She hobbled down the stairs to the kitchen where Tessa was attempting to make a pot of tea.

"Emma's gone."

"What do you mean?" Tessa said.

Tessa's emotions were jumbled and pulled apart. She felt like she'd been hit by a truck. Nuala had dragged every last detail of her life out of her and analysed it. It had been excruciating, like giving birth to a beast, with every possible emotion queuing up to gorge on her: anger, grief, pity, loss and loneliness.

Nuala could not understand all the lies; Tessa could not explain them. They both cried.

"She's left a note. It says, '*I think I know where Patrick is and am gone to fetch him. See you later.*'"

Tessa sat down. She was exhausted.

"Now I've to ring bloody Fiona Fox again," Nuala said.

"Have some tea first."

They sat at the kitchen table in Croydon and drank stewed tea, both a little raw from shared emotion. There were still so many questions unanswered.

"So many secrets," Nuala said.

"You think you're doing it for the best at the time," Tessa said.

"Don't I know?"

Tessa looked different now. A layer had been peeled away to expose a fresh vulnerability. "I have another secret. It's the last, I promise."

"Oh," Nuala said. She felt she had been punched in the face by revelations.

"I'm not from Kinshasa at all. I'm from the Eastern Congo, a place called Ubundu."

"Why would you lie about where you're from? What difference would it make?"

"I wanted to forget the place ever existed."

"Ah," Nuala said. "It's why Tom's father puzzled over the fact that you spoke Swahili and not Lingala all those years ago. I wondered at the time what he was getting at."

"When the UN got me out of there I wanted all traces of my past wiped out. Any memories of that man. But I can still see his face. It's impossible to forget what a rapist looks like, especially when your son is the image of him."

At Dover the train left the land for the Channel Tunnel and Emma felt a surge of excitement. She bought a cup of coffee and a bun from the snacks trolley and munched happily. The nun regarded her over her book.

The train rushed through the French countryside: fields and fields and villages and spires and red roofs all the way to Paris and Gare du Nord, which was huge. Daunting and dazzling and full of fashionable French, nice shoes, clipped sentences, whistles, and vagabonds and people rushing here there and everywhere. She tried to look as though she knew what she was doing but was pushed and jostled by rushing commuters as she tried to study the departure board. No trains for Saint Malo. In a café, she unfolded her map and knocked over her coffee and the waiter gave her a cold stare. But he turned out to be kind and was impressed by her French.

"Mademoiselle, where do you wish to go?"

"Mont-Saint-Michel, Monsieur."

"Not possible from here. You must go to Gare Montparnasse. Take a taxi outside but agree the price before you get in."

The taxi driver was Algerian and played French hip-hop. He was offended by her asking about the fare before she would get in.

Paris was magnificent, just as she remembered. A deep inhalation of sweet perfumed air, so vast so grand so ancient: Eiffel Tower, Montmartre, the Seine – a brief glimpse before Gare Montparnasse where she bought a ticket for Saint Malo.

As the train pulled out of Paris for Normandy, Emma switched on her phone and set her alarm. Then she fell asleep. When she woke up both her money and phone were gone.

It was nearly dark by the time the train pulled into Mont-Saint-Michel. She wandered to the water's edge and sat down. She didn't know what else to do. Across the sound, the island twinkled. Soon it would be dark and she had nowhere to go. Suddenly she felt alone and vulnerable and stupid. Falling asleep had been a mistake. It was cold. She opened her bag, pulled out her hoodie and her torch fell out. It rolled along the ground. She picked it up, shook it, switched it on and spelled out "I LOVE YOU PATRICK KIMBA" over and over. What was to become of her now? She turned off the torch and blew her nose and looked across to the island they'd always spoken of running away to.

She got up to start crossing the causeway.

"Where are you, Patrick?" she asked aloud and then, as if by magic, a light flashed across at her from the island. 'EM,' it spelled.

Then stopped. She stood there, squinting.

The flashing started again.

EMMA ME TOO, it spelt, and she knew she had found him.

# Chapter 55

At the pension the woman folded her arms over her huge bust and her head tilted at an angle that indicated suspicion. She wore a floral housecoat, one which had been altogether more fashionable during the war.

"What are you two running from?" she asked and her eyebrows arched impressively into a 'V' shape.

"We're on a camping trip and got lost orienteering," Emma lied. "Our leader told us to book into a pension for the night. In the morning, we'll catch the train to Paris to meet the rest of them."

"Paris? How lost did you get? You need to talk to whoever taught you orienteering, urgently."

"It's complicated."

"I'm sure it is," said the woman who knew they were lying but didn't want to know any more. Business was slow and they had cash. "Twin beds and no funny stuff. You're both a little young for it."

"We're just friends," Patrick explained.

"That's what they all say," said the woman and she turned to remove a set of keys from a pigeonhole. "Upstairs on the left, breakfast is at eight."

They showered and got dressed and went out in search of *moules frites*. It was squally and a wind whipped in off the sea. Lights beaded an outline of the mainland and in the dark the waves were luminous. Buoys made a clanging sound and accordion music played in a café.

They pushed open the door and light spilled out onto the cobbles. It was toasty inside and locals were drinking wine and coffee and eating beef and soup. Two old men were playing baccarat at the bar.

Their entrance caused a brief moment of interest. Diners paused mid-chew on rare meat, glanced, shrugged and resumed – two youngsters on a date, cute, pass the salt. The waiter nodded and put them sitting at a table under a painting of the island and they ordered a couple of Oranginas and *moules frites*.

"This is like a date, isn't it?"

"Hardly. We're fugitives. I have no money at all by the way. Can you pay for this too?"

Patrick nodded. "I withdrew some cash with my mother's card."

"I heard about that, nice touch."

"I had no choice. She banks my wages."

They sipped on their oranges. The ice clinked in the glasses. They ate and small-talked.

Afterwards they walked the cobbled streets. The wind kicked up dust and the church bell tolled. They climbed the steps to the church and sat down. Lights twinkled out to sea.

"You knew where to find me?" Patrick said.

"When I woke up, it came to me and I took off."

"To rescue me."

"You've rescued me lots of times. I owe you."

"Maybe I didn't want to be rescued."

"Too bad."

He started to cry then, quietly like an Irishman, impatiently, unaccustomed to showy emotion. She moved in closer. He was warm. The streetlights made circles of light on the cobbles and left them in shadow.

"What a waste of time, my whole life thinking about a man who doesn't exist," he said. "Why did she have to go and do that, invent this man? She even gave him a name. That's just fuckin' weird."

"She did it to protect you."

"From what? They didn't work out. So what? I could deal with that."

They had always been straight with each other, never cushioned the truth and Emma decided to be straight with him now.

"The man who fathered you was not a good man."

"Fathered me? Why are you speaking in Droid?"

"Your mam and I spoke last night. The soldier your mother talked about for all those years did father you but he wasn't your father."

He looked at her and frowned. "What are you getting at?"

"Their relationship wasn't consensual."

"What the fuck, Emma? Speak English, will you?"

"Your mother was raped, Patrick."

When she heard it spoken aloud, it sounded brutal like a smack. The words were tangible and sat in the air in front of them. She let them sink in. Moments passed, nothing was said. The wind made a tunnel sound, the sea grumbled at the shore, a door opened and shut, people said goodnight. *"Au revoir, au revoir."*

Patrick shook his head. "I am the son of a monster."

"You are your mother's son."

"I have the blood of a rapist. I'm doomed."

"You also have the blood of a brave woman who left her home so that you would have a good life."

"What if I turn out like him?"

"You haven't and you won't."

"How do you know?"

"Because I don't plan on turning out like my mother."

When it got too cold to bear, they went back to the café. It was the only place still open.

"Back again so soon?" the waiter asked.

They ordered tea. Patrick clutched the hot mug, hoping it would stop the shaking. He wanted to rip his skin off.

"You've had good influences in your life: your mother, Joe and Nuala. It's they who have shaped your life, made you who you are. Don't you think that between them they've done a better job on you than two parents ever could? Look at my house, my mother. It's a mess."

"Your mother is not a rapist."

"No, but she is insane. It was she who reported your mother to Revenue and Tarek to the Guards. It took me a while to realise it but I did."

"I'll kill her."

"Take a ticket, form an orderly queue."

They looked at each other across the table. Patrick looked into his mug.

"Where have you been?"

"My mother did a very good job of keeping us apart."

"I know now that you did an amazing thing by agreeing to go to that school but once you went there, you changed."

"I tried to fit in. It didn't work out. They told me about pony club – I told them about my father's Ukrainian girlfriend. They failed to see the humour."

Back in their room, they lay on one of the single beds and faced each other in the dark and for a time they were quiet until their eyes adjusted to the lack of light. Patrick reached to brush an imaginary strand of hair away from her cheek.

"Do you really love me?" he said.

She said nothing. He pulled her gently towards him.

"It's what your Morse read: I LOVE YOU. Is it true?"

She could tell by his voice he was smiling.

"Are you slagging me?" she asked.

"No. I love you too, you know that. And you know I've been thinking about that kiss ever since that day in Trinity by the cricket pitch."

"Me too."

"It has me driven demented."

"Is that right?" she said, smiling.

He leaned in to kiss her and she kissed him back for an age until they fell asleep.

When Emma woke some time later, Patrick was watching her, mesmerised.

"You're delicious," she said and she blushed self-consciously.

He kissed her again. "You're pretty gorgeous yourself." He ran his fingers through her hair.

"My ears!" she squealed and she brushed her hair back to hide them.

"Again with the ears! You're crazy." He brushed her hair back and kissed her ears.

"Cute moves. You've been practising," she teased.

"A bit. Not much."

"Me too. Mostly gross."

He locked his fingers with hers and they lay there just like that, looking at each other, smiling, kissing, looking, touching, talking.

"What now?" she whispered eventually.

"We stay here forever," he said and his eyes were dreamy.

They fell asleep again.

Emma woke in the grey dawn and counted the flower-heads on the wallpaper. She couldn't remember ever feeling so happy before. She got up and boiled the kettle and made two cups of tea. He sat up in the bed and watched her. They sipped and talked.

"The football was always for him, for a father I didn't have," Patrick said. "Now it means nothing. A father exists for sure but a bad one, an evil one, an anonymous one."

"Hardly."

"I'm through with football, Emma. I'm through with everything. I'm exhausted."

"Football isn't through with you. You might have taken it up to find your father but turns out you're good at it. And by the way, you owe everyone."

"Owe who?"

"Everyone who's listened to you, watched you from the sidelines in the rain, the snow, the ice, talked tactics, washed your jerseys, cleaned your boots, iced your injuries, filled water bottles and picked you up when you were feeling down."

"They didn't have to."

"They did it because they wanted you to achieve your dream. They – *we* believed in it as much as you did."

Emma pushed open the window and breathed in the sea air.

"Besides, I quite fancy being the girlfriend of a professional footballer."

He pulled her back down beside him and kissed her.

She reached up and put her arms around his neck. "There's something else too."

"Oh yeah?"

"You'll just never guess who called your mother the day you disappeared."

"Who?"

"Pim Van Hartenstein."

"The Ireland manager! No way!"

"Way. She said he speaks French terribly." Emma laughed. "And you'll absolutely never guess what he was ringing about."

"Try me."

"He said, 'Your son and me, we share the same birthday'."

"He called my mother to tell her that?" Patrick was incredulous.

"Of course not. He wants you to play for Ireland too."

# Chapter 56

The rest of the season was difficult for many reasons. For one, Innskeep was chasing the treble and it was all hands on deck. No one had any time for discussions about fathers or a lack of them. Training was tough and first team places were fiercely fought for.

It took a while for Patrick to get his game back. The image of his father, though fictional, wouldn't go away. The notion of father and football were so connected it was difficult to separate them and even more difficult to let go. For almost a decade he had rarely considered one without the other. The two were imbedded in his head as one and removing something out of your head, he discovered, took a conscious effort. Some days he actually had to shake his head to knock the memory of his father out. Other times he ached so badly he thought he was sick.

Then of course there was the whole coming to terms with his father being a rapist. He knew he never would quite get over that. Knowing that he was the result of a violent crime was like having the bottom of your world blown out and destroyed, your very existence brought into question. He went through a period of hating his mother. Hate was a strong word but he was pretty sure he hated her. She had lied to him since the day he was born. There was no excuse for that. They fought bitterly although Patrick did most of the fighting. For the most part Tessa sat in a catatonic daze and said nothing. She was suffering, reliving a nightmare she'd compartmentalised. She could even feel the pain of it, the shame, see the bystanders watching, looking on, doing nothing. Often she floated above the scene and could see it happening to her as if it were someone else. She found this profoundly upsetting. She wanted to reach out and help that woman, the woman that had once been her: a schoolteacher, a daughter, a person. The woman the soldier had taken away.

She didn't say anything to Patrick about what she was experiencing. It was hers to go through, but she did talk to Nuala for hours on end. Nuala rang her every day to check up on her. Tessa told her about the sensation of floating above the scene.

"I can't believe you had to go through that," Nuala said tearfully.

"I blocked it, now it's fresh again," Tessa said without emotion. "I can feel that man's body against mine."

"You need to see someone, Tessa, a psychiatrist. This is bigger than me. You need professional help getting through this."

There was silence at the end of the line.

"I'm so afraid I won't get through this," Tessa whispered. "I'm afraid I will go off the deep end."

"You won't."

"I feel overwhelmed."

"I'm coming over," Nuala said.

For the months that followed they took turns going over to London: Tom, Saskia, Nuala, Emma, Tot and Siobhán. Sometimes they all went together to see a match, everyone that is, except Joe. Joe was sorry about the father business but he could not forgive Patrick and Tessa for blaming Nuala and then walking out of her life without so much as a conversation.

"He'll come round," Nuala told Patrick.

But Patrick wasn't sure. He didn't blame Joe for feeling the way he did – Joe, who had sacrificed so much to help him get to where he wanted to be. Joe had believed in him and always listened. He had put Patrick at the centre of his world and had been more of a father to Patrick than any father could ever have been. His mother had forbidden that he get in touch but he could have easily without her knowing anything about it. He had been thinking about himself, afraid to put his Innskeep ambitions in jeopardy.

Patrick told Saskia about the aches.

"You're grieving," she said. "You've lost your father. Even though he was never real, you've still lost him. You need to talk to a grief counsellor."

Under duress both Kimbas got help and things started to get better.

Things got better for Emma too. She no longer feared her mother and told her that if she tried to pull any more fast ones she would be going to live with her father and Valentina and her brand-new half-brother. She also suggested that her mother use her PR skills to help immigrants, not all day every day, but often. It would help her case. There were several people who wanted her lynched. She also asked for her help getting Lavender Square FC back up and running. Joe had agreed to start coaching again if the residents allowed the garden to be opened up once more. When she told her that Patrick was her boyfriend, she didn't shout. She just turned and left the room with the dragging resignation of someone who'd lost a long argument.

Patrick texted Joe often but got no reply. He tried to talk to him but Joe never answered the phone. Even when Innskeep won the treble, he heard nothing. The season drew to a close. Patrick was tired and he knew there was only one place he wanted to be: at home in the square with Emma, with everyone. He knew his mother wanted that too, but without Joe's blessing it would be difficult. Nuala said she'd deal with it but Patrick wanted to do something for him. He didn't know what. He decided to sleep on it, and after five nights of doing just that, the answer came to him. He knew what he needed to do.

Before they broke up for the summer, Jacques Biet took Patrick aside.

"Quite the year you've had, Monsieur Kimba, and next year will be better. When you turn eighteen in a few months, we will talk about signing you as a professional and we'll talk about money. Now go home to Lavender Square and have a rest."

In Dublin he rolled down the window in the taxi and let the breeze brush against his face. It had been raining and he could smell the tarmac and the soil and it smelt like Ireland, like home. His room in Nuala's was the same as ever. The same wallpaper, duvet cover, picture of Pelé. The duvet cover was well worn now and smelt of washing powder. He looked out through his window. It was evening and turning gold. There was a gentle smell of lavender. People sat out on their steps and drank wine and chattered. In the walled garden, Joe was coaching a group of youngsters.

A car pulled up across the street. When Patrick saw it he ran downstairs.

The kids were finishing up and Joe was gathering the bollards when Patrick stepped through the door of the garden. Joe looked up and then looked away and continued tidying up. The young footballers gawked, wide-eyed.

"Look at this fine bullock of a lad," Joe said to them. "Do as I tell you and you might end up a superstar like him." There was a slight edge to his voice. "Now off with the lot of you," he said, "and remember, no beer tonight. You've got a match tomorrow."

Joe finished putting things away. Patrick helped him.

"I don't expect you to forgive me or to even speak to me. It's just I have a present for you and I'll leave you alone after that."

"What is it, a pony?"

"Yeah, something like that."

They inhaled the evening air and Patrick took the net of balls and the kit bag. Joe locked the door behind them. Patrick stood still and waited for Joe to turn around. When he did, he did a double-take and stood perfectly still before putting the kit bag down.

There was an Austin Cambridge parked at the kerb. Patrick handed him a set of keys.

"Where did you get it?" Joe asked. "It's just like my old one."

"Online," Patrick said.

"They sell Austin Cambridges online?"

"They sell spleens online."

Joe ran his hand along the bodywork.

"Come for a spin with me," he said.

They drove out of the square and up into the mountains. The city fell back behind them into a twinkling twilight and they climbed higher. They parked and got out and sat on the bonnet. The mountain air smelt of heather.

"Thanks, son," Joe said and he looked straight ahead.

"You like it?"

"I do."

"I'm sorry," Patrick said.

"Me too. I'm getting cranky in my old age."

"You were cranky in your young age."

"Less of your lip."

Dublin sat below them: a hub of gemstones, sapphire, ruby and emerald. The dusk was a purple silkiness.

"I never thanked you," Patrick said.

"For what?"

"For everything. It took me a while to realise. Clarity comes to you over ninety minutes. All your thoughts slot into the right places."

"Isn't that fierce profound?"

"You were more of a father to me than I could have ever have hoped for."

"Arra now," Joe said, shifting uncomfortably.

"Arra nothing. I was lucky."

"Then so were we, son. So were we. Didn't you save all of us from ourselves, lead us to redemption?"

"Like a saviour, a messiah or a king even?" Patrick suggested with a smile.

"Well, there you have it now," Joe said. "A king. Indeed. The King of Lavender Square."

"I like that," Patrick said approvingly.

"Who wouldn't?" Joe said. "Will we go home now?"

"We will."

And with that they got back into the car and drove down from the mountains into the valley and back to Lavender Square.

## THE END

If you enjoyed this book from
Poolbeg why not visit our website

**www.poolbeg.com**

and get another book delivered straight
to your home or to a friend's home.

*All books despatched within 24 hours.*

# Free postage on orders over €20*

Why not join our mailing list at

www.poolbeg.com and get some

fantastic offers, competitions,

author interviews, new releases

and much more?

 **@PoolbegBooks**

 **www.facebook.com/poolbegpress**

*Free postage over €20 applies to Ireland only